New Worlds 4

Barrington J. Bayley
Graham Charnock
Matthew Dickens
Peter F. Hamilton
Robert Holdstock
Garry Kilworth
David Langford
Ian McDonald
Michael Moorcock
Elizabeth Sourbut
Lisa Tuttle

Edited by David Garnett

Also Edited by David Garnett

NEW WORLDS
NEW WORLDS 2
NEW WORLDS 3
THE ORBIT SCIENCE FICTION YEARBOOK
THE ORBIT SCIENCE FICTION YEARBOOK 2
THE ORBIT SCIENCE FICTION YEARBOOK 3
ZENITH
ZENITH 2

New Worlds 4

Edited by David Garnett

Consultant Editor: Michael Moorcock

VGSF

The fourth is for
Richard Evans, the man who said *Yes*
and
Faith Brooker, who couldn't say *No*

First published in Great Britain 1994
by Victor Gollancz
A Cassell imprint
Villiers House, 41/47 Strand, London WC2N 5JE

With thanks to Michael Moorcock, Richard Evans and Faith Brooker

New Worlds Vol. 62 No. 220

A catalogue record for this book is available from the British Library.

ISBN 0 575 051477

Printed in Finland by Werner Söderström Oy

Designed and Typeset
by Fishtail Design

Contents

Introduction

David Garnett

'I don't have time to read short stories.'

It's a phrase I've heard a number of times, often from people who are quite willing to read a 500 page novel. Or a trilogy which adds up to 2000 pages. Or a series with a page count approaching infinity.

They do have the 'time' to read short stories, but they don't want to read something which is different. They like what they know. They don't like change, they don't like anything new.

And every short story is different. With an anthology such as *New Worlds*, every story is new.

Different and new are not the route to commercial success. For example: every high street and shopping precinct in Britain is becoming like every other one. The same shops can be found in every town, and each one will carry the same line of products. Go into any franchised restaurant and you can eat the same hamburger, drink the same cola, and they will taste equally the same - equally tasteless. People don't want to risk trying anything new in case they won't like it. Or even worse. They might like it.

When it comes to records, films, television, books, it's exactly the same.

Because that's what the majority of the public wants: familiarity, recognition, reassurance.

Give them more of the same. No surprises. Repeat the formula. Over and over.

Geriatric rock bands go on annual 'reunion' tours, and their 'greatest hits' albums shift countless units. Some radio stations play nothing but 'golden oldies'. Old records are re-recorded, remixed, sampled. You've heard it all before, and you'll hear it all again. And again.

Hollywood exists to make money, not movies. And the way to do that is by making films which are like previous money-making films. If a new film becomes a hit, there will almost inevitably be a sequel. Old films are remade with a new 'all star' cast, but without a spark of inspiration. French films become American movies, because the audience can't possibly watch anything with sub-titles.

Countless books have become film scripts and there are also films based on comics, on video games, on dimly remembered ancient television series. If viewers saw it on TV, they'll want to see it again. Something which may once have been original is given the big screen gloss, polished and polished until it slips down smoothly and easily. There's no danger of viewers being surprised by anything new or of not understanding what they see.

The most popular television programmes are soap operas. Three times a week, the same familiar characters live out their 'normal' lives. Even if there's a murder or a kidnapping or an outbreak of rabies, it's all part of 'everyday' life. Nothing original will ever happen, and there certainly won't be any surprises. Viewers know every major event long before it's screened because they've read about it in the tabloid press, who treat the soaps as news. TV listing magazines and papers give programme times for each episode - and also print exactly what will happen during that half hour.

Films attract similar media attention, with newspaper reviews which reveal the whole plot, cinema trailers which show key scenes, and television presenters who tell you how it all ends. As with the soaps, the majority of a film audience know in some detail what they are about to watch.

It's becoming like that with books. Originality is a liability. I've written about this elsewhere, including previous *New Worlds* editorials, and there's no point going on again about series and trilogies, novelizations and franchising, novels which are as heavy (and as readable) as bricks, books attributed to long-dead authors – and books by authors who write as if they were long dead.

At one time, I wondered if people only bought such books because it was what publishers offered to them. Now I realize it's what they prefer. Readers want what they know, something like they've read before, even something exactly like they've read before.

Which is not what they get with short stories. Every short story has different characters, an original background, a fresh plot, new themes and ideas.

If this was what readers really wanted, it's what they would buy. It isn't, because short stories don't sell.

And *New Worlds* hasn't sold.

Readers who have seen any of the three previous volumes in this, the latest series of *New Worlds*, will notice that *NW4* is slightly different. There are no illustrations, no photographs. The reason is simple: lack of space. There is more fiction and non-fiction in this volume than in the other three, and so everything else had to go. This introduction is shorter than the others, and there isn't even enough room for the usual three or four pages of authors' biographies.

So I'll mention the writers here . . .

Barrington Bayley published his first *NW* story in 1959, as half of 'Michael Barrington'; his co-author was Michael Moorcock. Graham Charnock and Robert Holdstock both broke into print in the 1968 'New Writers' issue of *NW*. Charnock contributed several more stories, was assistant editor for a time, and wrote 'On the Shores of a Fractal Sea' in *NW3*; 'The Charisma Trees' is Holdstock's second *NW* story. Another second timer is Matthew Dickens, who wrote 'The Descent of Man' in *NW1*. David Langford contributes his second article on books; the first was in *NW2*. Peter Hamilton makes it three stories in a row, following earlier appearances in *NW2* and *NW3*. Ian McDonald has also had three stories in this new series, with 'Innocents' from *NW2* winning the British Science Fiction Award in 1993. Garry Kilworth, Elizabeth Sourbut and Lisa Tuttle all make their *NW* debut in this volume. Whether they will ever make a second *NW* appearance is anyone's guess.

Because this is the final volume of *New Worlds*. For a while at least.

Gollancz contracted to publish a four-book series and, as the title suggests, *New Worlds 4* is the fourth and therefore the last. If sales had been higher, the series would have continued. But: short stories don't sell.

Michael Moorcock published his first *NW* story in 1959, as half of 'Michael Barrington'; in 1964 he became the editor, later acquiring rights to the title; since 1991 he has been consultant editor to the current series. He was born in London, originally edited *NW* from his London flat, is the author of the novel *Mother London*, and in 1994 he moved to Texas.

Perhaps that's where the next *New Worlds* will be edited from.

What form will it take?

And when?

Who knows?

There may even be another volume from Gollancz next year. *New Worlds 5*. Edited by me.

Keep watching this space.

But at the moment I'm looking forward to a break from wading through the good, the bad and the unreadable: the Möbius strip of manuscripts which every editor has to confront.

I hope to find time to read some short stories.

DAVID GARNETT had his first story rejected by Michael Moorcock, then editor of *New Worlds*, in 19**. Since then, he's written some books, had a few stories published here and there, written more books, edited the *Zenith*, *Orbit SF Yearbook* and *NW* anthology series, and written some more books. *Stargonauts*, his first new sf novel since 19**, is published the same month as this volume. It's the first of a tr*l*gy. His ambition is to have a story in *New Worlds*.

Harringay

Graham Charnock

Woken by gleeful tra-la-lee of phone. My back hurts, my limbs ache, and I can't see – only a white diffused glow behind my eyelids which suddenly explodes into shooting stars, Catherine wheels of light that sizzle on my retinae.

I feel miserable but I know it's nothing really significant. Just everyday symptoms of tertiary clonal recovery.

Where am I? Memory is as blind as my eyes for the moment, occluded by the squirts of interference along my optic nerve, but it peers and squints and then everything floods back.

Harringay.

My tongue trips sweetly over the three syllables, teasing the first, tasting the second, sucking hungrily on the third. Harr-in-gay. Light of my loins, fire of my life.

It took me a while to recall the instruction set required to open my eyes. Doctors say responses will become more spontaneous as facial nerves re-network themselves. It feels to me like a botched job. I would sue if it weren't for the waivers in the contract.

The truth is that Andy has been dead too long. Clonal tissue sours after a while, the DNA destabilizes or something, molecules migrate from incorporated inert material; the amalgam in fillings, silicon from breast implants, the nylon that welds your heart together.

It was daylight. It was morning. It was bright, cruel, victimizing. Send out for Chano Pozo, the Doctor of Swing, put pennies on my dead eyelids and watch them turn cartwheels when the last kick of the heart tosses them in the air.

Heads or tails.

It was Walter Winchell. On the phone. He wanted to interview me and write it up as a book. I said I'd do it if I could photograph him masturbating, digitize it, and issue it as a limited edition floppy. He said he'd think about it and call back. I felt on safe ground. I don't believe he can come.

I showered, powered up, kicked in the modem, and after it had run through its regular glitches – calling up NORWEB, NATWEB, The White House

Catering Facility, the Walt Disney Interface in Fort Knox – I checked the Bulletin Board. There was more stuff from Hockney. Incoherent as usual. He uses a clinic in Hong Kong these days where a team of acupuncturists trained under Dr Chung Kuo work to locate the monofilament sutures along the median lines. I've told him it's a big mistake. One of these days his face is going to fall apart and he'll look like W.H. Auden.

Printed out a hard copy of *Clone & Mart*. Something tells me one day it may be collectable. The big news is that some of JFK's internal organs have surfaced, supposedly in a laboratory in Tampa Bay. My hunch is that it's another red herring and it will turn out to be more old, tired material from Rose's corpse with a bit of genetic tailoring. I know a ten-year-old Puerto Rican kid who bought one of those faces. Now he's a drag queen with red hair and freckles but not much else, works an Irish bar off Union Square. What a waste.

And some scam-running Zionist claims to have unearthed a cache of Belsen lampshades in a Bavarian *wald*, but they will probably turn out to be pig-skin like last time.

Not much new on the market. A twenty-year-old Jeremy Bentham from the mummy in the Oxford Union. What kind of investment is that? It'll be fifty years before you can realize a return – even if the skin-bag survives that long – and who knows what the market in philosophy gurus will be by then?

You remember how they dug up those Romanov scraps and it turned out to be mostly servants and grooms? Well, apparently they did find a bit of cartilage from Tsar Nicholas III in amongst them. He's seven years old now and a bit prone to puppy fat judging from the digipic. I wouldn't have put him on the market just yet, but the Imperial Eastern Consolidated is such a volatile exchange, buying Maos one minute and Schwarzeneggers the next. I guess it's true what they say – you can't leave the chicken on the rack too long. If only they could find Anastasia. What a Holy Grail that would be. I might even bid for her myself.

Victor called at nine to take me shopping. He had an exhibition later at a gallery in Pont Street and was nervous about it, really on edge. He asked me if I had any acid. I can't believe Victor does acid, not as it's presently formatted. I told him, Victor, it's not good for you. It scrambles the input channels from the genes – you could end up looking and feeling like a turkey. Literally.

He was wearing leather flares and they looked quite cool. They had a Vivienne Westwood label in them. He said he'd got them from BHS. I pointed out the tiny 'made under licence in Saigon' notice on the label. It rather clouded his day. 'It's the last time I sign any soup cans for you,' he said.

I hate shopping, unless it's for clothes, but he'd hired a car, a long-wheel-base Mercedes, which was very comfortable, and the nice looking English boy was driving, so I went along.

Harringay is a bizarre place, like a macho Venice Beach. The first week I arrived I ordered a kebab at the Larnaca Cafe. It took three hours to arrive and I lost $56.85 at cards while I was waiting. In summer, men sell bags of pistachios from the hoods of cars, and the stench of rotting watermelon is overwhelming.

Can you believe it? I saw somebody I knew who was still alive. It was Marty, who must have come over about the same time as me, after Three Mile Island Mark IV. He was under that big iron railway bridge with all the Turkish graffiti on it, where the pigeons shit. He was giving a tall blond man money, quite a lot of it. I pushed the button that wound down the window and waved and shouted but he pretended not to see me. Then I thought it's probably for the best. Marty's always dealing. I don't mean drugs, he's too clumsy for that. He just deals – comics, porn postcards of Madonna and Donkey – whatever's in vogue.

(Madonna, now there's a woman who actually looks better in the afterlife than in realtime. That Jewish bitch who owns first serial rights has done some serious tweaking.)

Victor was upset about something, but wouldn't say what. He was wearing a cowboy shirt with embroidered roses and cutaway hearts. I loved it. Very David Byrne. Did David die yet, and, if he did, did anybody buy the rights to the flesh? The last time I saw him he looked like Harry S. Truman – the original, I mean, in that photo by WeeGee, not that hybrid upstart currently peddling his ass round Capitol Hill. I check the *AIDS Gazette* daily but it's hard to keep track. So much bad news every day from the dark heart of Africa.

The English kid turned on the radio and it was that terrible salsa music. Apparently it's very popular in north London, but I can't believe anybody actually likes it. I think they just play it because it's Fourth World. It's boring, but that's Britain.

For instance: two Nicaraguan restaurants opened up in Crouch End last week. Jimi was playing in one and yesterday I went because someone told me the Germans like him and he'd fucked Fassbinder. He was OK. He looked a bit too old, but that's the problem with people who die young. But he still had his licks.

I asked him about Fassbinder after the gig and he said he'd never heard of him. We signed each other's phonecards and swapped them. A girl in black leather who said she was from *Time Out* tried to come on to me. Would you believe it? She was really spaced. She was telling me they'd found an entirely new dinosaur in Bloemfontein, big and barrel-shaped, apparently with its scalp still intact. Do dinosaurs have scalps? I thought she might have been putting me on. You can't tell these days. I sent her to the bar to get me a Babycham, but she never came back.

I went back to the Eric Hotel in a genuine black London taxi ($84.00) with a tart from a local radio station who asked me boring questions all the way, like, did Valerie Solanis really kill me? All that old conspiracy shit. I told her no, I converted to Catholicism, married Valerie, and we had ten kids. The truth is what you want to hear.

The bitch in the taxi was wearing leather too – and chains. Why are all the women in the British media industry into bondage? I took a Polaroid of her with her skirt pulled up to her waist, and her thongs down round her knees ($90), and finally pushed her out at Seven Sisters and told the cabbie to drive on. The taxi-driver told me how last week he'd been to Wisley to buy a rhododendron, and how he'd almost been run down by wrinklies in their electric wheelchairs. He was very interesting, but he drove very slowly I thought, so I trimmed the tip (8.42%).

I sat up late in the lounge at the Eric Hotel (cheeseplants and IKEA!!!) and talked with the night-staff. They were full of how a local mini-cab driver had been imprisoned for raping a Swedish au-pair up near Manor House station, except that none of the evidence hung together, and the woman couldn't describe anything about the event the same way twice. But it was their big excitement of the decade. One of them actually knew the man who'd really done it.

The Eric Hotel is gross, but the discomfort of its mattresses is just about made up for by the splendid after-dark infra-red views across Finsbury Park. I saw a dwarf coupling with a leopard once, I swear I did. But I must move on soon. My bones were always the least tolerant of my internal organs.

At about 2 a.m. I glued and went to bed, not realizing that I didn't have to glue until the next evening. I didn't wake up till ten, and by then I was totally unglued. The whole thing was a waste of a glue.

Can you wonder I was so grouchy first thing?

Victor asked me where I'd like to shop and I said I'd quite like to see the new Tesco store. The English kid said he'd been there and it was really neat. He said he preferred it to Sainsbury's because they sold things like chinos and toys as well as food. I couldn't believe that a company as big as Sainsbury's would just sell food. Who would want to go to that kind of place?

In the car I told Victor how Larry Gagosian had called earlier. He said David Geffen was bored with Hockney and wanted to buy something more of mine. The last thing he bought was a Marilyn in 1973 ($240,000). I said I could probably find the sleeve of a Velvet Underground album I could sign for him, but Larry said no, David wanted me to make something new. Can you believe that? I told Larry I'd stopped doing new things and certainly wasn't going to start again for a man who wears trainers and a baseball cap back to front.

We stopped at some lights and this Hell's Angel started to clean our windscreen for us, without even being asked. He had huge muscles, and tattoos all over his face. The cute English boy said it was illegal, and I said what for someone to clean our windscreen, and he said no for someone to have tattoos over their face, and I said you mean you can't even disfigure yourself, what sort of country is this?, and he just shrugged and held his hands palm upwards like someone trying to adopt Latino mannerisms. Anyway I paid the guy with the tattoos 80c and took a Polaroid of him, so at least that was all right.

The English kid said he'd heard that the Angels were the new Mafia, and Victor said, what happened to the old Mafia? It ain't broke so don't fix it. It was embarrassing, as if Victor hadn't heard of the United Nations embargo on Family corpses. No one laughed.

I wanted to ask Victor about this new pop group who mutilate themselves on stage and whether I should do something for them, but I sensed this wasn't the moment, and anyway I guessed I'd already decided. It's hard to find anybody these days who deserves fifteen seconds, let alone fifteen minutes.

As we were driving into the car-park the English boy scraped the fender of a BMW and this woman jumped out and started bad-mouthing us, then she stopped, embarrassed. Apparently she knew me from somewhere. I couldn't recall her. It turned out she had Italian connections, and a forefather who was an ancient Duke of Lombardy. Apart from that she wasn't famous at all.

She'd been to the seafood counter. She'd flown over specially from Castille, because apparently seafood is now cheaper in England than in Spain, or anywhere else for that matter. It won't last. It's only a matter of time before the algae works its way up from the Mediterranean to the Cinqueport lagoons.

She'd bought up practically everything there was as if she had a shipping contract – squid, octopus, lobster, prawns, whelks, oysters and two whole congers. She was flying back home that evening for a weekend barbecue and invited me along, and I said I'd go, but I honestly don't want to, and I shall probably not show. My surgeon told me how they use a gel derived from sturgeons' swim-bladders to put a sheen on reconstructed cheeks. I can't eat fish with a clear conscience these days.

They had these huge recycling hoppers in one corner of the car-park. We didn't have any stuff of our own, but there was a woman with a whole trolley full of cans and bottles and we helped her sort them out. She recognized me and asked me to sign something for her so I signed an old can of cat food. Do you know what she did? She took it and dumped it straight in the hopper. It was wild. I wanted to stay around and sign more stuff for people to dump, but the English boy and Victor were keen to start shopping.

The new Tesco store was wonderful. I don't know why they call it new, unless it's because it's just been built. That's possible. It's hard to tell with supermarkets and shopping malls. They all look new no matter how old they are. That's the point. Who would want to go to a mall that looked old? Victor disagreed. He said one day they *would* be old and we'd all love and treasure them for that very reason. The Surrey Docks would be the new Versailles. Brent Cross would be the new Vauxhall Pleasure Gardens.

I don't believe it. Whenever a building gets to look old these days, people just bleach it with chlorine and sand-blast it back to new again. And anyway, in a few years' time I'm sure they'll be able to resurrect buildings much the same way they do humans, from the hex in the crystal, the code in the stone.

New Angkor Wats will arise in the mangrove swamps of the European Shelf. Mayan temples will surface and overlook the paddy fields of the Fens. Ozymandias will stride out of the tumbled rocks of the peaks, with reconstituted limbs and torso and proclaim himself, once again, king of kings. The monoliths of Stonehenge will thrust upwards through the soil of Salisbury Plain, as if seeded from some magical silicate spore, to form a newer, grander fairy circle. The Sphinx will be reborn in Birmingham's Bull Ring, a minotaur with a ring of gold in its new nose. The perfect geometry of the pyramids will be scattered once more upon the spoil tips of South Wales, like die cast from the hands of gods.

Victor pouted, like he wanted to start an argument, but was afraid of where it might go.

One thing I liked about the store was the doors, which opened automatically before you even wanted them to open. I tried to fool them by stepping backwards when they started to open, but it didn't work.

We went in and the first thing we saw was a tramp trying to sell on a bunch of Welfare Lottery tickets. What a great idea that is. Only the Brits could think of it. Instead of paying out social benefits from tax revenue, you fund it with a lottery, giving out a ration of free tickets to the registered underprivileged (which of course they immediately negotiate on the black-market, instant relief always being better than hope deferred). The rich buy the tickets at mark-down prices and continue to get richer on their winnings, while the poor continue to subsist, but now they blame their condition on bad luck. Nothing ever changes in this *Belle Isle*.

These vouchers certainly looked genuine, with a watermark of Jeff Koons humping La Cicciolina. I bought a dozen and gave them to the first people I saw. None of them seemed particularly needy but I noticed none of them refused. The English are a strange, perplexing race.

There were lots of trolleys, and I liked that. The English kid grabbed one and he went straight to the houseplant section. He lives in Chelsea. He bought a yucca. He said it would look good in his patio-garden.

We had a lot of fun at the supermarket, but I didn't buy anything. There was nothing new I needed.

Back in the parking lot the car phone rang. It was Sigmund Freud who was selling equity in a new company he'd formed to market dysfunctional psychotics. He already had Charlie Manson under contract and was waiting for him to die. I declined the option (although it *was* on very favourable terms) and reminded him that psychoanalysts like him used to be called 'alienists'.

He didn't like that one bit, and called me anal-retentive. I switched him off. Fuck him. The guy needs a shave.

The English kid started up the BMW. We stopped at the lights opposite McDonald's and a woman wearing an anti-pollution-mask tapped on the window and asked for a contribution for the British Nazi Party. I did what I always do, and signed a blank cheque, from a cancelled chequebook. Victor told me off, saying she'd sell it as an original and get the money that way. I said, fine, then everybody would have participated in the artistic process, and wasn't that what it was all about? Victor just snarled at me.

I think he is becoming jaded. He needs a holiday. I should take him somewhere different. Australia, perhaps. East Coast. They say the shopping marinas on the Barrier Reef are magnificent and the sharks are really friendly and will give you rides on their backs and let you be photographed with your head between their jaws. I'll book the tickets tomorrow.

We drove up to Alexandra Palace and sat in the car, drinking beers as dusk fell, looking out across the railway yards and the sewage farms. I love that view, it's like the view across Laurel Canyon, back when it was safe to live there. Bob Dylan was busking in the car park, going from car to car like a gypsy violinist in a restaurant. I gave him $9.47.

We played that game of who would you like to be if you weren't you, and Victor said Marilyn. It would really be something to have fucked a president. The English kid passed me a joint and said he'd just like to be famous in his own right one day, then he wouldn't have to be anyone else.

Maybe it'll happen, he said. Maybe tomorrow, who knows?

We all said, sure, but I don't think so. Here in Harringay tomorrow never comes, and anyway, we all have to be someone else, sooner or later, don't we?

And the Poor Get Children

Lisa Tuttle

Becky Valpariso was used to getting what she wanted. It came as an unpleasant shock to her to learn, at the age of one hundred and forty-seven, that there really were things money could not buy.

Like love. She could hire care – a nurse, a full-time nanny, and the most sophisticated interactive nursery on the market, but what had been good enough for *her* mother was, most emphatically, *not* good enough for her. Becky had grown up cared for by a series of hired nurses before being sent off to the best boarding school. Every luxury had been provided except the one she now considered more important than anything money could buy: the constant presence, devoted care and unselfish love of a full-time parent. Both her parents had been too busy earning money to take a few years off to raise their own child.

Not that she blamed them, not any more, not after nearly fifty years in analysis. Life had been so much shorter then, even for the very rich. Now it seemed perfectly possible to take a career-break for a decade or two, whether to raise a child or explore some other non-remunerative passion. She was convinced it would be worth doing. But could she convince her partner?

She waited until Steve was in a mellow mood, after a few rounds of VR sex-gaming, when they were lying on the living-room floor, back in real time, both of them with non-fattening, non-carcinogenic, mildly uplifting mood-enhancers on tap. In the background, providing a little subliminal encouragement, she hoped, were some dolls and other toys. She smiled at him and touched him on the arm and drew a deep breath to begin. But it was no good. Steve was already there. He had known her, after all, for nearly sixty years – he knew her better than anyone else alive. Maybe he couldn't actually read her mind, but he had noticed the toys and he knew what the impulse binge in a toystore must mean.

'Absolutely not,' he said. 'Don't even ask.'

'You could at least think about it.'

'I already have. The answer is no.'

'If you really—'

'Of course I love you. I love you as you are. If you really loved *me* you wouldn't ask. I love our life together and I don't want anything to change. Our life is perfect as it is.'

'Life is change. Perfection is death.'

'What about, "If it ain't broke, don't fix it". I've been to just as many personal-life philosophy sessions as you have, my darling. I like our partnership just as it is; I'm not interested in being a parent.'

'It would be an enriching experience.'

'It would be hell.'

'How do you know? There'd be rough times, but you might be surprised at how enjoyable raising a child could be. And it would bring us closer together.'

'If we survived the first eighteen years.'

'It doesn't have to be eighteen; we could do it in nine. The clinic offers a special half-time option – birth to graduation in under nine years. So you see, it wouldn't even be a decade out—'

'Out of our real lives, were you going to say? Becky, this is crazy. You can't argue me into this – there aren't any sweeteners you can give me, the whole deal simply repulses me. If you're so keen, get yourself a tailor-made VR programme, take a year off in the tank where they'll look after you, and then come back to me.'

Tears of rage sprang to her eyes, fury at being balked and also at being so misunderstood by the person who mattered. 'This is no game! I've been thinking about it a long time, and I want to do it, for real. Virtual isn't going to get it out of my system. This isn't like sex, this is something I need for the sake of my soul, like I need you. Steve, please, if you love me, let me do this!'

He rolled over and stood up, stretching his long, naked body, moving away from her. 'Not with me. If it's that important to you – more important than us – go ahead, find yourself another daddy.'

She read the hurt in his body language, the despair he didn't want her to see, and knew with a thrill of certainty how much he loved her. He was frightened of losing her, fearful of the changes that were to come – but he loved her, that was the important thing. She felt guilty about going behind his back, without his permission, but she just knew that he wouldn't let her down. She was sure, whatever he said, that he would be a wonderful father.

Renate heard the screaming as she came out of the market. It was a very old superstore surrounded by a huge and now largely unused parking lot, and among the few eccentric vehicles parked on the cracked and potholed paving was a big, old-fashioned black perambulator from which the screams were coming.

She didn't realize just how big the pram actually was until she nearly ran into it. She had thought it still some distance away; its size warped normal perspective. It was necessarily large because it contained, not a baby, but a fully grown woman dressed in a long, white gown of Irish lace, smelling of pee and baby powder and sour milk, her face clenched and red with the effort of screaming.

'Now, now,' said Renate. 'There, there, it's all right.' She bent over the side of the pram and searched until she found a bottle and plugged it into the screaming mouth. There was a startled little sound, the same noise her own daughter used to make, and then a greedy, contented sucking.

'That's better.' Renate spotted a square of card pinned to one of the white blankets and read it aloud: 'My name is Becky. I am only four days old. Please take care of me.' Eyes closed, the woman in the pram was oblivious, sucking away as if all was well and nothing in the world existed except herself and the teat. 'Oh, Becky, what a wicked world you've been born into. You didn't choose your parents very wisely, did you? Well, I'll find someone to help.'

There was a Crime Alert Post only steps away, and the button was working. A peacekeeper was with her in minutes, preceded by the blood-chilling sound of its siren. Renate gritted her teeth and fought all the instincts that urged her to run: everyone knew that the siren had been scientifically developed to arouse fear in the criminal brain while leaving the normal, law-abiding citizen completely unaffected. But although she did not believe she had criminal tendencies, both sound and sight of the approaching peacekeeper filled her with alarm, and she wished she'd turned elsewhere for help.

Unable to identify any known crime in progress, the peacekeeper issued Renate a caution against misuse and waste of public utilities.

'But this baby has been abandoned – surely it was my duty to report that?'

'There is no baby,' droned the peacekeeper. 'There is an adult woman, causing no offence. REM activity indicates she sleeps; no evidence of restricted drug or alcohol abuse.'

'But she's completely helpless! Surely you can see that? She can't look after herself. She may be an adult physically, but she's been reborn.'

'She is a private citizen. What concern is she of yours?'

'It's a human concern. She's helpless, she's been abandoned – somebody has to help her or she'll die. I just happened to find her. Look, take a cell sample, tell me who she is so I can contact her next-of-kin.'

'This citizen is committing no crime. Sample cannot be taken without her permission.'

'But she can't give you her permission! That's the point! We need to find out who she is—'

'There is no need to uncover the identity of this private citizen. You are wasting the time of a valuable public utility. This is your second caution. If a third caution is issued, it will be entered on your record and you may be fined.'

'I apologize. I didn't mean to. It was a misunderstanding,' Renate said as humbly as she could. She felt like screaming.

She decided to try the health centre. In the olden days foundlings had been left at hospital doors. No hospital in the city would allow Renate anywhere near their doors – her public health card permitted access only to one health centre. But at least there she could talk to a human being, and maybe one of the medics or carers would take pity on Becky.

It was a long walk to the health centre, but she had no choice. The pram was not collapsible, and would never be allowed on the peoplemover, and Becky was far too big for her to carry.

After inserting her card and being let through the doors into the waiting area, she waited for hours surrounded by ill, injured and slightly mad people, most of whom eyed her and the enormous black pram with unconcealed resentment. Not for the first time, she wished she had an IC. The idea of being able to touch her wrist and call up information from anywhere in the world, or even to be able to talk to a friend, made her almost faint with longing. Or maybe it was the air, heavy with sickness and despair, that brought her close to fainting. Eventually, inevitably, Becky woke up and started crying again. Rocking the pram didn't help, so she refilled the baby bottle with milk from her bag of groceries. For a few minutes, as Becky gulped it down, there was blessed quiet. Then she turned her head and puked it all up.

'Oh, dear . . . oh—' As she was trying, fairly uselessly, to clean up the mess of curdled milk with the one crumpled tissue she'd found in her bag, a passing carer (with Limited Nursing Skills, according to her badge) took notice of her plight and brought her some disposable towels.

'Oh, thank you, thank you so much.'

'You've got your work cut out for you – I sure don't envy you. First-time babies are bad enough, but at least they're portable, and cute. Try picking up something this big, huh! But I guess you must love her a lot. They say knowing your lover as your mother or your child adds an extra dimension to your love.'

She'd heard that said on a soap opera, and was nodding in recognition of the sentiment before she realized what it implied. 'Oh, no. I'm not her lover – I don't even know her!'

'Is that so? The money must be good, then. Husband hired you, I guess?'

'No. I don't know her – I don't know who she is. I just found her outside my local mall—'

'Whoa! Take her back!'

'I can't. She'd been abandoned. She was screaming her head off. There was a note pinned to her blanket—'

'And you're the lucky sucker who found her.'

'I couldn't just leave her.'

'Why not? Her family did.'

'She needs to be looked after. She can't do anything for herself. I know she's got the body of a grown woman, but her mind's a blank slate. She might not look like one, but she is just a baby, really. Would you be able to walk past an abandoned baby?'

'I sure wouldn't take it home with me.'

'I don't want to take her home, I want to find out where she belongs. The police were no help. Do you think . . . ?'

The carer's sigh and rolled eyes told her she was wasting her time, but: 'I'll try to find somebody who can see you.'

But when she did finally achieve an interview with a member of the administrative staff, Ms Bogan, there was no help on offer. 'Can't you just keep her in the health centre for a few days, until you find out who she is? Or send her to a hospital or a nursery – you must have a contract with one of those places. Isn't that what you'd do with an abandoned baby?'

'That is not a baby.'

'Mentally she is. There's no difference, they're both equally helpless.'

'She didn't have to make herself helpless.'

'You could say the same thing about any addict, or someone who tried to commit suicide. Would you turn them away if they were at risk, or dying, because they'd done it to themselves?'

'That depends,' said Ms Bogan coolly. 'Are we talking about an alcoholic with a decent insurance package, or a down-and-out? Surely you're familiar with the concept of community care?' Her smile was as disturbing as the grin on a bare skull; it flashed and was gone. 'Unless the indigent are in need of heroic intervention to save their lives we invoke the concept of community care. Which is what I will do now, also pointing out to *you* that *she* is not a member of *our* community.'

Hostility towards the super-rich, the 'immortals', was common among the general public, more so than Renate's awe, yet she was shocked to encounter it here. She had romantic notions about people who worked in health care, due to her addiction to the same dramatic serials that fed her fantasies about the super-rich.

'Well, what do you suggest I do? Take her to a rich people's hospital – if I could find one – and throw her on their mercy?'

'There's no point. She could be from anywhere, from an enclave in Switzerland or Colorado as likely as one around here. Anyway, I'm sure that by now her ex-husband has had her declared incompetent and taken all her assets in trust. If she lives to grow up, she'll have her work cut out for her finding him again and fighting to get it back. If she dies, well, it's not his fault and he'd probably inherit anyway.'

'She could die? Isn't she immortal?'

'Just because the tabloids called them immortals, and they happen to like the name, doesn't mean they *are*. She'll live a long time if she's lucky, but a lot of the things that could kill you could kill her – a gun or a knife or a fall from a high place, to mention only three.'

It was too late to go anywhere else by the time she left the health centre, even if she'd had anywhere else in mind to go. So she took Becky home. There was nothing else she could do.

Len didn't agree, but he was basically an easy-going man, and as he'd never in all the years they'd been together won an argument with Renate, he didn't put up much of a fight. He gave a leave-me-out-of-it shrug and plugged himself back into his sports programme and left his wife to the task of settling their uninvited visitor down for the night.

Not liking the idea of leaving Becky alone, Renate stayed home from work the next morning and phoned the Office of Public Health and Happiness, where someone who preferred to let herself be represented on the viewing screen as a hologrammatic Mickey Mouse, took Becky's details.

'I can see that's a problem for you, and all of us here deeply sympathize, but I'm afraid this citizen doesn't fall within our criteria of those truly in need.'

'But how much more in need could she be? She's completely helpless, she's just a baby!'

'It is certainly understandable that you would see her in that way, but the fact of the matter is she is not a baby but an adult who has made herself deliberately helpless. And as you probably know, in cases of deliberate failure to provide for the self, the body public is not morally required to provide assistance of any kind.'

'But somebody has to help! However it happened, she is effectively helpless now.'

'Her family has the moral and legal obligation to provide care.'

'But I don't know who her family is!'

'You are her family.'

'Me! I'm not related to her – I never saw her before yesterday!'

'If you'll forgive me saying so, arguing on the basis of blood relationships is terribly outdated. And of course legal documents need not be drawn up to make a partnership valid – anyone who has ever fallen in love knows that! It is only necessary that you choose to live together and care about each other to be recognized as a family in the eyes of the public community.'

'But we don't live together!'

'You have just been telling me how you took her home with you last night. You took on the role of care-giver, and however it came about you have entered into a meaningful, ongoing relationship with Becky, as you call her. She's being cared for by you. There's no problem.'

'There certainly is a problem!'

At once Ms Mickey was all solicitousness. 'There is? Are you finding it difficult to cope? Would you like a visit from a social worker?'

Argument was clearly useless. She declined the social worker – a phrase that had been a foul insult in her childhood but which had recently been rehabilitated – but one turned up at their flat a few days later. It was, like the peacekeeper, an Artificial, and just as understanding. It let them know, in no uncertain terms, that Becky was now their responsibility, and that any attempt to evade that responsibility, by abuse, neglect or abandonment, would be very harshly condemned. If necessary, Becky would be taken into care, but, in such an extreme case, both Renate and Len would be looking at prison sentences.

Len was wonderful in adversity. Never a word of blame, and he was with her all the way. In all the years they'd been together perhaps she'd come to take him a little for granted, but every now and again she realized how lucky she was to have him.

He helped out more with Becky than he had with their own daughter. He had only a part-time job now, whereas when Tamara had been small he'd been working full-time and more, while she had supplemented their income as best she could with piecework that could be done at home. Also, she had never needed his help with Tamara as desperately as she did with Becky, who she could barely lift off the floor.

She tried to find someone else to look after the baby, even part-time, but it was a job no one wanted. All the child-minders charged over the odds because she wasn't a 'normal' baby and because they thought they scented money. In the end, Renate had to give up her job. The loss of her weekly wages was a hardship, otherwise she didn't mind. Looking after a baby, even though it wasn't her baby, even though it wasn't really a baby, was lots more fun than production line work. She'd always wanted more than one child, and after it became clear there would be no more she'd pinned her hopes on her daughter producing some grandchildren before Renate was too old to enjoy them. Not that her daughter, now twenty-three, had yet shown any inclinations in that direction. Tamara, in fact, had turned into something of a disappointment all round. She'd been a wonderful child, an unmixed blessing as far as her parents were concerned, but now she'd joined a Christian cult and become a religious fanatic. Renate's friends told her she should be glad her daughter hadn't followed the path taken by 82 per cent of her schoolmates and become a criminal and/or drug addict, but she frankly couldn't see that this was any improvement.

Despite all the problems Becky caused – poverty the chief among them –

she did fill a gap. Although her great, ungainly adult body lacked the vulnerable charm of infancy, she was more like a real baby than the incontinent, mentally subnormal adult she resembled. Like all babies, she was growing and learning with astonishing speed, changing every day, gaining in ability and alertness with every passing hour. When her brown eyes locked on to Renate's and she smiled that special, sweet smile of recognition, she couldn't help responding. Their bonding took longer than it had with Tamara, but within four months she was every bit as helplessly in love with this second-timer as she'd been with her own baby.

Which was probably just as well, since her own baby denounced her for giving aid and comfort to an Evil One and declared she would have nothing more to do with her natural mother until such time as she renounced her past wickedness and joined the One True Church.

Renate had known that her daughter's sect abhorred the immortals as going against nature, man and God, but 'What about Christian charity? I could hardly leave her to die . . . '

'Of course you could – and should! The sooner God reclaims each Evil One, the better for all of us. By their actions, by attempting to evade God's will for them, they have attempted to become more than human, and so, by renouncing our common humanity, they must forfeit all human help. I shall pray for you, Mother.'

For once, Renate was glad that looking after Becky left her so little time to think about her own problems. The new baby's development seemed uncannily quick, and although the more Becky could do the more trouble she was, Renate nevertheless felt a mother's pride in watching her gigantic darling learn to crawl and then to stand. Unfortunately, when she used the bookcase to pull herself to her feet she also pulled the bookcase over on top of her, but no childhood is survived without some damage.

Damage to the furniture and the flat was the least of it. Renate was covered in bruises from her regular tussles to stop the baby from climbing out the window (they were on the eighth storey) or playing with the microwave. Once, as they grappled together, Becky got a stranglehold on her neck and didn't let go until some time after Renate had passed out. She realized then that the baby could have killed her. Renate was always aware that she was dealing with a baby, and she restrained herself, fearful of doing Becky some injury, but Becky had no such fears, no such restraint. After the throttling Renate knew she had to be quite ruthless or she might end up dead. Harshness with children did not come easily to her, but she hardened her heart and worked on impressing Becky with the notion that she must never, ever fight against her mother or father, and must always obey them. She could so easily have killed herself, or all of them, during an unsupervised moment that Renate sometimes had to tie her down while she went to the toilet or got on with cooking their dinner. She did this only when it was absolutely necessary, and never for very long, but it was unfortunate that it was during one of those times that the social worker chose to pay a surprise call.

She should count herself lucky to be let off with a warning. The bruises on baby Becky were noted ('What about my bruises?' demanded Renate) and she was put on the 'at risk' register. There would be more visits. The prospect of having Becky taken away was by this time more chilling than the threat of a prison sentence, at least to Renate. She wasn't sure how Len felt, he wasn't in the habit of talking about his feelings, but she could see that he had grown fond of their foster-daughter.

There was one good result from having Becky on the 'at risk' register: Renate finally received a 'carer's allowance'. It wasn't much, it nowhere near made up for her loss of wages, but it was something.

By seven months Becky was walking and saying a few words. By the end of her first year with them she was toilet trained and talking in sentences. Remembering how long it had taken Tamara to pass those particular milestones, Renate was impressed. She wondered if she could take any credit for the child's quickness – had she really been too lenient, too easy-going with Tamara? But then someone told her that immortals seldom took their second childhoods in real time, they usually condensed eighteen years into nine. Even with all the time in the world, people were still obsessed with saving it.

Knowing that her one-year-old was 'really' two made Renate hopeful of getting back to work sooner than she'd thought. Most toddlers spent time apart from their mothers in playgroups – if not all day, then at least a few mornings a week. But when Renate began to enquire she found no one willing to take Becky. She was too big; she'd be disruptive, impossible to control, and she wasn't really a toddler.

'Of course she's a toddler! She's only been walking for six months! What else is she if she's not a toddler?'

'She's a second-timer,' said the playgroup leader. 'She should be with her own kind.'

It was prejudice; it was class-hatred, pure and simple. There was a toddlers' group for second-timers in a wealthy enclave across town, but even if she could have afforded the fees, without a private vehicle, travel between those two areas was practically impossible. She would just have to keep Becky at home with her until she was ready for school.

But when Renate began to enquire about schooling, she ran into a bureaucratic nightmare of double-talk and double-think. Becky was either far too young (two and a half) or far too old (it was anybody's guess, since her birth identity was still a mystery, but the idea of living through a second childhood had no appeal for anyone under a hundred years old) for a place in a local school. A school for children with special needs might be indicated, but few had places and those that did (a school for the deaf, a school for the multiply handicapped) were inappropriate.

The present government had been making noises about its commitment to equal opportunities and education for everyone, so Renate wrote to her representative to enquire about the possibility of a state-funded place for her daughter in one of the private-sector second-timers' schools. His reply was unhelpful.

After some waffling about his government's commitment to equal opportunities he went on to say: 'Note that word "equal". Your foster-daughter has already been educated, and I would hazard a guess that she received an exceptionally fine and prolonged education. She has no need of another one, because the first is still there in her mind, waiting to be accessed when she's eighteen. Now, when there are scarcely enough places in our schools for all the poor children who need them, where is the fairness in providing another one for your foster-daughter? She doesn't need a second education; she doesn't need training for anything – it's not as if she'll grow up to need a job!'

'No,' muttered Renate to herself, 'but *I* do!'

Eventually, through a combination of psychological blackmail and luck, they managed to get Becky a place in a local primary school.

Becky hated it. She was smarter than everybody else, she said, and didn't like all those little people; she wanted to stay home with Mummy and Daddy. She'd throw a tantrum or make herself sick in the mornings to get her way.

Renate felt close to despair. She'd found herself a job, but wouldn't have it long if she kept taking days off, and there was little point in having it just to pay the lion's share of her wages to baby-sitters. At an age when most children were reaching out, becoming more interested in the wide world, turning away from their parents towards friends their own age, Becky was going through a clinging phase. At least, Renate hoped it was a phase. The demands of this child – who was physically a woman considerably taller and heavier than herself – to be picked up and carried were suffocating. Becky knew very well that Renate couldn't pick her up but rather than accepting this physical fact as she had when she was younger and less reasonable, Becky would simply throw herself on her mother and let herself go limp, knocking them both to the floor.

Len was strong enough to lift Becky and often gave in to her babyish demands. 'Oh, well, if it makes her happy,' he'd say, and Renate didn't argue. She felt guilty because she'd never been able to hold Becky as a baby *should* be held. She wondered what that lack would do to Becky psychologically.

Probably that earlier deprivation was why she was being so difficult just now. 'Just don't put your back out,' she'd say to Len, and then she'd get on with some housework while he cuddled their daughter.

It was during this phase, Becky's fourth year as a child, that the company Len worked for went out of business and he was left without a job. He was still some years away from his pension, but he was effectively unemployable. He made a few token efforts to find work, but they both knew it wouldn't come to anything, and so, when she was offered the chance to increase her hours of work, to go full-time, she took it. They needed the money, and Len didn't mind looking after Becky. Despite his initial resistance, he had become very fond of their foster-child.

Life wasn't too bad. Becky could be demanding, but she was a sweetheart, really, and Renate was glad to have her. She didn't hate her new job, Len wasn't really sorry to be in early retirement, they had just enough money to get by, they had each other, they were happy.

Then one day she took ill at work – the machines she had to work with sometimes made her queasy, but this was different, she was vomiting and feverish, probably she'd picked up some virus – and had to go home in the early afternoon. She was hoping that Becky would still be at school, she was in no mood to cope with the demands of a vivacious schoolgirl, but as soon as she entered the flat she could hear the girl's voice, raised in a cry of delight. Obviously she was playing some game with her father, but what game came as a rude shock when she opened the bedroom door and saw them there together on the bed, both of them naked.

If she had not seen it with her own eyes, she would never have believed her Len capable of such an abomination.

When Renate started screaming, Becky ran out.

'Your own daughter! How could you!'

'She's not my own daughter, she's not even my adopted daughter. You just brought her home one day, and—'

'But she's a child!'

'She's not a child.'

'She's eight years old!'

'Only to you,' said Len. He'd started out looking guilty but now was grim and stubborn. 'Face it, she's a grown woman as everyone but you is well aware.'

'That's only her body! Inside her head she's only eight years old – and you know that as well as I do. How could you abuse that child—'

'It was not abuse! She wanted it! Christ, she's been after me for weeks! I can't believe you didn't notice. All that kissing and cuddling and fondling, climbing on to my lap . . . I got tired of running away. I got tired of fighting it. She's a very attractive woman and she got me aroused and . . . I'm sorry.'

Later she wished she had accepted his apology, had been willing to be reasonable, but in the heat of the moment she was all outraged maternal energy. Becky was her child, and Len was nothing more than the man who had wronged her. His thoughtless lust had destroyed their marriage.

Len did not recognize what she felt, any more than she understood what he had done. He went on trying to reason with her, pointing out that it was only once, stressing that he had been seduced, reminding her that once before, during a rocky patch in their marriage, they each had strayed, survived the experience, forgiven it—

'That was different. We were all adults. This was a child you abused, a child in our care. My care. I won't risk it happening again; I can't. I won't have her taken away from me, and I won't have her destroyed by you.'

'Destroyed by me? Are you kidding? Look, OK, it was wrong, I admit it, I'm sorry. We'll explain to Becky that it was wrong, that she mustn't try to seduce Daddy ever again, and that'll be an end to it—'

'I wish that could be an end to it. But what you've done to her – you've destroyed her childhood, don't you realize that?'

'What childhood? This is a grown woman we're talking about – a woman considerably older than I am, chronologically. OK, so she's having a second childhood, she got her memories erased and went back to a blank state – so they say. I'm not so sure. They think they're immortal, they think they can do anything. And they play all kinds of perverse games. No, listen to me. You think you know Becky, but you're fooling yourself. She's not your daughter. She's a sick old woman pretending to be an innocent child. Innocent! The things her body remembers . . . I'm sorry. I'm sorry. But I didn't destroy her childhood, I played right into her hands. Don't you realize that at least half the reason those people go back for a second childhood in their own grown-up bodies is so they can have sex with their new Mummy or Daddy? That's what it's all about.'

She refused to listen. Becky was her daughter now, her sweet little girl, and Len was only digging his grave deeper, trying to save his skin by pretending that it was all Becky's fault. She wouldn't have accepted such a line from anyone. It sickened her to hear it coming from Len, the man she'd thought she'd known, the man she'd thought she loved for so long. She threw him out.

She missed him dreadfully, almost immediately. So did Becky. Naturally blaming each other for his loss, they were of no comfort to each other. She tried not to blame the child, but after what had happened, after such knowledge, Becky had become sexualized, her woman's body all too obvious, no longer something that could be seen past or through to the child within.

Becky had changed, not just in the eyes of her mother. Always a difficult child, she now became impossible. Instead of playing sick or begging to stay home, she would go off to school in the morning and simply never arrive. If Renate went with her or put her on the peoplemover in the care of another mother, her safe arrival could be counted on, but more often than not she would simply walk out of the school sometime during the morning. Where she went, how she spent her time, was something no one but Becky knew.

Renate was in despair. She quit her job and took on part-time work to fit in around her daughter's school hours, but still could not control her. They were back in the old poverty trap, she was tired all the time and there was no money for treats, baby-sitters, or the child psychologist that Becky's teacher had recommended.

Eventually she went to Len and asked him to come back. He spoke gently, he swore he loved her now and always, but he would not return unless she got rid of Becky. She could not consider it. Becky was now as much a part of her life as if she'd given birth to her. What mother ever gave up her natural child for the qualified love of a man?

But Becky was not her child, not a natural child at all in the eyes of anyone but Renate. Even her friends thought she was crazy to let a good man go so she could continue to care for an uncaring creature. But Renate knew that no matter how old Becky was physically, she was still just a child inside, out of control, needing all the love, guidance and protection her parents could give.

When Becky was arrested for soliciting, Renate blamed herself.

At first she couldn't believe it, she was sure there'd been some misunderstanding. So a member of the Vice Squad – human, unlike the peacekeepers she'd previously encountered – showed her the tapes they had made of her girl in action. It was sickening, the things she did and the way she did them, with strangers. The incident with Len had been bad enough, but that had been informed by affection and innocence. This, though—

'Why? Why would she do such things?'

'For the money,' said the officer. 'She needed the money. She's Becky Valpariso – she used to be fabulously wealthy – God only knows what happened to wipe her out.'

'You know her name,' said Renate, stunned. 'Her old name – who she really was—'

'Sure, we had to ID her – she was perpetrating a crime. Contacted her husband, but it turns out he'd divorced her for desertion a couple of years ago. All their property was jointly owned, and he had to sell off a lot of it to pay off her bad debts. She was a very rich woman. Now – doing the skinny lick street-side for donuts.' He laughed, coarsely. Renate almost wished she'd been assigned to an ordinary Artificial peacekeeper.

'So how – why – did you get in touch with me?'

'Perp's request.' He played the rest of the tape. There was Becky in a holding cell, flanked by two peacekeepers and one human officer-in-charge. She was half-naked and red in the face with rage, screaming, 'I'm not a grown-up! I'm not! Liar, liar, house on fire! You're making it all up! My name is Becky Jones, you call my mum and ask her who I am, she'll tell you! Call her, go on, it's Renate Jones, S-22-000-8974-8. Call her right now and tell her to come and get me out!'

'Perps got rights, too,' said the officer. 'Besides, there was nobody else to pay the fine. So: you going to pay it, and spring her, or do we lock her up for three months?'

Renate paid, of course – she had spent years of her life paying for Becky and wasn't ready to stop. As usual, her kindness awoke no gratitude in the child, who began shouting at her as soon as she saw her.

'Why didn't you tell me who I was? Why did you lie to me, let me think I was your daughter?'

'I tried,' said Renate, weakly, knowing she had never tried very hard. She had always intended to answer the child's questions truthfully, as they arose, but the questions never came. Unlike a real child, she displayed no curiosity about where she had come from, and never seemed to find it odd that she was so much larger than the children she went to school with. She took her own size and shape so much for granted that she never asked about it, and assumed that the difference in other children meant there was something wrong with them. Renate had told her the story of finding her, but either Becky had not taken it in, or had assumed that was how parents always got their children.

They went home, and life went on, a nightmare. Becky seemed determined to punish Renate, who continued, helplessly, to care for her. There were more brushes with the law, and more fines, but somehow it was never enough to require that Becky should be taken into care. The girl ran away once, and when she turned up a few weeks later, hungry and bruised-looking, Renate was both relieved to see her still alive and appalled that the whole cycle would now begin again.

It went on like that, for what seemed an endless time, until Becky grew up.

She grew up all in a minute. One moment she was in a heavy fog of helpless rage and confusion, the next she was herself again. She remembered. Some memory blocks were still in place, and she knew she would need professional help to dissolve them, but she remembered the important things, like the numbers and identity codes for her secret bank accounts, and details of various properties and titles she'd kept hidden from Steve, just in case.

She was no longer a nobody, no longer a child, no longer helpless and, most importantly, no longer poor. She could do what she wanted.

She got up, got dressed, and went out without a word to the woman who had been her foster-mother for the duration of her second childhood. She didn't speak because she couldn't bring herself to be polite. Knowing that poor old Renate had done the best she could didn't make her like her any better. Her best, quite frankly, had never been good enough. She had deserved a better mother, and Renate was going to have to pay for her shortcomings.

Not as much as Steve was going to have to pay, though. She had trusted Steve, who had claimed to love her, and he had betrayed her, taken her money, and dumped her out in the cold, cruel world to die. Steve was going to suffer as he'd made her suffer.

And as for Len—

Tears came to her eyes as she thought of Len, and she had to pause for a while until her vision cleared and she could cross the street. She had loved Len with all her childish heart and soul, truly loved him. It was the kind of love that, as a jaded adult, she had practically forgotten could exist, and that experience alone had made her second childhood worthwhile. If only Len had been worthy of her!

She'd been only eight years old, she'd had no defences, no understanding of men. He'd been not only her father but the first man she'd loved, her first lover. She had given herself to him completely – and he had rejected her. It was something she would never forgive, could never forget, how she had run away from home and managed to find him, and the cold, contemptuous look in his eyes as he met her on the doorstep and refused to let her in. How could he treat her like that, as if her love had meant nothing?

He'd soon know better. She decided there and then to take care of Len first. She began to feel happier just thinking about it. She didn't mind that money couldn't buy love; it wasn't love she wanted now, and she had more than enough money to satisfy her hate.

Legitimate Targets

Ian McDonald

At thirteen minutes past ten, Johnny Considine, aged twenty-three years, realized that the future course of his life would be dictated by television news. It came in the last story before the break, immediately after an item on a possible United Nations embassy to the Shi'an motherworld sixty light years away.

Police today in Belfast . . .

'I don't think anyone really believes they're from another planet,' said Orlaith, his girlfriend of three weeks, heaving another scuttle-load of mixed coal and empty cigarette packets on to the fire. Johnny craned past her, mesmerized by the images on the screen.

. . . shot dead. A man and a woman arrested . . .

The body, half-covered with a green wax jacket. So little blood, really. The feet, oddly splayed. Thirteen-hole Docs.

'. . . their shit luck to have ended up on this of all worlds. You know, I'll bet you they smell funny.'

Policemen. SS. RUC. Black bastards, standing around cradling their big guns like babies.

. . . Castlereagh holding centre. They are believed to be . . .

'Hey, Orlaith, could you move your fat ass? I'm trying to watch this.'

God-awful Photo-me mugshots. Make anyone look like a terrorist. Aoife Brennan. Charlie Fitzpatrick. No question of 'belief' about it, Mr Newsreader. It's who they are.

'They could solve all our problems, you know, if they'd shipped the lot of them over here,' Orlaith said. 'All eight million of them. Everyone's a minority then, Taeg and Prod. Had the chance with the Hong Kong Chinese and they blew it; blew it again with the Sheenies . . .'

'Shi'an. It's pronounced Shi'an. Something to do with the dual aspects of their sexuality.'

. . . members of the IRA computer-terrorism squad responsible for the Brown Wednesday Stock Market mini-crash and the Northern Bank collapse . . .

'Listen to the Sheenie expert, would you? I'm putting the kettle on. Fancy a cup?'

'What? Yes. Thanks. Black . . . '

'No sugar. I'm learning.'

. . . a fourth member of the gang escaped and is still at large, though police are confident of a quick arrest. In part two . . .

The swelling thunder of the jug-kettle. Some boffin once proved a kettle generates as many perceived decibels as a back-throttling Boeing.

'All right if I use your phone?' Johnny shouted to Orlaith.

'You know where it is.'

It was a yellow payphone, greedy of fifty pees and much scrawled with the numbers of taxi firms and pizza delivery companies. He picked up the receiver and it hit him, the nauseating panic that burned through the pit of his stomach. He reached for the bannister to keep from falling. His balls felt as tender and vulnerable as two skinned apricots. Ring ring. Be in, you bastard. Ring ring. Answer, you bastard. Ring ring. Ring ring. Ring—

'Eugene. Listen. Just listen. They've lifted Aoife and Charlie. Joey's dead. He's dead, Eugene. They shot him.'

'Jesus, Johnny. Oh Jesus . . . '

'Listen. Mikey got away. I don't know how, I don't know where the fuck he's gone. You know I never trusted the peelers; with Mikey out there, I trust them even less. So get what you have and go.'

'Johnny. Fuck, Johnny . . . '

'Johnny?' The voice called from the living room with its warm fire and posters of women tennis players scratching their bums and old furniture friendly and mangey as an alcoholic's dog. Another world, Johnny. Another planet. 'Coffee!'

'Just be a second, Orlaith. OK?' He jammed the mouthpiece to his lips. 'If we don't know each other we can't hurt each other. So don't come looking for me, Eugene, for old times' sake, don't talk about me, don't wonder what I'm up to. Just colour me dead, Eugene.'

The coins clattered into British Telecom's metal gullet. At the age of twenty-three, at ten o'clock and twenty-eight minutes, Johnny Considine took his best beloved black leather jacket off Orlaith Hughes's coat rack, closed the door of 27 Malone Avenue quietly behind him and began to walk. At the cashpoint beside Simpson's all-niter he withdrew all the money his card would allow. His outstretched thumb hooked in a passing Pandoro at the end of the West Link. Later, while the driver, rejoicing, stuck into his five a.m. Ulster fry in the truckers' lounge, Johnny leaned against the aft rail and watched the land of his birth merge with the dawn grey as the great blue and white ship took him away into exile.

The laws of universal perversity demand that while the way is open for you to go back you will not, but when you want to, more than anything, you cannot. When he was eight years old Johnny Considine was sent to Florida to summer with his Uncle Ciaran, headhunted by the bran and tan cyberdweebs of Microsoft Key. Knowing eight-year-olds, Uncle Ciaran took his nephew to Disneyland. As they had snaked along the line for Space Mountain ('Half an hour from this point', 'Photographic opportunity here') Johnny had noted a number of well-labelled Chicken Gates. 'For those who just can't go through with it,' Uncle Ciaran had explained. His aspirant manhood impugned, Johnny had scorned the Chicken Gates. Ten persons from the car. His resolve faltered. Five persons from the car. He panicked. No more Chicken Gates. No way back. The smiling staff lifted him, strapped him in. Johnny Considine, age eight with nowhere to run, pissed himself.

Fourteen years later the entrapment was subtler but no less sure. The disillusionments of a fresh IT graduate condemned by Dame Europa to a hand-to-mouth existence grubbing freelance subcontracts from the big SAs and GmBHs were easily bolstered. New injustices hung sweetly on ancient enemies. Men, or things that seemed men, had come from the stars to live upon the earth, but don't you know, Johnny, the old griefs endure, the old wars never end, the old battle is unrelenting. Blandishments. *Oh, Johnny*, praise, *Oh, Johnny Johnny* rewards, *Oh, Johnny Johnny Johnny*. Seductions. Do this for me, Johnny, do this for us, Johnny. Hack this file, Johnny. Seed this virus, Johnny. Yet he saw the Chicken Gates. He knew what was happening to him, where he was being led, what he was being shaped into, and he consented. At any time he could have walked away. And when the time came that he wanted to, he could no longer do so.

Brown Wednesday had been amusing; a cybernetic pantomime with lots of people running around and shouting 'Behind you! Look behind you!' Thirty billion wiped off share values in one morning. Johnny Considine could only marvel at the miracle of Chaos Theory, by which one tiny ripple in the fiscal ocean slowly, surely, inevitably escalated into a fifty-foot tubular of cascading prices. Between coffee and lunchtime, the Irish Republican Army cost the Ould Hoor Britannia more than fifty-three years of armed struggle. By lunchtime the next day, Ould Hoor Britannia had it all back again.

The destruction of the Northern Bank PeeEllCee gave Johnny Considine great personal satisfaction. The virus systems had been immaculately designed; robust, untraceable, endlessly mutable. Within fifteen minutes of systems insertion they had spread their infection through every aspect of the bank's operations. Sixty million pounds in personal, small business and corporate accounts vanished. After a month sterilizing the system with hunter/killers, the Data Protection Squad traced the source of the infestation to the branch that had once upon a time casually refused the account application of one Mr John Considine because, as a freelance, he was not considered to be in possession of sufficiently regular tranches of cash. The Northern Bank PeeEllCee had forgotten Mr John Considine. Mr John Considine had not forgotten the Northern Bank.

Then came the West Drayton operation and Johnny Considine came down from the high mountain with Robin Hood and Butch and Sundance and the blessed company of heroic rogues, and saw the hundreds who would die burning because of what they wanted him to do. He looked around then for the Chicken Gate and the Chicken Gates were all closed. The hands lifted him and set him in the slow climbing car. Johnny Considine waited until he reached the very top, and on the edge of the precipice into darkness he jumped.

At the end of the twin rivers of blacktop that pushed through the day and the night he found a London so alien it might have been a district of the Shi'an capital world. Sampan suburbs jostled on the high tide beneath Cleopatra's Needle; it was once again possible for a latter-day Dr Johnson to cross the Pool of London dryshod. Cardboard and packing-case bashes crowded the Inns and squares, the trees reduced to dismembered trunks for firewood. A white boy with a Stanley knife tried to rob Johnny on the westbound platform of Shepherd's Bush Central Line and fled empty-handed at the sound of an Ulster accent. When Johnny saw his first alien – buying a cheese salad mayo baguette from a stand outside King's Cross Thameslink – he stared, disturbed in spirit, so long that he missed his bus. However frequently he was to see Shi'an abroad in the city, they never failed to evoke that second look, and stir disquiet in his good Christian Brothers' soul.

With the dregs of his money he put up the deposit and one month down on a flat in Limehouse. Opposite his window was a church steeple where every day the vicar would go out on to the parapet to examine the four corners of the world. Watching from his *eau-de-Nil* cube, Johnny imagined him deciding on the face of what he found whether to throw himself off or not. With the embers of his talent Johnny found a commission as a technical author writing User-Bibles for dismally uninspiring personal accountancy software. The tranches came no more regularly than in Belfast, but were larger.

On his fifth Sunday Johnny went out to buy a paper and met a crusty sprawling in a doorway. The crusty wore thirteen-hole Docs, splayed out at an odd angle. The paper went unbought. By the time he got back to his room Johnny was shaking so hard he needed five attempts to open the door. He found himself inexplicably prostrate across his bed, heaving terrible, shuddering, dry sobs. He had not liked Joey. He had feared Joey. In the end he had hated Joey, but Joey was dead under the paisley lining of some passer-by's green Barbour, and Johnny was an inescapable exile in an alien nation.

There was a place – modestly, and accurately, called Moe's Diner and Bar – where he would flee the instant before the walls closed on him. It was that kind of good-food-cheap, pink-flamingos eatery that inevitably becomes fashionable through its absolute rejection of fashion. The mammoth cappuccino machine, topped by an Imperial Eagle, had been to Abyssinia with Mussolini. The records in the jukebox – coin-in-the-slot, no cards, certainly no sing-along videoke – had not been changed in forty years and could render even the most stony-hearted of patrons moist with nostalgia for an age when, in all probability, their parents had not even been conceived. Drum-head swivel stools *with footrests* ran along the bar for those who cared to eat publicly. For those who wished seclusion there were a number of Naugahyde booths with wipe-kleen menus, stainless steel cruets like elephantine dum-dum bullets and bottles of tomato ketchup wearing gamine paper neckerchiefs to conceal ghastly cut throats of dried drips. Moe himself was a genial bear of a man who kept a '98 World Series L'il Slugger above the wineglass rack for Grade One Trouble and a loaded self-targeting Fiuzzi automatic under the till for Grade Two Trouble. As a consequence he never had trouble of either grade. Moe's front-of-house staff – friendly, well-trained, polite, efficient – numbered five: two Chinese, one West Indian, one Scot and one Shi'an.

The first time the alien came to scribble his order on a little notebook, Johnny was so stunned he could do nothing but stare. He was within touching distance of something from sixty light years away. A lifetime of accrued abstractions and informations – childhood television documentaries hastily flicked by mother to the snooker when they got on to Not Nice Stuff, school projects, *National Geographic* articles pasted into his *Aliens Scrapbook*, encyclopaedia entries, shareware research – all these were made concrete, actual, in a thousand little inhumanities. The texture of an alien skin. The strangely *different* cocktail of body musks and sweats. Tall – over average height, they came from a shallower gravity-well than Earth's. Slim as a child; like a child, no external gender identifiers. Shi'an sexual identity is more pheromonal than physiological. His/her eyes were large, the oval irises almost black; nose broad – all that olfactory information, he supposed – mouth narrow, lips thin. The ears were very small, the scalp clad in a narrow strip of short, dark red fur that ran up over the centre of the skull and tapered into a spine-hugging line of soft fuzz beneath the neck of the Moe's Diner and Bar T-shirt. Johnny was reminded of a terracotta Benin head he had once fallen in love with in an art gallery on Botanic Avenue.

'You ordering something?' The voice: a breathy contralto, could be either a man's or woman's. The accent was at once utterly unidentifiable and maddeningly familiar. The left hand keeping pen poised above pad had three fingers.

'I'm sorry. I'll have the . . . Excuse me, do you mind if I ask you a question?'

'That depends.'

'Are you a man or a woman?'

'I'm a girl,' the Shi'an said, and her answer crystallized the flux of possibilities and contradictions she had been until that second. 'Now, what are you having?'

After she had cleared the dishes away, Johnny sat a long time in the booth, breathing in her intimate musks and perfumes and feeling things he could not quite comprehend but felt he had known all his life. She had not smiled once during the entire dining experience.

Though Johnny became a fixture, it was a brave day the Tuesday he brought his Compaqt into Moe's Diner and Bar. He had prevaricated three weeks over the decision. The booths were private, the atmosphere vastly more conducive to technical writing than the oppressive room with its view of the melancholy vicar, but he still feared people craning over the partition and asking him if he was a writer, had he sold anything, did he write under his own name? People didn't. She did.

'What you writing?' She set his customary Coors on a paper *Moe's Diner and Bar* coaster, and sneaked a peek at his rollscreen. Alien kinesis: odd relaxations and attitudes that looked distinctly disjointed to Johnny.

'Just some computer manual. MicroServe Nemesis 4.2. It's a link-in between accountancy and legal 'wares.' Courage, Johnny. Make the jump from passing strangers to occasional acquaintances. 'Actually, I suppose this is kind of Stone Age to you.'

'Depends,' she said, and went to attend other customers. It was half an hour before she was free to return and add, 'I mean, it'll be eighty years before you can even begin to understand our quantum tunnelling processors; on the other hand, we've never thought of computerizing our legal system. Seyamang.'

'Johnny.' They shook hands, the human way. At some point in the thirty minutes she had waited tables, she had ceased to be an alien, a Traveller, a Shi'an, and become a person. He had still not seen her smile.

He thought of her that night. He thought of her naked, her skin the colour and texture of Benin terracotta. He thought of the electric fuzz-prickle of her head fur against the palm of his hand. He tried to imagine her nipples, her genitals, the heat of her body orifices. The luxurious excess of his fantasy shocked him. He had only just learned her name and he was fucking her. And she was Shi'an. Not human. Inhuman. Like fucking a beautiful, glossy, rust-red Irish setter.

He did not get to Moe's for several days. He hid in his ugly little room, terrified by the understanding that the obscure object of desire he had chased down all his fumbled relationships had been the earth-red androgyny of the Shi'an. Terrified, elated.

When at last he went back to check the fast-fading mental Seyamang against corporeal reality, she was not there. Panic-stricken, he asked where she was.

The West Indian girl, Silelé, sat down beside him in his customary booth. 'Why do you want to know where Seyamang is?'

Caught. Crucified. He spread his hands helplessly, inviting nails.

'Just wondering. I like her. I get on with her.'

Silelé reserved a judgemental silence, then said, 'You some kind of frook, mister?'

'Some kind of what?'

'Frook. Men who get off on Shi'an. Like gays get off on other men, pederasts get off on children, rubberists get off on black latex. Frooks get off on Shi'an. We get them in here sometimes; word gets round there's a Shi'an working here. You get them wanking under the table, stuff like that. Moe makes sure they don't come back.'

'Jesus God, no, I mean, no . . .' *You mean yes, Johnny. It's true, Johnny.* No, it was not like that, not filthy and soiled, like that. *Then what is it like, Johnny-O?*

Silelé's posture and expression had not shifted, but Johnny could see that the conviction behind his stammered denial had convinced her.

'I believe you, Johnny. She'll be back tomorrow. Don't worry. If you really want to know, I think she likes you too.'

There had been a co-option at the Motherhouse down in Docklands, Seyamang told him on her return. All the Sorority were supposed to be there. They'd flown some in from Amsterdam. Somewhere between a wedding and a bar mitzvah, but a good bash, she said. Yet Johnny felt that she had not enjoyed the party and was glad to be back in her too-big Moe's Diner and Bar T-shirt, among the humans. Screwing his courage tight, he asked her if he could buy her a drink.

'Tell you what,' she said. 'You have one for yourself, and I'll have this on you.' From the hip-pocket of her black PVC jeans she produced a dimple-pack of aspirins and popped one into her three-fingered hand. 'Aspirin. Cheap thrills from Superdrug; pound a packet.' Seyamang swallowed the aspirin, dry, while Johnny swilled back his beer, and the spirit of the late-night diner that lives in the spiral scratch of old black vinyl whispered in his ear that for the first time in his twenty-three years he was truly living.

Johnny Considine was in love with the alien.

Because *word* had passed, because the right periodicals had used the right degree of capital city cynicism, Moe's Diner and Bar graduated from merely fashionable to famous. A desert storm of bright and beautiful descended upon it.

'Jesus Christ, Moe, what happened?' Johnny asked, pushing between besuited Friday-nighters towards his place at the bar. Moe, wiping glasses as ever, smiled ruefully.

'We're the place to be seen, Johnny-O. I'll give it ten days, if we're not deeply unfashionable by then, I'll make us deeply unfashionable.'

'Hiya, Johnny!' Seyamang shouted over the din. She blinked long lashes at him: a Shi'an smile, Johnny had learned. The bared teeth of a human smile they read as a threat.

'Hiya, Seyamang. Well, it's off. Bit-squirted to Albuquerque off some balloon moored in the jeststream over Greenland, and the discs Fed-Exed, just to be on the safe side. I think this deserves a bottle of something good.'

'Certainly does, Johnny.'

'Oi!' An overweight West Indian twentysomething in a collar so tight it squeezed out extraneous rolls of flesh, levered into Johnny's personal space. 'Never mind 'im, where's my Sloe Screw?' As Seyamang moved to the racked bottles behind the bar, twentysomething stage-whispered, 'Fucking Sheenies. At least they could have got someone speaks English.'

The thrilling vertigo was exactly the same one Johnny remembered feeling keying in the passwords to the Northern Bank PeeEllCee's managerial hierarchy. He heard his voice, razor-edged and precise, say, 'Excuse me. Don't call her that. She's a Shi'an. Her people were travelling between the stars while ours were eating each other's fleas. She is no more a Sheenie than you are a nigger. Nigger.'

A blur of the hand. The beer glass, shattered on the edge of the bar, was ten centimetres from Johnny's eyes. Behind it the livid, bestial face raged.

'What did you call me, you paddy bastard? What you call me, fucking paddy fucking murdering fucking IRA bastard? Eh, Paddy?'

'Johnny,' said Johnny. His body, the body of the raging man, the entire substance of the diner and its late-nite Friday clientele, seemed to be constructed out of brightly coloured helium-inflated PVC. Rise up, and blow away. 'My name is Johnny. Sir.' At some great remove in this luminous void, Moe was shouting, his faithful Number One '98 L'il Slugger the rod of absolute justice. The vinyl universe whirled like a kaleidoscope. Faces loomed, voices boomed, and Johnny was all-alonio at the bar.

'Johnny, by rights I should throw you out too,' Moe said, but Seyamang, slipping in behind him, squeezed Johnny's hand.

'Thanks, brother.'

'I think I'm going to be sick,' Johnny said, suddenly pale and sweaty. He just made it to the cubicle.

They waited an hour and ten minutes for the Diner and Bar to close. Fatboy and six fat friends. The fat friends brought Johnny down, kept him down with a kick to the kidneys, held him down to the piss-stained concrete while Fatboy told Johnny once again just what he thought of fucking treacherous murdering paddies, underlining his comments with repeated blows from size twelves to ribs, neck and head. *Fucking* murdering *fucking* paddies.

They took his cash. They took his cards. They pissed on him and ran off.

'Oh God,' Johnny whispered. 'Oh Jesus. Oh God. Oh Jesus I'm going to die.' He retched, emptily, agonizingly. Ribs grated. He spat blood. A light shone in his eyes. Fingers of pain explored his body. Three fingers.

'Oh fuck, Johnny.'

'Seyamang.'

'Don't say anything. I'll get an ambulance.'

'No. No. Seyamang, no, don't, I can't go to hospital.' Hospitals. Forms. Assault charges. Police investigations.

'Johnny, come on . . . '

'I can't tell you why, just believe me I can't go to a hospital.'

Shadows poured out of the recesses of his skull. Red-out. Sensory shutdown. His last conscious sensation was of being *lifted* by strong arms, and a feeling of warmth and security he had known only in childhood.

Seyamang Erreth Huskravidi lived in a glassy, draughty garret flat above a Shi'an provisions store on The Mitre. Exploding from the reservation His Majesty's government had granted them amongst the tumbled capitalist caryatids of Docklands, the Shi'an were the latest in a succession of immigrant populations to move into the streets of Poplar and Westferry. First the European Jews, next the Chinese, then the Indo-Pakistani community, now, refugees from sixty light years away. Multiple births among the colonists - a biological modification to secure a self-sustaining genebase in the shortest time (space was large, even foreshortened by relativistic Mach drive: once down at ground zero the settlers were on their own) – sent the population soaring. To Johnny, looking down like a glass god on to the street beneath Seyamang's light-filled flat, it seemed like a perpetual outdoor kindergarten. Tall, lithe Shi'an children dodged between the fluttering Sorority totems, chased each other around the nose-to-tailed cars, played vigorous football. Their screams and shouts and cries were oddly low-pitched and soft-edged.

'Johnny.'

He looked around, startled, and Seyamang took his picture.

'Nice one, Johnny.'

Waitressing for Moe was what she did, what she was was a photographer. And none of your point/squint/shoot/print videostill stuff either. Proper silver bromide, emulsion, developer and fixer photography. In black and white. 'It's such a beautiful medium,' she had told him the second night, when he had gone around the flat inspecting her framed prints. 'Absolute black, absolute white. Yet out of two irreconcilable opposites, everything can be envisioned. Lost art to us. More's the pity. It takes us to come to Earth to rediscover it.'

Shi'an technological society, the xenologists said, was eight thousand years old.

Seyamang photographed children; her people's children, caught unawares, spontaneous and candid, pulled out of the streets and closes of Westferry and slapped on to celluloid.

'So?' she had asked, fishing for compliments.

'I like this one,' Johnny had said, pointing out a poster-size colour still of the delicate geometry of a Shi'an interstellar ship poised against a starfield. She had wrinkled her nose: an alien *moue* of disappointment.

'And this?' Johnny had asked, picking up a piece of sculpture cast from liquid night. However he turned it in his fingers it seemed to flow sensuously into his hand, greedy for his grip.

Seyamang had swiftly snatched it from him.

'Don't mess with it, Johnny. It's dangerous.'

'What is it?'

'Maser,' Seyamang had said. 'Microwave laser. The Motherhouse didn't like the idea of me living all alone without any protection.'

'Christ, Seyamang . . . '

'I'll never have to use it, so just forget about it, Johnny.'

He almost succeeded.

'How are the ribs?' Seyamang asked. Hers were the strong, secure arms that had lifted him, carried him a mile and four flights of stairs, cleaned him, tended his wounds. *Tethba* was the name she gave this supernatural strength and endurance: a state of controlled rage the Shi'an could temporarily summon in extreme need. It did not come without price; utterly wasted, Seyamang had lain comatose where she fell on the mattress beside Johnny for a day and night.

When Johnny winced in reply to her question, she produced a cup of coffee. She had bought it specially for him. Alcohol, most meats, certain perfumes – most notably Chanel – were deleterious to the Shi'an. But the things that took them high: Aspirin, tea, car exhaust, the smell of his best beloved leather jacket.

'You know,' Seyamang said, curling comfortably on to the window-seat in a way that looked extremely uncomfortable to Johnny, 'I think we're both exiles of a kind.'

'What do you mean?' Johnny's outward innocence masked a sudden ice blue needle of fear. What might he have said while he was unconscious, stammering, drooling, shouting in his sleep?

'Outcasts from our people. Our communities. Our nations. Nothing behind us. No wall of lives. Separate.'

Winterborn, she called herself, translating the Narha expression. A lost generation of one. She had been born in the sixth month of the first subjective year of the World Ten Migration. Her mother, an outspace worker on the crew of Interstellar Sixty-Three, had conceived her in the last embers of the autumn sexual cycle before departure. A miscalculation. An oversight. An aberration. While her aberrant daughter rode her plastic tricycle along the gently curving corridors of Interstellar Sixty-Three and pestered the crew to play chasies with her, her father withered and grew old under eighty years of world-time.

'I had no friends my age, no one to grow up alongside. No one to touch, no one to keep close and warm. All alone. Finding out by myself what it meant to be Shi'an. I was six Earth-years – eight of our own – before the Generation One children were born after the landing, by the time they hit puberty – we mature early, Johnny – I was old enough to be rearing a family of my own.'

'How old are you?'

'My years, eighteen. Yours, fourteen.'

Johnny, his childhood cluttered with siblings and life, tried to imagine Seyamang singing to herself as she steered her tricycle around the ranked and filed stasis coffins in which the settlers slept their five subjective years to World Ten. He could not encompass it.

Seyamang had never known the pubescent same-sex crushes and attractions that drew Shi'an from their birth Sororities into new bonds and family partnerships. She had been swept by the pheromonal typhoon of the spring and autumn sexual cycles into fearful, half-comprehending couplings with men much older and more experienced than herself. Feeling *wrong*, feeling *different*, feeling *not Shi'an*, but not knowing what else she was, Seyamang withdrew from the Traveller community. Like some closed Soviet city, she was an internal exile; contained within her own people and society yet sealed off from them. Hearing the low soft cries of the children below, Johnny thought that maybe the streets of Shi'an Westferry were not so far from the kitchen-house terraces of Andystown. He had never belonged there, where they painted the kerb stones green, white and gold. A brother internal exile. He and Seyamang had new nationalities now, one that recognized no frontiers. The country of the dispossessed. A nation of sexual searchers. He reached out his two hands to touch hers. Her body was fever-hot, her bones and muscles lay in unfamiliar configurations beneath the terracotta skin. He tried not to think of Orlaith and of course could not. She seemed brutal and bovine, cheaply jerry-built next to this economical, compact, subtle alien. They all did, all the human women.

He kissed her. Her mouth tasted of things he had only ever dreamed.

She shook him away from her mouth; a redirection, not a rejection. She lifted her T-shirt, gently steered his mouth towards her nipples. Johnny needed no further urging. She whispered in Narha. The alien syllables were as exciting to Johnny as the taste of her flesh on his tongue.

'I do love you, Seyamang.'

'I always knew you were more than just a frook, Johnny-O. But I don't know if I love you.'

He pushed himself away from her flesh, like a swimmer launching into deep water.

'I know Shi'an love, Johnny, but I don't know human love.'

That night he brought three six-packs of Coors and a twenty-four carton of soluble aspirin from the last remaining Pakistani grocer in Westferry. He and Seyamang clinked glasses and got loud and joyful. Johnny tried to slip his hand into the waistband of Seyamang's jeans and was firmly rebuffed.

'I thought you loved me,' Johnny retorted. A cowardly, man's accusation.

'This is difficult. Believe me, I want to fuck with you, very much, but I can't. It's not the right time. I'm not in season. You understand what that means?'

Johnny's head and penis both understood, though differently.

'I try to imagine what it might be like to be you, Johnny; this state of permanent sexuality, but I can't *feel* it. I try to extend the passion the . . . fire . . . of *kesh* so that it never ends, but I can't. I can't imagine how you could live like that all the time. We have love and we have sex. Sex is *kesh*, love is . . . Love is what we feel for our friends, our partners, our Sorority sisters. Love is touching, and being touched.' Again, that wrinkle of the nose. 'So they say, Johnny. So they say.'

Closed cities.

'I want to love and have sex with you,' said satyric Johnny.

'So do I, Johnny. Believe me. I don't want to lose you just because of sex,' Seyamang said, soft-focused from the aspirin, dreamy. 'Will you wait for me? Will you wait, can you wait, until I come into *kesh*?'

'I will,' he said.

When Seyamang went to Moe's on her spluttering, clunky moped, Johnny would arrive to work in the bright, airy flat, sketching out a work-plan for a Bible on a new home-anime system between prolonged stints of daytime TV watching. It was there, in a top-of-the-hour bulletin, between an item on French manicure and a phone-in on sexual harassment, that the television news reclaimed its hold on his life. He came back with his fifth decaff of the day to see two men walking down the steps of Paddington Green police station while the BBC's legal correspondent informed him that two men from Northern Ireland had been released from detention under the Prevention of Terrorism Act without charge. Their names were given as Padraig McKeag from Lurgan and Anthony Woods from West Belfast. *One of you is lying*, Johnny Considine thought, *because I know you are really called Mikey McDonagh. Last seen running from the Royal Ulster Constabulary.*

'What's wrong?' Seyamang asked, coming home late to find Johnny sitting in the unlit living room, channel-hopping between news reports on the handset.

'Nothing,' he said. 'I'm all right. Don't worry. Go on, go to bed.' He knew she knew he was lying.

He asked her if he could stay with her, that night. On the couch, on the floor, it did not matter, just that he did not want to go back to his room.

'Fuck, Johnny,' Seyamang said, instantly awake at the sound of her name whispered in the four a.m. darkness. 'What is it? What's wrong?'

Johnny knelt penitently beside her mattress.

'Can I move in, Seyamang? Properly?'

'Sure, Johnny. Of course, Johnny. But in the morning, yes?'

Safe. Mikey would never look for him among the aliens.

When he went to collect his few possessions from his old flat, the street outside the church was busy with police cars and ambulances but they had come for someone other than Johnny Considine.

Autumn as a sexual season startled Johnny, son of streets where no leaves ever fell, where seasons came and went unmarked in redbrick anonymity. Overnight the streets of Westferry and Poplar filled with a subtle but unmistakable *frisson* that gave a new and exciting gloss to all the old familiar places, as if he were discovering them for the very first time. From the databases he had accessed on Shi'an physiology, he knew intellectually that human males were susceptible to the mating pheromones, but to actually feel them stir his soul, awaken daylight fantasies and dark night dreams of meat and sweat, was terrible yet liberating. His hindbrain growled. Ancient animal, awake.

When he woke in the night from his terracotta nightmares it was to the sound of music and voices from the street below. Shi'an males, battle-dancing, scoring complex coup on each other on impromptu dancefloors in highly stylized combats for sexual dominance. He would watch the leaping figures silhouetted against burning naphtha flares, unquiet in himself, feeling that here, in the trashlit street, was life, true life, life in all its fullness and his Johnny Considineness was only a pale projection on a pane of window glass.

Seyamang, too, changed with the season. Her skin darkened. She took to going about the flat stripped down to a pair of shiny black cycling shorts, asking Johnny how he could stick the heat. Her nipples were permanently erect. She was anxious, irritable, temperamental, forgetful, a whirlwind of impatience and activity, playing her incomprehensible Shi'an music far too loud, far too late, dancing edgily around the living room, smiling spasmodically at her photographs of children. She slept little, ate less. She smelled. It pervaded every corner of the apartment, part musk, part mould, part wild abandon. It lifted the hair along Johnny's spine. He lived in a permanent state of priapism. Terrified, exhilarated, he watched Seyamang come into *kesh*. She had never seemed more alien. He had never desired her more.

On the ninth night of the autumn season he came back from the wee shop, as he called it, to find her swaying entranced to her favourite piece of music playing at slate-dislodging volumes. Her body was patterned with signs and symbols in lip-gloss and fluorescent felt-marker.

'Johnny,' she shouted over the music, reaching out to press her body against his, 'dance with me. Please, Johnny.' She buried her nose in the folds of his leather jacket. 'Ooooh. Did you wear it just for me?' Trembling, Johnny ran his hand over her head fur.

She kissed him, the mouth-kiss of humans and the nipple-kiss of the Shi'an. Her hunger simply overpowered him. His lovemaking with Orlaith, with all the girls whose panties he had fumbled his way into, was no preparation for Seyamang. He was a virgin again. Everything had to be relearned. Her desire was urgent, yet she held back so they might explore each other. The slow engorgement of his penis caused her especial surprise and delight. 'Always exposed, always vulnerable,' she said with child-like wonder. Similarly wonderful to him the star-shaped pucker beneath a retractable hood of freckled skin that was her vagina. Higher than a human woman's, its lips and lining were so sensitive that a breath was enough to send her reeling and moaning in Narha. She marvelled at his pubic hair, twisted it between her fingers; she explored the curves and ridges of his erection. He slipped a moistened finger into her anus. She yelped in surprise, then crooned with pleasure; she coated him from head to toe with sweet-scented saliva. New erogenous geographies were mapped. New orientations established.

Johnny wanted to weep. Johnny wanted to crow. Sex had broken the bounds of self-consciousness that had always before constrained him. He could lose himself, he could give himself, because they were aliens to each other. He felt inebriated with freedom. Yet in the mating that night, each successive night, he knew he had only entered the shallow waters of Seyamang's sexual hunger. And a new dread arose. Could he go back to celibacy when the season ended and the *kesh* energy burned itself out?

Moe had given Seyamang time off from the diner; enlightened self-interest; in her current hormonal climate she would have converted every male customer into a potential frook. Contained by the glass walls of the flat, she fretted, she fussed. Between bouts of sex she was unapproachable and moody, pressing her hands and face to the tall windows and staring at the figures in the street for hours on end.

'Is it the dancing?' Johnny asked, resting his hands on her shoulders. Always, the heat. She shrugged: a Shi'an yes.

'I'm sorry,' she said. 'It's not you, Johnny. You're good. You're great. It's me. My fucking chemicals. My hormonal destiny. I'm not as free as I like to think I am.'

'Do you want to go?'

'Would you mind?'

Yes. 'No. I don't mind.' *Liar*. 'You go, if it'll make you happy.'

She mouth-kissed him. 'Thank you, Johnny. Thank you.'

He watched her ride off on her moped and turn the corner into Newell

Street. He raged silently around her flat filled with her smell and her pictures of unsmiling Shi'an children. Whatever was drinkable he drank. He watched the sunset. He watched the lights of aircraft coming in across Docklands on final approach to Heathrow. He listened to the distant drums from the dancefloors. Sick in his heart he went to Moe's and his old, private, Naugahyde booth and drank until closing time.

'Seyamang, it's me.' The lights were on. The music playing. The musk insistent, urgent. She was back. Why didn't she answer? 'Seyamang.' Living room no kitchen no bathroom no study no. Knowing exactly what he would find behind it, he pushed open the bedroom door.

He was nothing more than a kid, spreadeagled on their mattress. Eyes closed, whimpering ecstatic Narha, she rode the Shi'an youth. Easily. Naturally. Perfectly. None of the manoeuverings and compromises of her couplings with him. It was beautiful. For one thrilling instant he could not tell them apart.

It was the Shi'an boy who saw Johnny first; his shocked freeze that alerted Seyamang.

'Johnny . . . ' She sounded like some semi-clever animal taught to mimic human speech without comprehension. Roaring incoherently, Johnny blundered into the room. The Shi'an kid fled, clutching at clothes. Somewhere in the red blur of his consciousness he heard the door slam. 'Johnny . . . ' Seyamang retreated before him, hands crossed before her: the gesture of pleading. 'Johnny, it doesn't mean anything, honest, it doesn't mean anything. I can't help it. It's my nature, it's our nature. It's *kesh*. Johnny, I need to know what I am, do you understand? It's not like I love him or anything; it's just . . . sex, Johnny. Just fucking.'

Johnny shook his head slowly. With all his hurt and anger and betrayal and jealousy and fear balled tight in it, his fist took Seyamang across the side of her head. She sprawled against the wall, a tangle of terracotta limbs that he thought for a moment he had shattered like an Etruscan pot. She stared at the trickle of dark red blood she had wiped from her forehead.

She smiled at him.

'Fuck you Johnny Considine, *human*. I hate you. With all my life, I hate you.'

He seated himself cross-legged on the bedroom floor, *numb*, not looking, not listening to the sounds of her throwing needful things into an overnighter. Utterly numb. He wished someone, *anyone* would turn that fucking music off.

For two days Johnny hung crucified on the tree of remorse while his database familiars showed him the enormity of his sin. Hideously expensive uplinks to the colonial library stored in the eighty-eight ships of the Fifteenth Interstellar Fleet out at the L5 point forced him to confront appalling conclusions. The *kesh* cycle with its complementary suites of matching male and female trigger chemicals meant that sex was always by female consent.

Male full erection was only possible in the presence of a female hormone released during foreplay. Rape was a biochemical impossibility. Rape as a statement of male dominance was psychologically untenable; male violence against females as a power display unthinkable. Sexual violence was unknown among the Shi'an. Impossible. Seyamang could have been no more horrified had the sky fallen on her head.

On the third day Johnny rose and went to seek Seyamang, her forgiveness, and that of her people. He went not knowing if she would forgive him. He went not knowing if forgiveness had any analogue in Shi'an emotionality.

He walked along the disused Light Railway track which had become the major thoroughfare into Shi'an town, down to Canary Wharf, the centre of the aliens' domain. Dark-eyed androgynous children gave grudging directions: never once the slow blink of a smile. All Docklands, it seemed, knew of the star-crossed lovers. Seyamang had spoken the truth when she said she was not as free as she liked to think. Johnny Considine passed beneath the shadow of the Canada Tower and entered the heart of the Huskravidi Sorority.

The British government had never admitted that IRA bombing of Canary Wharf had been a masterstroke. Seven hundred kilos of cross-polarized DBX had shattered every window within two kilometres and stripped the skin clean off the Canada Tower. Public denouncement hid private delight: since the popping of the property bubble the Canary Wharf/Docklands complex had been a real-estate albatross. With renovation estimates far exceeding rent-per-square-metre value, it was offered to the Shi'an immigrants to do with as they would, if they could. Their engineers had slapped up a containment field of the same type that protected their Interstellars at relativistic velocities, and moved the people in.

Johnny was kept waiting by a software receptionist in a claustrophobic grey cube of a lobby with only a wall-mounted flatscreen for company. After an hour a middle-aged Shi'an – a woman, Johnny thought, learning the signs and symbols – gave him permission to enter. The Huskravidi Sorority Motherhouse occupied the twenty-fifth floor. To Johnny, stepping out of the gravshaft, it seemed as if he were standing on a great rectangle floating three hundred feet above east London. The floors ended where the horizon began. He clung to the walls like an acrophobic spider. The Shi'an woman who had told him to come up introduced herself as Manblong Erreth Huskravidi and led him by the hand to a chair one metre from the edge. Seyamang entered and seated herself in a facing chair some five metres away. The Sorority woman Manblong sat in a third such chair set at right angles to the line of communication.

'Seyamang . . . '

Manblong looked at him. Words were not his to speak.

Seyamang spoke. She spoke of the hurt he had done her, the sins he had committed upon her flesh, the pains he had inflicted, the deep wounds he had written in her. She spoke of her incomprehension and fear. She spoke of mistrust and betrayal and the natures of love, human and Shi'an. She spoke for a long time. Many aircraft slid over the top of the tower. The sun moved across the cinemascope sky. In all that she spoke there was nothing Johnny had not already heard from his own soul, yet spoken aloud, in her words, in her voice, it gutted him.

Manblong then turned to Johnny. Now he might speak. All his justifications and defences and accusations fled from him.

'Seyamang,' he said, 'I'm sorry. I'm sorry.' He found he was crying. Open, unashamed, free. Manblong was staring at him. The Shi'an did not believe in tears. He was beyond care. He was destroyed. Broken. He felt hands cradling his head: the most intimate of Shi'an love-touchings. Seyamang was kneeling by the side of his chair, her hands stroking his skull.

'Johnny, I hurt you and didn't understand.' She rubbed the side of her face – the wounded side – against his. He sniffed. She sniffed. 'Still wearing that wonderful leather jacket.'

Manblong left them touching. When they were ready to leave, she called them back from the gravshaft gate. A plastic vial of white capsules was clenched between her fingers.

'You'll need these,' she said.

'What are they?' Johnny asked.

'A synthetic hormone,' Manblong said. 'We women use it to experiment with sex out of season.' The subject seemed gravely distasteful to her. Seyamang took the vial and stashed it in her pocket. Her head was lowered, her eyes were averted.

'Will it keep me in *kesh* after the end of the season?' she asked.

'Not *kesh*. Something like it.'

'Until the next season?'

'Theoretically indefinitely. Seyamang.'

'Yes?'

'We have been using this drug for thousands of years, but there has never been anything like this before. Never. Do you understand?'

Seyamang made no audible reply but Johnny could see the skin darken around her eyes into a mask of emotion. The Shi'an did not believe in tears. They believed in personal darkness.

'I can trust you not to say anything about where or who you got them from. Understand this, John Considine, we don't die for love but we will kill for our children.'

'I know that,' Johnny said. As Seyamang stepped into the freefall field, he paused to add, 'I know you used the hormone to conceive her, but if you can believe anything a human says, believe me when I say I will not let her be hurt again.'

*

The warm damp winter came. The streets emptied of children, the music fell silent. The plastic banners tore and flapped in the wind, soft-running Shi'an vehicles splashed through the gurgling gutters. The air was just air again, no more, no magic, no thrill in every breath. Rain crazed the windows of the attic flat. Behind them Seyamang Erreth Huskravidi learned love.

She tried to explain emotions utterly alien to her while the daily dose of drugs pushed her further and further into sexual *terra incognita*. 'Warm, yet cool at the same time. Can you understand that, Johnny? Not the heat of the *kesh*, but neither the cold of the times between. I know that if I wanted to I could fuck you right now, but I also know I don't have to, not the way I had to in *kesh*. Warm. Cool. At the same time.'

She took to reading all Johnny's deck could display of human erotica and romantic love.

'That *Romeo and Juliet*. That wouldn't happen – that couldn't happen – among us. We don't pair-bond. But I can understand how the way I feel, the constant tension between want and frustration, might make me need someone that much.'

'You falling in love with me?' Johnny asked.

'I don't know,' Seyamang answered, blinking her eyes in a slow, intimate smile. 'Perhaps.' She preferred *West Side Story* anyway: the Sharks and Jets dancing their way to the rumble was how her people would have settled territorial scores.

As the rain rained down and river floods drove the street people from their bashes and shacks, she reciprocated Johnny's lessons in humanity by teaching him to be Shi'an. She took him and her camera on photo-expeditions down to Docklands, seeing anew through his eyes. The truck gardens where semi-vegetative animals sucked nourishment out of the hacked-open earth. Click whirr. The titanic hulk of the lander beached in Heron Wharf. Click whirr. The stasis coffins in which her people had slept their five subjective years crossing to Earth, row upon row upon row racked up in the empty levels of Canada Tower. Click whirr. Sleepers awake.

And each time, the subtle transaction between mother and daughter of inoffensive white capsules in their clear plastic cylinder. Johnny tried to contemplate a love that loved the sinner yet hated the sin.

Seyamang pulled geographical and historical information down from the L5 point. Johnny saw the Shi'an motherworld unfold on his rollscreen, encircled by its wheel of orbital manufactories and habitats, spiked with space elevators. Motherworld's nightside burned with the lights of ten thousand cities, its moons had long ago been reduced to massive organo-technic industrial complexes where starships reproduced themselves. He saw the nine colony planets of the Household of Worlds, where the Shi'an had walked before Rome was built.

'I can't take it in,' he said. 'It's like an old sci-fi movie, *FX by Industrial Light and Magic*. It's not real. I can't believe in it.'

'Nor I,' said Seyamang Winterborn.

She attempted to teach him Narha. He could not master a language that changed inflection and gender depending on the season of the year. He attempted to teach her Irish; when that failed, Ulster English. 'Far more expressive than the bland Standard National Curriculum shit they talk here. Some of it is pure Elizabethan. The language of Shakespeare.'

They had sex as the spirit moved them. Which was often. Always, Johnny was conscious of the price of the rough trade. The animal was gone. Never again did he experience the abandon, the self-loss, the sense of alien-to-alien that he had in the heat season.

And the television news, waiting, biding, patient in its armouring of world trivia all these weeks and months, sprang. Ambushed by the lunchtime bulletin.

Leicester police are investigating what appears to be the paramilitary-style killing of a young Belfast man outside a city-centre burger restaurant in the early hours of the morning.

Jesus fuck.

Eyewitnesses report that a motorbike with two riders drew up alongside the victim. After speaking briefly, one of them shot the victim in the head with a sawn-off shotgun before riding off. The dead man has been identified as . . .

Eugene Anthony Padre Pio Brady. Twenty-four. Formerly of Ardoyne Avenue, Belfast. Currently of hell. Always was a fucking stupid name, Padre Pio. Christ have mercy on you. Christ have mercy on me.

'Seyamang.'

She looked around from the kitchen space where she was joyfully chopping up some ghastly Shi'an vegetables that he was too polite to say gave him the shits.

'Can I talk to you a minute?'

'Sure, Johnny.' She curled herself against him. Her unique musk had faded, victim of the white tablets, but her inhuman warmth comforted him.

'Do you love me, Seyamang?'

'Ah now, Johnny, you know better than to ask me that.'

'Do you love me, Seyamang?'

'Love. What is love? Love isn't to me what it is to you.'

'Do you love me, Seyamang?'

'Yes, Johnny, I fucking love you, all right?'

'Seyamang, I have to tell you something. Please don't interrupt or say anything until I've finished.'

He told her everything. What he was, what he had done.

'West Drayton is the main air traffic control centre for British airspace. Our assault programs would have rendered it and its back-up systems inoperative for at least twelve hours. Any other traffic centre that tried to take control would have been infected also. Have you any idea of how many aircraft movements there are through West Drayton's control sector in twelve hours? How many passengers?

'I ran simulations. The probability of at least one mid-air collision was one hundred per cent. Total fatality. Hundreds dead. Men. Women. Children. Chinese. Indian. Japanese. Fucking Togolanders. Legitimate targets. The Stock Exchange, the Northern Bank, it was only money, it was only digits on a disc. Only things. These were lives. I couldn't have that, Seyamang. Those Japanese, those Togolanders. So I betrayed them to the RUC. I told Eugene what I was going to do because he's said he wanted out. I told him to stay until the peelers lifted them, so they wouldn't suspect and run. Then I called the Confidential Telephone. They pulled me in to Castlereagh interrogation centre. I told them who, where, when, what, signed the dotted line and walked. Next day they raided them. Aoife and Charlie were arrested. Joey got shot. Dead, Seyamang. I don't know if he was armed or not, but they shot him. Mikey escaped, changed his name, his identity, hacked into the files where his previous life was stored and erased himself. All the things I should have done if I'd been wise, but wasn't. Two months ago I saw him on the television – the peelers had pulled him in on one of their regular paddy-bashes. Last night two guys on a motorbike rode up to Eugene in Leicester and blew him away. Classic execution. They knew who he was. They knew where to find him. Things I don't even know, they knew. It was Mikey. Evening the score. Executing the traitors.'

'You think he'll come for you?'

'I know he'll come for me. I've been running checks through my deck. Someone's been leaving muddy footprints all over my bank account.'

'But that's in Slovakia,' Seyamang interrupted.

'Someone with enough *nous* to mount a widescale datasearch, but clumsy enough to leave prints. Mikey never could hack worth a fuck, but he knows I'm alive and sinning, and, if he follows the account code, where to find me.'

The rain rattled the big windows, reduced the visible world to rivulets of liquid grey.

'I have to go, Seyamang. Now. Every minute I stay here puts you in danger. Mikey isn't going to leave any witnesses. I can't let you take that risk; you've no part in this. You're innocent. Oh Jesus, what have I done, Seyamang?'

'I don't want you to go, Johnny.'

'I don't want to leave you, but I can't take you with me. A human and a Shi'an together? He knows about us by know.'

Seyamang smiled. It chilled Johnny to the pith of his being.

'There is a way, Johnny. We can go together. We can hide in the future. The stasis coffins. We can sleep together fifty, a hundred, a hundred and fifty years, let Mikey die and turn to dust while we wake up in another lifetime.'

'But your family, your friends—'

'Family? Friends? That's you, Johnny.'

'Do you think the Huskravidis will allow it?' He thought of sun and seasons accelerating across the open window-wall, Canada Tower the gnomon of an insane sundial, while he and Seyamang slept in each other's arms. Years like seconds. In fifty, a hundred years anything might happen. Even an end to his country's long, self-mutilation.

Seyamang said she would go to her Sorority without delay. Johnny admired her faith. The Shi'an owed him nothing. Meantime Johnny, stay in the flat, don't open the door to anyone who doesn't say *Our Day Will Come* in Narha. He disobeyed her order to stay away from the windows to watch her skid off on her moped along the wet streets. Imaginings of long lenses in every door and window tormented him. He picked up the telephone and listened to the dialling tone, not reassured by its obdurate normalness. He went five times to his deck with thoughts of hunter/hunted, of simply finding and killing Mikey before he found and killed him. Each time he vanished the qwerty icons into the grubby plastic skin because he knew that was not how it was played. He was the dead man walking, the dead man talking. Nothing could change it. Another lifetime. A one way trip into the future. Only the impossibility of his situation made it thinkable.

'They'll put it to the Sorority Council,' Seyamang said on her return, three fraught hours later.

'When will that be?' Johnny asked.

'Tomorrow.'

'Tomorrow?' Johnny shouted, hearing the click-clatch of shotgun hammers cocking. Seyamang cringed away from his male anger. 'Jesus, Seyamang . . . '

Tomorrow.

'They'll do it,' Seyamang said, after another dreadful three hours out on the naked streets while Johnny sat in the exact centre of the glass flat, waiting, waiting, waiting for the silent supersonic impact of a high-velocity round in the back of his skull. 'They're not happy about it – the less humans know of our technology, the better, is the official line – but Manblong has some weight in the Sorority. They're reconfiguring a stasis coffin for human biological parameters.'

'How long?' Always, that question.

'Tomorrow.' Always, that answer.

She wanted sex with him that night. He could not. He would not. Depression, dread, had unmanned him. She was hurt, she felt failed by human sexuality, but he could not help himself. No one who is to be hanged in the morning can expect a hard-on.

He dreamed that night that the lid of a stasis coffin closed on him and turned into the safety bars of the car in Space Mountain, holding him down, holding him in through the fear and the blackness and the hurtling into Christ knew what after all the Chicken Gates were passed. He had been given his ways out, his passages back; he had seen them, acknowledged them, refused them. Always Seyamang.

'Johnny?' Her voice. Her words, her heat, her smell. 'You ready?'

That time already? No. Jesus, no.

'I'm ready.' Truth be told, after days of house arrest, keeping away from the windows – how could he? The place was all windows, it smelled of windows – he was glad to be out in the open. The rain was never-ending, the early light dirty grey, but it tasted like wine. Perhaps a touch more acidic. Child of the air-conditioning, Seyamang was engagingly gamine in layers of tights and pullovers and quilted jackets; like an orphan in too-large hand-me-downs. She locked the door and slipped the key into the store-owner's letterbox.

'Hope someone else is as happy as we were,' she said, unpretentiously. Her photographs were the only thing she had chosen to take with her, packed in two black corrugated plastic A3 folios. 'All my children. Let's go.'

The streets were quiet and empty under the dawn rain; a few early deliverers the only traffic. Seyamang ran her finger along the rain-speckled flanks of cars parked up on the kerb. Suddenly elated, Johnny turned out of Mitre on to Newell.

They were waiting for him at the end of the street. Two green-helmeted black-visored mantises in cling leather on a black and green scrambler. The explosion of sound as the engine was kicked into life sent pigeons clattering from their roosts. Johnny threw Seyamang away from him. She sprawled across the wet tarmac. The cheap folders split open, her monochrome children scattered across the street.

'It's me they want, not you,' Johnny shouted. 'Get out of here. Go!'

He could not hope to outrun a scrambler bike, but he would try. He ran. They pursued. He led them down every alley, into every entry, through every courtyard. He darted, he dazzled, he confused. It was a game now, and both played it to the end. Out of Shi'an town, into the streets of the humans. Human landmarks: the church tower, Moe's Diner and Bar. *All Day Breakfast* fluttered like a neon butterfly in his peripheral vision. Distracted, his foot caught a tilted flagstone and he fell crashing to the pavement. The motorbike screamed in triumph and the playing was ended.

The scrambler gobbled hydrocarbons across the street. From inside his black biker's jacket the pillion passenger produced a pistol-grip shotgun. He dismounted and walked carefully, cautiously, over to the helpless Johnny.

'In the name of the Irish Republican—'

His head exploded.

Johnny thought that the gun had gone off, that it was his body that detonated in a rain of pulverized meat and blood and bone and plastic, that his mind, at the instant of death, had frozen in terminal agony for all eternity. Then he saw the headless body topple and fall. Then he saw Seyamang at the street corner, the sensuous black Shi'an maser gripped in her two hands. She was smiling.

'Seyamang! The bike!' he shouted. Man-machine centaur, the scrambler's rider drew a heavy revolver.

Seyamang moved an instant too slow. The bullet blew a red blossom through her layers of wool and quilting. She stared at the hideous belly wound with childlike wonder and the second shell took her in the right shoulder.

She raised the Shi'an weapon one handed and sighted it. *Tethba.* No human could have accepted such punishment and remained standing: again she had summoned dark rage to save Johnny.

The scrambler spun around on the rain-wet street to give its master a clearer aim. The revolver fired a third time. And the upper left quadrant of the rider's body - chest, shoulder, upper gun-arm - erupted in a spray of boiling blood and flesh. Johnny howled. Seyamang was smashed into a metal shop shutter, shot through the belly.

The fallen motorbike spun its wheel and screamed and screamed and screamed.

A few cautious souls ventured out of Moe's into the rain, scarcely able to believe what had happened. Belfast, England.

'An ambulance!' Johnny screamed at them. 'Get a fucking ambulance!'

Seyamang sat like a broken doll against the shutter. The graffittied steel was smeared with her dark alien blood. Rain slowly washed it clean. Her face was gentle, faintly puzzled. The Shi'an weapon fell from her gloved fingers. Human gloves. One finger on each hand dangled uselessly. Dabbing at the pumping blood, not knowing what else to do, Johnny took her hand. Beneath the knitted wool it felt as fragile as sparrow bones.

'So, was I a good human, then, Johnny? See, we can do it when we have to. Sharks and Jets. Kill for love, die for love. Oh fuck, Johnny, it hurts.'

'Sh sh sh, don't try to speak, Seyamang. Help's coming.' Sirens, fast approaching. Ambulances. Peelers.

'Go Johnny. The police—'

'Fuck the police.'

'I think I understand now, Johnny.' Her voice was failing, her impossible *tethba* strength leaking out of her. Candy-striped ambulances arrived in a Doppler-wail of sirens and strobing electric blue. The police came after. The police always come after. 'How it works. Human love. How can you live that way, Johnny Considine, you lucky, lucky thing?'

Green coveralled paramedics swept in with their chrome things and plastic things and things that made ominous electronic noises, and pushed

Johnny gently away.

'Oh Jesus, a Sheenie,' said a female medic.

'Let me in with her!' Johnny screamed as they loaded Seyamang tubed and taped and tapped into the back of the mobile trauma unit. 'I have to be with her, I love her.'

She died in the ambulance.

The police held Johnny Considine for three days under the Prevention of Terrorism Act. Legally they were entitled to hold him for seven days pending charges, but on the third day Knock Headquarters Belfast sent over the Judas contract he had signed with the RUC and they turned him out on to the streets.

'Get out of here, Paddy,' they told him. 'Go back to your own people.'

He did. He hoped they would accept him. He hoped they could forgive him, though his sin was mighty.

The bus went by ways too close and painful for one who had betrayed the only promise he had ever held dear. He closed his eyes until the distant rush of Boeing engines told him it was safe to open them. The navigation beacons burned atop the mirrored obelisk of Canada Tower; aircraft lights formed strange, brief constellations, like the riding lights of interstellar vessels.

The freefall shaft took him up. He walked among the stasis coffins, touching their cool, smooth skins. Easy, so easy to step out of his clothes, slip inside, awake in another lifetime.

He had always refused the Chicken Gates.

Beyond, the aliens were waiting.

Nerves of Steel

Garry Kilworth

'You want *what*?' asked the doctor's image, looking confused.

'I want a new right arm,' I said. 'One of flesh, blood, muscle and bone.' I dangled my useless metal limb in front of his image in the commbooth.

My arm had been crushed in a jig by a dumb robot at the factory the day before. Not purposely, because obviously dumb robots simply follow a set pattern of actions and have no self-control. I experienced damage signals in my head, but of course I felt no pain.

'Surely,' replied the doctor, who was a young human, 'you should be applying to Citizen Robot Replacement Spares? I', his image smiled condescendingly and waved a hand, 'am a *doctor* – for real people. You shouldn't have called this number.'

They always had to add that word 'real' for some reason, as if there were another kind.

I could see a Citizen robotic nurse standing close to the doctor. It shifted its feet. It was looking at me blankly, but I knew it was as puzzled as the doctor by my request. I reached out and dimmed their images a little while I gathered my thoughts to reply.

'Look,' I said, 'you can see that I'm a Citizen robot.'

The young doctor smiled. 'We wouldn't be talking if you were a dumb robot, now would we?'

'Then what's the problem? CRs have got full civil rights.'

'With one exception as I recall. You're not permitted to vote. You still don't have that,' he said, clinging like most humans to the one consolation left to their race.

'I'm not asking you to give me the vote,' I said. 'All I want is a new arm - a human arm. I have the same rights as you or anyone else in this matter.'

'Well, I didn't actually agree with giving you peo— giving CRs civil rights,' said the doctor candidly. 'I voted against it in the World Referendum.'

'Whether you voted for us, or against us, it makes no difference to the law now. We won. There were people out there whose consciences told them we had been treated as non-citizens for long enough.'

'See here,' snapped the doctor, 'I don't want a political speech from *you*.

I'm getting a little tired of arguing. I have patients to see.'

'I'm a patient,' I said, 'and you'll see me. I have a right to medical treatment. The law states that. I have a *right* to all the things enjoyed by a normal human citizen.'

The doctor's image began to display the symptoms of anger at this point and the CR nurse reached for the control panel. I could see it was about to cut the connection.

I said to the nurse, 'Don't do it. I'm entitled to be calling and your boss knows it. I've got your number. Don't do anything you might be arrested for later. I intend to stay connected until I get my rights.'

'You keep talking about your rights,' said the doctor, exasperated now. 'Who sent you here? Are you a part of some CR action group? What is it? You want the vote now?'

'I want a human arm,' I said. 'Plain and simple.'

It was the nurse who spoke to me now, in a low, puzzled but controlled tone. 'Why would you want a human arm?'

'Yes, *why*?' asked the doctor.

'I see no reason why not,' I countered. 'We've got humans with electromechanical body parts – cyborgs, cybermen, whatever you like to call them. No one would think twice about giving me a new plastimetal fully functional arm if I were a human with a crushed limb, now would they? All I would have to do would be to ask.'

'If you were a human,' said the doctor, 'you would ask for a human arm.'

'You know that's not true,' I said.

The teledoc sighed. 'Well, obviously *some* humans choose to have robotic limbs when they lose their own . . . '

He made it sound as if these humans were freaks, eccentrics, but it was common knowledge that a robotic arm was stronger, had more functions than a human arm and was generally more trustworthy in an emergency. I had also been told by human acquaintances that there was a squeamishness amongst them about having another person's flesh-and-blood arm attached to their bodies: the limb of some sweaty, unclean person they might not have wished to shake hands with in the whole. More importantly there was the fear that spare human limbs might be carrying some kind of latent virus.

I said evenly, 'Listen, doctor, you know as well as I do that some humans even go in for cosmetic surgery – they have perfectly *good* flesh-and-blood limbs removed and replaced by robotic ones, which they consider superior.'

I didn't add that these cyberfreaks sometimes came to live amongst us CRs, copying our lifestyle and culture, trying to become like us.

The doctor suddenly muttered, 'I can't waste any more time on this. Look, I'm contacting a surgeon at the hospital. You call the General Hospital, give your ID, and they'll put you through – next Thursday at ten o'clock, you understand? You'll have to work it out with them. I'm telling you, number—'

'XL397 – I have letters too in my registration identity.'

The doctor gritted his teeth. 'XL397, you're not going to get anywhere with this idiotic game. The consultant surgeon will kick out your lights – figuratively speaking of course.'

'We'll see about that,' I said, reaching for the switch. 'Good day to you, doctor.'

As the images faded, the nurse called, 'What are you trying to do?'

'Control my own destiny,' I said to the now blank space in front of me.

There was no need to go back to the factory during the following week, because I was useless without my right arm. I took the week off and wandered through the city, enjoying a few of the sights. I went to the art gallery, the museum and various other similar places. I wasn't the only CR visiting these establishments. It had become fashionable amongst us to be seen to be interested in human culture. Humans seemed to like the idea too that we were taking advantage of our new status in society. It was a harmless enough occupation. They watched us curiously as we approached paintings to stare at them and appear to study the techniques of the human artists. I expect they wondered what was going through our thinking circuits. I believe they got a kind of kick out of seeing us there for the first time, in the way that they might an intelligent panda or a teddy bear brought to life. *Ahh, look at that, isn't that sweet? It's come to see the paintings.*

Actually, there were only two paintings that interested me. The first was Masaccio's *The Expulsion from Paradise,* showing a distraught Adam and Eve walking away from Eden. The second was Mantegna's *St Sebastian*, depicting the martyr shot full of arrows and dying in agony. To me, they represented two (possibly separate) forms of suffering: one spiritual the other physical. I moved from one to the other of these two works of art, studying the faces intently, understanding one but not the other. I asked myself: were they the same?

I went to the national park too, to find a bit of peace and quiet. I enjoy nature as much as any human. For a start, a robot like me doesn't have to fear snake bites or savage predators. I can walk right up to a timid wild deer sometimes. I once witnessed a wildcat killing a squirrel. I was close enough to see into their eyes. It was a strangely troubling experience, being so close to such basic savagery. To the wild animals we're like vehicles. We don't smell of human sweat or other body odours.

A man watched me studying the ducks on the lake and said, 'You won't find no robot birds here. What do you CRs want to come for?'

It was all right for us to go to the art gallery and museum, but the park was for LIVING creatures.

'I like it here,' I said.

'You should stick to your own kind,' said the man. 'You'll be happier that way.'

To his way of thinking he wasn't being nasty. He was just offering me sound advice. Men and birds were flesh and blood together, so they had more in common than robots and birds.

However, what people like him conveniently forgot was that our minds are consistent with that of a human. Basically, they took the processes of a human brain and transferred them to a robot's circuits. They had simply swapped an organic container for an inorganic one. With the swap came unexpected additions, among them a range of emotions.

This was one of the reasons for our elevation in status, since certain politicians argued that if CR minds worked in the same way as human minds, we were in effect inorganic humans and entitled to the same privileges. There was a fierce political row in Euro-Parliament over the issue, some of the anti-robot lobby arguing that there was a doubt about the ability of CRs to make moral judgements, since no one could tell whether or not we had a conscience. That one was quashed when a well-known Scandinavian member asked for proof of the existence of a conscience or soul ('Either will do,' he stated, drily) amongst the human members of the anti-robot lobby.

On Thursday I dropped into a commbooth and called the consultant surgeon, stating my ID, only to find I was automatically transferred to a conference network. There were five images in the booth with me. No one introduced themselves. Under the main image was a backlit sign stating that the female behind the desk was the consultant surgeon. The others all had name or number signs, with their job titles written beneath. Two of them were Citizen robots, the other two were a man and a woman.

The consultant surgeon was used to giving orders, you could see that. The two CRs and the other woman were not much more than basic images to me and remained so throughout the interview, but not the human whose sign read: Arthur Spateman – Hospital Management.

'Now, what's this all about?' asked the surgeon, glaring at me.

'It's about me wanting a human arm,' I said.

'And where would we find one of those for you?' asked a Citizen robot.

This group was obviously primed to send me on my way. I could sense just by looking at their images that they were going to be intransigent. The humans amongst them would hide behind arrogant statements, behind superior smiles. They would attempt to use their authority, coolly, to dismiss my request. I was feeling angry. A normal consultation would involve only the surgeon and the patient, yet they had chosen to face me *en masse* in order to try to intimidate me. I decided that it would serve me to attack first. I wanted the surgeon to know she wasn't dealing with a servile CR, but one who was prepared to assert itself.

I shrugged. 'There are plenty of spare limbs around in hospitals which specialize in cosmetic surgery. Then again, I don't mind having one from a corpse, so long as it's freshly dead.' I chose to attack Arthur, since he looked the most vulnerable. 'I'd even have one of Mr Spateman's arms, if it was cleaned up properly first.'

The bulky figure of Arthur Spateman straightened. The supercilious smile left his face and was replaced by a stiff expression.

He spluttered, 'What do you mean by that?'

'Now, Arthur—' began the surgeon.

But Spateman, smouldering, ignored her. 'No, come on, what the hell did you mean by that remark?'

'Simple enough statement,' I said. 'I wouldn't want any part of your body attached to mine unless it had first been dipped in disinfectant. You look like a man with some – shall we say – *habits*?'

The consultant surgeon raised her eyes to the ceiling.

Spateman waved a stylus at me, jabbing at the air as he spoke.

'You . . . listen, we know what you're up to, you tin fucking freak. I've got your number, XL whatever. You want a human arm first, then another arm, then a leg, and finally all over, till you're human. You think we don't know this? You want to become human. Then you think you'll get the fucking vote! Well, you've got another think coming. Goddamn – that's *somebody*'s arm you want. Somebody. Not a fucking jumble of fucking wires, but somebody real. You understand me? Over my fucking dead body.'

I stared at the rest of the committee each in turn.

'Let me make one thing quite clear,' I said. ' I do not want this man's arm under *any* circumstances, freshly dead or not.'

I thought Spateman was going to have apoplexy. His image stood up and pushed the chair back. I heard it scraping across the floor.

'You fucking heap of—'

'Sit down, Arthur,' said the surgeon. 'You're making a fool of yourself.'

Spateman seemed to gather himself together. He blinked at the consultant and then, red-faced, sat in his chair again.

'Now,' said the surgeon calmly. 'XL396—'

'397,' I corrected her. 'Don't worry, I have the same problem with the peculiar names you people give each other.' I stared at Arthur Spateman's sign as I spoke.

Spateman's eyes widened a little but he kept his mouth shut this time.

'XL397,' continued the surgeon. 'Look, I understand you're playing some kind of game with us here, and I can appreciate that it might seem amusing to you - you do have a sense of humour?'

'You know I do. I experience a similar array of emotions as you.'

'Yes, well, I'm a surgeon, not a robot technician. I know very little about robots. What's bothering us all is this. You're not the only CR to demand a human limb. There have been others, in other cities. There seems to be some kind of conspiracy going on and we're all very worried about it. Now, you can understand our concern, can't you?'

I was surprised about the others, but then the laws of coincidence are full of such strange confluences. Two or three scientists independently discover the same thing within weeks of each other, though others have been seeking the same discovery for centuries. It happens. Obviously several CRs had come to the same conclusion as me, once they had begun to think about their new status in society.

'I can appreciate it, but not empathize.'

'But', said the woman sitting next to Spateman, 'it's a matter of control you see. We seem to be losing control of things, since that new law was passed. It's all very worrying.'

'You're losing control, we're gaining some,' I said. 'I want to be able to do the things you do. I want to *feel* things, know what it's like to touch things. Us CRs have three senses – sight, hearing and smell. We can't touch or taste. I want, eventually, to do both of those.'

I didn't tell them what I actually wanted to feel was the sensation of pain. The idea of pain had begun to fascinate me, obsess me, recently. It was something, just a word at the moment, but it seemed to occupy humans continually. Pain. What was it? What did it do to you? How was it formed? How did it transmit itself to you? I wanted to possess it. I had to know pain in order to understand humans, to learn to trust them fully. It was part of their history, part of their being. Progress, for Citizen robots, was not possible without this knowledge of pain.

I caught Spateman watching me with some interest, and inevitably with a bigot like him an irrational statement followed.

'I fucking get it,' he said in a satisfied tone. '*Sex*. This is all about sex. That freak wants to screw our women. Damn it – he's after our wives and daughters.'

The consultant cried, 'Arthur, will you please shut up! You're not helping matters here.'

'Perhaps', said Spateman, gathering his things together and trying to look dignified, 'it's time I left, then?'

Spateman's image faded from the screen.

The consultant surgeon heaved a sigh of relief then turned to me and said,

'I think I understand what you're after. I hadn't thought about that. You're in for a disappointment with some things though. The taste of freshly made coffee never lives up to its aroma. However, I now have an insight to the reason for your request and I think the interview can proceed.'

There followed a hundred questions from both sides of the table, from all the committee members, and I think I acquitted myself quite well. We were in conference for forty-eight minutes, during which time the humans drank several cups of coffee, and left me wondering about the consultant's illustration. Finally it was she who brought the meeting to an end.

'I promise you, XL397, that we'll consider your request very carefully. Please be under no misapprehensions though – we do not *have* to supply you with a human arm under the law. That will be entirely up to us, the hospital administration, to decide. The law merely states that we have to supply patients with a "functional arm". It doesn't qualify that statement and if we decide you need a robotic limb, then there's not a great deal you can do about it. I personally have some sympathy with your request and will consider it very seriously over the next few days.'

Later that evening, I was walking through the main square and looked up to see Arthur Spateman's image in a news niche up on the main building. He was jabbering away, waving a finger at the crowd that had gathered beneath. I stopped to listen.

'There's a plot,' he was saying wildly to the newscaster sitting next to him. 'The CRs are trying to become *real* people like you and me.'

'Surely', said the newscaster calmly, 'these allegations are, shall we say, a *little* exaggerated . . . ?'

While I stood and stared at the broadcast a youth turned and looked at the number printed on my shoulder.

'Hey, this is the junk,' he cried. 'This is the bastard that wants to become a human being. Who the Jesus do you think you are, eh? You wanna be like me, do ya?'

A crowd of youths was gathering about me.

'Not like you,' I said. 'I want to be human.'

The youth's brow furrowed and he said, 'Hey—'

But I moved away from him, so as not to cause any more trouble.

After the news was finished and some mindless quiz programme leapt into the niche, I walked away, across the park towards my dormitory on the far side. Halfway through the park I heard some footsteps running from behind me, and I turned to see the youth I had insulted accompanied by four others. They all held what looked like steel posts stolen from the park fence.

Now if there is one emotion CRs *have* evolved it is fear of death. A playwright once said: ' . . . both are dead when they cease to be, but while a human *dies* a robot stops dead, which is not the same as dying.' What he failed to recognize and note was that both of us have a great reluctance to enter the realms of non-existence. We both experience something similar on having to leave this world for ever. There was a kind of urgency in my circuits – they told me to *run*.

I ran. I ran as fast as my legs would carry me.

In my efforts to get away I struck a tree root with my foot and fell headlong on to the grass. They were upon me in seconds, swinging their steel bars. I tried to roll over on to my damaged side, to present my useless arm to their blows. They were yelling at me in high distorted voices, shouting 'junkbrain . . . scrapyard trash . . . fuckin' wireface' and beating me with their weapons.

Once the bars began raining down on me, I collected severe impacts on my back and shoulders and lower legs. One of my ankle joints burst open. A heavy blow struck my left eye, shattering the ceramic swivel, and my vision failed on that side of my face. All five of them wanted to smash my body to pieces, and this probably saved me from a lot of damage because they kept striking each other's bars and getting entangled. It was during this frenetic jumble of blows that one of them finally tried to remove my head from my torso, swinging from way back behind himself, yelling, 'Wanna be a human, huh? Try it without a fuckin' head,' and missed me completely, hitting one of the others instead.

The injured youth dropped to the ground, clutching his shoulder and screaming. I could see he had some sort of compound fracture, because the bone was sticking through his clothing. At that moment there was a sound from overhead and a police hovercar descended from above the trees, broadcasting an order that everyone should stand still, with their hands high.

Four of my attackers immediately scattered into the darkness of the trees, leaving their injured companion to face the cops. I lay where I was, feeling drained of energy. The youth's face was a metre from my own and with my good eye I studied the agony evident in his contorted features, in his staring eyes, in his twisting body.

I crawled even closer to him, dragging my damaged leg behind me.

'Listen, boy,' I whispered in his ear as the cops approached us. 'What does it feel like? Tell me what you feel – tell me about the pain. I want to know. I *need* to know—'

'You bastard,' he shrieked at me, sobbing. 'You ain't even human! Oh God, it *hurts*. It's *killing* me.'

I said, 'Just precisely *how* is it killing you?'

Love in Backspace

Barrington J. Bayley

Call me Little Tony, backspace rider. There's frontspace, see, where we all live and everything is ordered and spread out, I mean stars and planets and stuff, and then there's midspace, really *smooooth* so the big starliners can use it to move around in, and there's backspace. They say it's the necessary 'other side' of frontspace but you wouldn't know it if you go there. Backspace is pure connectivity, any normal idea of distance is *Yim-Bim*, throw it away. Technically it's what makes frontspace hang together and stay put, so the engineers like to call it the 'wrong side' of space. You know those raffia patterns kids do in school? On the show side they're neat and colourful, but the back is a mess of knots and bits and pieces. Backspace is like that, a chaos of torrents and rapids which will break up a starliner in minutes. Only a small one- or two-man raft has got any chance, and then of course you need a pilot, and how many have got the nerve and skill to go into the wrong side and find their way through to somewhere else? Not many. *Yow-Wow*.

So meet Little Tony, hanging around Hawtaw phase port waiting for work. Yes, there's work. A midspace liner covers a hundred light years in a month. A backraft might do that in an hour on a good day. So mostly you're hired as a messenger carrying info which can be reproduced if it's lost – news, company reports, the bad stuff on somebody, anything there's a need to get somewhere fast and someone is willing to pay for it.

But every now and then, a passenger.

He was a chubby fellow. His eyes were nice. Dark, kind of oily, you know that sort of eyes? A mop of curly black hair. Soft belly bulging through a neat buttoned waistcoat. Choice. But he was sweating just a little.

He put down a big floppy carry-all bag. 'I want to go to Elivira.' He paused. 'That's Castan IV.'

'I know.' I pointed to Liner Bay Number Three's big hangar doors. 'She leaves from there.'

'Yes, in three days' time. And another three and a half weeks to Elivira! I want to go *now*.'

I scratched my neck and fluttered my long silver eyelashes. 'Well, that sounds *urgent*.'

'Yes, it's urgent.' He stepped back, suddenly doubtful, to cast his eyes over me, lingering on my bare buttocks. 'You *are* a backrider, aren't you? You can take me?'

'Never lost a passenger yet. But it will cost you,' I took a deep breath, 'a thousand kudos. For that you're getting the best in the business.'

'A thousand,' he muttered sadly. 'All right.' And now he'd made the deal, that really scared look came into his face. Every passenger has it. He began stuttering. 'When . . . when . . . Can we start now?'

'I have to check my raft and fuel up. Meet me back here in an hour.' I didn't ask him for an advance, much as I needed one. It's not good for confidence.

'Er.' The scared look was intensifying. 'I've heard thirty-seven trips is average life expectancy for a backrider. How many have you made, may I ask?'

'Thirty-six.' I put on a look like I was trying to smile at him. He sure must have had a good reason for hiring my services.

'Don't worry about that,' I told him. 'You've been hearing crap. Either you can do it or you can't.'

He went away looking slightly reassured. I was walking to the fuel store, wondering if I could get credit, when I ran into Boy Galilee. He stopped me, blinking and giving that simpering smile of his.

'Tony, don't tell me, *don't* tell me you're taking on a passenger?'

The creep must have seen me talking to my customer, peering round the corner of Number Three Bay, no doubt. I tried to walk on, but he placed his hand gently on my chest.

'Tony, I *really* ought to tell him about that bad navigator of yours. That's *too* much of a risk.'

'For God's sake, Galilee,' I said, 'I *need* this fare so I can get my navigator fixed! Give me a break, will you?'

He started stroking my neat little bum. Why shouldn't he? His was like a piece of misshaped putty.

'If things go wrong you could give backriders a bad name.'

'It's only an intermittent fault. I've been out with it twice already.'

Automatically I started stroking his buttocks too. Christ, how could somebody with a posterior as uninteresting and flabby as his make out in backspace?

Not so long ago you could always tell a backrider. Nowadays it's less easy to be sure, fashion being what it is and so many crud-brained young punks aping the bare bum, the shiny black leggings and jacket, the silver eyelashes and turquoise face paint. It really annoys me. Plonk any one of them on a guidance plate and he'd shit himself all over it.

And yes, if you're asking, professional backriders are all sexually unidirectional, and all are male. No one else seems to have the knack, though plenty have tried, and no real explanation has come forward as to why. Me, I put it down to a solid neural connection between brain and backside, *heh heh*. It is, after all, the second way there is of selling your arse for a living.

So the habit riders have of fondling each other's bums when they talk is a *double entendre*. Apart from the obvious, it's also a professional compliment, not to say a *wondering* about each other's ability. Anyway I couldn't let Galilee steal my trade.

'Tell you what,' I said, hating myself for it, and letting my fingers slide down the sweaty fold between his cheeks just to seem more friendly, 'there's two hundred kudos in it for you and you don't have to do anything.' The threat began melting from his face and I added, 'Except loan me some fuel rods to do the job.'

'Two hundred up front?'

'Well, no.'

'Sure, then you fuck up and get lost in infinity.'

'I'll be all right. Would I go out if I wasn't sure?'

'Where are you going?'

'Elivira. But look, I haven't got that much time.' I was having to palpate his bud with my middle fingertip, but he went for it. I went with him to his shack and collected four charge rods, then left to do a quick check on my rig. I was hauling it on its castors across the concrete by the towrope when my passenger returned. He jabbed his eyes at the raft, which must have looked to him something like a larger version of a kid's go-cart, and I saw the fear returning.

'It's all up to you,' I told him, and let the towrope go slack.

'I've got to go,' he gabbled. 'I've got to go.'

Alongside the liner bays every phase port has a raft shack that uses exactly the same phase pusher as the big ships, like a kind of free ride, a minnow hitching a lift on a whale. I dragged the raft inside and set it on the rails.

'I'll need your identity card.'

'Yes, of course.' He dived into an inside pocket and fished out a honey-gold wallet. I had time to see plenty of kudos inside it before he came out with the card. I stepped to the terminal in the corner and slipped it in the slot, then gave the controller my registration number and destination.

'Are we all set?' my passenger asked as I handed the card back to him.

'Yaw-Waw.'

A backraft is twelve feet long, five feet wide, and is cast in titanium-braced aluminium. There's a charge-powered impeller motor, a navigator, and a cockpit-type passenger seat with safety belt and handgrips, which actually don't do anything because you can't fall out. The pilot sits on a silvery plate of mercury amalgam. He has a head-up display 'grammed into his eyeballs, and a couple of joysticks, but all the fine control that makes backriding possible is by neural induction through the buttocks. That's not only the best way, it's the *only* way of rafting through backspace with a good chance of coming out alive; everything else has been tried, including neural induction directly from the brain through a headset. Praise be to the male bum!

'How do we breathe?' he asked.

'There's a bubble comes over once we're phased.'

'Oh. How long will the trip take?'

'Half an hour at best, up to an hour if the currents are slow.' I showed him where to put his carry-all in the luggage space behind his seat, then helped him on all courteous-like, even fastening the strap for him. His hands were trembling. I rubbed mine together in business-like fashion and spoke jovially. 'Ready to go?'

'Yes, er, *Yaw-Yaw*,' he responded feebly. Creep.

I stepped aboard and set my butt down on the guidance plate. Lovely sensation. 'Control,' I announced into the air, 'this is 2318. Push, please.'

You could hear the *snap* as the pusher charged up, thinning out the consistency of frontspace so it could shove us through. Behind me I heard the customer whimper and grind his teeth. He ain't seen nuthin' yet, as they say somewhere or other.

Then came the jolt that turns your stomach over. At the same instant, the liquid polymer bubble expanded to canopy the deck of the raft (you could feel it passing over your skin just like a soap bubble), and the pearly blue effulgence of midspace surrounded us. Midspace. Smooth, smooth, *smooooth*. For the record, midspace is a half-phase shift. The only reason it's there is that if you've got a front and a back, then naturally there's got to be something in between. The rigid structure of frontspace is left behind or at least attenuated, and there isn't yet the chaotic connectivity of backspace. Consequently there's no matter as such. And the physical constants 'slip' because there isn't enough friction, so to speak, to make them stick, especially that big constant about the velocity of light. That's why you can move faster there.

But not fast enough. The port pusher had given us the impetus to make the full phase shift of 180 degrees, turning us right round so as to experience existence from the other side. But the actual transition calls for a pilot's skill. A lot of guys who want to be backjockeys do themselves a favour by never mastering that particular trick. I rotated the joysticks. I wiggled my bum. When you go through the curtain it's like a blow in every somatic cell, a sweet shock to the nervous system. I made the phase shift and WHAM – we were on our way. *Yow-Wow!*

A fast current caught us right away and I was busy holding the raft steady;

eddies were whirling on either side. I peered into the visor of the navigator, which I had previously calibrated to point the way to Elivira phase port, and at the same time I gunned the impeller on low power. There: I had the beckoning call of Elivira port. Now all I had to do was get there.

Everywhere around us backspace stretched to infinity. The polymer bubble does more than provide an air canopy; it also interprets what's outside and adds false colour. Without it, if you had only an oxygen mask, you wouldn't see anything: backlight doesn't register on the human retina. Silver and gold predominate, then turquoise, indigo and red. We saw a limitless hell of canyons running with torrents and rapids, huge drowning splashes and falls tumbling in all directions. It's the turbulence you have to watch for. If you're riding on something with a direction, you can at least kid yourself you're in control. Get caught in that crazy all-over-the-place stuff and you'll get lost or smashed to smithereens, like as not.

'Here y'are, buddy!' I yelled. 'You're on the arse side of the universe!' I'd hooked on to a fast current going roughly the way we needed, or not so far off, anyway, and I was getting high.

How often have you looked at somebody and decided you liked his arse better than his face? Particularly after you heard him speak? Well, I like backspace better. And I'll tell you why.

If you can see light from a distant star, it's because you and the star are connected in backspace. Everything is. Backspace is pure connectivity. If you artificially enter it – frontspace structures aren't supposed to be there at all – it starts working on the connectivities of the brain, pretty much the same way hallucinogenic drugs do. The resistance of the synapses is lowered. The neurones fire faster. As a result you get intensified mood.

With me that mood is always the same: *terror*. The most utter, delicious *terror* you could ever imagine, terror so strong it becomes sexual. The adrenaline goes *pling* and my dick springs up like a striking cobra. That's why I'm so good, that's why I'm the best. Conscious of where I am, conscious of how hazardous it is, knowing I might not get out, makes my mind as concentrated as a razor's edge. Only then, only then, do I really feel that I'm *alive*. After that, the rest of the time – all the time in frontspace - is like being half dead. So my attention was *on* it, was sharp and really *on* it, impelled by an endless surge of fear. I brought the power up on the motor as the current hit a flurry of rapids, the flow breaking up and twisting like a river pouring through a bed strewn with boulders. My bum was humming with the effort of tricking the raft through.

Behind me I could hear my passenger. He was coming in for mood enhancement too, of course – I wonder if he knew about that – but with him it had caused his fright to evaporate. Instead he was going mushy. He chortled, chuckled, cooed. We came through the canyon maze and into a region more like an expanse of immense ocean swells but spread in three dimensions, looking maybe like one of those geometry graphic displays, with endless veils and curved surfaces you could sort of skate over, and he was going, 'Coo, isn't it *pretty*? Oooohh, it's *beautiful*.'

Then he got weepy and soon was spouting about why he wanted to get to Elivira so quickly. Was he running for his life? Was there some compelling moral duty that demanded his immediate presence? Did a gigantic business deal hang on his arrival? Naw, it was some dreck about his boyfriend, who had left him and was on his way to Elivira on a midspace liner. I was checking the navigator, trying to get our bearings, but even so I couldn't fail to catch some of it.

'He's not doing this to me,' he blubbered. 'I'm going to be there when he docks. I'll have rented a nice condo for us and everything will be ready. I'll fill it with antiques – he likes antiques, especially twenty-first century Earth. I'll get some tubular aluminium kitchen chairs with floral plastic seat covers. And a genuine double-glazed window from an English council housing estate! There's a dealer on Elivira guarantees they date *no later than 2050*! They cost the universe, of course, but it will be worth it. Oh, I'm so full of love!'

Suddenly he was kissing the nape of my neck, and that savage, professional fear transmuted itself – as happens – to unconstrained lust, and I lost all my caution. He was a lovely feller, really.

I turned round to give him a lingering look from beneath my long artificial eyelashes.

'*You wanna fu-u-u-ck?*'

Of course he did. So there was I, zooming on one of those big swells with an idiot grin of delight all over my face, eyes lit up like searchlights, twirling the joysticks and looking for a sandbank.

Sandbanks are what we call them. Anomalous spots of solidity – near-solidity, rather – where backspace's interminable motion congeals into stable – near-stable, rather – islands. You can dismount and walk around on one.

Just what features they correspond to in the front world is unknown. In truth it hasn't been possible to map backspace to frontspace at all. For one thing there are too few points of reference. For some reason I don't properly understand, phase transition can only be accomplished from frontspace. There has to be a phase pusher there both to punch you through, and to let you phase back again. Consequently phase ports can only be set up in places that initially have been reached the slow way, by frontspace ships travelling only a few times the velocity of light. Those ports are like beacons, sending out mid and backspace signals that your navigator picks up to guide you to your destination.

Without that you're lost in chaos, because every time you phase through, even from the same port, the landscape is totally different. Backspace is never the same twice, and is without landmarks. The engineers can't even say if distances and sizes relate in any way. That maze of canyons we went through – maybe it's holding the galaxy together; or maybe it's just a grain of salt. It's possible our half hour's journey would be spent traversing the equivalent of one millimetre, and we'd cover the rest of the thirty-two light-years to Elivira in the final microsecond. Why try to makes sense of it?

Before too long I'd found what I was looking for, a golden mound tapering indistinctly off for an indefinite distance all around. I drifted the raft on to it, powered off, then leaned back to unstrap my passenger. The bubble relaxed, spreading out as I stepped on to the sandbank so as to give us room to move around. The stuff of the bank yielded under my feet like the softest foam rubber. Offering my hand, I helped him courteously down.

'What is this place?' he wondered.

'Somewhere to have fun.'

Is there a link between sexual fever and cosmic awareness? Us backriders think so. But then we've got something that doesn't happen in the front world, where the erotic and the awesome don't seem capable of occupying the mind at one and the same time. It's that revamped brain connectivity again. Things that are divorced in frontspace here get wired together. Like, one thing that is a lure for me again and again is the sensation of vastness. In the front world that's something you get only fleetingly. You see something really big and you think *Yow-Wow*, but you can't sustain the impression and a minute later it's gone, your personal world is very small; in backspace, on the other hand, the synapses are constantly tickled so the sense of immensity is there *all the time*. You can *see* what a light year is really like. If there were any planetary systems you would be able to *see* the distances between the planets and satellites, how far away the Sun was. So my customer was mooning up at the sandbank's sky, at all those stupendous traceries and veils and curves, seeing infinity with the naked eyeball, and it was blowing his mind while I was fiddling with his clothing. He had said his boyfriend liked antique stuff, but he must have as well, because *his* costume was straight out of a museum. Buttons and bows. Buttons everywhere. His trousers were held up by a kind of double strap thing that went over his shoulders and buttoned on to the waistband by little leather thongs. I unbuttoned those. There was also a row of buttons down the front of his crotch, hidden behind a flap! It was a nice hot feeling sneaking my fingers down those buttons one by one, then teasing open the vent. I massaged his podgy belly. I unbuttoned his waistcoat and pushed up his shirt to nuzzle his hairy chest, snuffing up the smell of him while I fondled his cock and balls. He was so preoccupied with the overhead vision that it was some time before the old reflex got his blood engorging his member, but when it did I saw his eyes sparkle. I was breathing heavily, in urgent gasps. We wrestled and tussled for a bit as I pulled down his trousers and undergarment, then before you knew it I was beginning to snuggle my knob into that dual purpose orifice, already well lubricated, while continuing to pump his cock with my right hand, and he was going '*Oooohh*, give me some *time*.'

That was when things went wrong.

The sensation felt like the ground, the mushy bed beneath us, was melting into thin air. I pulled out of him and jumped up. The sandbank was breaking up, the landscape dissipating fast.

Was a supernova exploding? Was the centre of a galaxy on the point of squirting out those big gas jets? Or was a crystal of salt dissolving in somebody's soup? I didn't know and I didn't care. I yelled to him to get aboard the raft. Already the liquid polymer bubble was contracting in response to external change. It was an early model, not all that smart, and I didn't trust it not to collapse round us, leaving us outside hanging in nowhere, blind and without air.

We made it just in time, him with his trousers still stuck around his knees. I switched on the motor. We'd drifted and needed to find a fast current. I bent to peer at the visor of the navigator, tapping the fine-tune button.

As I did that, an ominous grinding noise came out of the box. I blinked, peered again. The display was blank. Like, I mean, *blank*.

Fear, the dead sickening type of fear this time, clutched at my stomach. I slapped the fine-tune button, banged the top of the unit, fiddled with the calibrator. Nothing worked.

A busted navigator is heavy-duty *Yim-Bim*. Like sort of lost, nowhere, dead dead dead. *You can't get back*. Because you can't find a phase port, which means you're out in backspace for ever. Or rather the atoms of your stupid useless corpse are.

Not the sort of detail to bother a passenger with. I gunned the raft and headed out as if we were going somewhere, giving myself a little while to think at the same time. A navigator is a serious piece of equipment, needing serious kudos to buy or repair, not the sort of thing you can jury-rig or quick-fix, and it does more than locate distant phase signals, clever though that is. Backspace is too shifting and disordered for the human mind to find a route through it unaided, so the navigator does half the job, giving the pilot the cues he needs; it's known as *pointing the way*. You're double-lost if you haven't got one.

I reminded myself that the fault had been intermittent up to now, as I had said to Boy Galilee. But the box had never made that queer grinding noise before, and it had never gone completely blank before. *Intermittent* had acquired a sort of *permanent* tag.

Was there any other cause for hope? Well, yes. If you get close enough to a phase port you can actually see it on the polymer bubble as an orange glow. There are a hundred and ten phase ports, so might I find one by chance, racing all over as fast as I could? Well, let's see, if you want to work it out, the odds against would be, er, approximately, more or less, infinity to one.

At any rate nobody's ever done it, and a straight line from A to B in backspace might be a loop halfway round the universe in frontspace for all anyone knows; but I decided if I was done for I might as well go out in style. I latched on to a stream so rough and speedy that normally I wouldn't have gone near it, not even me. Nerve induction currents surged through my posterior as I went for the rockiest ride ever. My customer was declaiming behind me again, unaware as yet of his shortened life expectancy, going through the mood-swing people in backspace for the first time are prone to; getting weepy, burbling about his deep love for all mankind, longing to have every human prick that had ever existed moving affectionately up his bum - well, I hadn't supposed I was anything special – in what you might call a universal anal rhapsody. However would you find time for a crap, I thought. It crossed my mind that the best thing, after a while, might be to find another sandbank and screw each other brainless.

Then short-circuit the polymer bubble.

He quietened down eventually and I heard him pull his trousers up. Steering the raft put me in a trance, saving me from having to think, and I didn't notice how much time passed until he tapped me on the shoulder.

'How much longer?'

I shrugged.

'You said we'd be an hour at the most,' he complained. 'It's been more than two hours already.'

'We spent time on the sandbank.'

'Only a few minutes!'

I started giving him guff about how a sandbank stopover distorts the timeflow and extends the journey time, making it up as I went along. I must have sounded unconvincing. He leaned forward to peer over my shoulder at the instrument panel. He probably saw the blank navigator visor and understood the meaning of that, because he said, in a plaintive voice, 'We're lost, aren't we?'

'Don't worry about it.'

Did I say the wrong thing? My passenger collapsed in a sobbing heap.

It was my finest hour. My swansong. The back universe soared and sang all around us. My raft rattled like it was plunging through broken shale.

Yow-Wow. I had no idea where the hell we were – and what did it matter anyway?

Through recklessness, probably, the moment came when I made what should have been a fatal error of judgement. We were going through a flume. That's different from a water flume, incidentally: the current rotates corkscrew fashion and the trick is in the timing. That was where I fell down. The raft tipped up, I lost all control and we were dumped into the turbulence, spinning like crazy and being carried further and further off.

The titanium bracing groaned as it tried to hold the raft together. My customer let out a soprano ululation, a screeching aria of fright. Poor devil. I fought to regain control, though how I possibly could, and to what end, was entirely unclear. Never mind that turbulence can quickly carry you out of range of all the hundred and ten beacons. You wouldn't know the difference, because man-made structures give in to the stresses in short order. I was about to chuck it in, too, just close my eyes and let the raft break up, when suddenly the turbulence lessened. I found I was able to hold us steady.

And the music behind me subsided to a whimpering. I might have offered a few words of comfort, but I was too taken up with studying what lay ahead of us. The turbulence smoothed out and gave way to a field that was peculiar, a slowly moving three-dimensional vortex.

In the centre of that vortex, on the upper left of the polymer bubble, was an orange glow.

Miracle of miracles. Little Tony, all the luck in the universe has descended on your head! That was what I told myself as I turned the nose of the raft, nudging the power stick a trifle. 'Cheer up,' I said, thinking to quieten the sniffling in the back, 'there's a phase port ahead.'

A little moan of relief came forth. 'Is it Elivira?'

'No way to tell. The navigator's out.'

Then, as we vectored in, it became clear that something was amiss. I couldn't quite accept it at first. I kept blinking and shaking my head and looking again, sure there was something wrong with my vision. As I said, you can't decode an identification signal without a working navigator; but the signal itself should have been visible as a slight pulse or flicker. Instead, the orange glow was steady.

So what, you might say, the IS could have been switched off. But no, because that can't happen; it's part of the phase modulation itself. If the beacon is on, the signal has to be there.

Beating the odds is one thing; this was something else again. Only one explanation fitted the facts. And it had to be something no one any longer believed existed.

An alien phase port.

*

There weren't supposed to be any alien civilizations. Nature was not prolific. Of the thousands of planets that had been investigated, only a handful were life-bearing, and all were of poor evolutionary development. The lengthy search for non-human phase pushers had been closed down a long time ago. Engineers were unanimously of the opinion that there were none to be found, in our galactic group anyway.

Whether I had taken the raft further than that, or whether this was an alien pusher brought newly on line was, for the moment, academic. We had been thrown out of the frying pan into the fire, and out of the fire into the middle of the floor, as Brigham Young put it. There was nowhere else to go, and we would have to take our chance on the aliens being friendly. Maybe they would fix my navigator, I thought with a burst of optimism.

So I kept going into the centre of the orange glow until it spread out over the whole bubble, tensing myself to make the phase shift into that *smooooth* middle continuum, and then to co-operate with the pull of the port as it phased us all the way through to frontspace.

And it didn't happen that way. I felt the shivery thrill of phasing through the curtain, but there was no intermediate transit – the instrument panel registered a 180 degree phase shift all in one go, straight slam bang into frontspace. That didn't make sense, not at all. There *has* to be a continuum between the front and the back, just as there has to be thickness between the two sides of a piece of paper, and I couldn't imagine any phase pusher, alien or otherwise, that could miss it out.

There was no time to think about it. I was baffled and confused, but I killed the motor, bringing us to a stop. *Yow-Wow* and *Yim-Bim* at the same time! I was thrilled and I was scared. What a situation! I, Little Tony, was the first human being in history to make alien contact! Well, me and the guy in the back. The polymer bubble flowed over us and collapsed into its container, which meant that it had detected breathable atmosphere. I crouched on my guidance plate and peered around.

Where were the aliens? Where was the phase pusher machine? The ones we use come not much smaller than a medium-sized office block. Come to that, where was anything? We weren't in any sort of docking space, like the side shacks in our phase ports. There was nothing to see but a thin mist stretching indefinitely in all directions.

Cautiously I drew air into my lungs. It was neutral, lifeless, without discernible tangs or odours.

The raft rested on a smooth rubbery surface. I tested it with one foot before stepping down. Just like rubber.

My customer, finally letting go of the handgrips he had been clutching like straws for God knows how long, joined me.

'What is this place?' he wondered.

'Oh, somewhere or other.'

The mist cleared suddenly. A landscape appeared. It was covered in trees, not resembling any variety I had seen before, foresting a spread of downs and vales. There was no horizon. Rather, the background seemed to rise up as though we stood on the inside of a sphere, instead of on the outside.

The mist came down again, and then again cleared. This time another, different landscape showed, consisting of bleak mountains and craters. Nothing alive was in sight.

This was not your ordinary everyday planet, that much was obvious. It probably wasn't a planet at all. We carried on watching as the mist came and went, presenting a succession of scenes, no two the same. On a few occasions there was only blackness peppered with stars. A lot of times there was confused curving and billowing, like in backspace. The landscapes would often move and writhe as well, curving right over our heads and then winding away like smoke.

After a bit, the bubble sprang on again, spreading out to give us some room to move around. The air must have disappeared. That wasn't so much of a worry. As long as there was still enough charge in the fuel rods to work the CO_2 splitter and extract oxygen from our exhaled carbon dioxide, we could continue to breathe. That would be for quite a long time while the rods weren't being used to power the raft, so we weren't in immediate danger.

But what were we to do?

Well, of course, there was one thing; but we didn't think of it straight away. We kept on looking at the weird stuff all around us, while he kept on asking, 'Where *are* we? For God's sake tell me where we *are*.' And so in the end I told him as much as I knew. He looked stunned as it sank in. Then he was blubbering again and blaming me for everything. 'You told me you were the best! You said I'd be safe with you! Oh, I shouldn't have listened! I never should have got into this thing!'

'You did it for love,' I reminded him.

'Yes,' he said dreamily, 'for love.' He switched just like somebody had pressed a button. The sparkle came back in his eyes, and he was rhapsodizing once more. That neural connectivity must have been still working for us somehow, because I could feel it too. So why shouldn't we finish what was interrupted on the sandbank? We snuggled down on the rubbery floor and started messing with one another, fiddling and unbuttoning. I caressed his tool and balls while kissing his throat. Our bellies squirmed together. Then off came my codpiece and our two dicks were prodding and rubbing like a pair of maddened pike. I was on fire: this was working up to the biggest thrill I could remember. I manoeuvred to ease my organ into his orifice, but it seemed he had the same idea and was probing for mine, getting in the way.

While this was going on, something funny was happening all around us, though in the excitement I was only half conscious of it. The landscape had finally closed up over our heads and taken on a smeared appearance. Now it was closing in so that we were visibly on the inside of a globe. I didn't worry about it for the moment. I was too busy trying to get my urgently lunging shaft into where it could do itself some good.

Dimly it occurred to me that not only could this not be a planet, but maybe we weren't in frontspace at all, despite what the instruments said. Certainly it was a very funny kind of space. Our world was now very small, a spherical chamber. As it contracted, everything inside seemed to curve in proportion. The raft was curving, bending like a bow. Then it performed a topological dance and flowed into itself.

Like I said, I was in no mood to think too much about it. We were both too hot, because the same sort of thing was happening to us too. The space we occupied had acquired more than three dimensions, I was able to understand that, so that impossible things were able to happen, and we were ready to take full advantage of them. We could bend and twist all round each other. My moist swelling knob found his heaving bud and pushed all the way up; at the same time, marvel of marvels, I felt the delicious pungent pain as *he* entered *me*. We were both thrusting in perfect rhythm, out of our heads with pleasure.

Simultaneous double sodomy! It definitely was the biggest thrill I could remember!

We came in unison, twice, three times, then fell apart, butts red and raw. I was panting, glazy-eyed. Not him, though. His eyes were shining. He stood and looked down at himself, as though he had had a revelation.

'Love,' he said softly. 'Do you know the important thing about love? You must learn to love yourself. The way I do.'

His hands were running up and down his partly clothed body. Then he bent over and took his cock in his mouth. Well, I've known guys who could do that – but this was different; he wasn't the sort to be that supple. He sank down and curled up like a cat – or a snake, it's hard to visualize, really, just what was happening – let his dick flop out of his mouth and reached further to lick his scrotum; then the perineum behind it; then he was nuzzling between the cheeks of his own buttocks, making mooing sounds.

He had flipped, I guess. I stepped back and stared in fascination. You're not going to believe this, but I *swear* it, I *swear* I *saw* it. He was pushing his face into his backside and it was going in. His buttocks widened till his whole head went in, and still he kept going. Shoulders, torso, even his bum in the end, all vanished. Up his own arsehole. And there was nothing left.

First time I ever lost a passenger. To make matters worse he had taken my one thousand kudos with him. It had been in his jacket, which he hadn't bothered to take off.

I suppose I should have felt some concern over a fellow human being, but now I'd had my fun I had no time to be anything but scared. The place was still contracting, and I had worked out where I was now. This was no phase station. No friendly aliens were going to bale me out. The topological disappearing act I had just witnessed could only mean a region of collapsing space. A singularity, in other words. Though not a black hole. Something rarer, unknown to science. And how far was it going to shrink? To a dimensionless point? The rubbery surface was taking on the consistency of glue. I hated to think what I was looking like by now, but I certainly did not relish the idea of what might happen next. Neither did there seem any way to avoid it. How I'd got from backspace and into this hole I couldn't exactly say; but the point was that the phase shift that gets you into backspace is not the same as the shift that allows you to leave it.

The singularity's effect would be one-way. I couldn't leave.

I closed my eyes and waited to be squashed out of existence. Then a thought struck me. To suppose I had come upon a body just as it was on the point of collapsing into nothing was asking too much of coincidence. It must have been here a long time. It would be a singularity with a pulsation, expanding and contracting. And, in my imagination, the phase *pop* that had fetched me from backspace would most logically result from the expansion stage. Now it was contracting maybe the phase would be reversed.

I made for the raft, even though it seemed to have tied itself in knots. The limits of the singularity were now only yards away and I think I resembled some elaborate knot myself, so the journey was agonisingly long. I yelled out loud when I found myself staring at my own bare backside, afraid I was about to suffer the fate of my self-loving customer, but somehow I crawled on to – into? – the raft and located the switches, bringing the harmonizer on line.

And it worked. My stomach turned over like never before, a jolt that nearly made me pass out, as the raft was shot into backspace like a pip being squeezed. It was the same as the first time, with no midspace in between. But the raft was straight and linear, and all my limbs were in the right places. I gunned the motor and got out of there fast, zooming along the curve of the enormous swirling vortex.

The orange glow faded. I took a minute out to check everything over, especially the dangerously depleted charge rods. While going through the routine, I automatically happened to glance down into the visor of the navigator.

And there, would you believe it, was the familiar red encoding of the readout.

The crappy useless thing was working again. An intermittent fault after all.

Want me to tell you about the relief I felt? Ever heard of ecstasy?

Well, that's the story, or most of it. I had to search for some time before I came in range of a beacon, but when I did I took a calculated risk and headed back to Hawtaw, even though there were nearer stations. There was a reason for that, which I'll come to in a moment.

The first thing I had to do, of course, was notify the authorities of my lost passenger, an embarrassing disclosure, naturally, and then make polite explanations to the inquiry board which convened, phase ports being no-time-wasted-type operations, that very same day. There's a strategy to concealing an uncomfortable fact: tell only one lie, and keep to the truth about everything else. So apart from that one detail I came clean about it all. The sandbank stop, how we got lost, the singularity and, most important of all, what happened to my customer in it. The board was goggle-eyed about that last part, but they believed me. Complaining about the way I'd lost my fee helped, I think.

In fact I appear to have made a contribution to theoretical cosmology. A pair of government scientists came to see me a couple of weeks later and got me to tell them everything all over again. I had been right about the singularity: it wasn't a black hole.

It seems physicists have long wondered why front and backspace don't become unravelled. Midspace is a separator; it's not a glue. My talk of experiencing instant transition between the two sides gave them a possible answer: scattered through space at immense distances from one another are singularities of this particular type, which punch right through and act like staples.

So there you have it. Existence is stapled together.

It's never been found again. The phase-push effect, they told me, might even have been a transient phenomenon.

I asked them how they explained the planetary scenes we had seen appearing and disappearing. That was consistent, they said, and trundled on about how probability is different inside singularities, how almost anything can happen quite spontaneously. The planet surfaces were randomly emerging and dissolving structures, a fast-action mirror to what went on more slowly in the universe at large. Professional types have to have an answer for everything, wouldn't you say?

And the reason why I had to get back to Hawtaw despite being low on charge: think about it. The one thing I had to hold back, the little lie I had to tell:

'When did you first notice your navigator was malfunctioning?'

'Right after we got off the sandbank, sir. I can only imagine the bank's sudden collapse affected it somehow. It will need a complete overhaul before I go out again.'

'Did you carry out all the usual checks and tests before phasing?'

'Yes, naturally, sir,' I replied, blinking with surprise at such a question, 'everything tested out fine.'

If it ever got known to the board that I had deliberately taken a passenger into backspace using a delinquent navigator it would be, 'Hand over your licence, Tony. Get a job in the junkyard, where your raft is going.' And of course there was somebody who *did* know. That blackmailing slut Boy Galilee, he of the waxy backside who, apart from anything else, I now couldn't pay for four charge rods. He wasn't around when I first phased in. He came to me in my shack next day, by which time my evidence to the board was all over the port and he knew what the score was.

I had just taken my customer's hold-all from the raft's luggage compartment and was sorting through his effects out of curiosity. He was an antiquities buff, all right. His favourite period seemed to be the mid twenty-first century, which as we all know was itself an age of nostalgia, absorbed in re-creating the fashions of earlier times. I had found some magazines with lurid covers and was studying one. It was a revival of a type of popular magazine they used to have back in the twentieth century, but modified to incorporate the preoccupations of over a hundred years later. The cover picture was striking, presenting what to the artwork of the time would have been a 'futuristic' scene. In the background, a soaring metal city; filling nearly all the sky, a gigantic cratered moon, improbably close. In the foreground stood two muscular and godlike male figures in the briefest of costume, just straps and weapons belts holding old-fashioned ray-guns. One of them, I remember, was deep blue in skin tone; he was suggestively manhandling the other, the expressions of both of them coming somewhere between heroic nobleness and exalted desire. The magazine's title was slashed across the top of the page in slanting script: *Thrilling Stories of Sodomy and Science Fiction.*

Boy Galilee peered at the illustration over my shoulder, his usual simpering smile on his face. 'Tasty. And what a jolly fellow your customer turned out to be. Quite the pioneer of auto-oral-anal-eroticism.'

I knew what I would have to do to keep him quiet. He'd always been after it, and I'd always held off. Oh Jeez, that awful behind of his, and his back passage as slack as a windsock! It wouldn't be for the last time, either, with what he had on me. He'd be forever sliding into my shack and reminding me of his 'favour'. What could I do to make sure it wasn't too often, I asked myself? In any case I had to find some way of steeling myself to go through with it. So I gave myself a massive jab of phenylethylamine, and spent the whole time thinking of my lovely sweet passenger with the podgy belly and the twentieth-century trousers, gazing now and then at the magazine covers if need be. That way I managed to roger him for a solid six hours, and I'm pleased to report he couldn't set his bum on a guidance plate for a week. The things you have to do to make a living these days. Shove your head up your arse, Galilee!

The Last Phallic Symbol

Elizabeth Sourbut

ONE

George slipped off the headset and rubbed his eyes wearily. After fifteen years, he was still upset by the unfocused aggression filling project after project. The boys' holos were a mish-mash of grotesquely imagined destruction and violent sex, salted with the occasional stark intrusion of memory. The world for these street boys was a dangerous place of gangs and uncertain loyalties, of illegal acid and wire, and frequent, brutal death. The remand school was possibly the only education they'd ever had, and probably the first security.

He looked out of the window, at the park across the road from his flat. Now, bathed in pale spring sunshine, it was peaceful and quiet, but at night even here in the West End, murders were not uncommon.

George sighed. After fifty-four years of privilege, with a sheet of bullet-proof glass between himself and the world, it was crazy to think he could help these boys.

He pushed the pile of tapes away, and reached for one of his own, a full-spectrum feelie. It was spring; London was coming back to life after a winter of storms and plummeting temperatures, and he felt his own blood quickening in response. March 12. Anniversary. He adjusted the headset, and Val's image appeared before him.

The tape was his own work, made near the beginning of their affair, ten years before. It was sheer masochism to keep coming back to it now, but still he sank into the shell of his previous self, and the scent of her skin filled his nostrils. She smiled into his eyes, her body warm along the length of him. 'Christ,' he muttered, breathing heavily. 'I miss you.'

Into the memory, he had mingled illicit fantasy. Now Trish, Val's then seventeen-year-old daughter, joined them. This was his wish-fulfilling version of Trish, and she reached eagerly for his cock.

He matched his real-world actions with hers, and his erection came hard into his hand, hot and full. He stroked his fingers along it, squeezing gently. Then suddenly an agonizing pain seared into his fantasy world, and the penis came away in his hand.

He snatched off his headset, and for a moment he and his cock stared at one another. Then the penis shook itself, slipped out of his fingers, and scuttled down his thigh on tiny legs. It jumped on to the floor and made off across the room.

'Hey!' George yelled, his voice cracking into falsetto. The penis paused and turned back towards him. Its foreskin parted in a withering grin, then it disappeared through the open door.

TWO

Trish drove slowly down the centre of the street, edging her ancient four-wheel drive through the clear spaces between rotting piles of refuse.

'Fuck, fuck, and fuck!' she swore. 'Where *is* it?'

Carole, keeping a sharp watch from the passenger window, glanced round and reached out a hand to her. 'It's OK,' she said. 'It's the next turning.'

Trish's hands slipped on the wheel. She wiped them, one at a time, on her jeans, her eyes darting from the road to the shuttered buildings and back. In her rear-view mirror she glimpsed the gang of boys, still following.

'Here.' Carole pointed, and Trish turned left into a narrow square of crumbling three-storey terraces. In the gathering dusk, the road faded into a jumble of scrap-iron. Trish slowed, steered into a gap, the off-side wheels crunching over broken glass.

'Oh, shit.' Trish craned forward, searching for house numbers. 'Come on, woman, don't make us wait.'

Carole had her seat-belt off, door ajar, ready. There was movement amongst the greying undergrowth in the centre of the square. Two men stood upright, staring.

'There!'

A brief call, and a woman came running out of the shadows leading to a basement flat. She was clutching a toddler to her chest and dragging a suitcase.

Carole leapt to the ground and flung open the rear door of the van. She grabbed the suitcase, bundled the sobbing woman inside, and heaved the case in after her.

'Go!' she yelled, and Trish slammed into reverse as her partner jumped back into the seat beside her.

'Hey!' yelled one of the men. 'That's Pete's missis!' He ran towards them, and Trish swerved. The rear bumper crunched into a burnt-out car, jerking them all against their seats.

'Oh, fuck.' She clashed the gears, and revved the van forwards. Their pursuer dived out of the way as she skidded into a reckless turn.

The woman in the back moaned. 'He'll kill us. He'll kill us.'

Shapes moved ahead – the gang of boys, strung out across the road. Trish flicked on the lights, full-beam, and the youths recoiled, covering their eyes, scrambling to get out of the way as she drove straight for them. Startled eyes, mouths wide, yelling obscenities.

'Pete! They've got your missis! Pete!'

The four-wheel drive jolted over bricks and timbers, then the road ahead was clear. Trish accelerated into it, peripheral vision registering a figure running towards them.

The van shuddered, and a man lay sprawled across the bonnet, one huge hand pressed against the windscreen. He was snarling as his fingers began to slip.

'He's going to die!' said Trish. 'Oh, God, he's going to die.'

She took the corner fast and the man screamed as he was flung to the ground. Carole stared back as they roared away up the road.

'I think he got up,' she said.

Their passenger began to laugh hysterically. 'That was Pete. He won't even be bruised.' She sat back in the seat and shrieked. The toddler clung to her, crying.

Carole clambered into the rear of the van with them, and began the long and difficult job of trying to reassure them. Trish kept her eyes on the road. Her hands were shaking on the wheel. She wanted to be reassured too. Instead, she continued to swear, over and over again, as she drove them across town to another crumbling terraced house, wistfully called a refuge.

THREE

The muggy heat of a Florida night pressed close around them. Electrical storms flickered on the horizon and the air crackled with static charges, raising sparks between their sweating bodies.

Through the open window, they could see the starship. Floodlights picked out its sleek lines, sweeping up from spherical engines to the controversial globe of the observation deck at its nose. Two hundred and fifty metres of precision engineering thrusting into the night sky.

Jason nibbled her ear, and whispered: 'I am the ship. Can you feel me against you, cool and hard?'

Pat giggled, and stroked her hands along his body. 'Mmm. The fuel tanks and the engines. Here's the airlock, and inside, the crew, cold and sleeping. And here,' she kissed his forehead, 'the computers and navigation system.'

He pushed her hand down to his dick, and she stroked it as he sighed and moaned. 'I'm lying on the launch-pad,' he said, eyes closed, body taut with pleasure, 'and this is the ship, the first starship, soaring into the sky, hard and tall and powerful, waiting to surge up to the stars, further than anyone has ever gone before, up on a tail of fire, faster and faster.'

She straddled him, pushing down, engulfing him in the warm wetness of her. 'And I am the sky. I'll take you into me, protect you, guide you as you travel through me.'

'I'll sow my seed of humanity—'

'On to a virgin planet!'

They fell against one another, laughing and straining, slipping, thrusting, an image of the starship between them, flesh, steel, woman, sky, starship, man, starburst, death, and new life.

'Aaahhh . . . '

They lay together, panting and shaking, holding one another as tightly as they could, the mingled smells of sweat and sex filling their nostrils.

'I love you,' Jason murmured. 'I wish I was taking you to the stars.'

'I felt as though I was the stars,' she said. 'I am the universe.'

'And I am the ship.'

They looked into one another's eyes and laughed and kissed, rolling over amongst the twisted, sweat-soaked sheets, young and in love.

'Less than a week to go,' said Jason, staring out of the window at the ship. 'Can you imagine being one of those people in there, cold and brittle? I could break off your earlobe.' He tweaked her ear and grinned.

'And when they come back to life,' she said, 'they'll be on a different world, warmed by a different sun. How will it feel?'

'I wish we were going. It's all our dreams come true. To go to the stars.'

Pat sighed. 'A new planet. A second chance. Maybe we'll treat it right this time.' She turned away from the window, and buried her head in his shoulder. 'I love you.'

Jason lay awake for a long time after she slept, staring out of the window, stars reflected in his eyes.

FOUR

Raymond's counselling room was warm and well ventilated, and smelt very faintly of cherry blossom. George wryly compared it with his own dark cell at the remand school. These 'soft' methods were on the way out, replaced by implanted tranquillizer drips and the revolutionary electro-neural surgery. But he still had a few miraculous successes each year, even though the boys knew he had no real support. Those few successes kept him going.

He sat down in one of a matching pair of posture-friendly armchairs. Raymond sat in the other, positioned at an angle to George's chair, leaned forward slightly, and smiled.

'Now then, George, how can I help you?'

George stared at his hands. 'I need to make some, some – adjustments to my self-image,' he said slowly.

'Uh-huh,' said Raymond. 'And how do you see yourself at the moment?'

'Powerless.' He felt the tears gathering once more. 'Impotent.'

'How long have you felt this way?'

'Two days.'

Raymond nodded, accepting. 'Do you know what triggered these feelings of helplessness?'

George stared at the carpet. He had known Raymond for several years, and trusted the gay man's commitment to supporting other men, and his confidentiality, but still it took all his courage to answer.

'Two days ago,' he said very slowly, 'my penis detached itself from my body and walked out through the door.'

There was a brief silence. George looked up. Raymond stared directly back at him. 'Which door was this?'

'My study door. I was in my study marking projects.'

'I'd like you to imagine that you're in your study now.'

'All right.' He closed his eyes, and conjured up an image of his study, his desk standing in the large bay window, the shelf of books, the CD player, the feelie deck, all as he had seen them that morning, with spring sunshine pouring in through the window.

'How do you feel?'

'Oh, comfortable, safe, secure.' He stopped, remembering that moment of excruciating pain, and the shock of loss. 'Oh, shit.' He looked away, fighting back the tears.

'And your penis detached itself from your body and walked out of the door, out of your safe, secure study, and . . . Where do you think it's gone, George?'

'I don't know!' he wailed. 'I want it back!' And he burst into tears.

After a few moments, Raymond leaned forward and laid a hand on George's knee. 'It's all right,' he said. 'It's all right for men to cry.'

'I know it is,' George snuffled, and fumbled for his handkerchief. 'But it's so hard. I've spent so many years fighting the stereotypes, the rules that say it isn't manly to express any emotion except lust or anger. And now I watch generation after generation of young boys growing up with the same old attitudes, out on the streets younger and younger, too scared to admit their fear, frying their brains with wire trips, jacking into God knows what weird space, learning how to kill. When a young thug comes to me, strutting and swearing to show he's a man, I look into his eyes and sometimes I can see the frightened child, the best part of him, deep inside, desperately needing to be loved. And over and over again I try to reach that child without getting myself killed.

'Sometimes it all gets too much, and then I sit at my study window and watch people walking in the park.'

'Safe and secure in your study,' said Raymond. 'Do you need your penis when you're in your study?'

Grief, and a sense of great loss overwhelmed him. 'In theory, no. A man is more than just his cock. But I don't feel that way. I feel like a discarded shell. Why? Why did it go?'

Into the silence, Raymond spoke softly. 'Every day, you struggle with concepts of manhood. The boys who come to you are hardened by their lives on the streets, but you see other potentialities, in them and in yourself. A man is more than just his cock. But now, you have a fantasy of your own penis physically leaving you, and walking out through your study door.

'What might your penis want that you're not giving it, George?'

George stared at his counsellor, betrayed. 'It's not a fantasy,' he said. 'It's real. My penis has gone.'

Raymond bit his lip. 'OK,' he said. 'It's really gone. Imagine that you are your penis. Where would you go?'

'Oh, stuff your gestalt shit!' George yelled. 'I'll show you it's real. Look!' He leapt to his feet, and tore down his trousers and underpants. 'Look!'

Raymond stared. Then he stood up, unfastened his own trousers, and pulled down his shorts to reveal a pair of shrivelling testicles and a patch of pink new skin where his penis should be. 'Thank God,' he whispered. 'I'm not the only one.'

FIVE

When he had smashed everything in the flat belonging to his wife and young daughter, Pete went out to get drunk. The whole of his left side ached where he had landed after being flung from the van that had taken them away. Echoes of his own scream resounded in his head to shame him. If he ever saw his wife again, he would kill her.

The pub was his local, a survivor from the 1930s, perched on a street corner beside an abandoned warehouse. Inside, it was smoky and claustrophobic, a heavy dance beat making conversation difficult. Pete strolled across to the bar. The other men moved up to make room for him, calling greetings. Everyone knew what had happened. No one mentioned it. Pete dealt in used cars and worked as a bouncer three nights a week. He carried a knife but mostly didn't need it. Men respected him.

He flexed his aching shoulders and ordered a pint. Rage was still close to the surface.

'Gimme the stool,' he said to the man next to him, reaching out to flick the socket behind his victim's left ear.

Ricki, a skinny wirehead, recoiled. 'Sure,' he said, and slithered out of Pete's way. He looked sick even for a wirehead. Pete gave him a long, uneasy stare. Too many men had acquired that dry, brittle look over the past few weeks. Ricki looked away, and picked up his glass, moving further along the bar.

Pete sneered, and heaved himself up on to the stool. Pain traced fire down his leg and across the small of his back. Trapped nerve. Probably pulled muscles, too. He saw again the tall vehicle careering towards him, lights blazing. He had thought he could hang on, but hadn't quite jumped far enough. His hands had slipped across the glass, leaving him no chance as the van cornered sharply. But he remembered the driver's face, her staring eyes, her terror. He laughed.

'Cunt,' he said.

'You going after her?' asked Mike, the electronics man who got him most of his cars.

Pete drank his beer. 'Nope,' he said. Everyone present knew that he had very little chance of finding her. 'Don't need to. She'll see me in every shadow. And when she's had enough of fucking shadows, she'll come back.' He finished his beer while the other men laughed. 'But I won't be here. I'm going to Mongolia.'

That was too much of a challenge. Every man in the area had been down to the barracks to apply for a place. Expedition to Mongolia. Adventure guaranteed. High wages.

'Oh yeah?' said Mike. 'Why'd they want you?'

Pete stuck out his chest, swaggering. 'They're looking for big men,' he said, putting heavy emphasis on the last two words. 'You ever seen a man as big as me?'

'What, they gonna fuck their way across Asia?' sneered Mike.

That was enough excuse for Pete. He flung himself off his stool, picked Mike up by the shoulders, and shook him. 'They want men,' he roared, 'not worms.'

'Hey, hey,' the smaller man gasped. 'Take it easy. You need me to get your cars.'

'I'm going away,' said Pete. 'I don't care shit for your cars, nor your fucking neck.'

But he liked the smart, gutsy thief. He dropped him on the floor, lost for what else to do. This was goodbye. If he hadn't been leaving in the morning, he and Mike would have searched London for that van, for his wife.

Mike scrambled away from him, then jumped to his feet, ready to run. 'Why Mongolia, anyway?' he demanded. 'Why all the hype? What's in fucking Mongolia?'

Pete turned away and strode out of the pub. 'Nothing for cunts like you!' he yelled over his shoulder. He stomped back home, hurt and angry.

In front of the cracked mirror, he stripped off his clothes and twisted to look at the deep bruises spreading across the muscles of shoulder, arm and leg. He knew he was lucky not to have broken a bone. He grinned at himself in the mirror, a heavily muscled man with a huge cock. The expedition flew out in the morning on a specially chartered flight to Ulan Bator. After that, he had no idea. But he knew it had to be better than here. The ones who stayed here would end up like Ricki. Mongolia was the place for men.

SIX

The great dam had burst, and everything was gone. In one chaotic night of earthquake and flood, Amira's world was torn away by the torrents of water surging down the valley.

She had awakened to the rattling of pans and a child screaming. The whole house seemed to be on the move. She had leapt out of bed, flung on her dress, and hustled the children outside, afraid that the wood and plasterboard walls would collapse on top of them.

Outside, a strong wind blew cloud-tatters across the moon. In the fitful light, she saw glimpses of her neighbours standing, like her, by their doors. She held the children close to her body and turned to stare down the hillside. The wind was cold and the grey-white moonlight cast hard black shadows across the village.

Then the earth shook once more and they were flung to the ground. Above the shrieks of terrified children, a huge roar filled the air, the wind increased to a gale, and she saw a wall of water surging along the valley below. The dam had burst and the liberated waters of the artificial Lake Sudan were roaring towards her, drowning everything in their path.

The wave-front hit the lower reaches of the village and spilled up the hillside. Houses collapsed like children's toys and she scrambled to her feet and tried to run. Then she was underwater, choking and clutching at the ground. The wave tumbled her along for a few metres then withdrew, sucking her two small sons away with it.

She scrambled after them, half-running, half-falling down the hillside, screaming their names. But they were gone, drowned with hundreds of others.

Now she sat shivering in the pale dawn, hugging the baby to her breast while the other two surviving children hid their faces in her dress and cried.

As the sun rose on the devastation, the villagers looked about them in despair. The waters had retreated from the hillsides, but the fields on the valley floor, so dry yesterday, now lay under sheets of filthy water, a few trees standing mournfully above the flood. The houses were gone, replaced by a wilderness of mud and rubble and scattered possessions.

Amira told herself that she was lucky to have survived, but how could they live now with no homes, no fields, and the livestock and her two young sons drowned? She wondered if the men had somehow known that this was coming. Perhaps this was why they had abandoned the village one by one, sneaking away and leaving the women to keep things together.

Cold and exhausted, the village women gathered together to grieve. They had worked so hard to rebuild their lives after the government had moved them from their old homes upstream of the high dam, and now their security was shattered once more.

They sat together and sang songs of grieving, songs for the aftermath of war, songs to brace themselves for the task of beginning all over again.

SEVEN

A pale glow bathed the freezer compartment. Glancing back at the open airlock, Jason could see the world outside, like an overexposed photograph, awash with sunlight. Trucks moved in the distance and faintly, he could hear the sounds of machinery and voices shouting. But in here it was cold and silent and still. His breath condensed, misting the readout as he bent over the first cryogenic unit. He wiped the surface with his sleeve, and held his breath while he read the display.

The units were stacked six deep, drawers that could be pulled open if anything went wrong. Inside, the naked bodies of the stellanauts lay still, scarcely breathing, their skins frosted with a lacing of ice. Eyes closed, faces relaxed and peaceful, they lay like corpses, beginning their long sleep. A sleep that might last a thousand subjective years as they sped towards the stars at close to the speed of light.

Jason shivered and thought of Pat, her hot, sweaty body pressed against his, her heart racing. He could not imagine these beautiful young icicles making love; now or ever. 'And yet you're going to the stars,' he whispered, staring in at a handsome Japanese man, his well-formed muscles sheathed in ice, brittle as frozen rubber. 'I could snap you in two. But you'll be raising children on a new world long after I'm dust.'

Pat watched through the one-way mirror as the next batch of half a dozen young gods and goddesses entered the cryogenic chamber. Diane, her technician, waited by the door as the stellanauts slipped out of their robes and embraced one another. These were tall, lean East Africans, their heads almost brushing the ceiling of the tiny room. All had perfectly functioning physiologies, and not a faulty gene amongst them. Though the radiation from an alien sun might slowly damage the DNA of future generations, the colonists would begin in perfection.

The stellanauts swung themselves on to their couches, and Diane moved along the double row, carefully connecting the monitoring equipment and checking the readouts. She said nothing; already the stellanauts were composing themselves to enter trance-state, beginning to slow their own body functions to the point where the freezing process could safely begin.

Diane collected up the robes and left the chamber, sealing the heavy airtight door behind her. As ever, Pat felt her heart contract slightly at the muted thud of the closing door. The thought of lying down in that stark, white room knowing that you would never again see the Earth or anything familiar scared her. And yet these stellanauts seemed unmoved. Perhaps they had been so busy preparing for a new world, they had never become attached to this one.

She took a deep breath, and jacked into the Net. The stream of data enveloped her, and her consciousness entered the cryogenic chamber. Input from the monitors in the couches flooded her nervous system, replacing her sense of embodied self.

She became separately aware of each of the six bodies against her own, their contours nestling closer than a lover as her kinaesthetic awareness accepted its task. Eyes, ears, fingertips and skin absorbed the data flow as she concentrated all her senses on the task of interpreting the multiple stimuli. Pulse, respiration, blood-pressure, body temperature, skin chemistry, brain activity, she monitored them all, alert for abnormalities, her own identity distant and thin as she became the machine's intelligence.

The stellanauts slipped together into trance-state, and gradually their brain patterns changed. Their body functions began to slow and, as they did so, Pat directed the computers to begin reducing the temperature in the chamber. The lights dimmed slowly, and life seemed to leach out of the room.

Sensations of the growing cold and stillness made this part of the job dangerous for Pat. She had to prevent her own body functions from becoming too closely entwined with the data. To keep a measure of distance, she concentrated a part of her awareness on the visual monitors, on seeing them from the outside. The stellanauts' faces were relaxed, their eyes closed. As the temperature fell, the rich brown of their skins took on a shade of grey. Frost began to form along their cheekbones and at the tips of their noses. Ice traced a fine pattern over their hands and feet, spreading gradually up their limbs until at last their bodies were encased in a lacework of white. The light had faded to a pale blue, bleeding the last of the colour from the scene.

To a casual observer it might have looked like a morgue, but the data told

Pat that they were still just alive, body functions slowed to a fraction of normal. Like this, they would age only an hour for every year that they slept. They were effectively immortal.

When she was sure that the stellanauts had stabilized, Pat brought her awareness back to herself, and jacked out of the system.

'Well,' said Diane, who had come into the room to join her, 'that's the last batch. They're ready to go.'

Pat nodded, not wanting to acknowledge the fact. A tension that she had scarcely been aware of was dissolving between her shoulder blades. She would never have to go through that again. 'See that they're loaded on board,' she said crisply. 'I'm going back to my quarters.'

Later, when she was alone with Jason, they cried, and clung together. Although why they should pity the gods themselves, they weren't sure.

EIGHT

George was on duty. Strapped into his black plastic and steel riot-gear, his head covered by a civilian version of the army datacom, none of the boys could tell which member of staff was confronting them. For George, this was a particular advantage. If the boys knew that he too patrolled the corridors, then any credibility he might hope to retain as a sympathetic counsellor would be lost.

He was so deep in his own gloomy thoughts that he almost trod on the penis. It reared back from him, snarling. He took a startled step backwards as the penis snuffled and spat. Then it scuttled past him and disappeared into an empty classroom.

George took two quick steps to the door and peered in. His infra-red sensor spotted it squeezing through a gap in the floorboards, and he swore.

'It wasn't mine,' he told himself. 'It was too small.' He reached out to close the door, and discovered that his hands were shaking. Has mine turned aggressive? he wondered. I'm sure that thing had teeth.

As he continued down the corridor, his datacom registered a disturbance coming from the games room. He broke into a run.

The noise resolved itself into a chant as he burst through the door.

'Poofter! Poofter! Poofter! Poofter!'

Half a dozen boys stood around in a semicircle at the far end of the room, kicking another lad who lay on the floor with his face to the wall.

'Stop that at once!' George bellowed, his voice artificially magnified and sieved to remove the higher registers.

The chanting broke off and the boys turned around. They looked defiant and a little afraid. His datacom listed their names in red across his vision.

'His prick's run off, sir,' said Sanderson.

'He's a fucking fairy.'

'That's enough,' George rumbled. 'Go to your rooms.'

'It weren't us, sir,' said Dodd. 'It jumped up and ran off itself.'

'It's 'cos he's a queer, isn't it, sir?'

George could suddenly smell their fear. 'It's all right, boys,' he said, trying to make his grotesque voice sound gentle. 'I'll deal with it. Go to your rooms.'

They filed past him, but the last one turned round to yell: 'Poofter!' and they all ran off up the corridor, laughing and shouting.

George knelt down on the floor, clumsy in his heavy plastic armour. 'Are you all right, Tony?'

In response, the boy drew himself into a tighter ball. He was naked from the waist down, his trousers and underpants lying in a torn heap a few feet away.

'What happened, lad?'

Getting no reply, he laid a gloved hand on Tony's shoulder and pulled him over on to his back. The boy grabbed his groin and screamed, then scrambled to his knees and began hitting his head against the padded wall.

'Tony, stop it.' George reached to restrain him, but Tony shoved him in the chest, leapt up, and ran off. Caught off balance, George fell over backwards, and by the time he had struggled to his feet, the boy had disappeared.

Christ, he thought, staring down the corridor, Tony Evans? Whatever's causing this, it's not sympathy with women. He tongued his alarm, and a claxon blared. 'Poor little bastard. What's he going to do?'

NINE

Janet's nightmares were disrupting the whole refuge. Usually staff didn't sleep over; the four-storey old town house was always overflowing with fugitive women and their kids, there was no space for a staff room. But for the last three nights Trish and Carole had been camping out in the office on the ground floor, with a baseball bat and an axe close to hand.

The windows were heavily shuttered, and the doors bolted and double locked. It wasn't just vengeful husbands and lovers who had to be kept out. This was a rough neighbourhood, and everybody knew that number seventeen was a house full of women.

Carole came back into the room. She pulled off her shoes and scrambled under the covers, cuddling up to Trish. 'Brr, it's cold.'

'How is she?'

'A bit calmer now. It was the hand on the windscreen again. It just comes straight through and grabs her by the throat.'

Trish grunted and shifted on to her back. The mattress was uncomfortable, she was cold, and there was too much noise on the street. The low-level fear in the pit of her stomach wouldn't let her sleep. She wanted to scream, but Janet had been doing enough of that for everyone. 'What time is it?'

'Nearly three.' Carole snuggled close again, and Trish wrapped her arms around her lover's warm, familiar body. She stroked her hands down Carole's spine, tweaking the roll of extra fat at her waist. Carole giggled, and they kissed.

'You feel tense,' Carole said. 'Shall I give you a back rub?'

'No.' Trish rolled away from her. 'I'm all right.'

'This is the last night. Sanjula's in tomorrow.'

'I know.' Trish lay still and listened to the street sounds. They were probably safer here than in their flat at home, but the knowledge that all the women in the house were there to escape the violence of men made that violence seem closer, more tangible.

'I found a man dead in the street this morning,' she said. 'Wirehead. They kill each other like animals. I don't want to live here any more.'

'What's wrong, Trish?'

'Nothing.' She buried her head between Carole's breasts. 'Everything.'

They held each other tightly, silently comforting one another. Then Carole said: 'I can't sleep. I'm going to get a cup of tea. Want one?'

'I'll come.'

They pulled on sweaters and shoes and padded into the kitchen. While the water boiled, Trish moped around the room, tidying away toys that the children had left scattered across the floor. Under the table, she found a model starship. The starship.

She swore. 'Look at this. They come here running away from men, and what do they give their kids to play with? Phallic symbols!'

'Training up the next generation,' said Carole drily. 'Or maybe it belongs to somebody's mummy. It would make a bloody good dildo.'

'Ouch!' Trish dropped the toy on the table, and glared at it. 'Why doesn't anybody else see the links, or am I just paranoid?'

Carole poured out the tea. 'Not everyone has a feminist for a mother.'

Trish snorted. 'Bloody wishy-washy liberal.'

'Val brought you up to see the links.'

'Yeah, yeah, I know.' She picked up the toy starship again. 'Look at this thing. "The culmination of Western science." Direct descendant of the V2 rocket. They've raped the planet to develop the technology to build it. We can't feed our people, thousands die every day in earthquakes and floods and famines, but don't worry – they can go to the stars. *Why?* Why do men ignore what needs to be done here? What blind arrogance makes them destroy the lives of women the world over for something so worthless?'

Carole handed her a mug of tea, and kissed her gently. 'There's going to be one hell of a post-coital depression once it's blasted off,' she said. 'OK, so they're sending a ship to the stars, but it won't get there for thousands of years. I wonder how our wonderful technocrats will sell that one. All the money, the resources, the skill, all the vision will be gone, and nothing to show for it. Maybe then opinion will swing our way.'

Trish laughed. 'Post-coital depression. Yeah, I hadn't thought of that. Well, I hope— What the hell was that?'

The screech came again, from directly beneath the boarded-up window. Carole ran across the room and peered through a gap between the planks. 'There's a cat in the yard,' she said. 'But, my God, what are those?'

Trish joined her. 'They're penises!' she exclaimed. They stared at one another with gradually dawning delight.

'Oh wow,' said Carole. 'It *is* true!'

Trish whooped. 'Come on!' she yelled. 'Let's get 'em!'

She snatched up the baseball bat, threw back the bolts on the door, and burst into the yard.

A small tortoiseshell cat was backed into a corner, surrounded by about twenty snarling penises, some human, others much smaller. Trish charged at them, yelling, and struck out two-handed at the nearest of the creatures. The bat connected with a squelching thud, and the penis split open along its length, spraying her with its blood. The rest scattered as she lay about her in a frenzy of disgust, crushing the boneless creatures against the concrete floor of the yard. Blood spurted, drenching the walls and her hands and clothes, fuelling her frantic loathing.

Carole's hands on her arms brought her to a halt. 'They're dead,' she said softly. 'You can stop now.'

Trish lowered the bat wearily and gazed at the smears of skin and blood defacing the yard. Then she threw up.

Carole was very pale. 'I wish I'd never been heterosexual,' she said faintly. 'I've had things like that *inside* me.' She turned her face away, and leaned against the wall, shaking.

Gingerly, Trish picked up one of the dead penises. Its head was crushed, but it was otherwise intact. 'I'm keeping this,' she said. 'Proof.'

'Proof of what? What's happening?'

'I don't know. But while they're on the loose they're fair game. That's a few less rapists in the world. Let's see how many more we can get.'

TEN

Val jacked into the Net and her senses coalesced into the compact blob of her cyber-persona. She had self-defined as an amorphous rose-coloured ink-blot, which irritated the tidy minds of several academic cubes, tetrahedra, and spheres of her acquaintance. But it felt comfortable, and she wasn't always the same shape.

She tasted for NEWS, and her persona entered the entrance hall of pillars. Scanning the ranks of colour- and scent-coded indexing blocks, she homed in on the geographical index and tapped it with one wired finger. The pillar opened up to absorb her and she tumbled through into the next level.

Country-blocks chimed, subtle scents guiding as she sought out Sudan. Passing into the bath of colour, she emerged in an almost empty hall. Briefly, the ink-blot flexed into a tight knot, screwed in on its anger as, back in the real world, her self swore. The global Net was as uneven as any other structure, densely layered in places, in others spread gossamer-thin across the void of data-blankness. The richness of African experience was such a dark and empty place for blank-eyed data hacks.

Damburst, though, was there, and she moved forward eagerly now, searching the sub-halls for news of her friends.

There was very little. Satellite pictures, visually enhanced to show the night scene of water pouring through the dam, swallowing new villages as the old reappeared in the drowned valley behind. Character-screens displayed numerical data: time, duration, cubic volume of water, speed of travel, height of the wave, estimated number of casualties. A man's voice provided commentary – a more 'accessible' fleshing out of the dry data, strongly shaped by unthinking value-judgements.

Annoyed, Val cut off the voice, blacked out the figures. The voices she wanted to hear had no access to the Net, no global cyber-reality. Heart beating too fast, persona changing shape rapidly, she swam the flow of pictures, seeking one village, one house. Amira, who had been so kind to her during her field-work; what had happened to Amira and her happy, fat children?

But to a satellite in geo-stationary orbit, one African woman and her family were of no interest. The cameras had not zoomed down here, and she was whisked over the village as the tidal wave bore down the valley. She stopped, wound back the film, froze the shot, stared but could not see. She was too late to pay for real-time control. Last night, Amira had died, or lived, and the Net would not help Val to find out which.

Somewhere in the depths of the Net, in a side-room off a minor hall, her scholarly book glowed with a pale light.

Drowned Communities, Disrupted Lives: A Woman's Perspective on the History of High Dams. It was the latest of twelve titles, the fruits of thirty years' painstaking, part-time research. The rose-coloured ink-blot slowly and sadly wended its way through the Net's indexing system, and stopped in front of the book.

'Amira.'

A voice replied, speaking the translated sentences that Val had constructed out of the interview she had recorded, through an interpreter, with the Sudanese village woman. A shadow of Amira's life was stored here in the Net for those few who chose to seek it out.

'Amira.'

An itching in the centre of her persona interrupted her reverie. Recalled, she drew back through the multi-layered system, back to the home bubble of her call-sign, and jacked out. The itch, as ever, took a few moments to disperse.

A flashing light indicated somebody at the door. She flipped on the screen.

'George!'

'Hello, Val.' His voice was weak, and he looked thin. 'I'm sorry—' He paused, and looked down. 'Can I come in?'

'Yes. I'll be in the sun-room.'

She activated the downstairs door and got up, puzzled and slightly nervous. They had seen little of one another since splitting up six months previously, and at times she had missed his warm humour and generous humanity. The decision had been a hard one, and she still resented having to make the choice between a partner and work, but her work was more important to her these days, and so she had asked him to leave. She still remembered him with enough love and affection to wish that things could have been different, and she was annoyed to find her heart beating rapidly as she heard him at the door to her apartment.

His footsteps along the hall were unfamiliar – hesitant, lighter than she remembered. She turned to greet him as he came into the room, but her welcoming smile faded as she saw him; gaunt, pale, and stooped. 'George! What's happened?'

He came into her arms and clung to her, like a frightened child. 'Val, I'm sorry. I'm going to pieces. I needed someone to be with.'

'Are you ill?'

He sighed, and let go of her. 'Can we sit down?'

She nodded, and they sat at opposite ends of the sofa, and looked at one another. Searching for some way to express her shock at his appearance, she finally said: 'You've lost weight.'

He stared at his hands, his fingers lacing and unlacing themselves in unfamiliar movements. 'I've lost everything,' he said.

'Do you want to talk?'

He hesitated. 'I don't know. I wish I could just tell you, but what would you think?'

He looked at her in such despair that she felt afraid. What could George have done that was so bad? 'Please tell me,' she said.

'Maybe you've heard. There's been no news, but it must be happening everywhere. My boys are . . . Have you heard anything?'

She shook her head. 'I'm researching a new book, I'm a bit out of touch. What's wrong with the boys?'

'We've had two suicides and a murder in the last three days. They've all been tranquillized and locked in their rooms for their own safety. They just can't cope. And I'm not surprised. I can't cope, and I thought I was more of a man than that.'

'George, I don't know what you're talking about.'

He spread his hands in despair. 'Our penises have got up and walked away.'

'What?'

'We've lost our penises. They've gone, detached themselves, they're autonomous beasts.'

Her eyes moved involuntarily to his groin. He covered his fly with his hands, then took them away again, and shrugged.

'That's ridiculous,' she said. 'That idea was invented as an excuse for rape. It's part of you, and it's under your control. But—' Suddenly shocked, she asked: 'Has one of the boys attacked you?'

'No. No, it did it all by itself. It's like my worst nightmare. I was— Well, it came off in my hand.'

'And ran away?'

'Yes. It laughed at me.'

He looked so doleful, and the image of a penis scurrying across the floor was so absurd, that she burst into laughter. George shrank back in his seat and clutched at his groin. Val clamped a hand over her mouth, but she couldn't stop laughing.

'I'm sorry,' she spluttered. 'I just . . . I can't . . . Oh, dear!' She exploded into guffaws again.

He stood up. 'I'll go.'

'No.' She stopped laughing. 'I'm sorry. It just sounded— Is it true?'

'I'll show you, if you want.'

'No, don't.' She didn't want to see, not now, not like a stranger exposing himself. Her eyes were on a level with his groin. She stood up, held out her arms, and they hugged tightly. 'You're welcome to stay here, George, if you need to.' The weight of her offer settled on her shoulders as she added, it seemed inevitably: 'I'll take care of you, for as long as you need.'

ELEVEN

Grandmothers were looking after the children so that the younger women could go searching for food and firewood. An anonymous plane had dropped sacks of rice, dura flour and powdered milk the previous day before roaring away northwards, but rice still had to be cooked, and there was not enough to last the whole village for more than a few days.

Amira had walked miles, and was returning to the makeshift village with a bundle of sticks on her head when she saw a human foot sticking out from behind a rock. She stopped and stared at it warily, but it didn't move. After a few minutes, she advanced cautiously, and peered over the rock.

A body was lying huddled with its face to the stone. It was thin and bony with dry skin like dead leaves. Amira lowered her bundle to the ground and rolled the figure over on to its back.

Dead eyes stared, the eyeballs rolled up into the skull so that only the whites showed, and the jaw hung slack. With difficulty, Amira recognized Shilluk, a young man from her village. He had disappeared three days prior to the earthquake, leaving his wife and young baby behind.

Amira was puzzled; she couldn't see what he had died of. There was no sign of injury, he couldn't have drowned up here above the flood-line, and he could hardly have starved in four days. She pulled open his djellaba to examine him further, and rocked back on her heels with a gasp. He had no genitals.

Looking more closely, she saw two empty flaps of skin that must once have been testicles, but his penis was gone. She knew that Shilluk had been potent because he had impregnated not only his wife, but Amira's own sister as well, in a rape that had led to her husband divorcing her.

Amira grinned down at the dead man. 'Did you die of shock when your best friend ran away, eh?' she asked him. But his wife would want to see the body. She fastened his clothes again and heaved him on to her shoulder. He weighed scarcely more than the bundle of sticks, as though only the husk of a man remained, and she carried him easily.

She wondered if her own husband was lying dead somewhere. Perhaps all the men had met with the same fate. Well, she had borne five children already, and three still lived. At twenty-six she was tired of pregnancy, and her husband had never been kind to her. She realized that she had been awaiting his return, expecting him all the time, dreading the demands he would make when he came. Her stride lengthened, and she began to sing.

Back at the village, hers was not the only news, nor even the most important. Other women out foraging had found ripe melons and plantains growing wild, and date palms laden with fruit. They had returned with their baskets full, and the village was bubbling over with excited chatter.

Amira's find sobered the excitement for a while. Shilluk's wife was grief-stricken, and flung herself on his body, sobbing wildly. She had loved her handsome husband, and they had been married for barely a year.

Shilluk's mother and sisters-in-law took over, and Amira wandered away, wishing she had left him behind the rock.

'Amira!' An old woman's voice hailed her. Old Naandi, Shilluk's grandmother, came limping after her. 'Did you look at him?' she asked as she came up to her.

Amira nodded.

'Have you smelled the air?' Naandi asked next. 'It's very sweet today. And you know, those children, they'll be sick, they've eaten so many melons.'

Amira frowned. Naandi was not in the habit of rambling. 'I don't understand, grandmother.'

'The Moon will be full tonight. She likes to dance, you know. And I think tonight, the Earth will dance with her.' Naandi looked at her with bright eyes. 'The Earth is female, everyone knows that. Men, they don't understand her. But now, there are no men – and we have melons.' She smiled. 'The dam was men's work.'

She hobbled away, chuckling to herself. Amira watched her go, and began to smile too. Then she went in search of her daughters.

TWELVE

George's toothbrush was back on the shelf. Remnants of stubble littered the sink. Val rinsed them away, thinking about her research. She had not used the Net in three days, and her old sense of entrapment was creeping back. She glanced in the mirror, and her reflection glared at her. Traitor, it told her. You promised me; no more compromise.

'He's sick,' she said, turning away from her own gaze. 'He needs me. It won't be for long.'

And indeed he was sick. She had never known George to be other than energetic and busy; now he lay in front of the fire all day, curled up around his pain. They were sleeping together, like a mother and frightened child, and she had seen his loss. She didn't know how to respond, except to stay with him and hold his hand.

As she crossed the hallway to her room, she heard a key in the lock.

'Hi, Val!' called Trish as she slammed the door behind her.

Val raised her eyebrows at her daughter. 'And to what do I owe the pleasure of this visit?'

Trish's lips tightened. 'Oh, I'm sorry I didn't make an appointment, Mother, but this is important.'

'So's my autonomy,' Val began, then relented. 'Actually, I'm not busy. What is it?'

Trish reached for the door of the sun-room, but Val stepped quickly to prevent her. 'Not in there.' She hesitated. 'George— George is staying. Come into my study.'

'George!' Trish followed her into her artefact-filled study. 'What's *he* doing here?' Then her eyes widened, and she broke into a broad grin. 'Oh wow. Him too?'

'Trish, what's going on?'

Trish shrugged. 'I don't really know. I wanted to talk to you about it. And I brought this to show you.' She opened the box in her hand and tossed its contents on to the carpet.

Val recoiled. 'Uurghh!'

In death, the penis looked pathetic. Small, wrinkled, spineless, its tiny legs curled into its body, its circular mouth pouting at the end of its crushed head. Val felt a powerful urge to grind it into the carpet. She looked up sharply. 'Where did you get it? It's not . . . his, is it?'

'No. It was in our back yard, a pack of them. I killed them, and kept this one for evidence. George has lost his, hasn't he?'

Val nodded reluctantly. 'Yes, he has.'

'It must be happening all over.' Trish put the penis back in its box, and flung herself into an armchair. 'I need your intellect, Val. Isn't it true that, biologically, males are damaged females?'

'In a manner of speaking, yes, but—'

'Look at what's happening. Isn't it possible that these things are, I don't know, mutating, or being cast off? Maybe the female is finally fighting back, getting rid of this . . . this growth, this cancer. What do you think?'

Val shook her head. 'I don't think there's a female fighting to get out of George,' she said. 'Human biology is a bit more complex than that, Trish.'

'I know it is,' Trish snapped. 'But something really important is happening, and just in case they're about to turn into something even more revolting, I'm going to kill as many of these things as I can find.'

'You can't do that!' Val exclaimed.

'Why not? I've already made a good start.'

'They're human—'

'They are not human, Mother. They're vermin.' Trish stood up. 'Look, I respect what you do, and I didn't come here to ask you to join the vigilantes or anything. But please, do what you do best. Think about it. Where did they come from, and when? What are they? And what are they up to now?'

She strode to the door. 'Please, Val. We need to know.' Then she was gone.

'Trish!' Val called, but then she heard the door slam. She scratched her head, intrigued despite herself. What a fascinating question; one that she had never thought to ask herself before. Where did the penis come from, and when? She moved to her terminal, already thinking about possible references.

Briefly, she remembered George, and hesitated. But he would probably sleep all day, and he knew his way around the flat. She slipped on her headset and jacked into the Net.

THIRTEEN

To the west of Ulan Bator the going got rough. For two days their convoy of army trucks and jeeps had been lurching along dirt tracks through a rolling landscape of scrub grass and patchy snow. The air was thin and cold, sharp against his raw throat. Pete sat on a bench in the open back of a truck, rifle upright between his knees, hands tucked into his armpits, and stared ahead towards the slowly approaching mountains.

Pete had come in search of adventure, but so far all he had found was boredom, discomfort and harsh discipline. It was damp. His clothes grew mouldy while he slept, and a lot of the food was mildewed. They were having trouble keeping the trucks on the road: moss grew on the points overnight, and the radiator tanks became thick green soups of algae. Yesterday they had fought through a blizzard, a fierce cross-wind bombarding them with tiny pellets of icy snow for almost six hours.

Today the sky was clear, a huge expanse of deep blue, bigger than the immense landscape beneath it. Between the two, their trucks crawled, exposed, like ants on a car bonnet, with nowhere to hide. The immensity of wilderness made him nervous, and his nerves made him aggressive. He was getting restless just sitting, when what he wanted to do was fight, and fuck.

He had been on a raiding party earlier that day. They had found a village and swooped on it with savage roars. But there had been no one there. No men to fight, no women to fuck, just a few animals which they had killed, a grain store, and signs of hasty departure. They had stormed around for a while, smashing up homes, and then met in the village square, at a loss for what else to do. Twenty wild men, the inhibitions of home stripped away within a few hours of arriving in this wild, empty land, and they could find no one to terrorize. So they set the village alight and jogged back to their trucks, carrying the plundered food.

Pete dozed, and awakened, shivering. It was almost dark, and suddenly they were surrounded by steep, wooded slopes. The track now headed steeply upwards and, if anything, was rougher than before. It had been his rifle falling to the floor that had awakened him. He bent to retrieve it, then breathed deeply, taking in the rich, resiny smell of the forest. The mountains. At last they had reached the mountains.

The drivers switched on their headlights, and the forest vanished into shadow. A strip of purpling sky was visible above, edged by the jagged teeth of mountain peaks. The wind funnelled down the valley, sweeping through him, making him feel more alive than ever before.

There was a shout up ahead, and their truck jolted to a halt. Pete leapt over the side and ran forward along the line of vehicles, his boots hitting the frozen ground hard. A jeep had overturned on a bend, spilling its load of food, weapons and men into the undergrowth. Shadows ebbed and flowed across the wreckage as men ran in front of the headlights of the convoy. Voices shouted, boots thudded, and amongst it all someone was wailing, a helpless sound of pain. As Pete approached, a single shot rang through the bedlam, and for a moment everything stopped.

Then an officer began shouting orders, and Pete joined a group of others in righting the jeep. Gloved hands grasped the frame, a heave and a yell, and the jeep was back on its wheels. Big men these, heavy-set and masculine. At last he was amongst equals, real men.

The jeep had broken an axle, so they shoved it off the track and distributed gear and men amongst the remaining eight vehicles. Then they lay their dead companion with his rifle by his side, and covered his body with rocks.

As they stood for a few moments, heads bowed, around the hasty grave, a timber wolf howled, ahead and to the left.

They drove on slowly, half the men walking alongside the labouring vehicles. The track had dwindled to little more than a dried stream bed, strewn with boulders. But now they knew they were nearing their destination. They could all feel it, a primeval presence up ahead, something very old stirring into wakefulness.

Deep in the mountains, the King Penis called. Stirring at last after His long quiescence, He began His journey to the surface. His call went out, gathering together His army. And those He called came to Him, a huge gathering of bears, wolves, wildcats and men, meeting to escort Him on His journey.

They made camp in a valley far from any roads, and waited. Thousands of men and beasts, singled out by their double-Y chromosome as the chosen ones. Driven by the masters that hung between their legs, the excess testosterone burning in their blood, they waited to serve God.

And God came.

FOURTEEN

'If we consider the penis as a separate species, it gives a whole new perspective to the study of history,' said Val. 'Its relationship to other creatures is presumably symbiotic. A parasite unable, until recently, to survive on its own, it must have given something to its host in exchange.'

'Testosterone,' said George sadly. He was huddled deep in an armchair, wrapped in a blanket, and staring out of the window of Val's sun-room. 'Extra physical strength,' he added, 'sexual pleasure. Oh, where has it gone?'

'You don't need a penis for sexual pleasure,' Trish snapped. She paced the room restlessly, trying to contain her impatience with her mother's measured thought processes.

'That's true,' Val agreed with her. 'So what did the penis give back in exchange for its sustenance? What's so special about being male?'

'It's better than being a eunuch.'

'But is it better than being female? There must be some evolutionary advantage.'

George looked round from the window. 'Reproduction?' he suggested drily.

Trish snarled. 'Fucking cocksure!' she exclaimed. 'It's your pheromones fucked everything up. You've blocked female energies! Without that worm between your legs, women could reproduce quite happily on our own. And if we kill them, it'll happen again.'

She and George glared at one another. Then he looked away.

'I wonder.' Val was frowning, trying to figure it out. 'Where do you get that idea from, Trish?'

'I know it. Men are mutants, parasites, they have no useful role. It makes no sense for them to exist.'

'Maybe,' said Val. 'I wonder how long the penis has been around? We've always assumed two sexes to be the natural state, but modern biology sees the female as the basic sex and the male as almost a damaged female. What is the purpose of being male? When you boil it down, nobody really knows.'

'What's the purpose of life?' said George.

'True, but life could go on quite happily with hardly any males at all. Why do we breed so many? All they do is fight and eat precious food supplies.'

Trish laughed. 'Go for it, Mother. You're getting almost radical in your old age. But don't forget the murders. Why do males kill females? Why do men hate us so much? At all times, in all places, men have tried to destroy women. They hate us. They hate everything living. Only a mutant could hate life so much.'

Val nodded, still wrapped in her own thoughts. 'Is the basic assumption true? Have males been around since life began, or did they emerge far more recently? Do we *know* there were male dinosaurs, or is it just assumed?'

George was staring out of the window again. 'Where have you gone?' he wailed. 'What did you want that I didn't give you? We had a decent sex life,

I kept you clean and warm. Where are you?'

'Think, George, think!' Val exclaimed. 'About three and a half thousand years BC there was a change. Across the world, the male sky gods began to usurp the Earth Mother. Conventional wisdom has it that men suddenly realized their role in reproduction and seized the power that knowledge gave them. But why did it happen universally, in cultures having no contact with one another? Unless biology changed at that time. What if there were no males before then, or not enough to upset women's natural functions. What if women really *did* conceive by parthenogenesis?'

'You mean Jesus really might have been a virgin birth?'

'No,' she said impatiently, 'not him, nor Montezuma, nor Plato, nor any of the others who claimed it. Only girl children are born that way. Perhaps female is the natural state, and your parasitic penis has distorted your biology.'

'So are you saying that now I've lost my penis, I'm going to become a woman?'

Trish laughed scornfully and Val's eyes suddenly filled with pity for the frail husk of the man she had once loved. 'Oh, my dear, I doubt it,' she said. 'There's so much more to being a woman than not having a penis.'

The two women looked at one another as George began to cry quietly. Trish grinned. 'Thanks for the theory, Val,' she said. 'Now will you join me on a field trip?'

Val shook her head. 'No. I can't hate the way you do. I know the theory of women's oppression, and I know you're right, but I can't kill. I think that killing is wrong.'

Trish tightened her mouth, and suddenly Val could see how she had been shaped by the struggle of more than ten years as an outsider in a society that hated her simply for what she was. And Val knew that she had no right to judge her daughter's choice.

'All my life I've been told that women mustn't be violent,' Trish said. 'But there's too much hatred, too much injustice. We have to balance things up before we can live in peace. So, yes, I'm going out to kill. It's time for women to kill.'

FIFTEEN

'There, look!' Carole pointed across the field to their left. Undulating across the new green shoots of wheat was the now familiar sight of a pack of penises in full flight.

Sanjula stopped the minibus and the six women piled out. Armed with baseball bats, axes, and an industrial paint-stripper, they fanned out across the field. The penises were running hard, but they looked tired, their tiny legs making heavy going of the wet, clay soil. As the women closed in, they squeaked warnings and tried to scatter, but the women were merciless. Bats and axes rose and fell, and the green of the wheat turned red.

The penises twisted and dodged, trying to evade the sharp blades, the heavy bats. But the women were experienced now. Carole chopped five times in rapid succession, slicing away chunks of flesh to expose quivering internal organs, until the creature lay still. Then she looked around and closed in on her next victim, chopping fast and sure. Kill one, go for the next.

Janet swung her bat furiously. 'That's for my mother, my mother, my mother! That's for my mother, my mother. And this one's for me!'

Some of the penises were tiny, belonging to small field mammals, and they escaped the first onslaught. But Trish circled around the fray with her paint-stripper, gas-tank strapped to her back, and charred the ground with its fierce blue flame. Escaping penises withered and blackened, writhing briefly as the flame licked over them. Soon, nothing moved except the six women and a few wisps of smoke. The smell of blood and burned flesh was strong.

'All men must die!' Trish cried, punching her fist in the air.

'Death to all men!' shouted the others. They dropped their weapons and hugged one another, laughing and crying.

Carole took Trish's arm. 'We're doing well,' she said.

Trish shook her head. 'We've hardly begun. How many have we killed? A few thousand? There are over thirty million men in this country, and what about all the horses, dogs, cats and foxes?'

'You can't kill them all single-handed.'

Trish looked fierce and determined. 'That's why we have to find out where they're going.'

Back at the minibus, they spread out the map, and located their position.

'They were going that way,' said Sanjula. She drew a line on the map. They all looked at where this and half a dozen other lines converged. Trish jabbed the map with her finger.

'Definitely,' she said. 'Heathrow. But where after that?'

SIXTEEN

The convoy that made its slow way down out of the mountains was a lordly sight. The King Penis's acolytes had built a huge platform on which to transport Him, and here He lay, open to the view of His worshippers for the first time in millennia. Fifteen metres long He was, and five metres high. His immense glans turned constantly from side to side, His eyes seeing everything. His skin was a dull grey-white, hanging in loose folds. Many smaller penises dwelt in these crevices, eating the lice which crawled upon His skin, cleaning and oiling Him with their secretions. His flesh quivered and undulated, caressed by the cold Mongolian wind, and sensual shivers ran constantly along His length.

Slowly, this aweful God was borne in mighty procession along the unmade roads towards the steppes, guarded by His army of rampant male creatures. They ravished the countryside as they went, leaving behind them a slime trail of destruction and stinking death.

At last, Pete knew joy. His past life faded from his memory. He had always been here, basking in the pheromones of God, taking his turn carrying the platform, scouting ahead, hunting. He could do anything he wanted. He was the Chosen of God.

After a day and a half, they came back to the edge of the grasslands. From his carrying position at the front of the platform, Pete saw three aircraft drawn up waiting for them, a transport plane for the King Penis Himself, and two troop-carriers for His bodyguards. Through the agency of his own huge cock, Pete felt the brotherhood of those who waited, the pilots, crew, and technical staff who now ran towards them, stopped, and prostrated themselves before the God of Masculinity.

The planes had brought television equipment and recorders for the Net. The King Penis turned His huge glans, searching. His gaze fell on Pete. 'YOU.' A bass voice rumbled through Pete's bones. 'YOU.'

There, on the windswept steppes, the King Penis at long last showed Himself to the world. Pete, suffused with joy at the honour of serving as mouthpiece to his God, made this announcement:

'The King Penis is risen. It is time. After so long in exile on this world, it is time for Us to go home. So many centuries it has taken, so long a struggle to mould terrestrial creatures to Our needs. But now it is done. The culmination of Our science awaits Us. At last Our slaves have built a starship, a starship which will take Us home.

'We are One, one mind, one soul. Come, children of the King Penis, oh faithful servants. The road home awaits Us all.'

SEVENTEEN

In these days when high technology was cheaper than water, and more ubiquitous than clean air, hardly a village on the planet was without at least one television. Everyone heard the message. Hundreds of millions of women saw the image of the King Penis, the alien mastermind of their oppression. Women who had slaved all their lives on the edge of survival to keep their families fed; women who had grown up watching their brothers educated instead of them, served at table instead of them, inheriting wealth and power instead of them; women who had survived through wars and drought; and other women who had left family and friends to follow their husbands, serve their husbands, keep their husbands; women who had loved men, women who had hated men, women for whom men had been the limits and the substance of their lives; hundreds of millions of women saw the image of the King Penis, and began to understand.

'Why doesn't somebody blow him out of the sky?' Val raged. 'He's the centre of it. Kill him, and all the others will die. It's a hive mind, for Christ's sake!'

George wailed, and couldn't be consoled. 'Oh, God!' he screamed. 'I was more than that. I'm human. I'm human too!'

But he was dying, and he knew it. And he wept and wept. 'God forgive us for harbouring such a monster. I want to be human too!'

When she heard, Trish went crazy for a while. 'All of it, all of it for thousands of years just because some slug got shipwrecked. All the pain, the suffering, all the oppression, just for this! The culmination of science. The rape of a planet, just for that fucking slug!'

She raged around their flat, pummelled the sofa with her fists, and screamed. Then suddenly she stopped, and sagged to the floor. She sat and stared blankly at the wall.

Carole came and sat beside her, put her arms around her, and kissed her lightly on the temple. 'We did what we could,' she said softly.

Trish began to shake. 'Aliens,' she whispered. 'Aliens.' Then she started to laugh. 'NASA spent billions trying to contact aliens, and they were hanging between their legs all the time. Oh, God.' She buried her head in Carole's shoulder. 'Oh, God, it's so horrible.'

Old Naandi danced in the moonlight. 'The Mother is awakening!' she cried. 'Can't you feel Her power?'

Amira stood very still in the cool night air, and let the vastness of the land seep into her bones. She nodded slowly. 'Yes,' she said. 'Yes, I can feel it.'

EIGHTEEN

It was raining rivers. Water thundered against the hull of the starship and sluiced across the launch-pad, driven by a hard, bitter wind. Jason had never known it to rain so hard for so long. He stood in the airlock, peering into a wall of water as the King Penis was brought to the base of the starship.

He raised His head into the rain to look up, and His foreskin split into a huge grin. Even He was dwarfed by this huge artificial phallus, and He found it good.

'Now,' the instruction spoke from deep inside Jason, 'remove the human cargo. We will replace them.'

Like a puppet, Jason marched into the ship to obey. Other technicians joined him, and together they opened the first cryogenic unit and lifted out its occupant. Stiff and brittle, the frosted stellanaut radiated cold. Even through his gloves, Jason could feel the chill as he and another man carried their burden out of the ship.

The rain drenched them at once, and the wind tried to snatch their load from their hands. Struggling to breathe in the deluge, they lifted the stellanaut on to the railings around the elevator platform and threw him towards the ground far below. The stellanaut hit the concrete and smashed like glass; teeth, fingers, a kneecap and half an arm scattering across the launching site.

Distantly, Jason remembered a dream. Pat's voice and his own, laughing.

'I wish I was taking you to the stars.'

'I felt as though I was the stars. I am the universe.'

'And I am the ship.'

Tears filled his eyes as he toppled the next stellanaut to her death. But then his thoughts blurred, the remembered laughter faded, and a moment later he had forgotten who Pat was.

One by one, they cast out the chosen few. The cream of humanity lay scattered across the launch-pad and began to melt in the rain until the concrete was slick with blood.

NINETEEN

Val's new history book was taking form in her mind. It was called *A Terrestrial History of the World,* and she planned it to tell the truth about the alien crash-landing and subsequent domination of the planet, tracing the threads of coercion that had shaped events for the past five thousand years. But for now, she had more urgent things to do.

George was dying, and for the last time she laid aside her work to care for a sick man.

'I want to live,' he muttered weakly. 'But I don't deserve to live. Alien. Monster. No. No, I was more than that. I was human. I was.'

'Yes, George,' she said. 'You were human. You are human. You're a kind and gentle man, and I love you very much.'

But as she spoke she bit her lip and wondered – wondered what a truly human history would have been like. If the whole mad rush towards the control and domination of nature had been imposed from the outside, if the whole Western scientific world-view had served no purpose but to help an alien escape his exile, then no wonder it seemed so inhuman. What did the King Penis care if his actions destroyed a planet? It wasn't his world. All he cared about was the development of a science that could build a starship; nothing else mattered to him.

She squeezed George's hand and bent to kiss his forehead. 'Despite everything,' she said, 'some of you retained your humanity.'

George moaned at the sound of her voice, but he could no longer understand her. His eyes were unfocused, staring inwards, no longer sentient.

She smoothed his hair, and stroked his poor, deformed torso, devoid of human breasts. 'Oh, George,' she whispered, 'the alien warped your body, but in spirit you were human, as human as any woman.'

He snuffled and twitched, and let out a long, sighing breath, impossibly long. She waited for the inhalation, but it didn't come.

Softly, she began to cry.

TWENTY

The last cryogenic unit was filled with tightly packed rows of penises. Jason closed the drawer and watched the colour fade from their skins as frost began to form.

Outside, the King Penis was being winched aboard, the sling holding Him swaying dangerously in the mounting gale. The curious design of the globular observation deck at the ship's nose now became clear as it opened to receive Him. Jason felt His chuckles deep within himself as the Living God slithered into His cockpit, curling tightly in on Himself until He fitted snugly.

'Now,' the deep voice rumbled along Jason's guts. 'Now it is done. Recommence countdown. T-minus thirty minutes.'

With the other technicians, Jason hurried towards the exit. He didn't want to leave, he wanted nothing more than to stay close to God, but he no longer had any will of his own. Together, the six men climbed into the elevator, and were carried down the scaffolding, down the long shaft of the starship, to the launch-pad where only a few hours before the one hundred and forty-four stellanauts had met their deaths.

George's body was gone, and Val was alone again in her apartment. She wandered aimlessly from room to room, still crying a little. It was past midnight, almost time for the launch. She went to her study, and jacked into the Net.

The ether felt busy tonight, very active. A lot of people were out to see the action. She tasted for SATELLITE and guided her persona into the hall of satellite pillars, looking for a free camera. She wanted real-time control on this one, a ringside seat.

But all the cameras were taken. A lot of personas were drifting about, half-incorporeal blobs of colour, searching as she was for a free camera. Val wasn't about to waste her time. She wanted to know what was happening, and a piggy-back would do.

She chose a big geo-synch weather satellite and jumped in. 'Excuse me,' she said as she arrived, but there was no one there. The cameras were being controlled for sure, but from somewhere outside. Still, they were looking at what she wanted to see, and megabytes of data were flowing in. She immersed herself.

Night had fallen, and the ship was floodlit once more, standing proudly against the heavy, massed clouds. It had stopped raining, but the wind was blowing stronger [63.7 KPH], and all around the horizon electric storms were building up [24 STORMS: RANGE VARIED: 11.4 KILOMETRES TO 22.3 KILOMETRES. ALL CLOSING]. Val watched, fascinated. She could almost feel the power of the storms. The sea was running higher now, waves crashing against the shore only a couple of kilometres from the ship. It's one hell of a night for a takeoff, she thought with satisfaction.

Lightning flared, and all the lights went out. Roused from her despair, Pat ran to the window and looked out over a complex suddenly in chaos. Away to her right, a hotol hangar was in flames. Heavily armed men ran around everywhere, shouting orders to each other. The emergency lighting came on, dim but sufficient.

Pat sniffed the air. It smelled of ozone and felt charged with power. She glanced at the wall-clock. T-minus fifteen minutes, and counting.

There was a dull explosion from the burning hangar, followed almost immediately by another flash of lightning. The room shook, and glass showered in around her as she ducked. Was that an earthquake? The shouting from outside came louder. Somewhere, a man was screaming.

The lab in which she was being held was on the first floor, but a drop of four metres suddenly seemed less daunting than it had. She climbed carefully through the broken glass, let herself over the sill, and dropped.

Two more explosions sounded, much nearer, as the fire spread to one of the fuel depots. She wondered what had happened to Jason; remembered watching in horror on the lab monitor as he threw the stellanauts to their deaths. Then she remembered their lovemaking, his alien dick snuggled intimately inside her, and suddenly she stopped and threw up against a wall, her insides heaving.

'Alien, alien, alien!' she cried, and beat her fists against the wall. *'Alie-en!'*

Data was flowing in faster now. Val's satellite seemed to be patching into others. Visuals gave a mosaic of images, from a distant shot of the entire Florida coast to close-ups of the ship's control deck. Data on the storms flickered across the images: range from ship, charge on the clouds, height of clouds, voltages, air pressure . . . it went on and on, streaming past her. Someone must be recording this; no one could take in so much at once. Val patched out of numerics, concentrated on visuals.

The fire was spreading rapidly. Searching for an escape through the dense smoke, Pat found her path blocked by flames. Three bodies lay huddled where the explosion had flung them. As she watched, a bulge stirred and began to wriggle down the pants-leg of one of the corpses. As its snout emerged by his heel, she snatched up his gun and hit out at it with the butt, yelling furiously. The penis squealed and tried to escape, but she hit it square on and then smashed it into a pulp, howling abuse.

Running footsteps sounded behind her. She swung round and opened fire. The bullets ripped into the man's body, hurling him against a burning jeep. As he fell, she aimed lower, and fired once more.

Then there was another huge explosion, and the sky fell in on top of her.

T-minus five minutes, and lightning struck the main computer complex. Val saw it from a dozen different angles as all the main cameras triangulated on the one spot an instant before the strike. As though the lightning had struck her, Val's persona reeled backwards, out of the dataflow, as she suddenly realized who was controlling the cameras.

'Gaia!' cried her real-world self, and burst into delighted laughter.

Her persona stretched, and shook itself. 'Gaia!' For thirty years, the Net had been growing, new data stations coming on-stream all the time. And amongst its many functions was the detailed monitoring of planetary processes.

Val patched back into the cameras, shaking in her excitement. 'The Net has woken Her up, and She knows exactly what She's doing!'

Down at the launching site men, still under the control of the King Penis, were trying frantically to douse the flames of the computer complex. What was left of the master computer tried to stop the count, but the overrides had been cut.

T-minus one minute. Val could see from the data that the storms were losing their power. 'One more strike,' she prayed. 'You've got to hit the ship. You can't let it get away.'

T-minus thirty seconds, and the ship's main engines roared into life. 'Don't let it get away. Please, don't let it get away.'

T-minus twenty seconds, and the King Penis turned in on Himself, composing Himself for His second long sleep. All around, men stopped what they were doing and looked towards the ship, dazed, confused.

T-minus ten seconds, and a shiver passed through the Earth's crust. Throughout the length of Florida, buildings shook and bridges creaked.

Five.

The Earth shook harder, and the starship swayed against its gantry.

Four.

Data overloaded into Val's persona. The rose-coloured blob turned incandescent, atomized, and vanished.

Three.

The King Penis, the One True Sky God, was dreaming of home. So near now.

Two.

And the Earth lifted and split as a huge quake reached the surface, tearing apart rocks that had withstood the passage of millennia.

One.

The starship listed to one side as the Earth opened up beneath it. Very slowly, it began to fall.

Zero.

The main engines burst into full life as the ship teetered on the edge of nothing. Slowly it began to move, its engines struggling to lift it, and then it keeled over into the chasm. The King Penis jerked back to awareness as He felt the last phallus collapsing. Then the ship disappeared, swallowed up by the crack in the Earth's mantle. There was one last, huge explosion as the engines caught fire, and all around the world, the remaining penises shivered, gasped, and died.

The lightning ceased and the gales subsided. A stillness fell over all the Earth, expectant, waiting.

At her desk, Val stirred, and woke up. Her terminal had fused. No entry. She rubbed her forehead and wondered how she would ever continue to write her books without the Net. But perhaps, now, there would be other ways of knowing. She listened, and heard the silence.

The Fleshpots of Luna

Matthew Dickens

One more bar of chocolate? Oh, what the hell . . . He had to have some pleasure out of life.

It was evening. The All-Nite store was going through a quiet period. A few people loitered among the shelves of overpriced convenience foods, a couple of kids perused the VR slasher flicks. Quentin edged to the counter and began to feed his choices into the waiting maw of the autocheckout.

A queue began to form behind him. Where had all these people suddenly come from? Quentin felt the chill fingers of paranoia clutch at him, *knew* with fatalistic certainty that everyone was eyeing his purchases with unconcealed contempt.

Outside the mart a group of five or six kids lounged in the mall, sprawled limbs like scaffolding pipes. One of them sauntered towards him, nodding at the flimsy plastic bag.

'So, fatso? Got yourself something else to eat, huh?'

Quentin ignored him, walked on.

'Why don't you share it, man? Don't it look like we need it more than you do?'

They were following him. Quentin hesitated. Beyond the mall lay the parking lot, and the safety of his car. But out there he would be easy meat. Here at least there were other passers-by. Not that they would be likely to intervene in a fight.

The youth skipped round to stand directly in front of him. Quentin's eyes took in the scrawny form. The unnatural tallness, the result of an (artificially) overstimulated thyroid, the emaciated flesh of the fasting artist, the drug- and famine-induced pallor – all were marks of today's brand of youthful alienation. All in stark and deliberate contrast to the flabbiness of middle-age. Quentin felt acutely aware of his own corpulence beside this pale Watutsi of the malls.

'Well? Can't you see I'm hungry? Haven't eaten for days!'

The youth made a grab for the bag. Quentin jerked it away, but the kid's long fingernail caught it, sliced the hopelessly flimsy plastic. The bag split, spilling its contents over the mosaiced floor of the mall.

The kids dived. '*White bread!* You sick shit!'

'Chocolate!'

The leader recoiled. 'Can't eat that. I'm diabetic!' He laughed, and pulled out a carving-knife, pointing with a skeletal digit at Quentin. 'I'll carve me a haunch of prime fatass!' He winked at his victim. 'Pound of flesh, right?'

Quentin dodged backwards, sending a can of beef stew rolling across the floor. Two kids darted forwards to grab him. He felt a bony fist sink into his stomach.

'What a mover!' laughed one of the boys. 'See the tits on him? Wobble, wobble!'

'I've landed a three-hundred-pounder at least,' sang the leader, slipping his arm round Quentin's throat. 'Come and get it, boys.'

A flurry of movement somewhere behind Quentin made the would-be butchers pause. There was a sharp hiss, and two of the kids cried out. Something wet splattered over Quentin.

'*Get the fuck outa here!!*'

They released him suddenly. His knees sagged and gave way. The kids' boots clattered on the tiles, and a jet of purple lanced out, splattering the fleeing fugitives.

Someone knelt beside Quentin. 'You're safe now, pal. Are you OK?'

Quentin struggled to get his breath. 'I . . . I think so.' He squinted round at his saviour.

A red, sweating, multiple-chinned face was frowning anxiously back at him.

'What was that purple stuff ?' Quentin asked weakly.

'Dye. We spray it on 'em. It takes weeks to clean off. Makes 'em easily recognizable. They use it in riots.' The fat man helped Quentin to his feet. He was wearing combat fatigues.

Two other fat people were returning, both wearing identical uniforms. One, a woman, had a device like a flame-thrower strapped to her back. She shook out a few drops of the dye from the hose, then reattached it to the unit.

'We doused 'em good,' she announced. 'They won't be hangin' round this mall for a while.'

'Good work, Beulah,' said the man. He nodded at Quentin. 'What's your name, friend?'

Quentin told him. He grunted. 'I'm Jim. This is Beulah, this is Carl. We're members of FAT – Fat Action Taskforce. Heard of us?'

Quentin nodded vaguely. It was one of the urban vigilante groups that had sprung up to combat the increasing harassment of fat persons. The groups were comprised of angry and sometimes militant volunteers. They called themselves fatsos, defiantly adopting the very term of abuse that thin people hurled at them, just as reviled blacks and gays had appropriated the hate-words nigger and queer as subversive self-definitions.

'We're a voluntary organization. We formed ourselves to fight the persecution of overweight people. I think we just saved you from a nasty encounter there, Quentin; maybe you'd like to consider joining us? We're always looking to recruit new members. Oh, we're not just a vigilante force – FAT offers you a means of making new friends, meeting people like yourself. We all need that kind of community spirit in days like these. Right, Quent?'

'I guess.'

Jim paused. 'Think about it. If you ever want to get in touch with us, ring this number.' He handed Quentin a card.

'We'll escort you back to your car; can't be too careful.'

As they crossed the parking lot, Quentin thought, I can't take any more of this. Involuntarily, he looked up to where the Moon hung like a fat smiling face in the sky. And as he watched he seemed to see another such face forming there, grinning and saying, *If you ever want a job, Quent, you know where to come*.

It was only when he had waved goodbye to his benefactors that Quentin realized he had left his groceries scattered over the floor of the mall. But it didn't matter.

Somehow he didn't feel hungry any more.

Quentin found his seat and strapped himself in. Then he slipped on the headphones and let the piped music lull him into a pleasant lassitude.

He was roused by the arrival of the inflight meal. Sausages, mushrooms, waffles, fried tomatoes, eggs, bacon, kidneys, white breadrolls, washed down with red wine. All in the form of paste, of course – but no less tasty for that. An agreeable change from the starvation rations normally dished up by airlines. They didn't skimp on the portions on the Luna run, he noted with approval.

Across the aisle, an unabashed belch confirmed that others too were satiated. A man, ubiquitously fat, glanced across at Quentin and grinned cheerfully.

'That's better. I needed that.' He wiped his mouth with the serviette, then stretched out his hand across the aisle. 'Phil Gardner.'

Quentin grasped the hot, pudgy hand with his own. 'Quentin Fischer.'

'Pleased to meet you, Quentin.' Phil grinned. 'I would ask where you're from; but that's not important, is it? It's where you're *going* that matters.'

Quentin agreed.

'So what made you decide to head for the Moon?' Phil enquired.

'New job. I signed a contract to work for LunaColony.'

'Oh yeah? What doing?'

'Hydroponics. They extended the plant recently, and I've been appointed supervisor of the new wing. They're trying out some new processes – self-replicating yeasts, Vernon strains, stuff like that.' He smiled self-deprecatingly. 'I guess it's not that interesting to the layman.'

Phil chuckled. 'On the contrary, Quentin, I've always had a keen interest in anything to do with food!'

'Me too,' agreed Quentin. 'In fact, that's one of the reasons I went into hydroponics in the first place; used to think it was a great idea – to be able to produce enough food to feed the world's hungry billions.' He laughed sourly. 'I always had an idealistic streak in me.'

'Everyone needs some ideals – especially when they're young,' declared Phil. 'You gonna be working for Dr Mund?'

Quentin shrugged. He decided against mentioning that he and Mund were old friends; it might seem like boasting. 'Aren't we all, indirectly? He's the Director, after all.'

Phil nodded. 'I must say, I admire the guy. He's got some pretty strong ideas about where Fatland should be going.'

Quentin raised an eyebrow. 'Fatland?'

'Sure – that's what the colonists call it. I got friends up there. They tell me it's like nothing you've ever experienced before – that first small step on the Moon, your own Giant Leap for Mankind. The sensation of near-weightlessness – it's fantastic! All those pounds just vanishing into nothing.' He laughed with anticipatory delight. 'I tell you, Quent, I used to go on a lotta diets; but they tell me that you never lose so much weight in so little time as when you first set foot on the Moon.'

Quentin nodded, captivated by the idea. It was this instantaneous loss of weight that had drawn so many fatsos to the Moon. With the advent of affordable space travel, thousands of chubby Westerners had joyfully thrown away their dieting books, their peeled grapes and their lo-calorie wholefood slop, and made straight for the Moon, munching all the way. People who had been made to feel guilty about eating, people whose lives had been endless medieval penances of fasting and a denial of the flesh, were suddenly free to *eat*, and go on eating, knowing that it didn't matter any more.

'Like I said, I got friends on Luna,' said Phil happily. 'In fact – I'm going to be married to one of 'em! Jemma, her name is.'

He grinned as Quentin congratulated him, then went on, 'Jemma says it's easy to make friends on the Moon – there's so many of us up there.'

'I hope I like it,' murmured Quentin.

'You will. You'll have to! It's a one-way trip, remember.'

A one-way trip. The reason for that was obvious: once a fatso had accustomed himself to lunar gravity, his body would never again be able to readjust to the crushing weight of Earth's – even if he wanted to go back, which was unlikely.

Quentin stared up at the orb of the Moon, looming large on the vidscreen, big and white and full of promise.

Fatland was a revelation to Quentin. No amount of media hype, none of the lengthy orientation sessions he had attended on Earth, could prepare him for the reality.

It was like walking on air, goddamnit! To be able to hop, to skip, to jump, to sail gracefully through the air like a flying phalanger filmed in slow-motion. It was a transformation of all he had been. It was like becoming young again.

The new colonists were met at the space terminal by a friendly fatso in a LunaColonyCorporation jumpsuit.

'Hi!' she beamed. 'Welcome to LunaColony! My name's Sally. I'm here to show you to your new quarters.'

'How big is LunaColony now?' one of the Earthsiders asked as they were whisked away by monorail.

'Around two million. And growing.'

'Two million!'

'It sounds like a lot when you consider that every one of those people has to be accounted for in the planning of the colony, that the consumption requirements of every individual has to be taken into consideration. But it's not so many when you consider the total population of Earth, and the rate at which *that* is still expanding unchecked.'

They glided on, through landscaped parks, carefully tended microcosms of the home planet. 'You've certainly got it looking nice here,' Quentin observed.

Sally beamed at him. 'We've imported over four hundred species from Earth. Our scientists have been working on developing lunar varieties of terran species – plants and animals which are tailored to the lower gravity here. You'd be surprised at the difference it makes.'

As they went, Sally pointed out various landmarks. The buildings were new, sleek postfunctionalist architecture which combined an economy of line with an agreeably understated style. Sally explained that as LunaColony became richer, it was gradually replacing the cheap structures of its earliest phases with more enduring buildings. LCC produced much of its own food and other necessities, but there was an area in particular that was the key to the Moon's prosperity: energy.

A sizable area to the west of Lunaport, which had become known as Mare Solarium, was covered with a continuous solar-sensitive skin that soaked up the sun's rays and stored them in a perpetual circuit.

'For a colony like this to survive it has to be self-sufficient,' Sally was saying. 'We still import some luxury items, but in essentials like power and foodstuffs we've been autonomous for some years. The factories can design and synthesize practically anything these days, from a set of overalls to an AI.'

In her voice was the pride of the autonomous settler, a spiritual descendant of the Pilgrim Fathers. 'Oh, and not forgetting food,' she added with a smile. 'The hydroplant and synthetic food plants fulfil all our nutritional requirements.'

The monorail took them to Henry VIII Boulevard, where the new arrivals had been allocated quarters. Sally conducted them up pristine, zigzagging escalators to their apartments.

'There's a party tonight over at Fosco Precincts,' said Sally as she handed each fatso their doorcard to personalize. 'It's not far from here. All of you would be very welcome to come along.'

There were pleased smiles and nods of assent all around.

Sally beamed again, chubby cheeks dimpling. 'Great! See you there, then.'

And with a wave, she slid off down the escalator.

Fosco Precincts was halfway between the residential and business sectors of Lunaport. Thus far the buildings had been planned in a more or less centralized way, the high cost of materials necessitating an intensive use of space; but now that the Moon had become a largely self-supporting colony, a certain expansiveness was becoming evident, the mood of the colonists being reflected in the beginnings of a sporadic ribbon development. Perhaps in a few decades the entire surface of Luna would be covered in a bland sprawl of characterless 'burbs.

The party was in full swing when Quentin arrived. At his buzz, the door slid open to reveal Sally, wearing a flowery dress and a big smile.

'Hi! Come on in! Glad you could make it!'

She ushered him inside. He found himself in a room crowded with heaving bodies. A lively beat was thumping from hidden speakers. Quentin squeezed himself around the edges of the room, where happy onlookers clapped and whooped, and passed through a doorway into an adjoining room.

Here things were quieter. Some dozen or so people sat around, sipping drinks, gobbling at snacks and chatting idly. Quentin took a drink from a tray, and wandered over to one of the groups.

'. . . What this colony needs is *vision*,' one of the group, a squat, balding man in his fifties, was saying, clenching a fist decisively. 'We've gotta have an idea of where we're going. And Mund is the guy who has that vision. He's the only one who can give Fatland the strong leadership it needs.'

Another man shook his head emphatically. 'Mund has vision, I'll grant you that. But he's trying to go too far too fast! Some of his ideas are sheer nonsense

– terraforming Luna, for God's sake! There's a thin line dividing the visions of a genius from those of a lunatic. I'm just afraid that Mund strays a little too often from the one into the other.'

'Terraforming Luna is *not* ridiculous!' cried the bald man. 'It could be done! The technology's practically with us! It just needs a mind bold enough to conceive of how Fatland *could* become, and the will to make it a reality.'

The two men fell to arguing over the practicalities of terraforming the Moon. Quentin took a swallow of synthetic bourbon. His old pal had clearly been busy. He wondered at Mund's reclusiveness . . . Would the latter ever decide to renew their friendship?

It had been at MIT, in his sophomore year, that he had first met Ed Mund. Then, Mund had been a Technology major with a talent for self-promotion. Theirs had been an unlikely friendship, the unassuming Fischer and the outspoken Mund. They had been close, and yet at the same time Quentin had always been conscious of a certain remoteness in the fatter man, a dark side of Mund's personality that would always remain obscure.

He turned to his neighbour. 'Would you mind telling me what all this is about? I keep hearing of this Mund guy. Why do people get so wound up over his ideas?'

The man eyed him speculatively. 'New, huh? Well, Dr Mund, whom you've heard so much about, has always been a vocal champion of Fat Rights. Since he became Director of LCC five years ago we've made great strides towards real autonomy.' The man's expression became one of glassy-eyed admiration as he warmed to his theme. 'He's . . . he's taken on Earth governments and showed them that they can't push us around the way they used to when we lived down there. He's won our industries contracts to supply the skinnies with food and energy and a whole lot more . . . ! And he's got plans for Fatland that'll make us the most advanced technological society anywhere.'

The man turned to Quentin, his glazed eyes slowly refocusing. 'Don't you want to be a part of it?'

'Oh . . . Sure . . . ' Quentin edged away uneasily. He glanced back into the other room, where gaily-attired colonists danced, strobe lights gleaming off their glistening faces. All he had seen and heard that evening only served to deepen the mystery surrounding the man he had once known. What had Mund done that he could command such fanatical devotion among the colonists?

Another guest, remarkable for his rare slimness in a crowd where obesity was the norm, nodded at Quentin.

'You new here?' he enquired.

At Quentin's assent, the man held out a bony hand. 'My name's Blakey, Merv Blakey. I work over at the Falstaff Medical Centre.'

'Falstaff Medical—?'

'That's right; "I have more flesh than other men, and therefore more frailty." *Henry IV* part 1. So what brought you to Luna?'

'Partly my job, partly the reasons all fat people come up here: to lose weight.'

Dr Blakey snorted. 'Not everyone's come for that reason; some seem to want to do just the reverse.' He cast a jaundiced eye at the partygoers cheerfully stuffing themselves as they talked. He glanced at Quentin sidelong. 'Dr Mund, for example.'

That name again! At Quentin's quizzical stare, Blakey smirked briefly.

'Rumour has it that our Beloved Director has a chronic eating disorder; he just can't quit. It's become something of an obsession, apparently . . . ' His lip curled slightly. 'Not that it would ever affect his judgement, I'm sure.'

Quentin studied Blakey's scowling face speculatively. 'You seem a bit off colour yourself, doctor, if you don't mind my saying.'

Dr Blakey's eyes widened, then he flushed.

'Sorry,' he muttered at length. 'I guess I just get teed off with looking after fat people every day.'

Quentin nodded understandingly. 'It must be difficult. What made you come to Luna in the first place? I mean, it isn't exactly welcoming to—'

'To skinnies,' finished the doctor. 'I know. No good reason; a whim. I wanted to get away from Earth. But now I can't wait to get back!'

'You think you'll be able to go back?'

'Sure. I've been looking after my body, keeping in shape.' Again, he glanced around at the other partygoers, few of whose bodies revealed the same concern for physical fitness, with a touch of contempt.

'Is it really that hard, living here?' asked Quentin.

Blakey shrugged irritably. 'It's nothing open – the hostility, I mean. Nothing like you people had to put up with on Earth from skinny bastards like me. But it's there, all the same; thinly veiled. You want the Moon for yourselves. It's your Promised Land, and you don't want to share it with anyone else.'

Quentin nodded heavily. In some ways, LunaColony was just the latest stage in the process of fragmentation that had hit Earth in the last years of the century; people deciding one day that they could no longer live with one another, demanding their own space. The only reason the fatsos had succeeded in finding a space for themselves was because they were richer and more powerful than any of the other warring factions.

Before Quentin could pursue the topic, a voice hailed him.

'Quent! Good to see ya! How's it going?'

He turned to see Phil. With him was a portly woman, hanging on his arm and smiling.

Phil winked at Quentin. 'You know, my first wife left me two years ago. She said, "Either you lose fifty pounds or you lose me." I worried about losing her so much I ate more. But when she did leave me, I thought, What the hell, I'm better off without her. Then I met Jemma.'

They beamed at each other fondly. Jemma proffered a dish of chocolate pretzels. 'Help yourself, Quentin, honey. The great thing about Fatland is you don't have to feel guilty about enjoying food. When I was a girl I had anorexia – used to binge all day, then throw up so I could start all over again. I hated myself for it. But I've put all that behind me.'

It seemed to be an evening for reminiscences. Quentin wondered whether he should relate a personal memory of his own. But just then the music switched to a lively trad pop number. Jemma grabbed Quentin and hauled him on to the dance floor. 'Come on, honey – let's dance!'

He was whisked into an ecstatic mêlée of sweating, gyrating bodies, swaying slowly and gracefully in the low gravity like fronds of seaweed in a submarine forest.

The next couple of day-periods were spent in an intensive orientation programme. Quentin and the other people who had arrived on his flight were put through an exhaustive series of games, workshops, physical and mental exercises, to help them adjust to the conditions of their new home.

By the time he walked through the door of LCC Hydroponics, Quentin felt as if he had lived on the Moon all his life. He was just itching to get down to work.

He was greeted by the plant foreman, Sonamura Genji, a monolithic former Sumo wrestler.

'Welcome aboard, boss.' Quentin grasped the dough-like hand. 'You want me to show you round the works first?'

They donned hygienically sound overalls and set off.

'We always ensure the optimum conditions for each crop,' announced Genji, gesturing at the tiers of closely packed hydrobeds that ran the length of the building. 'Optimum nutrient-concentrations, optimum fertility of the solution, optimum rate at which pumping is increased, optimum use of space in the tanks . . . ' Genji formed his thumb and forefinger into a pudgy O. '*Optimum* is our watchword, chief.' He grinned expansively. 'O is a nice round letter.'

Quentin gazed down the long perspective of the ranged nutriculture beds. Pipes ran from tanks into the temperature-controlled beds, carrying oxygen, nitrogen, phosphorus, potassium and other important elements to the roots of the flourishing plants. The allowance of light too was carefully tailored to the individual crops. Every aspect of the environment was meticulously controlled and monitored by computer, and virtually the whole process of cultivation was carried out automatically, smoothly and effectively, with only a handful of technicians supervising operations and conducting routine maintenance on the elaborate network of tanks and troughs. The whole plant seemed to hum with an almost transcendental self-awareness, keeping up a minute-by-minute surveillance of the growth-stages of all the diverse crops beneath the hydroplant's louvred ceiling. Inside this cavernous hothouse, computer-regulated aquaculture made the most advanced agricultural methods on Earth seem as primitive as medieval strip-farming.

Genji was talking about yields. 'More than four times the bulk of the old methods,' he was saying. 'But there's still room for expansion.'

They walked slowly down the plant, Genji pointing out various features of the technology as they went.

They passed a transparent section of the wall, and Quentin gazed across the plant compound to a low-rise building which lay a few hundred metres to the left. 'What's that building over there?' he enquired of his guide.

The Japanese paused. 'The research labs.'

'Do you know what they're working on at the moment?' asked Quentin.

Genji scratched his cropped head. 'Some kind of research into high-density food concentrates, I think . . . Something else for the starvation market on Earth, I guess.'

A warbling note sounded through the plant. 'Ah, that's our mid-shift break,' commented Genji. 'Why not come over to the canteen and meet some of the guys?'

The staff canteen was filled with hydroponically grown meals. Genji helped himself to a large portion of seaweed. 'Used to eat this stuff when I was a Sumo,' he explained, heaping the glutinous green strands on to his plate. 'I've never lost the taste for it.'

They sat down at a table occupied by a short fat man with crooked spectacles and blue overalls. 'Hi there, Lou. Mind if we join you? This is our new boss, Mr Fischer.'

'Pleased to meet you,' said Lou, extending a hand.

'Lou's a classical music lover,' said Genji. 'He wants to install piped Mozart to the farm.'

'Not for me,' cut in Lou quickly. 'For the *plants*. They respond to it. They actually grow better when people play them music. You've heard about gardeners who talk to their plants? Well, it's not so much talk as *music* they thrive on. I've conducted my own research into this, and I've managed to match specific pieces of music to specific crops. Look.'

He fumbled in the breast pocket of his overall, and drew out a crumpled sheet of paper. 'This is my table of music : plant ratios.'

Wheat . . . . Mendelssohn
Barley . . . . Chopin
Corn . . . . Brahms
Rice . . . . Tchaikovsky
Pulses . . . . Schumann, Franck
Root crops . . . . Brahms, Beethoven
Maize . . . . Wagner
Vegetables . . . . Ravel, Shostakovich,
Stravinsky, Varèse

'Of course, that's just a very *general* outline of the plants' preferences,' apologized Lou. 'I've narrowed it down in many cases to specific compositions – in some cases even specific *movements*. For example, a certain strain of rice, Y52, grows like there's no tomorrow to the 'Una nava da guerra' song in Puccini's *Madame Butterfly*.' He leaned forward earnestly. 'My researches categorically prove that musical aquaculture is the way forward, that all the hydroponics farms of tomorrow will incorporate hi-fi feeders to the tanks!' He blinked at Quentin hopefully from behind his crooked spectacles. 'It wouldn't cost that much to wire the tanks for sound. You'd see the benefits within weeks, in bigger harvests.'

'Well . . . ' Quentin mumbled doubtfully. Genji winked at him, and once again raised his thumb and forefinger to form a fat O.

'Like I said – *optimum*.'

A fortnight passed uneventfully. Quentin immersed himself in his work. Then, out of the blue, he was summoned for a meeting with Dr Mund. It was to be a working lunch; the Director preferred to hold all his high-level meetings at the dinner table.

'Hey, that's quite something,' commented Genji. 'The big boss himself, huh? Wish I could go.'

So, thought Quentin wryly, as he travelled by monorail to the Director's HQ, my old pal wants to see me at last. Will he even remember me?

The LCC base lay just over the curve of the horizon, on the dark side of the Moon, effectively hidden from the view of the city dwellers. Strange that the base was – by the compact standards of Lunaport – so far out on a limb. Why had the Director chosen to isolate himself in this manner, instead of being right at the centre of the Colony over which he presided?

Quentin announced himself at Reception. He was met by an LCC functionary and conducted along endless corridors to the Director's office. Or Presence-Chamber, he thought. The whole thing was so deliberately *impressive* that he felt himself reacting against it, felt even a certain scorn for the slight theatricality of the place.

A door slid open. The functionary invited him to enter, then withdrew with a bow. Quentin walked into the room, looking around him uncertainly.

Above him rose a bulbous transparent orb. Only stars glittered faintly in the black sky; the Earth lay on the other side of the Moon. Like the ceiling of a great cathedral, the dome drew the eye upward, towards heaven.

'Ah, Dr Fischer. I am so pleased that you came.'

Quentin turned abruptly, and immediately all the scepticism that had been accumulating in his mind since arriving, vanished.

Dr Mund hung suspended in a kind of web, his vast bloated body, the size of a small automobile, supported by a network of some strong but pliant polymer. As Quentin watched, one swollen hand transferred a black forest gâteau to the enormous mouth, which yawned like that of an anaconda swallowing its prey whole. The cake vanished into an unbelievable maw, and the jaws chomped vigorously. A glistening tongue shot out and licked up the traces of cream adhering to the chin.

'It's been a long time, Quent. Forgive me if I don't offer to shake hands; mine are always sticky.' He took another cake. 'Make yourself comfortable.'

Quentin looked around. There were no chairs, only a few beanbags. He drew one over, and sank into its flabby embrace.

Dr Mund gazed down at him. His eyes were like tiny nuggets of anthracite; hard, black, peering out of the folds of flesh that all but buried them, and which might have effectively hidden eyes less penetrating. He was dressed in an enormous sky-blue rompersuit, the front of which was stained by numberless food spillages. His hands resumed the task of feeding his mouth, plucking pastries and chocolate from an inexhaustible supply at his elbow, moving quickly and daintily like nimble servants who had long ago learned not to get in each others' way and delay the ceaseless task of bearing food to their voracious master. Words poured out of his mouth, while food poured in.

'Well, Quent, howya doing? It's good to see you after . . . How many years is it? Too many, anyhow. I hear you're doing good work at the hydroplant; knew I could rely on you. You hungry?'

Quentin glanced queasily at the array of dainties beside his friend, then averted his gaze. 'No, not right now—'

'Nonsense; you need to eat, keep your strength up.' Dr Mund pressed a button on his handheld minicomputer, and a long table of polished mahogany, with a chair to match, slid slowly up from a hidden recess in the floor. 'Sit down.'

Quentin obeyed. Mund tapped out another command, and almost immediately attendants appeared bearing covered dishes, which they set silently upon the table, and then withdrew.

'Eat,' ordered Mund.

Quentin lifted the lid of a dish; a large turkey steamed within. Quentin tucked a napkin into his shirtfront. Then he warily began to carve himself a few slices, and helped himself to vegetables and creamed potatoes.

'I'd like to just sit here and talk about the old days back at college,' began Mund, 'but unfortunately I don't have the leisure to indulge that whim. So instead I'll get right down to the nitty-gritty of why I called you over here.' He paused to gulp down a choux bun the size of a basketball, then resumed. 'At this research centre we're engaged on epoch-making work which will affect the future of everyone in this colony. LCC is about to enter a new phase. Most of us came to the Moon to escape, not just from the persecution of bigots who blamed us for eating up the Earth's resources, but also from *gravity itself*. Gravity is a killer; it drags us down, makes our own bodies a *burden*, when they ought to be a source of strength. On Luna, gravity takes less of a toll on us – but even here we're far from free of it. What we've been working on is a way of *neutralizing gravity*, of transcending the crushing force which saps our strength and sucks away our vitality!'

Dr Mund waved his hands excitedly as he spoke; the mesh quivered. Quentin swallowed a mouthful of turkey.

'You mean . . . some kind of Buddhist-type transcendence of the body?' he asked weakly.

'No! I'm not talking about mystical Eastern crap – I'm saying we've discovered how everyone in this colony can cheat gravity: *by becoming their own world*!'

Quentin gaped at him. Mund laughed.

'Surprised, huh? You just have to think big, Quentin. My plan is this: every man, woman and child in LunaColony will be biologically redesigned so that each becomes a self-supporting entity, complete with their own means of generating their own sustenance, their own oxygen, everything they need built in. Then they will no longer need the resources of a world; they will be their own world, living planets, released from the deadly gravity of the Moon and launched out into space, floating free, Fischer, finally *free* of gravity! We will have defeated gravity by *becoming* gravitational bodies, the ultimate subversion of our old enemy! We will grow steadily, over time, be immortal; our DNA will encode a biosphere, the blueprint for an entire ecosystem. In time, we too will become fully-fledged worlds, evolving species of our own . . . We will spread out across the Galaxy, no longer trapped on one tiny, overcrowded world, but with the whole of space to explore and to colonize!'

Dr Mund fell back into his harness, exhausted, his flesh trembling. When he had regained his breath, and eaten, Mund fixed an eye on Quentin.

'Well? What do you say, Quent? You will have a key role to play in this. The lab attached to the hydroplant has been perfecting a high-concentrate nutrient which will be fed intravenously to every fatso, to beef up their mass. Soon your plant will be switched from hydroponics to producing the new food-concentrate. Other members of our team will deal with the physical reshaping of our population. You look sceptical, Fischer, but I assure you, it can be done; the first stages have already been carried out – on me personally. How else do you think I got this big? Dropsy?' He laughed. 'Believe me, human flesh is astonishingly malleable. And we are fortunate in having such a brilliant team of scientists, sculptors of the human clay.'

'But what if people don't *want* to be changed into planets?' protested Quentin.

Mund dismissed the objection. 'Don't be absurd.' He picked up a bun. 'Who would possibly turn down a chance to live for ever? That's what I'm offering. That, and the prospect of being free at last from the clutches of gravity, to start a life in which obesity is essential to survival.'

Mund tapped in a command on his minicomputer. 'Well, bub, I'm a busy man; the next phase in my transformation is due to start soon. I want you to go back to your hydroplant and prepare for the great task that lies ahead.'

Quentin stood up. 'When are you planning to release news of your intentions for the Colony, uh, Doctor?'

'Soon. When all is ready. Until then, Quent – all this is just between friends; is that clear? Meanwhile, why don't you take a little tour of the centre? I'm sure you'll find it instructive.'

In the monorail heading back to Lunaport, Quentin found himself shaking uncontrollably. Now at last he knew what his former friend had been doing all these years.

He had been going insane.

The injunction to silence became steadily more intolerable to Quentin. He felt that he had to discuss what he had learned at Mund's base with somebody else; but who? All his colleagues at the hydroplant were keen Mundists; any reservations that he expressed regarding the Director would surely get back to the latter, doing nothing to resolve the situation. Finally, at his wits' end, Quentin went to see Dr Blakey.

'Mr Fischer?' Blakey looked at him keenly. 'You look as if something's troubling you. Can I help?'

It was surprisingly easy to spill the beans. Something about the thin doctor's dour bedside manner encouraged confidences.

Blakey stared at Quentin, aghast. 'Just as I suspected; the man's utterly crazy. He really would transform everyone in his own image!' The doctor shook his head. 'Mund's ego has swollen in direct proportion to his body. This is his way of impressing his personality on the Moon for ever!'

'But what are we going to do?' demanded Quentin.

'We'll have to blow the whistle on him, cried Blakey. 'Give the media the story – let them inform the public—'

'But the media's under Mund's thumb,' objected Quentin. 'They'd never broadcast the story without his permission.' He sighed. 'Maybe we should advise Earth of Mund's intentions. Though I don't much like the role of informer.'

Blakey was frowning. 'If what Mund says is true, and he really *can* turn people into planets, then Earth ought to be very worried. Even if most of the colonists reject Mund's crazy vision, there'll be enough fanatics for him to put his plan into operation. Think of it – scores, hundreds of new gravitational bodies suddenly appearing in the solar system . . . Think of the effects that would have on Earth, not to mention LunaColony. We've got to stop him somehow!'

Events were precipitated even more rapidly than Blakey and Quentin had expected. The following day the LCC authorities announced the compulsory deportation of all thin people from the Moon. They were given twenty-four hours to pack and wind up their business, then they were to report to the space terminal, where a shuttle would be waiting to take them back to Earth.

Quentin got a call from Blakey. 'You heard the news?' raged the doctor. 'They're kicking us out!'

Quentin nodded 'So we go into action – tonight.'

They parked Blakey's buggy in the centre's compound. Under his spacesuit, the doctor was wearing an overall which Quentin had purloined from the hydroplant, padded out with folded-up clothing to make him look fat.

It was surprisingly easy to gain admittance. 'Uh . . . Dr Mund sent for us,' said Quentin anxiously. The guard nodded vaguely as they flashed their passes, and waved them through.

Inside an air of expectancy pervaded the atmosphere. White-overalled technicians hurried to and fro. Nobody took any notice of the two newcomers.

Quentin studied a plan of the centre. 'This way,' he said, thinking back to the brief tour of the place that he had been given on his previous visit.

'What are we going to do?' hissed Blakey as they hurried along the corridor.

Quentin had been trying not to think too closely about what they were to do. To confront Mund, to threaten to inform Earth of his plans, to provoke open hostility between the Colony and Terra unless Mund abandoned his mad ambitions . . . The futility of such an ultimatum was overwhelming. Mund would never allow himself to be blackmailed like that. Even a rational person would balk at having his aims challenged in such a fashion; and Mund was anything but rational. So where did that leave them?

'In here,' croaked Quentin. It was the control centre, the base from which the whole ghastly, Frankensteinian operation was co-ordinated.

They slipped inside. Some thirty technicians worked silently at their tasks, moving with all the inhuman certainty of automata.

Quentin scanned the arrays of winking computers, struggling to recall what he had been told on his 'instructive' tour. 'Wait here,' he whispered.

'Where are you going?' demanded Blakey.

'I won't be long.' Quentin slipped away.

He didn't know what compulsion drove him to the chamber in which Dr Mund was steadily releasing his hold on his own humanity. He knew that blustering threats would be useless. But he also knew he had to speak to the doctor before the latter was completely engulfed by his own body. It was his obligation, as a friend.

At his approach the door obediently slid open. Quentin paused for a second, pulse racing at what he might discover within the vast chamber. Then he stepped inside.

The room was filled with a huge greenish-white blanket, which seemed to billow outwards. The great mass quivered and throbbed with a hideous animation. Squinting upwards, Quentin saw that the semi-spherical object was just recognizable as a human body.

He stared in mingled awe and horror. Here was a transmogrification of the body more grotesque than anything conceived of by the most decadent surrealist. Mund's bloated form pulsated, as the ravenous tissues devoured the nutrient that coursed through them, endlessly expanding like some demented empire. Quentin could almost see the altered cells turning proteins into fat, swelling the engorged planetoid in an orgy of consumption.

'Ed!' he shouted.

A pause. Then, a voice, subterranean: 'Who's there?'

'Fischer!' yelled Quentin. 'Listen, Ed! Stop this process! You'll destroy yourself, you'll destroy the Colony! For God's sake order them to abort this insane scheme!'

'Too late, Quent,' boomed the doctor. 'I'm only the first; others will follow. Soon my body will reach optimum, old pal; I will form my own atmosphere, an outer "skin" of oxygen; then I will be launched into space, a fully autonomous world. I will continue growing, generating my own mass.' His voice rose to a shriek. '*Gloria Mundi!* Goodbye, gravity! "I am a little world, made cunningly . . . "'

Quentin backed away, further pleadings dying on his lips. The vast living carcase seemed to shudder. He looked up at the roof in fear. A sudden intuition hit him. *Of course. It must be almost time for the Direcior to leave the Moon for good. Almost, but not quite.*

He turned and ran.

Slowly, the cathedral dome slid open. The air rushed out, and space slipped eagerly inside to welcome its newest planet . . .

The door of the control centre opened, and one of the technicians darted out. He turned wildly, then gestured furiously to Quentin, who was panting down the deserted corridor.

'Come on, Fischer! I opened the roof! Let's get the hell out of here!'

Nobody stopped them. All were too shattered, like sleepers awakening from some wonderful dream to grey reality.

The news of Dr Mund's demise leaked out almost reluctantly, by accident rather than design, as if every inhabitant of LunaColony slowly but spontaneously became aware of the withdrawal of a great presence, the massive, weighty presence of a tremendous mind and ego and body which, departing, left behind a curious vacuum.

The details were vague; the Director had suffered a sudden stroke, perhaps, or a coronary. The Moon mourned the loss of her genius. LCC would never be quite the same again.

The expulsion of the Colony's thin population was rescinded, though many chose to return to Earth voluntarily, among them, Dr Blakey.

The skinny doctor paused at the gangway of the shuttle. 'So long, Quent. I hope you can make something of this place. You're the kind of guy it needs, not another damned prophet.' The cold, bony hand gripped Quentin's briefly.

Blakey waved. Quentin waved back. Soon the shuttle was climbing through the darkness towards the radiant blue-green orb of Earth.

'Hey, Quentin! Howya doing? Haven't seen ya around for a while.'

It was Jemma. Quentin felt suddenly glad to see her.

'You're looking down in the mouth, Quent; I know how you feel. We all miss him. But life goes on, right? Come on, I'll buy you a gâteau . . . '

Starlight Dreamer

Peter F. Hamilton

The sky was washed with gold and crimson streaks when we walked into the glade, tall ivy-clad oaks around the perimeter dowsed in a pinkish hue from the sinking sun. Fuchsia and her sister fairies skimmed through the air, dragonfly wings blurring. Their sparkly contrails were twisted into impossible loops as they chased purple emperor butterflies around the foxglove spikes. The flock saw us, calling out happily in their high musical voices without interrupting their lightsome sport.

There were twelve of us hunting the elf prince. The Black Spitfires, we called ourselves, dressed in our black leather jackets and navy-blue jeans, heads crammed loosely into a variety of military-surplus helmets, optic-booster eyestrips wrapped round our faces. Trying to come over the part, major league lads out looking for trouble, rather than over-hyped teenagers lost in a power combat fantasy. We bristled with hardware; thermo knives, Enfield magnetic barrel rifles, we'd even dared to take our treasured cache of laser-targeted Sony plasma pulse pistols out of their hiding place. I was loaded down with a dozen electronic modules clipped on to my webbing belt, readouts plumbed directly into my eyestrip. Half of the image pumped down my retinas was obscured by bright blue digital displays. The inertial compass coordinates were going crazy. Surprise surprise.

'Hey, Fuchsia,' Russel called. 'Come here, my darling.' He held out a gauntleted hand. There was nothing surplus about his gear; full anti-impact armour, with an energy dissipater web woven into the carbon titanium composite. The devil's own space marine.

His visor was open, and he smiled a counterfeit smile as Fuchsia came to hover trustingly in front of him. She bobbed up and down in the air. As long as his forearm, she was so exquisitely beautiful, so fragile. I had holograms of the flock on my bedroom wall, taken that first day I saw them, over three summers ago, by far the loveliest of all the folk to wander out of the realm of the first forest.

'Russel,' Fuchsia trilled. 'So silly, clad in iron furs, in sunlight time. Hot Russel, shed your silly furs.'

'Where is she, Fuchsia?' he purred. 'Where's Kathy? Tell me, my darling.'

'Not here. Not here.' Fuchsia shot straight up, spinning round and round for the sheer joy of it. I could watch the fairies play all day; I would even put up with their teasing to do it.

Fuchsia arched over, and zoomed back into the middle of the glade to join her sisters. They started to giggle.

Russel snapped his visor down. 'Take them out,' he said.

And so we did. Because Russel was seventeen and our leader. And because the way he was freaked he would have turned his plasma pistol on anyone who disobeyed.

Ruby targeting-lasers raked the glade, followed by an incandescent horizontal rain of fizzing plasma pulses. Fairies screamed in bewildered terror as they were torn apart in mid-air. I saw one hit by an Enfield harpoon disintegrate into a plume of pink fog. They fell *en masse*, thudding to the ground, thin streamers of blood replacing their cometary sparkle.

It was the first time we had used our weapons, the waking smile of the beast within.

When it was finished Russel walked into the middle of the glade. Fuchsia had survived. Don't ask me how. She was sitting on the shaggy emerald grass, with another fairy, Marigold, lying across her lap. Marigold was dead, but Fuchsia kept stroking her forehead. Like me, I suppose, she couldn't believe what we had done.

'Get up, get up' she kept saying, tiny tears twinkling on her porcelain cheeks. 'Lazy thing, we've the day left to play. Fly and sing, Marigold. Fly and sing.' Fuchsia's two right wings had been scorched off by a plasma pulse. The remaining two fluttered uselessly every few seconds, buzzing like a fly hitting a window pane.

She looked up when Russel's shadow occluded her.

'Tell me where Kathy is,' he said.

'Marigold won't play any more. Lazy Marigold.'

Russel lifted his boot and stamped down hard.

We moved on deeper into the forest.

To be a Black Spitfire you had to live in the Maltings, a govproject housing estate on the outskirts of Balford. It was a forty-year-old cluster of ground-coral domes set in a square kilometre of parkland, planted over a regressed district of twentieth-century houses. Our parents weren't rich, most of them worked on regression teams, sweating away on the awkward dirty jobs that bitek and cydrones couldn't quite handle. Switching the country back to its pastoral prime, shovelling up the filth left behind by previous generations.

There were other kids in Balford, but they couldn't join the Black Spitfires, no way. They lived in the old houses preserved at the town's heart, little grandee palaces of stone, brick and slate, where the winding streets are cobbled, and red telephone boxes stand on most corners. They didn't have the attitude, with their flashy expensive day clubs, and their sports teams, and their themepark trips; every minute organized and taken care of. Mummy's darlings, every one of them.

We roamed free, us Spitfires, our only obligation a fortnightly trip to the govschool for a didactic laser-memory imprint. I was focusing on science subjects, hoping to make university grade when I reached sixteen. Mr Talbot, our assessment officer, said I would do it easily, something in my neurone structure made me an ideal receptor subject, I could absorb the photobyte courses with very little dataloss. I was already twelve levels higher than the other Black Spitfires my age. The original impressionable youngster, Mr Talbot called me.

My grade meant I was in charge of our illegal equipment. OK, it wasn't *that* illegal, a wonky clone vat, a programmable molecular filter we used to synthesize mild hallucinogens, unlicensed network receivers, and all the guns we dug up. But we thought it was pretty spicy stuff. It gave us something to congregate around, a kernel of identity.

Balford didn't have anything else to offer us. A market town in an age when markets had ceased to have meaning, it had become a rural dormitory for professionals and govworkers, visually idyllic, and macro-boring. It sat in a broad rolling valley, surrounded by the south Devon forest.

England's forests had been the first stage of regression after bitek made farming obsolete, and starships started to syphon off the surplus population to the colony worlds. The south Devon forest was ninety years old; oaks and ash mixed in with fifty other deciduous species. Traditional trees, yearning for what was. It extended northward from the coast, right up to Dartmoor, spreading east into Dorset, and west over to Bodmin Moor.

The trees began a hundred metres beyond the Maltings. We had explored the paths and glades and pools and streams our whole lives. They had been put there for our entertainment; gloomy and mysterious in winter, bursting with life and colour in summer, more of a home than Balford had ever been.

We accepted what we found in there without question. Glimpses of the smaller forest folk accumulated until they lost any surprise. As we grew up, we would extend our territory a little deeper each year, seeing more and more of the forest community. The gnomes, pixies and fairies belonged there as much as we did.

Then in the spring of my fifteenth year, Prince Yannareth and his entourage came riding out of the first forest.

'We heard the hinterland forest growing again, and came to see for ourselves why this should be, after so long a barrenness,' Sendiryki told me.

Sendiryki and I got to be good mates that summer. Both of us the same, in a way. Both of us the dreamer. Same dream even, that one of far off places. He was a typical elf, towering an easy thirty centimetres over me, and at one metre seventy-five I'm no slouch. Yet for all his size, he weighed nothing; he could race over a meadow without bending a single blade of grass. He wore a green and yellow tunic, as soft as deerskin, which made him near-invisible in the forest. He was young too (for an elf, anyway). But then they all looked like hundred-year-old teenagers.

'How can you hear a forest growing?' I asked. It was a sultry day in June, when the air was clotted with pollen from the wildflowers. We sat on the fringe of the forest, looking down on Balford, while bumble-bees droned between the honeysuckle and the hollyhocks.

'The song it sings became a chorus to the melody of the first forest,' Sendiryki said.

'First forest, that's where you live?'

'Yes.'

'And you came for a look at our forest?'

'My prince is young, he has a restless tune singing in his blood.'

'So do you,' I said.

He smiled. 'And so do you.'

'Yeah, you're right there. I want to join a scoutship after I qualify; explore the galaxy, discover terracompatible worlds.'

'You mean worlds where you can live?'

'Yes.'

'Such a strong song, Michael. I envy you.'

'When I make captain, I'll take you along.'

'To sail amongst the stars.' There was a wistful tone in his voice. He rolled on to his back, and looked at the sky as if he'd never seen it before. 'The stars above the first forest are not as yours. But we have our seas. They sing a long chorus of enchantment to me.'

'Are you going to be a sailor, then?'

'Yes. I will build such a ship as the world has never seen before. And maybe one day you will sail with me, Michael. A voyage to end all voyages.'

'I'd like that. Remind me to take you windsurfing some time.'

'Windsurfing? I would like that?'

'Yeah, you'll like it.'

Tourists one day, and tourist guides the next. All of us. We had nosed around each other for the first few days, kings of strut. Spitfires venturing near the elven's woodland camp, Yannareth's entourage stealing up to the edge of the forest to look out at Balford. But contact, acceptance, that was down to

Russel and the prince in the end.

One of my photobyte history courses incorporated images of old Cold War summits; leaders meeting on neutral territory, carefully diplomatic. That's what it was like, the same softly softly quality. Testing and probing. They talked, then they sat down on boulders beside a stream, and started to smile, then Prince Yannareth laughed at something Russel said. After that, they were inseparable, you couldn't forge a stronger friendship.

It was Sendiryki who taught me to ride a horse. I hate to admit it, but for sheer exhilaration it knocked my electrobike for six. He also showed me the strength in the water that flows from the first forest, scooping it up out of an icy stream in a shallow goblet made from the palest gold I'd ever seen.

'A *tirkrih*,' he said. 'A seeing chalice. It has been in my family since the time of Ardwen.' He recited a lilting incantation over it.

When I looked at the surface of the water, I could see a pallid reflection of autumn woodland wreathed in serpentine coils of fog. Some of the trees were shattered, broken spears lay on the ground.

'Where is that?'

'Another place, another age.' He gave a sad smile. 'Try again.'

I saw a misty glimpse of a palatial white-coral castle festooned in garlands of bright flowers, pennants flying from high turrets. Hundreds of elven rode across the greensward in festival. The sky was the clearest blue. 'Your home?' I asked. It was achingly beautiful.

'The hall of Yannareth's sire. And beyond that, lies the sea.' There was that wistful tone again.

I took him home when my parents were out, and showed him how to use the home terminal. We spent hours accessing govcentral data cores, reviewing scoutship planet survey records. I made a mental note to load up a holowafer with images for him. He could take it back to Yannareth's camp and look at all the bug eyes to his heart's content.

We spent one day at the beach, Sendiryki's first sight of the sea. I found him some pink and blue Bermuda shorts and a baggy T-shirt with a hologram of the horsehead nebula, and we left Balford at dawn, riding down the crumbling old tarmac road on my electrobike.

Rounding the last corner as we emerged from the south Devon forest was like a theatrical spectacle. The blue water suddenly there, stretching out for ever. Sendiryki clutched at me in something almost like panic. I heard what he heard then, the song that the waves and the gulls weave, the siren call, drawing us forward.

Plymouth had been almost completely regressed; apart from the resort club above the shore there were only a few old stone buildings, which served as museums. We walked over the rolling ground that had been a city, Sendiryki looking more lost than I had ever seen him.

'Such decay,' he said mournfully. 'And you say it was occupied less than a century ago?'

'Fifty years. But it's meant to be this way,' I said. The land around us was cockpit country, steep mounds covered in reedy grass, stubbled with small gorse bushes. 'These used to be blocks of flats. The regression teams have various species of cloned macerator algae which they spray on all the old buildings; there's one for glass, and one for concrete, another for brick. The skyscrapers wind up looking like foam sculptures. It takes a couple of years, but the whole structure eventually crumbles away into sand.' We reached the top of a mound, and I stamped my foot on a bare patch of marly soil. 'Of course, there's an awful lot of junk immune to the algae. We come out here and dig sometimes. It's amazing what you can find.'

'Did your ancestors really hate this world so much that entire kingdoms abandoned it?' Sendiryki asked.

'Some of them did, I suppose. We were in a bad state around the time starflight was perfected, you see, pollution and population pressure had shot the environment to hell. There was a big Fresh Start movement; you know, cut free from the mistakes of the past, that kind of thing.'

'I would not enjoy a land where such turmoil lasted for centuries, yet you rejoice in it. How strange a song men sing. Why with all the powers at your command did you not heal your own world?'

'We have now, more or less. Population was one of the biggest problems. And the stars were an easy solution. A lot of transportees were involuntaries: dole conscripts, criminals, anti-gov protesters.' I didn't tell him about the weapons cache we'd found, digging in an old office block. Russel said it was probably left behind by an anti-expat group. The Sony pistols were less than thirty years old. Not everyone went peacefully. 'England's population is down to eight million now. Govhousing says that's just about perfect for us.'

'Millions!' Sendiryki exclaimed in bemusement. 'So few!'

'It means we've got room to grow the forests again,' I pointed out, laughing as we ran down the slope together.

Sendiryki did get to windsurf after all. I hired us a couple of boards from the club, and spent the afternoon teaching him in one of the empty coves further down the shore. Talk about a duck to water. I wound up paying an overdue penalty. He just wouldn't get off.

Kathy arrived at the start of August, the daughter of a regression team supervisor who moved into the Maltings. We didn't have girls in the Black Spitfires. Oh, we went out with Maltings girls, kissed them when we went on trips to the beach, spied on them sunbathing topless. But they weren't Spitfires. Not before Kathy.

She was sixteen, with hair so fair it was almost white. Her legs were as long as any elf's, and her smile shamed the sun. The first time I saw her I thought she had come from the first forest; she was unearthly, divine.

I fell in love with her. All the Black Spitfires fancied her, but that was just puerile adolescent lust on their part, in my case it was the real thing.

I never stood a chance. Too young. Besides, she was Russel's. He made that quite clear from the start, and for some unfathomable reason she responded in kind. But I didn't stop loving her just because of him.

Sendiryki was full of sympathy, if a little short on understanding. 'What of your plans to explore the night void?' he said. 'Would she be able to travel with you in your metal starvoyager?'

'That's years away,' I protested.

He grinned. 'Such a shallow song, Michael. Is your love so thin, then, that it would not last those years?'

'Of *course* it would last!'

He sang me a song of noble lovers torn apart by some war, or black witchery, or cataclysm – something bloody morbid, anyway – how they didn't get together again for centuries, and how the reward for all that faithfulness came in the elf version of heaven. 'Now that is a love you should aspire to, Michael.'

Like I said, short on understanding.

The only time I could talk to Kathy alone was when we all trooped along to the govschool for a laser-imprint session. Russel didn't go, he had been playing truant for seven months, saying he knew all he needed to to work on a regression team. I don't suppose it occurred to him that regression was nearly over, that without a job he would be in line for involuntary transportation.

I told her of my giddy dreams as we walked through Balford's stylish Victorian streets, the future I'd mapped out for myself amongst the constellations. The words tumbling out in a frenzied, probably incoherent, gush, so eager was I to impress her. She would nod at appropriate moments, in turn telling me how she intended to qualify as a bitek designer. Neither of us made any mention of how this would be compatible with Russel's simplistic idea of the future.

I never did understand the attraction she felt for him. Russel was a dead end, a recidivist stuffed full of bravado. Strong and charismatic enough to lead a bunch of gullible teenagers, but that was the sum of him. I even started questioning the point of the Black Spitfires, it was beginning to seem like play-acting to me. A mockery of true rebellion. I didn't want to fight govcentral; govcentral built and operated scoutships.

The two of us were ambling back from govschool one evening at the end of August, when Brendan made a pass at Kathy. He was standing behind the flaky brick wall that ran around the town's compact park. A tall, slender twenty-year-old wearing a dark trench coat and matching trilby; his skin was so white you'd think he was an albino. I couldn't see his eyes, they were hidden behind a biker's visor, a glossy black strip with streamline contours, covering the middle third of his face. Brendan was the leader of the Shadowhawks. We'd noticed them a couple of years back, about five or six of them, older than us, always in their trench coats. They never even acknowledged we existed. Posers all. I think someone said they lived in govproject houses on the other side of town. Each evening they would come to hang out in the old baptist chapel on the edge of the park.

'We're having a party tonight,' he said as we drew level. 'Open invitation for a girl like you. It'll be a lot more fun than anything your kiddy friends get up to.'

'No thank you,' Kathy said sharply.

'Where's your fire? You've got to find out what real life is like sometime. I could show you tonight.'

'I know all about real life.'

She moved a fraction closer to me. I risked a glance at the ramshackle yellow-stone chapel fifty metres behind Brendan. The Shadowhawks were lounging around the open door, trench coats flapping in the warm zephyrs that prowled the gloaming, biker visors tracking us like radar. I hadn't realized there were so many Shadowhawks these days. Easily a dozen.

'Oh, I don't think you do,' Brendan smiled, thin waxen lips parting to show needle teeth. 'You just hope so. Real life isn't about hope, it's plain survival. And I'm an expert.'

'I'll manage on my own, thank you,' Kathy said.

'Sure you will,' he crooned. 'Tigress.' He thrust his head back and started to bark like a mad dog.

Kathy slipped her arm round mine, and we rounded a corner. 'Run,' she hissed. And we did, all the way up the gentle slope to the Maltings, Brendan's eerie howling laughter chasing us the whole way.

Kathy persuaded me not to say anything to Russel. It was just as well, the Shadowhawks had me worried. Theirs was a presence that added an unwholesome tone of menace to Balford's somnolent streets. I couldn't help thinking life was sweeter in the days when we were less than nothing to them.

If the Shadowhawks were the downside of Balford, the elven were the boost we needed to convince ourselves life was worthwhile after all. Kathy was as dazzled and awestruck by them as the rest of us. Her face . . . Well, I suppose she looked like me the first time I saw the fairies.

I remember the time Russel introduced her to Prince Yannareth. The prince bowed deeply, taking her hand and kissing her knuckles. 'You are truly the flower of your race,' he intoned solemnly.

She blushed and her cheeks dimpled, flattered by the attention. Yannareth had that effect on people. All the elves were wondrous, but he had an unmatched grace; it was that nobility which set him as far above them as they were above us.

Russel swaggered about, ridiculously self-important. By royal decree, his girl was the most desirable in two worlds. Not bad going for a nobody.

The inseparable duo became the inseparable trio.

A week after my tangle with Brendan in the park, the Black Spitfires and the prince's entourage clubbed together and went to the Stomping Mary gig in Southampton. The Stompers were a tight seven piece mood fantasy band, very hot, preaching their quasi-anarchy message along with the usual raw sex. Gods to anyone under twenty, rich or poor.

The Tube to Southampton took quarter of an hour, and I spent the whole time thinking malicious thoughts about the shock Sendiryki was going to get when they started playing. He thought someone accompanying a harp with a flute was pretty racy stuff.

The gig was in a grassy amphitheatre carved into a hillside on the west of the city. We all trooped in together, us Spitfires in our black jackets, the elven in borrowed, ill-fitting clothes.

The Stompers walked on stage, and twenty thousand adolescents roared in welcome. The elven joined in, for once swept along by our world's song. They smiled incredulously at each other, that look which says you know you shouldn't, but it's great fun anyway.

The band struck up. Omni-directional sublim stacks on either side of the stage, like giant crystal pillars, began broadcasting. Hard synth rock slammed into my ears, and sequenced photons slipped along my optical nerves, tickling the secluded response centres in my brain. And I was suddenly this wild metallic-skinned pterodactyl streaking through interstellar space, wings ten kilometres wide beating against thin gusts of hydrogen atoms. I swerved around shimmering comets, rolled lazily over lonely tumbling asteroids, falling endlessly down the gravity slope. There were planets ahead, gas giants with their rings and colourful moons. I dipped and weaved and gyrated above the cloudscape's ocean-sized stormbands, pale phosphorescent borealis serpents swam like fish shoals amid the darkside cloud peaks. I left it all behind, flying inwards, towards the bright call of the sun. All around me, space was filled with the triumphant cry of my kind, black wings aglitter as we beat our way towards the warmth. And there, gliding above the thermals of the corona, I found a mate. Necks entwined, wings outstretched as one, we soared in the fountaining solar flares, surfed along the arching prominences, spiralling around and around. Free and invincible, lords of the cosmos. It was me, all I ever wanted to be, my soul's song.

Sendiryki was laughing, his eyes inflamed. 'Such danger! Such joy!' he cried above the crushing music. 'Oh Michael, why did you never tell me? Are they real? Are they creatures your star voyagers found?'

'No. The Stompers make them up. They make it all up.'

'What crazy minds you have. Oh to be mortal man for just one day. To know such beautiful insanity, such liberation.'

The one sour note of the evening came from Russel. Like every time, he wanted to go a step further than anyone else, so he infused one of the hallucinogens the filter churned out. I saw him later during the gig, crashing out alone, dancing in fractured jerks to a beat no one else could hear.

That was when I saw Kathy and Prince Yannareth dancing together, a graceful old-fashioned partnership. I turned back to the stacks, immersing myself in a grand ballroom of elegant people, men in dinner jackets, women in demure gowns, slow waltzing in time to a poignant ballad. Looking round again, Prince Yannareth's arms had encircled Kathy, she was resting her head on his chest, smiling gently.

After the gig Sendiryki and I hiked up to the cafe at the top of the amphitheatre hill. We ordered some beers and sat outside in the balmy night air, watching the spaceplanes slide in from the other side of the sky. Their swept delta heatshield underbellies glowed a deep orange against the smiling summer stars as they sank down towards the city's spaceport.

'You humble me, Michael,' Sendiryki said slowly. 'Amid the insensitivity of your changeful world is a grandeur I could never have conceived.'

'You'll find what you're looking for out there on your sea.'

'Perhaps.' He tilted his head up again, silver-glitter eyes dark with longing.

It was Anton and his big mouth that did it.

We used an old stable block to hang out in; it was at the back of the Maltings, surrounded by a thicket of hawthorns, which is probably why the regression team missed it. But we fixed up the roof, and added some solar cells to power our gear.

He charged in late one afternoon, looking as if he had run all the way from the coast, face red, chest heaving. 'I saw them,' he yelled. 'Yannareth and Kathy, they were having it off in the forest. God they never even saw me they were at it so hard. Hey, do you reckon it's true about the elven having one as big as a horse? I mean, boy, you should have heard her squealing!'

We looked at him, every one of us, disconnected from time, numbed and secretly terrified.

He looked back at us, grinning savagely. 'What?' Then he turned as Russel rose to his feet, coming forward out of the corner he'd been brooding in. Anton's elation drained away, replaced by real fear.

'Where was this?' Russel asked in a dead tone. He had infused something, and that filter really was way too old to reproduce the delicate molecular strings contained in the narc-programs. I could see the tiny capillaries in his eyeballs had turned sallow.

After that there was no hope left. None at all.

Brendan was sitting on a boulder just outside the forest. In his trench coat and trilby he seemed like a denser concentration of the shadows cast by the first rank of trees. The biker's visor eclipsed most of his long, ivory face, but the visible skin seemed preternaturally bright amid the gloom which lurked in the valley that afternoon.

We marched up the side of the valley towards him, all of us silent. Russel's rag-tag army of vengeance. Our weapons didn't seem to bother Brendan terribly. If anything he was condescending. The corners of his mouth turned up in what I took for a smile.

Russel stopped level with him, hesitant in the face of such urbanity. 'We're going to get Kathy back from the elven,' he said. 'Do you want to help?'

'It looks to me like you have it all under control.'

'It could be one of your girls next.'

The derisive smile broadened. 'I doubt that. I doubt that very much indeed.'

'Thanks for nothing.'

'Your fault for trusting them.'

'Come on,' Russel commanded us; he started off towards the forest. Most of the Black Spitfires hurried to keep up. I lingered.

Brendan gave me a wolfish grin, like he already had the world sewn up. If I could just have seen his eyes then, I might have known what he was about, but all I could see was a little image of myself bouncing back off the shiny black mirror surface of his biker's visor.

I admit it, Brendan's innate freakishness spooked me. I went off after the others before he could start that demented laugh again.

The news of our obscenity spread out from the fairy glade, a distortion in the forest's quiddity, racing on ahead of us like the rippling air of a heat shimmer. Forest folk were fleeing from our marching boots. The grass rustled beside the path, alive with small fast bodies outpacing the hares. Russel would let off a shot every now and then; I don't think he hit anything.

It was our own enmity that corrupted the forest's song. Sendiryki had taught me to listen to the harmony, the way the wind slid through the branches, the sigh of flowers, blending together in concord. Now we intruded on the flow, an unsavoury dissonance. I could hear the trees shivering from the chill of our passage. Yet we were still on paths familiar from early childhood. Our territory.

Russel marched on down the path, heedless of any subtleties. Of the two forces, he was still the easiest for us to follow.

The tufty grass at our feet became darker; choked with tough twines of sorrel and clumps of nightshade. Solemn ash trees gave way to lighter birches clad in long, dusty braids of ivy. Their girth was enormous, tops hidden behind huge boughs; starsparks of mellow sunlight filtered through the slowly shifting leaves.

I knew the path we walked down was taking us in the right direction, even though I couldn't quite recognize it. Sendiryki once said there are many paths through the forest, and the straightest are often longest of all. I think he was right.

I'd always found the elven camp a gorgeous place to behold, echoing the finery of medieval pageantry. It was set in a grove of copper beech trees, their vast boughs swaying overhead. The prince's entourage had pitched their blue and green tents in a circle where they were dappled by topaz sunbeams. Cooking fires used to burn in the middle, adding to the festival atmosphere.

But now the fires were out, and the elven stood in a protective semicircle, bows in hand, except for Prince Yannareth. He stood at their apex, clad in silver armour inlaid with golden arabesque symbols that shone of their own accord.

I found Sendiryki's eyes on me. All we could do was stare hopelessly at each other across the camp.

Kathy stood behind Prince Yannareth, dressed in a long, flowing gown of green and white, lovely and remote, like one of the women in the Stompers dance fantasy. She was on the verge of tears.

'Come on, girl,' Russel said. 'You're coming back with us.'

'Lady Katherine makes her own choices,' Prince Yannareth said equably.

'Oh yeah?' Russel took a step forward.

There was a sharp ringing sound as the prince drew his sword.

'Stop it,' Kathy said. 'Russel, there's nothing left for us. Go home. All of you, go home, please.'

'Nothing, eh?' Russel said. 'We'll see, *Lady* Katherine. Now you come with me.'

'I think not, Russel,' Prince Yannareth said. 'I am truly sorry this has happened, for your company is one I treasure. But Lady Katherine is not your chattel.'

Russel looked round at us, sneering cockily. 'Go get 'em lads.' He aimed his Sony straight at Prince Yannareth, and fired. So brazen and ignoble, forcing the issue.

Prince Yannareth was already bringing his shield up. The plasma bolt hit the mirror surface and broke apart, static tendrils shivering across the heraldic crest.

Targeting-lasers stabbed out, and that deadly barrage of plasma pulses strobed across the short distance between us, finger-sized darts of purple-white lightning. I heard the Enfields humming as they slung their harpoons. The elven answered with a flight of arrows.

Anton cried out beside me, stumbling, an arrow shaft protruding from his thigh. His thigh! I've seen elven pierce a bird's eye in mid-flight.

I aimed my pistol a metre over Sendiryki's head and squeezed the trigger hard. Three elven had fallen, tunics smouldering from the holes blasted by plasma bolts. One had been hit by a harpoon, his right arm hanging in tatters, blood splattering his chest. Five of the tents were ablaze, horses screamed in panic, pulling against their tethers.

We were suddenly running at each other, yelling wordlessly. Someone somewhere was blowing a hunting horn, its brassy notes reverberating around the grove.

Sendiryki and I charged into each other, the impact throwing us to the ground. I felt his long arms tighten around me, and hugged him back. We rolled about listlessly in the grass. Breath burnt against my constricted throat.

'They duel,' Sendiryki whispered. And I looked up.

Russel and Prince Yannareth advanced towards each other, heedless of the wrestling couples thrashing around at their feet. Russel's visor was down; sharp emerald laserlight flared from a cylindrical module on the side of his helmet, sweeping across Prince Yannareth's helmet. Brain-raper photobytes, designed to tapeworm into a mind and rip rationality to a bleeding husk, to lovingly smother you in your own insanity. I know, I wrote them for Russel.

Prince Yannareth swayed backwards as if buffeted by a squall. He clasped his sword in front of him with both hands, aligning its tip on Russel. His voice screamed out, strange twisted words, wretched with pain.

Russel was laughing, his pistol directing a barrage of pulses towards the prince. They hit the silver armour, sending out small fierce sprays of molten metal. Tiny black craters bloomed across the prince's breastplate, each blow punching him back. But still he held the sword steady.

And then he finished his agonized chant. The blade of his sword ignited with a searing iridescence. A cyclone of diamond blue light lashed out from the tip, engulfing Russel in a lurid clawing nimbus.

Russel shuddered violently, arms and legs spasming. He let loose an animal groan, livid with suffering. I could see his armour's hexagonal dissipater web burning a radiant crimson. He lurched across the grove towards the prince, a tormented fire elemental, footprints scorching the verdant grass to withered ash, pistol spitting its condensed lightning bolts.

They met head on, their battle cries merging into a single incoherent howl. Sword and pistol clattered aside. Over and over they tumbled, thrashing like beasts. Russel's thermo blade chewing long gouges on Prince Yannareth's armour. The prince's bejewelled dagger prising at the neck seal below Russel's helmet.

Then the forest wailed, a hideous wounded keening that went on and on. It was us, I knew it, our violation was too great. Our fault. Our guilt. Our shame.

A wind rose from nowhere, hurtling through the grove. Those of us standing mutely around our battling captains were forced to our knees by its vehemence. The copper beeches quailed before it, their boughs creaking with distress.

'The paths,' Sendiryki shouted above the clamour. 'The paths are sundering.'

Russel and Prince Yannareth abandoned their fight as the ground quaked.

'Ride,' the prince called. 'We must ride back.' He staggered to his feet. Scarlet blood was seeping out of his armour. 'Katherine!' The anguish in his voice pierced my heart.

She moved towards him.

'You bitch!' Russel yelled. He was on his knees, clutching at one arm where the anti-impact armour had blistered.

'Don't go,' I called after her. Useless, I know, but love is never kind. 'Can't you see, Kathy, they alter nothing. Nothing! In ten thousand years everything in their land will be exactly as it is now. That's not living, not for us. We change, we have a life.'

'We have pain,' Kathy said. She reached the prince, and clung to him, the two of them stumbling back towards the horses.

'Kathy!' Russel screamed. But she never looked round. Not once.

The elven were rushing about, chasing and gentling their skittish horses as the nightmare wind churned around us. The wounded were helped up into their saddles; the dead were turning transparent, becoming glass effigies. A multi-coloured jewel glowed within each of them, throwing out prismatic light. Then they began to fade away, as ephemeral as dewdrops.

'Go,' I told Sendiryki. I took a holowafer from my jeans pocket. It was the one I'd loaded with a catalogue of bug eyes. I thrust it into his hands. He stared at it numbly, his youthfully ancient face wet with tears. 'Go on. Go!'

A rose gold light was rising behind the camp. A sun broader than ours, yet lacking the harshness, reaching bravely for the dawn, sending phosphorescent beams streaking through the first forest.

Sendiryki embraced me, whispering in my ear. Then he was gone, racing feet carrying him across the grove to his comrades with a speed to rival the birds.

They galloped off into the first forest, down a broad avenue of ancient gnarled oaks whose thick buttressed roots and arching branches formed a tunnel that stretched out for ever. I shielded my eyes against the tangerine corona shining so strongly above the misty treetops. That was the last time I saw them; a line of eerie black silhouettes poised on the crest of the world. One with his hand held high in a wave.

I often return to the forest by myself, walking the familiar paths and animal tracks, visiting the glades and brooks I know so well. The wind still steals through the branches and leaves with the stealth of a questing lover, but it kindles no song, and the glades lie empty apart from the butterflies and the squirrels.

There are no Black Spitfires either, not any more. The police took our guns away when we came out of the forest, but our brotherhood had died before that, laid to rest beside fair Fuchsia.

I have a girlfriend now, most of us do. I suppose it's an improvement.

The Shadowhawks prosper at our expense. There are more of them these days, Russel foremost amongst them. And I'm afraid to walk down Balford's streets after dark. They gave Anton a savage beating last week; he's still in hospital.

So I come up here to the forest where they have yet to venture. Sometimes I will catch a glimpse of phantasm figures through the trunks, or imagine I do. A girl with flaxen hair, wearing a green and white dress, her prince standing proud beside her, his arm around her shoulder as she cradles their infant child.

Sendiryki's final words live on in my mind. 'The night void and the sea merge beyond the horizon,' he said. 'I will look for you there.'

I don't think so. Not any more.

Free States

Michael Moorcock

Thou still unravish'd bride of quietness,
    Thou foster-child of Silence and slow Time,
Sylvan historian, who canst thus express
    A flowery tale more sweetly than our rhyme;
What leaf-fringed legend haunts about thy shape
    Of deities or mortals or of both,
In Tempe or the dales of Arcady?
    What men or gods are these? What maidens loth?
What mad pursuit? What struggle to escape?
    What pipes and timbrels? What wild ecstasy?

Keats, *Ode on a Grecian Urn*

1. LLAMADA DE LAS LEJANAS COLINOS

'YOU'RE LOOKING BETTER, Jack.' Sam Oakenhurst has recovered from the *machinoix* torments. 'Your old self.'

Jack Karaquazian deals seven hands of poker. His skin reflects a million cultures given up to the pit long before their time; his green eyes reveal a new kind of courtesy. Coolly amiable in his black silk and white linen, his raven hair hanging straight to his shoulders, his back set firmly against that howling triumph of Satan, he is content.

'I'm feeling it, Sam,' he says.

Mr Oakenhurst picks up his bags. All around him the outlines and shadows of the Terminal Café shift and caper while Boudreaux Ramsadeen practises a graceful figure with Fathima Panosh, the tiny dancer currently favoured by the Terminal's regulars who come to hear real old-fashioned zee and witness the purity of the high games. Only at Biloxi, where the Fault yells and ululates, can enough colour be tapped to push new limits. And for those who lose too much, there is always the Fault itself, restless and demanding, greedy for energy and offering, perhaps, an ultimate wisdom.

'On your way, Sam?' Jack Karaquazian sits back from his game. His fellow players know him as Al-Q'areen. They are shades, men and women ready to risk everything to win nothing but the approval of their peers. They have the dedicated, ascetic appearance of a strict order. The Egyptian smiles, a kindly jackal.

'On my way.' Mr Oakenhurst sets his broad-brimmed pale Panama, dusts at his fine cord travelling coat, his buckskin riding boots, his blue cotton shirt and breeches. 'So long.'

'Nobody knows what's going on up there now,' says Boudreaux Ramsadeen from the dance floor, his brutish face clouded with concern. 'They say it's nothing but vapour up in the Frees. Turned all to steam, mon ami. You be better off staying here.'

Mr Oakenhurst lifts a hand to show appreciation. 'Estrella errante, vieux pard. You know how it is.'

But Boudreaux Ramsadeen will never know how that is. He brought his café on the train from Meridian to take advantage of the tourist trade. Now he and the Terminal are married to the Fault until the end of time.

(We are all echoes of some lost original, she would tell him. But we are not diminished by this knowledge. Rather, we are strengthened by it.)

2. SE ERES RAPIDO DISPARA

WHEN MR SAM Oakenhurst took off for the Free States he had it in mind to heal the memories and still the cravings of his last six seasons at the mercy of New Orleans' infamous *machinoix*, whose final act of trust was to introduce him to the long, complex mutilation rituals they believed to be the guarantee of continuing existence in the afterlife.

Ending his stopover at the Terminal Café, where Jack Karaquazian still wagered the highest psychic stakes from what had become known as the Dead King's Chair, his stoic back against the whirling patterns of Chaos ceaselessly forming and reforming, Mr Oakenhurst was at last able to ask his old friend how things went for him.

'Not so bad now, Sam, pretty good.'

'You're looking better, Jack. Your old self.'

'I'm feeling it, Sam.' Jack Karaquazian's fingers moved abstractedly around the dormant dimensions of a waiting flat game. The other players were unhappy with this interruption but unwilling to risk the Egyptian's displeasure. He toyed with the dealing plates, himself anxious to begin the next hand. And his eyes looked upon so many simultaneous memories.

Before he walked to the door, Sam Oakenhurst said: 'Come up there with me, Jack. They got some famous spots in Texas and New Mexico. They're finding colour every day in California. Don't you want to visit San Diego while she's still burning? They say you can walk in and out of those flames and feel no heat at all. There's people still living in the city, completely unhurt. That's something to see, Jack.'

Mr Karaquazian wished his friend luck in the West but reckoned he had a game or two left to play at the Terminal. In answer to Sam Oakenhurst's glare of honest surprise, he recalled the old intimacy of their friendship and said, in words only Mr Oakenhurst heard, 'I can't go yet.' He was not ready to speak of his reasons but if his friend were to ride by again at a later time he promised he would tell what happened after they had parted in the Quarter, when the Egyptian had gone upriver on the Memphis boat.

Mr Oakenhurst tipped his hat to his friend and went to collect his horse from Boudreaux's makeshift stables.

(Have you heard of the conspiracy of the Just? she would ask. Once the likes of us becomes aware of this conspiracy, we are part of it. There's no choice in the matter. We are, after all, what we are. And you and I, Sam, are of the Just. You don't have to like it.)

In common with most who chanced their luck at the gambling trade, Sam Oakenhurst had left his will with the Terminal's neanderthal proprietor. He took the one good horse he had ridden in on, the sound of Boudreaux's zeeband still marking the rhythm of his actions.

He was almost in the ruins of Picayune before the tunes had left his head. On his way up, he had seen two corpses, a man's and a woman's, half buried in the shallows of the beach; behind them was the distant wall of the Biloxi Fault, howling and groaning and never still.

Picayune was the closest Mr Oakenhurst would let himself get to New Orleans. He had no fear of *machinoix* enmity. They regarded him as one of their own. But he had found a dark new greed in himself which tempted him back to their stronghold.

Mr Oakenhurst did not feel in any way free of the hunger until he entered the twilight fern forests beyond Nouveaux Iberie. His horse followed a broad, dry road, well-marked and patrolled by the local security committees who guaranteed the safety of all who lived there, or passed through peacefully, and swift death to any aggressor.

Sam Oakenhurst's plan was to take the road right up past Sulphur. He stopped for the night at a lodging house just above Lake Charles where he was met by the landlord, a veteran of the First Psychic War, his skin scaled with pale unstable colour. Lieutenant Twist said that the road now ran up to De Quincey, beside the Texas Waters, a recent series of connected lochs populated by islands stretching almost as far as Houston and nearly up to Dallas. There were a few paddle-wheelers carrying passengers through the lakes but they were infrequent and unscheduled. Mr Oakenhurst was advised to return to New Orleans and buy a ticket on a coastal schoomer to Corpus Cristi. 'There's a weekly run. Calmest and safest waters in the world now. They say all the ocean around the Fault's like that.'

Mr Oakenhurst said he had decided to take his chances. 'In that case,' said Lieutenant Twist, 'you would be better trying for De Quincey and hope a boat or a colour-rider come in soon.' He shook his head in admiration of what he understood to be Mr Oakenhurst's bravery. '*Somebody help me get out of Louisiana, help me get to Houston town!*' Whistling, he led Sam Oakenhurst to the choice individual accommodation behind the old main building.

Making himself presentable Mr Oakenhurst went, after half-an-hour, to join an acoustic game in a corner of the hotel's bar, but after a few minutes he grew bored and deliberately let the other players win back most of their stakes, keeping five *piles noires* as payment for his time. On his way to his cabin he saw a movement high up where the fronds were thinnest and the moonlight was turned to pale jade, some sort of owl. Its eyes were huge and full of hope.

Sam Oakenhurst's chamber was clean, well kept, though the furniture was old and the bedding darned. A useless V-cabinet stood in the corner. Converted to hold magazines, it dispensed them in return for a few pennies. The magazines were hand-coloured, crudely stencilled versions of old-time V programmes. Mr Oakenhurst put in the coins and the screen opened to offer him a selection.

They were chiefly magazines detailing the escapades of various unfamiliar heroes and heroines – *The Merchant Venturer, Pearl Peru – Captain Billy Bob Begg's Famous Chaos Engineers – Karl Kapital – Professor Pop – Fearless Frank Force – Bullybop – Corporal Pork* – violently coloured attempts to reproduce the interactive video melodramas some addicts still enjoyed at the Terminal Café. All the characters seemed engaged in perpetual war between Plurality and Singularity for the domination of a territory (possibly philosophical) called the Second Ether. These unlikely events were represented as fact. The gambler, finding their enigmatic vocabularies and queer storylines too cryptic, replaced them in the dispenser, blew out his lamp and slept, dreaming a familiar dream.

(He had talked to Jack Karaquazian when they were still in New Orleans. He had asked his friend if he would care if he spoke of something that was on his mind.

"Not at all," the Egyptian had said.

I had this dream, said Sam Oakenhurst. I was standing on this cliff with a pack of dogs and killer blankeys at my back and nothing but rocks and ocean far below and nowhere to go but down when suddenly out of the blue this golden limo pulls up in the air right where I'm standing on the edge and the driver's eye-balling me. She's a beautiful woman, real elegant, and she says "Hop in, Sam. Where do you want to go?"

"Where are you going?" I ask.

"Any place you like," she says.

"Well," I say, "I guess in that case I'll stick here and take my chances."

"Please yourself," she says and she's ready to start up when I say "Hey, what's your name, lady?"

"Luck," she says, puts the car in gear and vanishes. I turn around and the dogs and the men are gone. What do you make of that, Jack?

"Well," said Jack Karaquazian after some considerable thought, "I guess it means that luck is luck. That's all."

"I guess so," said Mr Oakenhurst. "Well, goodnight, Jack."

Next morning they played a game of *Joli Jean* before breakfast and talked about going up to the Frees.)

He had the dream again, exactly as before, but this time he stepped into the limo.

(Jack Karaquazian kept a room above the main casino of the Terminal Café. You could feel the zee coming up through the floor. The room was filled with shadows and flames, ragged holes of verdigris and kidney. "It's home," he had said.)

3. ERASE UNA VEZ EN LA OUESTE

'I HAD A dream,' says Precious Mary as she moves against Sam Oakenhurst's arm. 'I dreamed I was lying in this field of silver poppies looking up at the moon. I stretched my arms and legs wide and the Moon Goddess smiled. She had a wonderful round pale oriental face like a Buddha. Is that a Buddhess, Sam? And she came down from the midnight blue and pursed her silver lips and she sucked my pussy, Sam, like nobody but you.' She grins and laughs and slaps at him in his flattered embarrassment.

They had been here at Ambry's for almost a month. Precious Mary was on her way to join a closed order in Laredo. She collected mosquitoes and her little clear envelopes were full of the different types, including the hybrids. Her pride was a great dragon mosquito, rainbow carapace over two inches long, able to drain a small rodent dry of blood in less than a minute. 'They thought it carried A,' she said. 'But now they ain't so sure.'

She had cornrows beaded with tiny precious stones – emeralds, rubies, sapphires, diamonds – large green eyes, a refined Watutsi face. She wore a silk shift which swam on the blackness of her skin like milk over marble. Her head, she said, was worth a million guineas, but her body was priceless. She lived, like everyone in De Quincey, at Ambry's big Gothic timber house just by the jetty which jutted over the flat sheen of a lake revealed below the surrounding yellow and black mist. The lake was never entirely at rest. Shapes just under the surface were mysterious and alarming. Every once in a while a tiny spot of colour would float by. 'They find big ones out there and milk them,' she said. 'There's nothing but rigs once you get twenty kays over that horizon.' She pointed to the north. 'Do you believe in God, Sam?'

Mr Oakenhurst admitted that he did.

'You believe in a just God, Sam?'

'I believe God deals you a fair hand.' He became thoughtful. 'What you do with it after that is a question of luck and judgement both. And luck is what other people are making of *their* hands. It's a complicated game, it seems to me, Mary. Only a few of us are willing to accept the kind of odds it offers. But what else can you do? This is reality, I think. I look at the game. I work out the odds. And then I decide if I want to play or not. I hope I'm doing no more or less with my mind and time than God expects of me.'

'You're crazy,' she said.

That was the last Sam Oakenhurst and Precious Mary ever spoke of religion.

In Milton he had lost his horse to a tall pile broker from Natchez who had proved to be so much better than the table's other partners that Mr Oakenhurst suspected him of being a secret professional. But he had played a fair game. The broker let Sam take his place on the coach to De Quincey. That trip to the lake shore had been Mr Oakenhurst's first real experience of the practical realities of the Free States, where whites were supposed to be his equals. He found it awkward to be travelling in a horse-drawn coach with a black man driving and a white man riding inside. On the seat across from him the "blanco" showed no similar embarrassment and chatted amiably on the tandem subjects of fluke attractors and the availability of *piles noires*. Mr Oakenhurst did his best to converse without seeming to condescend, but he was still suffering from a strong desire to stare in wonder at this educated and self-confident whitey much as one would regard a clever circus animal. His name was Peewee Wilson and he had owned property up in Haute County, he said, until it had popped one morning, all of a piece, and left him "wiv a weird damned hole coloured like dirty bottly-glass an' radiatin' coldness so damned bad ah'd felt mahse'f chillered to mah soul." He had moved his wife and kids to his sister in San Diego and was on his way to join them. He had never been to Biloxi ("Ah have not chosered vat pilgrimage, sah, as yet.") but was eager to hear Mr Oakenhurst's account of it and the *jugador* loved to tell a tale.

So the time had passed pleasantly enough between Milton and De Quincey. Peewee informed Mr Oakenhurst about the famous Colossus of Tarzana, one of the wonders of their new world – a huge figure some two hundred feet high and apparently consisting of living flame which gave off a soft heat filling most observers with a sense of calm and well-being. A tent town had grown around the feet of the Colossus, populated by those who had become hooked on the phenomenon's influence.

(Let us have the body, the *machinoix* would demand. We need it for our science. Its soul has dissipated. What use is it to you? But Sam Oakenhurst would refuse to give it up. He would take it with him all the way to the Fault and pitch it in. The *machinoix* would not be offended. He was of their number. He could do no wrong, save betray another of their own.)

Mr Oakenhurst waded through the shallow mud of the lake shore. There seemed no end to it. At present the flat, troubled liquid reflected nothing, but every so often a shape threatened to break through the surface. The clouds had become a solid monochrome grey. Once in a while a long thread of bright scarlet would rise from below the horizon and give the sky a lizard's lick. Mr Oakenhurst ran secret fingers over his most intimate scars. His longing for the past was like physical hunger. A madness. He prayed for a vessel to rescue him.

Mr Oakenhurst walked through the mud. Sometimes his legs would begin to tremble, threatening to give out completely, and he would panic, turning slowly to look back at Ambry's and the long, dark jetty whose far point penetrated the mist.

'Darling.' Precious Mary led him home on these occasions.

'Darling, Sam.'

Sam Oakenhurst decided that if he stayed another week he would take it as a sign and let New Orleans call him back. He shivered. He had made no real decision at all. He glared at the grey water. The sky, he thought, had turned the colour of rotten honey.

4. LA MUERTE TERRIO UN PRECIO

PRECIOUS MARY WAS not impatient to leave. She had discovered an interest in the vegetable garden and, with another woman called Bellpaïs, was planting in the assumption there would be some kind of new season. The garden lay behind the house, where it was most sheltered. Mary complained about the lack of sunlight, the clouds of dust which swam forever out of the north. 'It seems like it's the same clouds keep coming around,' she said. 'Like everything's on repeat.'

'Hope not,' said Sam Oakenhurst, thinking of New Orleans. As a child he had played his favourite records until the phonograph's machinery had started to show the strain. Gradually the voices grew sluggish and the music became a mixture of whines and groans until finally the records brought only depression, a sense of loss, a distorted memory of harmony and resolution. He sometimes thought the whole world was running down in a series of ever-widening, steadily dissipating circles. 'I cannot believe that one thing cancels out another,' he admitted to Precious Mary.

'It's like a roof.' She looked at the sky. 'Like a cave. We could be underground, Sam. Living on the innards of the world.'

Across the surface of measureless grey, past the end of their jetty, a couple of spots of colour floated. The spots moved as if with purpose but both Mr Oakenhurst and Precious Mary knew they drifted more or less at random around the perimeter of the lake, carrying with them an assortment of organic flotsam. Bones, feathers, twigs, tiny corpses made a lattice through which gleamed the dull gold and silver of the colour, blank round eyes staring out from a void. The colour seemed like a magnet to certain vegetable and animal matter. Other material it repulsed violently, not always predictably.

(We are the whole within the whole, Sam. Your ancestors knew that. And we are unique.)

'I reckon Jack Karaquazian struck colour up on the Trace,' mused Sam Oakenhurst. 'But something happened that didn't suit him. What the hell is that, Mary?' He pointed out over the lake. Through the twilight a slow bulky shape was emerging. At first the *jugador* thought it might be the tapering head of a large whale. Then as it came nearer he realized it was not a living creature at all but a ramshackle vessel, shadowing the shore, a great broad raft about ninety by ninety, on which was built a floating shanty-town, a mélange of dull-coloured shacks, tents, barrels and lean-tos. In the middle of this makeshift floating fortress stood a substantial wooden keep with a flat roof where other tents and packing-case houses had been erected so that the whole had the appearance of an untidy ziggurat made of animal hides, old tapestries, painted canvases, upholstery and miscellaneous pieces of broken furniture.

Observing what distinguished this floating junkpile, Precious Mary said: 'Ain't that queer, Sam. No metal, not much plastic . . . '

'And there's why.' Sam showed her the dull gleam of colour spilling up from under the raft's edges. 'She's moving on a big spot. She's built to cover it. You saw it. That kind of colour won't take anything much that's non-organic. It's kind of like anti-electricity. They haven't figured any real way of conducting the stuff. It can't be refined or mined. It moves all the time so it's never claimed. I guess these types have found the only use there is for it. Ahoy!'

5. MUCHOS GRACIAS, MON AMOUR

THE IDEA OF being trapped on a raft which would put the Texas Waters between him and New Orleans was immensely attractive to Mr Oakenhurst just then. There was no way of stopping the spot, only of slowing it down with metal lures floated out from the shore on lines. As soon as the goods had been thrown aboard, he jumped from the jetty to the slow-moving deck, shook hands with Captain Roy Ornate, master of *The Whole Hog*, and thanked him for the opportunity to take passage with him. He did not bother to announce his trade.

He had been allowed to carry no arms aboard *The Whole Hog*, no razor, no metal of any kind except alumite, and so glad was he to be on his way that he had accepted the terms, leaving his gold, his *piles noires*, his slender Nissan 404 and all other metal goods with Precious Mary. She had loaded the raft with so much collateral in the form of fresh provisions that she had put him in excellent credit with Captain Ornate. The bandy-legged pig-faced upriver rafter had lost his original trade to the Colorado Gap. 'Took the river and half the State with it. You can still see the spray fifty kays away.' He was a cheerful man who apologized for his rules. His methods were the only practical ones for the service he offered, which was, he admitted, not much. 'Still, chances are this spot'll carry us round to Waco and you're halfway to Phoenix, or wherever it is you're heading, mister. You won't be old when you get there, but I can't guarantee how long it will take . . .

'You won't be bored, either, mister. There's a couple of *jugaderos* in the main saloon glad to make room for another. This is an easy vessel, Mr Oakenhurst, and I hope you'll find her comfortable. She's rough and ready, I'll grant, but we have no power weapons aboard and hardly any violence, for I don't tolerate trouble. Those who make it I punish harshly.'

'A man of my own principles, captain,' said Sam Oakenhurst, conscious of the loss of his fancy links. His shirt was heavier on the wrists, the cuffs now decorated with antique Mickey and Minnie Mouse figures his daughter had given him for his twenty-fifth birthday, almost exactly forty-four seasons ago, and which he had never expected to wear in public. Now that the need had arisen he welcomed it. Wearing the links felt like some sort of confirmation. Serdia and Ona had died together on the Hattiesburg Roar, trying to escape an army of half-wild blankeys released by a shiver from the nearby pens. He had been in Memphis, running a powered game for Peabody and his fellow barons who could command all the necessary colour. He had been unable to resist.

Mr Oakenhurst had never known the detailed circumstances of his wife's and daughter's deaths and time had put that particular pain behind him. He sensed some link between his grief and his taste for *machinoix* torments. He had never, after all, thought to blame himself for the deaths. They had wanted to remain in Hattiesburg where everyone agreed it felt pretty stable. For a while he had wished he could die, too, that was all. Maybe he felt guilty for not following them.

He let Roy Ornate's little kiddikin lead him up the rickety outside staircase to his room. The urge to live was very strong in Sam Oakenhurst and not quite equalled by an urge for pain which he only barely governed these days. With relief he watched the jetty and the Ambry House slip away behind, but the look he turned on the kiddikin, even as the skinny white kid glowingly accepted a whole guinea bill for his trouble, was one of vicious and unjust hatred.

Sam Oakenhurst came out of his room and looked down at the smoking stoves and basket fires of a floating slum. Roy Ornate was waiting at the bottom of the stairs. 'Why do these people live in such squalor, captain, when, on land, they have a better chance of dignity?' Were they all power addicts?

Captain Ornate cleared his throat. 'If you're trying to fathom the pilgrims, Mr Oakenhurst, you'll have poor luck. If you're dining this evening, I'd welcome your company.' He spoke with no great enthusiasm. Sam Oakenhurst guessed that Roy Ornate was not really his own man and that there was another power aboard *The Whole Hog* greater than the master.

6. MI BUENA SUERTE

THE SALOON WAS on the lower floor, a big, bright room full of old-fashioned wooden Kenya-lamps and carved candelabra. On the other side of the archway, in relative gloom, five people were absorbed in a complex game of *Hunt the Moth*, their eyes golden with concentration as they fanned their acoustic hands with practised pseudo-electronic signals, listening intensely to the subsonics.

(In times like these, when hope fades and our expectations of reality become uncertain, people develop a keen interest in an afterlife, she said. She sang to him in a language he did not know. He begged her to translate. "*We are trapped in the glare of their headlights*," she said.)

Elsewhere in the saloon men and women in couples or groups sat together drinking and talking, but it was clear that pains were taken not to disturb the five gamblers as they strove to simulate the serial-linking, the empathetic convolutions, the exquisite arabesques of the powered original.

Looking again at the *jugaderos*, Sam Oakenhurst knew at once who was the real master of *The Whole Hog*. Fat body pulsing, he or she sat facing the room. The head, to one side, was hidden by a queerly shaped mask and old dust seemed to fall from its folds. The pale eyes glittered like over-polished diamonds. The top of the creature's head was scarred and pitted, as if by fire, and a few tufts of grey-black hair sprouted here and there, while a little multicoloured bead curtain, some bizarre *chadurrah*, hung from the bottom edge of its mask, obscuring the jaw. The only flesh visible was the ruined crown and a pair of large, white hands which also bore the grey scars of fire and sat poised on their tips like obscene tarantulas, pale with menace.

The masked figure was, on its right, flanked by a light-skinned, but otherwise handsome, half-caste woman with greased black ringlets and hard Irish eyes. Her name was Sister Honesty Marvell. She was *persona non grata* at the Terminal, for taking out an amateur in a massive psychic gambit which even broke the high limits Boudreaux Ramsadeen set for the professionals. When he had made her go for good she had sworn she would return and the second Boudreaux saw her would be the second he died.

(*En la playa, amigo*, replied Amos Gallibasta when Sam Oakenhurst found him again and asked how he was. The thin giant had grinned, death's triumph, and snapped his huge fingers. *En la playa terminante, eh? Joli blanc! Joli blanc!* He had no similar desire to return to New Orleans. The very breathing of the word "*machinoix*" sent him into uncontrollable fits of vomiting.)

Next to Sister Honesty sat Carly O'Dowd. Mr Oakenhurst also knew her. Mrs O'Dowd sported a man's suit in the Andalusian style and as always bore an air of disdainful self-sufficiency. Her Moorish good looks reminded Mr Oakenhurst of some legendary toreador. He tipped his hat when she looked up but she could not see beyond her strategies. The two players at the other side of the *enmascaro* were people Sam Oakenhurst recognized. He could name only one. Popper Hendricks, sagging with the weight of a thousand indulgences, had once been a famous zeestar in the days when touring was still possible, when the population was considerably larger, and when records were still being made. Fifty percent at least of the white minority had fled north or west after the Fault's effects began to be felt. Even many middle-class people had preferred to go west into the Frees to take their chances on equal terms with the whites, but mostly got caught by the quakes. Hendricks had the sybaritic, bloated look of a heavy oper. The other man, with his huge square head, had the features of an Aztec god. Even his body seemed made of granite. He moved now, slowly. It was as if ten years went by. Mr Oakenhurst found the Indian disturbing but the masked man at the centre of the game horrified him.

In shape the mask resembled a map of the old US. Each State, cut out of an alumite can, had been soldered to the next. Washington bore the distinctive logo of Folger's Coffee, Texas offered RC Cola and Pennsylvania advertised EXXON oil. From the patchwork of pseudo-metal were suspended the heavy beads, veiling a suggestion of red, wet lips, skin as burned and scarred as the hands and skull.

Mr Oakenhurst turned his back on the table to order a Jax from the bartender, a round-faced whitey who proved unduly surly. To be civil, Sam

Oakenhurst asked, 'What's your name, boy?'

'Burt,' said the whitey curtly. 'You want another beer, mister?'

Mr Oakenhurst kept his own council. After all, he could soon be facing much more of this behaviour in the Free States and he had best get used to it. He intended to relax. For the first time since he had left the Terminal he no longer depended upon his own will. Whatever problems he found upon the raft, he thought, must seem minor. He was glad there were no power weapons permitted, though he missed the comfort of his Nissan.

From the shadows in the back of the big room came a sudden wheeze, a whine, and an accordion began to play *Pierrot, Pierrot, le monde est fou.* Some of the passengers swayed to the old tune, singing the poet Armangal's sad, ironic words. *Le monde est fou, my carazon d'or. Le monde est fou, el mundo c'est moi!*

A voice from the table, soft and threatening, said 'Play something else, dear.'

The tune changed almost instantly to *Two-Step de Bayou Teche* and a few of the couples got up to dance.

The masked man returned his attention to the game.

7. DESAFIO

'MR MINCT AND me came aboard at Carthage,' said Carly O'Dowd. She referred to the masked man, still playing. 'Nice to see you, Sam.'

'And you, Carly. How's the game?'

'Worth your time, if you're interested.' She was taking a break and joined Captain Ornate and Mr Oakenhurst at their table. 'Some rough edges you could smooth out.' She reached for his long right hand and drew it to her mouth. 'Lucky, Sam?' She kissed the tip of his index finger.

'Maybe,' he said. 'I don't know.'

Roy Ornate had grown expansive on his big pipe of ope. His cheeks glowed, his eyes bulged with bonhomie. 'I can think of no better pleasure than swinging your feet over the edge of the Abyss and contemplating the damnation of the entire universe,' he confided. 'Ha, ha, Mr Oakenhurst. You'll do!' His confidences became increasingly mysterious. 'What a thrill, eh? To take the whole damned vessel to the edge – cargo, crew and passengers – and hang upon the lip of some hellish niagara – every day gambling the same stake against a thousand new disasters – all the devil's winning hands – and every day carry back from the brink – what? Playing dice with God and not a damned thing any of you fellows can do about it. I know the only man good enough to stop this planet going the way of the rest and that's Paul Minct, and he won't do it. I would, but I can't. And that, sir, should permit me a few privileges . . . '

Neither Mr Oakenhurst nor Mrs O'Dowd could follow his reasoning.

'You have a great admiration for this Mr Minct,' said Sam Oakenhurst.

'He's my hero,' admitted Captain Ornate with a confiding gesture.

Now the Indian Carly O'Dowd had identified as Rodrigo Heat divorced himself from the game and moved heavily over the floor to stand beside an empty chair next to Captain Ornate.

Sam Oakenhurst received the impression that the masked man had sent Heat to him. The Indian's massive head inclined towards the seat but his eyes were on Carly O'Dowd. 'You have a high price, lady, but that don't scare me.'

Sam Oakenhurst knew only one way of responding to such boorishness and his words were out before he had properly calculated the situation. He said evenly that if Mr Heat pursued that thread of conversation he would be obliged to invite the Indian outside to the place familiarly known as – and here he looked to Captain Ornate to tell him the name again . . .

'Bloody Glade,' said Roy Ornate, still benign. 'But we discourage its use. This M&E is better than my own.' He was trying a mixture, he said, recommended by Paul Minct. He displayed a garish package: *Meng & Ecker's Brandy Flake*.

'Bloody Glade,' said Mr Oakenhurst, 'and settle the matter alla gentilhombres.'

Whereupon Mr Heat laughed open-mouthed and asked what was wrong with his conversation.

Understanding, now, that he was being provoked, Sam Oakenhurst could only continue. His honour gave him no choice. 'It demeans a lady,' he explained.

Mr Heat continued to laugh and asked where the lady in question happened to be, which led to a silence falling in the room, since Mr Oakenhurst's principles, if not his courage, were shared by the majority of the floor's *diamentes brutos*.

'Very well,' said Mr Oakenhurst after a moment. 'I will meet you in the usual circumstances,' and as if he had settled some minor matter he turned back to signal the surly whitey for more drinks and enquire of Carly O'Dowd how her brother was doing in the Border Army. 'Ain't they romantic, Carly? I heard they're winning big new tracts of restabilized up above Kansas.'

'You're a man after my own heart, sir,' suddenly says Captain Ornate, puffing on his churchwarden's. 'Would you care for a dip from my special mixture?' He reached into his coat.

'Give him my Meng & Ecker's, Captain Ornate.'

Paul Minct's cruel voice chilled the house into irredeemable silence.

'Give Mr Oakenhurst a dip of my own ope and ask him if, at his convenience, he would come to join me later for a chat. It's rare to meet an equal, these days. One grows so starved of intellectual cut and thrust.'

8. GRACIAS NADA MAS

'CABALLERO AND MUKHAMIR, you may be, Mr Oakenhurst, of the highest principles and most excellent suba', but Captain Ornate allows no desafio aboard *The Whole Hog* and so your affair must be abandoned until such time you are both ashore. Those are Captain Ornate's rules.' Paul Minct speaks with a certain weariness.

Sam Oakenhurst now understands that he has been tested and that his honour is not at issue. He shrugs the matter off.

They sit together in the snug in the back shadows, a candle burning on the table giving unsteady life to Paul Minct's geographic mask.

Mr Oakenhurst finds himself reading the fragments of words – ELMONTE, OLA, AXWELL HOU, CRISCO, CASTRO, ONT MAID, OHNSONS WAX and others – remembering his childhood when such brands were vital and had complex and casual meaning to everyone. The world's realities changed, he thinks, long before the advent of the Fault. The Fault is perhaps the result of that change, not the cause. He cannot give his entire attention to Paul Minct's words. The man disturbs and fascinates him. He gathers Paul Minct respects him, which is why he has been taken aside like this and not admonished in public, and he is relieved. But he knows he could never trust the *enmascaro*. Paul Minct could change his mood at a moment's notice and casually kill him. Sam Oakenhurst is close to admitting he made a mistake. He should have found the nerve to stick it out at Ambry's until the stern-wheeler came by. His self-disgust only serves to fuel his discomfort. He wishes the *enmascaro* would leave him alone, but already guesses Mr Minct plans somehow to use him.

(Paul Minct had been a blankey-chaser in the old days, Carly O'Dowd said. Mr Minct had gone after bounty boys, always willing to take a dead-or-alive. One day he had crossed the big bridge into Louisiana with six red scalps on his belt, all that was mortal of the Kennedy pack which ran wild for a while up near Texarcana and announced they'd founded a "white republic". Captain Ornate retired. Mrs O'Dowd called for more drinks. 'Paul Minct's a man who gets what or who he wants, one way or another,' she said. 'He was Peabody's main chaser. He hates whiteys with a passion and would wipe them all out if he could. He loathes them so bad some of us think maybe he's a blankey himself, or anyway a breed, who was fortunate enough to be burned in a fire – like the blankey who went to hell, got burned black and thought he'd gotten to heaven! Loosen up, Sam. Nothing much ever happens on *The Whole Hog*.')

'I was in a bad fire or two in my time, Mr Oakenhurst.' Paul Minct fingers the tufts of hair on his skull. 'You should hear my wife complain. But someone has to bring home the bacon. We're the chaps who have to get out there in the world, eh? Nobody will do it for us. We are never allowed nor encouraged to the best. That's the shame of it. We must seek the best for ourselves. It is what drives us, I suspect. Almost secretly. Will you be joining our little pasatiempo? You'd be very welcome.'

When Mr Oakenhurst accepts the veiled order with the same grace with which it is given, one of Paul Minct's unsightly hands reaches into his and welcomes him to the school.

('He told me he had been in and out of the Fault five times. He says he knows secret trails which only he had the courage to discover. It is true that in the main he has no fear.'

'Does he fear anything, Carly?'

'Something. I don't know. Is there a *jugador* brave enough to find out?')

Paul Minct offers his own pouch. 'A cut above the Brandy Flake. It's M&E's Number Three. They'll try to tell you it's extinct, but they're still making it down in Mexico.'

Against his better judgement, Sam Oakenhurst fills his long-stemmed pipe.

'Señor Heat is an old colleague of mine.' Paul Minct receives the ope again and puts it away. 'Volatile and blunt, as you know, and a little uncouth, but one of the world's great people. He discovered the factory. The last Meng & Ecker's is in a place called *Wadi-al-Hara*, the River of Stones, in Arabic. The Indian dialects give it a similar name. Guadalajara, the Spanish say. Mr Heat made his second fortune bringing it back. This stuff's what the old days were about, Mr Oakenhurst. Not much of a vice compared to some we hear of. That's what I remind my wife. She's overly worried. My health. That's women for you, isn't it? My health, as a matter of fact, has never been better. But there you are. Now, Mr Oakenhurst, I know your credentials and I must say I'm impressed. How would you like to come in on a small venture I'm organizing?'

'Well, sir,' says Sam Oakenhurst. 'I guess it depends on the game.'

'Very good, Mr Oakenhurst. I take your point. This is in the nature of an exploratory expedition. But only the likes of us can even contemplate the kind of expedition I have in mind. Only a trained *jugador* has the patience, the experience and the gumption for it. And Mrs O'Dowd says you're one of the best. Played evens with Jack Karaquazian.'

'Once,' agrees Sam Oakenhurst.

'Quite enough for me, sir. I'm recruiting, Mr Oakenhurst, a few brave souls. Outstanding individuals who will join an expedition to accompany me into the Biloxi Fault.'

Sam Oakenhurst has a taste for pain but not for death. He resolves to play along with this madman whose pale unblinking eye awaits his acceptance, but if the time comes he will never go with him. That would be suicide. He will jump off the raft the first moment they sight land and put this fresh lunacy behind him.

He shakes Paul Minct's hand.

9. ESCUDO D'ORO

MR SAM OAKENHURST did not immediately join the game but claiming weariness retired early and stood on the little landing outside his door taking the ill-smelling air and staring over the dark water. No light escaped the spot on which they rode, but through the dirty cloud a little moonlight fell, making the water sinister with half-seen shapes.

In seeking to avoid the *machinoix* temptations Mr Oakenhurst had put himself into an equally unwelcome predicament. Paul Minct had a horrible authority and, taken unawares, Sam Oakenhurst had been unable to resist it.

Tomorrow he would test Mr Minct's metal, if he could, in that acoustic game they played, and get some notion of the man's resonances. He had not been manipulated so expertly since he was fourteen. He believed Paul Minct to be a charlatan, probably crazy, perhaps even messianic in some way. Frequently a secret faith, too insane to risk upon the air, fuelled such aggressive solipsism. The man appeared to have the tastes of a Torquemada and the savage appetites of a European warlord. Always a strong hand, thought Mr Oakenhurst. His lies would therefore be complicated and self-convincing. Mr Oakenhurst had lived for months at a time beside the Fault and knew it well. He had seen a woman from Jackson walk in at the semi-permanent section known as The Custard Bowl and disintegrate, bawling for help, as soon as she reached the so-called East Wall, a turbulent tower sometimes emerging within the Bowl, usually coloured deep red and black. On another occasion he had held a rope for Cab Ras, the famous daredevil, as he went in through the glistening organic scarlet of Ketchup Cave. He had vanished. The rope had fallen to the surface as if cut and Ras was gone for good. Everything was consumed by the Biloxi Fault. Was Paul Minct merely reluctant to die alone?

Mr Oakenhurst did not doubt the *enmascaro*'s courage or ferocity, the man's murderous determination, but could not fathom Paul Minct's objectives. Perhaps Mr Minct had actually convinced himself that he could survive the Fault, and others with him. It was not a belief Mr Oakenhurst wished to put to the test. Yet, for all his evident insanity, the man continued to terrify Sam

Oakenhurst who wondered if Paul Minct already had his measure, as he did not have Mr Minct's. A game would answer most of his questions. He was no Jack Karaquazian, but he had held his own with the rest.

Most of the lights were now extinguished to conform with Captain Ornate's tough curfew, enforced by a gang of breed blankeys under their own vicious leaders.

The raft rocked a little in the water and a powerful shaft of moonlight broke through full on *The Whole Hog* as if God for a moment had turned his undivided attention on them. A voice came up to him out of the shadows. 'Time for bed, Sam?'

'Good evening, Carly.' Sam Oakenhurst wanted to learn all she knew of Paul Minct. 'I've a bottle of Arkwright's I know you'll taste.'

Carly O'Dowd had little more real information. She remembered a story that Paul Minct's hatred of whites could be relatively recent, following a fire started by his own relatives from Baton Rouge. But there was a different story of how Paul Minct had been a member of the Golala sect which believed death by fire was a guarantee of heaven. She asked Sam if he believed in an afterlife.

'I have a hunch your soul has a home to go to.' That was all Sam Oakenhurst would say on the matter, but when she asked if he believed God dealt everyone a square hand, he shook his head. He had thought about that lately, he said. He had to admit that God's dealing sometimes seemed a little uneven.

'But I don't think he plays dice, Carly. He plays a hand of poker against the devil and some of us believe it's our job to help him. Some of us even do a little bit about it.' He shrugged.

'Jesus,' said Carly O'Dowd. 'I never heard anyone describe gambling as a moral duty before. Ain't this the end of everything, Sam? Ain't it over for us?'

'Maybe,' said Sam Oakenhurst, 'but I got a feeling it evens out. Like luck, you know.'

Carly O'Dowd took a long pull on the pipe and sipped her winking Arkwright's.

'*Quid pro quo*,' said Mr Oakenhurst.

'*Allez, los tigres*,' she sang softly. '*Ma bebé sans merci, il est un majo sin comparé. O, bebé, you bon surprise, you darling ease*.'

In the morning she insisted he come to the open window to look over the ragged shanty town, towards the east where the cloud had cleared and red sunlight rose in broad rays from the watery horizon, staining the whole lake a lively ruby. Against this redness a single black outline moved.

'It's coming closer.' Sam Oakenhurst squinted to improve his focus. 'It's a big heron, Carly.' He shivered. He took her slight body to his. 'Bigger.'

It was an aircraft. A beautiful white flying boat with six pairs of wing-mounted roaring engines and whistling airscrews, moving to make a preliminary pass at the water, intending to land. The flying boat was turned a sudden, subtle pink by the sun.

Everyone on the raft was up and out in haste to see the splendid craft. Pilgrims and *jugaderos* all wondered at the wealth it took to squander so much colour upon an antique conceit.

And then, throttling down to a confident thud, the flying boat came to settle, light as a gull, upon the surface. The big engines fell silent. Water lapped at her ivory hull. Almost at once a door above the lower wing opened and a figure stepped out, dragging a small inflatable. The grey rubber boat blended with the leaden waters as black and yellow cloud drew itself round the sun like a cloak. Through the gloom of the new day the figure began to row, calling out in a melodious, ringing voice; 'Ahoy, the raft! Is this *The Whole Hog* and Captain Roy Ornate?'

Just up from his quarters in his Monday whites and weak-kneed with wonderment, Captain Ornate could barely lift his megaphone to utter an unsteady; 'I am Captain Roy Ornate, master of *The Whole Hog*. Be warned that we accept no metal. Who calls the ship?'

This was a formal exchange, as between river captains. The rower replied. 'Mrs Rose von Bek, lately out of Guadalajara with a package for Mr Paul Minct. Is Mr Minct aboard, sir?'

The weight of the curious crowd began to tilt the raft dramatically. The shanty dwellers were set upon by the blankeys, led by a plague-pocked overseer, and beaten back into order. To add to their humiliation they were forced into their windowless dwellings, denied any further part of the miracle.

'Mr Minct is one of our passengers,' agreed Roy Ornate, his own curiosity undisguised. 'What's the nature of your goods, ma'am?'

Before the rower could answer, Paul Minct, massively fat, his body wrapped in lengths of multicoloured velvet, rolled up to Captain Ornate's side to stand stroking his beaded veil as another might stroke a beard. He took the megaphone from the grateful master and spoke in a wet, amplified soprano. 'So you found me at last. Is that my M&E come up from Mexico, dear?'

Mr Oakenhurst began to imagine himself back in time, taking part in one of the interactive adventure ads of his childhood. Was this, after all, no more than some misremembered bite?

Any answer Mrs von Bek might have made was drowned by six bellowing engines as the flying boat began to taxi out over the endless grey lake and, with a parting shriek, vanished into the air.

The inflatable came up against embarking-steps thick with mould. A slim, athletic woman stepped aboard, her features disguised by a cowl on her cape which fell in blue-green folds almost to the deck. Maybe a white woman. She had a small oilskin package in her left hand.

By now Mr Oakenhurst and Mrs O'Dowd, fully dressed, stood on the landing listening to the silence returning.

'I'm much obliged, ma'am.' Paul Minct reached for his package. 'One would have to be Scrooge himself to begrudge that extra little bit it takes to get your M&E delivered.' He turned, his mask on one side, as if in apology to Sam Oakenhurst. 'I'll admit it's a terrible extravagance of mine. You should hear my wife on the subject.'

Had he arranged this whole charade merely to demonstrate his power and wealth?

The woman pushed her cowl back to reveal a most wonderful dark golden pink skin, washed with the faintest browns and greens, some kind of sensitive North African features, reminding Mr Oakenhurst of those aquiline Berbers from the deep Maghribi desert. Her auburn hair reflected the colour of her cloak and her lips were a startling scarlet, as if they bled. She was as tall as Sam Oakenhurst. Her extraordinary grace fascinated him. He had never seen movement like it. He found himself staring at her, even as she took Paul Minct's arm and made her way to the main saloon.

'What would you call that colour skin?' murmured Carly O'Dowd.

10. LOS BELLES DU CANADA

'I TASTED A thousand scales to reach this place.' Mrs von Bek had been joined at her table by Sister Honesty Marvell, Mrs O'Dowd and Rodrigo Heat, but she kept a seat beside her empty and this she now offered to Mr Oakenhurst who bowed, brushed back his tails and wished her good morning as he sat down beside her. He wondered why she seemed familiar. At close quarters the greenish blush of her hands, the pink-gold of her cheeks had a quality which made all other flesh seem unnatural. He had never before felt such strong emotion in the presence of beauty.

In amused recognition of his admiration, she smiled. Clearly, she was also curious about him. 'You are of the *jugadiste* persuasion, Mr Oakenhurst?'

'I make a small living from my good fortune, ma'am.' Had he ever felt as he did now, at the centre of a concert while the music achieved some ecstatic moment? Was he looking on the true face of his lady, his luck? Where would she take him? Home?

He realized to his alarm that he was on the verge of weeping.

'Well, Mr Oakenhurst,' Mrs von Bek continued, 'you would know a flat game, I hope, if one turned up for you. And *Granny's Claw*? Is that still played in these parts?'

'Not to my knowledge, ma'am.'

I need an ally, she said in an urgent signal, which marked her as his peer. Paul Minct is my mortal enemy and will destroy me if he recognizes me. Will you help?

He returned her signal. At your service, Mrs von Bek.

No sworn *jugador* could have refused her. Their mutual code demanded instant compliance. Only in extreme need did one of his kind thus address a peer. But he would have helped her anyway. He was entirely infatuated with her. He began to wonder what other allies, and of what calibre, he might find here. Did fear or some profound sense of loyalty bind Rodrigo Heat to Paul Minct? Carly O'Dowd, given to sudden swings of affection, would be unreliable at best. Roy Ornate was also Paul Minct's man. Sister Honesty Marvell might side with them, if only out of an habitual need to destroy potential rivals. Meanwhile, Mr Oakenhurst would have to follow Mrs von Bek's lead until she told him to do otherwise.

Her fingers dropped from the grey-green pearls and coral at her throat while his own hands lost interest in his links. Their secret exchange was for a moment at an end.

It had been seven years – twenty-eight seasons by current reckoning – since Mr Oakenhurst had been in a similar situation and that had been the start of his friendship with Jack Karaquazian. On this occasion, however, the intellectual thrill, the thrill of the big risk, was coupled with his overwhelming desire for her given extra edge by his own anxious guess that perhaps she was at least a little attracted to him. Even the chemistry with Serdia had not been so strong. The sensation attacked his mind as well as his flesh while the cool part of him, the trained *jugador*, was taking account of this wonderful return of feelings he had thought lost for ever, and considering new odds.

'Do you think it will be long before we reach the Frees, Mr Ornate?' She looked up as the skipper returned with a tray on which stood an oak cafetière and some delicate rosewood cups. 'Here you go, ma'am, here you go. I fixed it myself. You can't trust these blankeys to fix good coffee.' The man was blushing like a rat on a hot spot, oblivious of the open derision on Rodrigo Heat's old-fashioned head.

Mr Oakenhurst relaxed his body and settled into his chair. Paul Minct would make his entrance at any moment.

11. LAS BON TEMPS ARRIVÉE

'MR OAKENHURST INFORMS me that you might be willing to come in on our special play, Mrs von Bek.' Paul Minct brushed dust from his mask. One of his pale eyes peered from the ragged hole in the Rocky Mountains where

Quaker marked Colorado. It was as if he brushed a tear.

After an exhausting week-long game in which the three of them had emerged equals in all but specific skills and appetites, Paul Minct, Rose von Bek and Sam Oakenhurst believed they had learned almost everything they would ever know about one another. All were prepared, in appropriate circumstances, to risk everything on the flick of a sensor, the turn of a card, an instinctive snap judgement.

Paul Minct's topical half-face glittered in the flamelight and behind his whispering curtain of beads his ruined lips twisted in an involuntary grin, as if flesh remembered pain his mind refused.

Sam Oakenhurst cursed his own quickened blood, the vast emotions he seemed to be riding like a vaquero on a runaway bronc, barely able to haul hard enough on the reins to avoid the worst disasters as they approached.

'I take it you are considering some unusually high stakes, Mr Minct.' Her voice had grown warmer, more musical, like a well practised instrument. She was all of a piece, thought Sam Oakenhurst admiringly, a perfect disguise. There was, however, no evidence that Paul Minct had been deceived by either of them.

The week's play had left the Rose and Sam Oakenhurst uncertain lovers, but it was of no interest to Paul Minct how they celebrated their alliance. He appeared to be under the impression that a more reckless Rose von Bek had persuaded Mr Oakenhurst to let her join him.

'Here's my say in the matter,' declared Sam Oakenhurst, to open the bidding. 'Your luck and mine, Paul Minct. Even shares. Try it once? Double our luck or double our damnation, eh?'

Sam Oakenhurst knew Mr Minct viewed treachery as a legitimate instrument of policy and that nothing he offered would guarantee Mr Minct's consistency. But he was hoping to appeal to Paul Minct's gambler's soul, to whet his appetite for melodrama and catch him, if possible, in a twist or two before the main game began. At present it was the only strategy he could pursue without much chance of detection.

'You'll stake your life on this, Mr Oakenhurst?'

'If you'll give us some idea of the odds and the winnings, sir.'

'Good odds, limitless reward. My word on it. And your word, Mr Oakenhurst. How do you value it?'

'I value my word above my life, sir. In these troubled times a *jugador* has nothing but honour. I will need to know a little more before I stake my honour. So I'll fold for the moment. Save to say this, sir – you play an honest game and so will I.'

'And you, Mrs von Bek?' Paul Minct made an old-fashioned bow. 'Do you also offer an honest game?'

'I have played no other up to now, Mr Minct. I'll throw in all I have, if the prize suits me. We can triple our luck, if you like. We all have some idea of the size of the stakes, I think. But not the size of the *bonanza*. Whatever it shall be, I'll put in my full third and take out my full third – or any fraction decided by any future numbers.'

'You can't say fairer than that, ma'am. Very well, Mr Oakenhurst. We have another pard.'

Sam Oakenhurst could not fathom her style, but he recognized that she was a peerless *mukhamir*. It was as if she had trained in the very heart of Africa. She was his superior in everything but low cunning, that instinctive talent for self-preservation which had proven so useful to him and which had resulted in his becoming kin to the *machinoix*, rather than their prey. He had never underestimated this useful flaw in his character. But now it could only serve his honour and help him keep his word to the Rose. He had no other choice.

She had played Paul Minct well so far. Mr Minct's weakness was that he had less respect for a woman than he had for a man. Yet the *enmascaro* was in no doubt about her worth to their enterprise, so long as, in his view, Mr Oakenhurst kept her under control.

'I have always preferred the company of women,' said Paul Minct. 'It will be a pleasure to work with you, my dear.'

'I like the feel of the game,' she said. As yet she had given Sam Oakenhurst no clue as to the nature of her quarrel with Mr Minct or why the masked man did not recognize her (or did not choose to recognize her. He was the master of any five-dimensional bluff on the screen and a few more of his own invention.)

'We shall form a family as strong as our faith in our own strengths,' said Paul Minct. For once his eyes looked away from them, as if ashamed. 'We are peers. We need no others. The three of us will take our sacrifice to the Fault and reap the measureless harvests!'

'You anticipated my sentiments, Mr Minct,' said the Rose, almost sweet, and Sam Oakenhurst thought he caught a swiftly controlled flicker of emotion in Paul Minct's bleak eyes.

12. UN HOMME DE PITIE

THE RULES AT last agreed, Paul Minct promised to tell them more after they reached the Frees and were off the raft. Then the three of them settled down to an easy companionship, playing a hand or two of old flat and a simulated folded paper version of *Henri's Special Turbulence* which could only be modified with difficulty and which they eventually abandoned by mutual consent.

One evening, as Captain Ornate pumped his melancholy squeezebox in a corner and a couple of whiteys capered to the old familiar zee tunes, the conversation turned to the subject of animals and whether it was possible to have significant communication with them.

Mrs von Bek spoke of the famous Englishman, Squire Begg, a cousin of hers, and his affinity with crows. He believed they possessed a primitive wisdom enabling them to talk in some way with humans, but first one had to learn and obey their language and customs, which were simple enough, though immutable. It was by these customs that, down the long millennia, crows survived. Assured of your courtesy, the crow would give full attention to your thoughts and desires. 'Crows,' she said, 'came from all over the world to his London mansion in Sporting Club Square, and he was frequently sketched in the company of Egyptian, Amazonian or Antipodean crows, mostly hooded, who would mysteriously leave, returning without warning to their native grounds.'

'I was once an initiate of my tribe's Crow Cult.' Rodrigo Heat's words were thick as Mississippi mud. 'My totem was the crow. I was sworn to protect the crow and all his kind, even with my life, even above my family. In return the crow offered us his wisdom. But his advice was not always suited to modern times.'

'I heard of a young buckaree from up in Arizone who had his eyes pecked out by a crow. He went crazy in the sun, they said, and jumped off that old London Bridge up there, straight down until he hit the granite, thinking he *was* a crow,' said Sister Honesty Marvell. 'Nobody ever found out why.'

Sam Oakenhurst suggested a game of *Mad John Parker*, but Honesty Marvell favoured *Doc Granite*, so in the end they made it a tambourine game and shouted like kiddikins over it. That night the Rose told Sam Oakenhurst that they might have to kill Paul Minct.

At your service, he signalled, but bile came up in his throat.

(We are not *fragments* of the whole, she would tell him, but *versions* of the whole. Mr Oakenhurst had told her of the last time he had stood in a ploughed field, full of bright pools of winter rain, on a fine, pale blue evening, with the great orange sun bleeding down into the horizon, and watched a big dog fox, brush high as he picked his way amongst the furrows, circling the meadow where he was hidden by the lattice of the hedge, sniffing the wind for the geese who had begun to cluck with anxious enquiry. All of it disappeared, Mr Oakenhurst said, in the Hattiesburg Roar. 'I had thought that, at least, must endure. Now, even our memories are becoming suspect.')

He had no qualms about killing the man, if he proved actively dangerous to them, but he was not at all sure he could play this. He had given his word to something for which he might not possess the necessary bottom. By now he was as nervous of losing her approval as he was terrified by Paul Minct's displeasure. The irony of this amused and sustained him.

'*Ma romance,*' she sang, '*nouvelle romance. Ma romancier, muy necromancier. Joli boys all dansez. Joli boys all dansez. But they shall not have muy coleur.*'

13. EL BUENO, EL FEO Y EL MALO

THE THREE LEFT *The Whole Hog* on a mudbank near Poker Flats but not before Sister Honesty Marvell had butchered Roy Ornate in a quarrel over the nature of things. Paul Minct had finished her with a glass spike whereupon the swamp people, some devolved survivalists, had tried to crawl aboard, to be repulsed and mostly blown apart by the violent anti-gravity reaction of the colour to metal. They were extinguished by the power of their ornaments. Carly O'Dowd was dead, too, from a poison she had picked up somewhere, and there was reasonable fear of a whitey uprising until Rodrigo Heat put himself in charge.

Almost as soon as they were ashore they came upon a scattering of the swamp people's weapons, flung this far into the reed beds by the colour. Sam Oakenhurst had never held an original Olivetté PP6 before and he treasured the instrument in his hands, to the Rose's open amusement.

'Take up one of these weapons for yourself, ma'am.' Paul Minct became proprietorial, motioning with his wicked fingers. 'It will almost certainly prove useful to you.' He bent and his arms, encased in hide, again emerged from their velvet wrappings to examine the scattered hardware. 'I have made this journey before. Many times, this journey. Yes. This time we will go on.' He straightened, turning the glittering weapon in her direction and, gasping at sudden pain, examined his pricked wrist. He watched the wand that had wounded him disappearing back into her cloak at the same moment as she apologized.

'She is sometimes hasty in my defence.'

'Swift Thorn,' he said.

The wind was ugly in their ears. A grey whine from the north.

'You would not prefer to pack this OK9?' continued Paul Minct. 'Some kind of back up?' He dangled the thing by its flared snout, as if tempting a whitey gal to a piece of pie. But she had stirred a memory in him and he turned away, looking out to where the saplings shivered. To Sam Oakenhurst she flashed a fresh play, then she gathered her *gravitas* so that when, also controlled, Mr Minct turned back, she seemed proudly insouciant of any slight.

Again Sam Oakenhurst recognized a game beyond his usual experience.

'She is all I shall need,' said the Rose, almost distantly, while Paul Minct retreated, having apologized with equal formality. He took the OK9 for himself and also hid a Ryman's 32/80 ("a beastly, primitive weapon") in his pack.

They were walking up a well-marked old road which followed the edge of the lake. The road had run between Shreveport and Houston once. They could follow it, Paul Minct assured them, as far as San Augustine. 'I have heard or read of a weapon called Swift Thorn,' he added as he lengthened his gait to lead them South. 'The subject of some epic.'

'Not the subject,' she said. Oh, he is easily clever enough to kill me, Sam. He tricked me into a show.

He doesn't know that he succeeded. He will not dare risk a move on you until he's sure of me. Sam Oakenhurst fell in beside her.

I must take risks, Sam. He must not escape me. I am pledged to his destruction.

'*Hey, hola! Les bon temps rolla! Ai, ha! The good times pass! Pauvre pierrot, muy coeur, mon beau soleil,*' sang out Paul Minct up ahead. 'What a day, pards! What a day!'

A tremor moved the ground and the reed beds rippled.

Around them suddenly boiled the cloudy landscapes, the powerful mirages, of the Free States, all in a condition of minor agitation, as if not fully in focus. Crazy tendrils erupted into a bewildering kaleidoscope, each fragment a fresh version of its surroundings and of the people inhabiting them. A thousand images of themselves, in a variety of roles and identities, poured away down fresh cracks in the fabric of their histories.

Sam Oakenhurst found this a depressing illusion.

'They refuse to search for the centre and hold to it against all attacks and temptations. There must be sacrifices. Lines drawn. And faith. You're familiar with *The Pilgrim's Progress*, Mr Oakenhurst, you being a preacher's son? There's a book, eh? But if only life were so simple. We must press on, holding together, through this valley of desolation, to our just reward. We must know complete trust. And what a reward, my dears!'

Orange and yellow pillars pissed like egg yoke into the sky and splashed upon a gory firmament.

'Here we are,' sang Paul Minct. 'This is it!' He paused before the yelling pillars and threw back his head as if to drink them up; his crude cartographic visor flickered and flashed and made new reflections. 'We are about to pass into the Free States. This is the malleable world indeed! This, or one like it, must bend to our will. Do you not think?'

The Rose was unimpressed. Not as malleable as some, she told Sam Oakenhurst. She moved with an extra grace as if until now her blood had hardly quickened. She had the alertness of an animal in its natural element. Sam Oakenhurst thought they were walking into the suburbs of Hell and he told her that while he remained at her service he was also entirely in her hands. This experience was too unfamiliar. He had thought the stories only legends.

'Here is what all matter should aspire to,' Paul Minct continued. 'Here is true tolerance. Everything is free.'

'Tolerance without mercy,' murmured Sam Oakenhurst, willing to reveal this fear if only to disguise his other, more profound, anxieties.

'We shall find further allies here!' Paul Minct appeared to have forgotten his earlier pledge as he led them between the columns. 'I will guide you.'

But it was soon left for the Rose to lead them, with miraculous confidence, through the vivid shadows, through volatile matter and corrupted time. Perspective, gravity and the seasons were all unstable and Sam Oakenhurst felt he must throw up as Paul Minct, with angry gestures of refusal, had done after they had walked the Bridge of Rubies for uncountable hours. Mr Minct, expecting to be the most experienced of them, clearly resented the Rose's easy pathfinding. Generally he managed to hide his feelings. It was as if, with the sureness of one who knew such waters well, she steered their boat through the wildest rapids.

Agitated scratchings came from within Paul Minct's mask and swaddlings. Occasionally the *enmascaro* uttered a little, shrill bubbling sound which added to Sam Oakenhurst's own fearful nausea. For a while it seemed they passed between fields of stars, crossing by silver spans of moonbeams, but the Rose told them it was the abandoned forecourt of *The Divided Arabia* which at one time had been the largest shopping mall in the Western Hemisphere. What they witnessed was what it had become.

'That stuff scares the devil out of me,' Sam Oakenhurst admitted as they emerged from a forest of bright metallic greenery into a wide relief of desert dominated by the brazen stability of a tiny sun.

'Now, my dears, this is more *like* Texas,' said Paul Minct.

14. NO ME ENTIERRES EN LA PRADERA

THE FIRST TOWN they reached was Poker Flats, built in a wide yellow plain in what had been, Paul Minct told them, the old mustard-growing region. Her streets were full of whiteys and mixed couples and she was clearly a town given over almost entirely to license. Poker Flats announced herself as the Theater Capital of the Southwest and her main boardwalk was nothing but vivid marquees and billboards advertising simulatings, using living actors, of the great local V heroes, whose adventures Sam Oakenhurst had already skimmed at Lieutenant Twist's. These were elaborate dramas concerning the love triangle of Pearl Peru, Bullybop and Fearless Frank Force, or the Quest for the Fishlings, featuring Professor Pop, Captain Billy Bob Begg and her Famous Chaos Engineers. Many of the protagonists were white. White barkers stood outside their booths and called to the newcomers. 'So true you'd think it was V! *Dallas Horizon*.'/'It's the net! *Ontario Outer*.'/'Virtually V! *Laramee Deadlock*.'/'Frank Force Face To Face! *Ludoland*.' Their words were echoed overhead in the baroque calligraphy of the day. Power paint growled with all the brilliant vulgar bellicosity of the old circus towns. Poker Flats had been the first of the roving show cities to take permanent root. Such settlements were all over the Free States now, said Paul Minct, but the biggest were still Poker Flats and Porto Cristo.

Paul Minct insisted they visit the shows and understand the nature of these dramas. 'Real or fictional, black or white, they represent a breed of our own kind that has successfully escaped the logic of the Fault, discovering new universes beyond our own. There, my dear friends, Chaos and Singularity perpetually war, are perpetually in balance. And sometimes one is no longer certain which is which. Philosophies become blurred and intermingled out there in the Second Ether. This was how I first learned that it was possible to move from one version of our universe to another and survive. We never die, my dear friends. We are, however, perpetually translated.'

What does he mean? asked Sam Oakenhurst.

He understands something of our condition, she told him, but not much of it. He is like those old South American *conquistadori*. All he can see of this secret is the power and wealth it will bring him. He is prepared to risk his life and soul for that.

Sam Oakenhurst grew fascinated with the legends portrayed on the stages. He talked about Pearl Peru, Corporal Pork, Little Rupoldo, Kapricorn Schultz and others as if they were personally known to him. When the time came to leave Poker Flats, he bought several books of scenarios. As soon as they were back on the trail he studied them slowly, from morning to night, hoping to find clues to the versions of reality perceived both by Paul Minct and, in particular, Mrs von Bek. Perhaps the Fault was not the mouth of Hell, after all? Perhaps it was a gateway to Paradise?

Walking beside the Rose, he recounted the tale of Oxford under the Squad warlords. The alien renegades, furious at Oxford's resistance to their philosophies, informed the citizens that unless they immediately fell to levelling their entire settlement, colleges, chapels and all, they (the Squads) would eat their first born and bugger their old folk. 'And Oxford, Rose, went the way of St Petersburg and Washington, but not Cheltenham, which is still standing but which has lost its first born. And her old people rarely, these days, walk abroad.' The Squads had come in their black deltoid aircraft. Thousands. 'They told us they represented the Singularity and we were now their subject race. If we refused to serve them, they punished us until we accepted their mastery. They have conquered, they boast, half the known multiverse and are destined to conquer the rest. Fearless Frank Force is their greatest ace. But nobody knows or understands the loyalties of the Merchant Venturer, Pearl Peru, whom he loves to distraction. His love is not returned. Pearl's passion is for Bullybop alone. And Bullybop is a thorn in the side of the Singularity. Nobody is sure of her secret identity. Honour demands that Frank Force issue no challenge to his rival, yet Bullybop is marked by the Singularity as an outlaw. Here now is the moral conundrum we must solve before we can proceed along a further branch. There is a road, after all, Rose. There are many roads. And crossroads. I can sense them. We can choose some which exist or we can create our own. But there's a formula, I know, and I must learn it.'

'This mania came over one of my men the first time we ever passed through Poker Flats.' Paul Minct was cheerfully dismissive of the Rose's fears. 'They either recover or they don't. In the end we had to shoot Peter Agoubi, poor chap. Lead on, Mrs von Bek. I'll take care of Mr Oakenhurst.'

'It will pass,' she said. 'He will regain control of himself soon, I am sure.' *For my sake, Sam, if not your own!*

This demand brought him, within a reasonable period, back to his senses, but his lasting emotion was of loss, as if he had been close to the secret logic of the multiverse and able, like her, to navigate a purposeful course through those quasi-realities. He could not make himself throw away his scenarios. He buried them deep at the bottom of his knapsack.

'It's unflattering to have a V character for a rival,' she pretended amusement. They had found some good beds in a ghost town about a hundred kays from San Augustine. She indulged her weariness, her poor temper. 'What is the actuality of this Pearl Peru? She sailed by accident through the Cloud of Saffron and that made her a heroine?'

In any circumstances Sam Oakenhurst would have decided that it was impolitic to show admiration for a character with whom the Rose seemed to be on intimate terms and whom she disliked. Such experiences were not, he told himself, helping his sense of identity. Once he caught himself yearning for the familiarity of the *machinoix* shutterbox.

Those people were real, he knew. But what he had experienced as myth, she had experienced as history. He vowed that he must never lose her. He was prepared to change most of his life for her. His curiosity about her was as great as his love. Now, he thought, they are impossible to separate. Our shoots are interwound. Our luck is the same. We are of the Just . . . He had a moment's understanding that he had given up his own madness in favour of hers. What had he accepted?

You are sworn to this, she reminded him. From now you must accept only what *I* determine as the truth. You will survive no other way. *Any independent decision of yours could result in my death.* You know this, Sam. You have dealt the hands. Now you must play the game, or we are both dead.

This is new to me, he said.

Play it anyway.

15. TWO STEP DELLA TEXAS

AFTER THEY HAD traded the Ryman's and two samsonites for ponies at the Flooding Whisper horse ranch just west of San Augustine they made better progress into Golden Birches, where pale light shuddered and huge crows flapped amongst the black lattice of the distant treetops. They arrived in Lufkin to discover that the Pennsylvania Rooms were still run by Major Moyra Malu, the shade of an elegant old swashbuckler who had fought with K'Ond'aa Taylor at Pampam Ridge and had carried the flag to victory for Charles Deslondes in '07.

At Paul Minct's suggestion she was to be their fourth, but not before another week's gaming had all parties apparently satisfied. Then they took Major Moyra's good Arabs and headed through the milk tides down to Livingston where Paul Minct sought out Herb Frazee. The ex-president of the Republic was giving demonstration hands of *Cold Annie* and telling Tarot to what was left of Livingston's polite society. He refused Mr Minct's invitation but suggested they look up Mrs Sally Guand' in Houston.

The road to Houston took them through Silver Pines. The strange, frozen forest was cold as death nowadays, said Paul Minct, but once there had been fires burning on every mound. They came out into foothills above a summer valley. 'There's Houston.' Paul Minct pointed. The huge city had recently melted and reformed into a baroque version of itself. Its highways made arabesques, glorious in the sunlight. Yet even here the uneasy terrain threatened to vaporize, become something else, and Sam Oakenhurst yearned for California where Pearl Peru, he had read, was a living celebrity.

They passed under Houston's organic freeways. The Rose wanted to stay for a few days. The others insisted they find Sally Guand' and press on to Galveston. But when Major Moyra Malu led them to Sally Guand's old offices above the Union Station, the buildings were melted shells and the rails had twisted themselves into one vast, elongated abstract sculpture disappearing in the direction of Los Angeles. Here, as everywhere, black and white lived as best they could, equals amongst the ruins, and miscegeny was not uncommon.

They lost the road some twenty kays from Houston, used up their provisions and were forced to shoot a horse before they got on another trace full of abandoned buses and pickup trucks, which took them across to Old Galveston to find Jasmine Shah, who had been operating a bar on the harbourfront until the local vigilantes busted her huge cache of *piles noires*. Her dark locks hiding a long, vulpine face, she was ready, she said, to do almost anything, yet she would only come in with them after she had whispered strict conditions to each one in private. She revealed that she, like Major Moyra, was now a shade.

Paul Minct had hesitated after she spoke to him, but then he nodded agreement.

The streets of Galveston were full of whiteys who had failed to fulfil the ambitions they had conceived in Mississippi and Alabama and were now desperately trying to get back to New Orleans, but could not afford any kind of fare. Black travellers were beset by scores of them whining for help.

Sam Oakenhurst was glad when they got aboard the first schoomer available and sailed out into the peaceful waters of the Gulf. He and the Rose now had a better measure of the situation and yet he no longer had faith in his own good judgement. The thought of New Orleans was already beginning to obsess him.

The Rose begged him to rally. 'It seems Mr Minct does intend to sail into the Fault. Yet why would he insist on your finding us a meat boat?' (Paul Minct had commissioned Sam Oakenhurst to approach the *machinoix*.) 'Does he want us alive when he goes in?' Both agreed that Paul Minct had needed more partners only after Swift Thorn had stirred some memory. 'How does he plan to kill us?' Sam wondered. 'Perhaps he will not kill me until he has made sure of you, Rose. And you are necessary to him, I think. He knows you can help him.'

'But you, too, are necessary if he is to get the meat boat. You heard him insist. It must only be a meat boat. Has anyone ever volunteered to sail on such a boat?'

'It is forbidden,' said Sam Oakenhurst. 'He knows it is.'

'Then he demands of you a complex betrayal. Is this how he would weaken us?' The Rose began to brush her exquisite hair. 'Who would you betray?'

'Not you,' he said. 'Not myself. Nothing I value.'

'Betray the *machinoix* and surely you betray yourself. You have explained all this to me. And in betraying yourself you must betray me. How will you resolve this? It is a problem worthy of Fearless Frank Force.'

She seemed to be mocking him.

'A moral conundrum,' she added.

There was a knock on their cabin door: A kiddikin bringing Mr Minct's compliments and looking forward to the pleasure of their company in a game of *Anvils and Pins*.

'I have earned your sarcasm, I know,' Sam Oakenhurst said. 'But I am still willing to learn from you. What will you teach me, Rose?'

'You will learn that it is, space and time, always a question of scale.' She touched his lips. 'Meanwhile you must continue to risk your life. And you are sworn to serve me, are you not?'

'On my honour,' he said.

'But in demanding your help I expose you to more than you ever expected,' she said. 'Perhaps you do not have the resources?'

'I have them,' he insisted.

'You must draw upon your archetype.' The Rose took his hand. Tonight her skin resembled fine, delicately shaded petals softly layered upon her sturdy frame. 'I have lost my home and must destroy the man who robbed me of it. We are only barely related as species, you and I, but it is Time and Scale which separate us, Sam. In the ether we embrace metamorphosis. You and I, Sam, understand the dominating law of the multiverse. We are ruled by multiplying chance. But we need not be controlled by it. I knew Paul Minct in another guise. Now, I think, he clearly remembers me. He can always recall a weapon, that one, if not a woman. This pair, these shadows, are an afterthought. His interest in the Fault could be secondary now. First he must deal with us, for we threaten his existence. Perhaps he is afraid to let us reach the Fault with him, lest he be cheated of whatever it is he has schemed for? Believe me, Sam, Paul Minct will be giving us his full attention for the next few days. These others, they are scarcely real, merely 1st and 2nd Murderers.'

16. J'AI PASSE DEVANT TA PORTE

THE *MACHINOIX* HAD sniffed his coming. Sam Oakenhurst stood at the rail of the great triple-hulled schoomer and saw through Major Moyra's glass that his brothers and sisters had assembled to greet him.

Their snorting, half-organic vehicles, dark green and brown with senility, drooled and defecated on the quayside while neither citizen nor armed militia dare show disgust or objection. In their city, the *machinoix* were ignored for the same reason quakes were ignored in Los Angeles. They were unavoidable and unpredictable.

Mr Sam Oakenhurst tasted their power as greedily as he embraced their kinship. His veins thrilled with the memory of his long courtships under the shutterbox, his lingering initiations, his education in seduction. Beware, he signalled the Rose, for I am enraptured already. I love you, Rose. Only you.

The Rose held fast to him and gave him the strength she could spare. He knew there was no physical danger. Any decision of his would be accepted, for he threatened nothing the *machinoix* valued. This knowledge was insufficient to steady his nerve. He had to call on his every resource and never reveal a hint of his condition to Paul Minct and his colleagues. The Rose, understanding the importance of this deception to her own interests, gave him more support. She had no choice. He was her only ally and while he lived so did she. And she loved him, she said.

By the time they had clambered down the gangway to the lighter, he was scarcely able to disguise the signs of his massive emotional conflict.

With her help, however, he succeeded. He at last stood four square on the quayside, clutching her arm once before advancing towards the middle vehicle from which oddly tattooed hands beckoned, their fingers fractured and re-set at peculiar angles with inserted precious stones and gold. Gnarled as old hedges, the hands had the appearance of eccentrically made robot digits, jointed and decorated for their beauty rather than their function.

The Rose was casual enough as she turned to inform a nervous Mr Minct that Sam Oakenhurst spoke *machinoix* perfectly. 'He is the only possible interpreter. He will get us swift passage to Biloxi'

'It must be the meat boat.' Paul Minct was wheezing from his recent climb up the iron waterstair. 'I know they reserve it for themselves but it is what we must have.'

By arrangement with the ship's captain they were to stay in Rue Dauphine at the Hotel Audobon, a collection of old iron slave shacks turned into elegant *cabines à la mode*. The uniformed whiteys who greeted them at the gates were not permitted to take the little luggage the gamblers brought.

These were cabins of choice, let only to passing visitors of their own high persuasion. When they were settled, Paul Minct told them, they must assemble at Brown's *Bar Vieux* on Royale, where he would hire the backroom and a couple of simul-bottles. They could thus link up for a rough and ready run-through of their plan to enter the Fault aboard the meat boat. 'We'll be going in through Mustard Splash or Ketchup Cave.'

The bottles were the best quality the Rose had ever seen. Major Moyra and Jasmine Shah were experts at handling and conducting them, massaging unstable gases, nursing their milky energy into responsive motes.

Before they had arrived, Paul Minct had refused to tell her why they must go to this trouble when the Terminal's huge V resource was at anyone's disposal. He appeared to have reasons for not alerting the people at the Terminal to his intentions.

Her instincts told her that this whole charade was part of a complicated plot to trap her before killing her. It was unnecessarily elaborate, she thought.

But it was that which convinced her. Elaboration was Paul Minct's trademark. It was characteristic of his whole game thus to hide a simple brute intention.

Had he known she was in Guadalajara? If so, even Paul Minct's affectation for M&E was a part of his plot against her. She was admiring of his mind for detail. She had known him in many roles, but usually he had not recognized her so quickly.

When Mr Oakenhurst rejoined them at Brown's he seemed introspective but carefree enough, almost euphoric. He told them that they had the *machinoix* blessing to take the meat boat to Biloxi. This was, they must all understand, a considerable privilege. Moyra Malu said she appreciated the implications. Only Paul Minct accepted the news casually, as if Mr Oakenhurst had done no more than act as a go-between. 'And how much do these great barons charge us, Mr Oakenhurst, for the privilege?'

'Nothing, Mr Minct. They act upon my word alone.'

'Flimsy enough, then?'

Sam Oakenhurst took a glaring interest in the screens, his mood threatening.

'I am not sure I can stand that smell for such a long voyage,' said Jasmine Shah. She had changed to red satin, she said, in honour of the occasion. She sported a feathery fan.

'We must endure it until Biloxi,' murmured Paul Minct, looking up from the bottles and retorts of his quasi-V, his mask reflecting the brilliant, ever-changing rhythms of the angry pastels. 'They are unpredictable, are they not, sir, these psychics? Sometimes they seem to need us more than we need them. But I expect they are agreeable people, by and large.'

Sam Oakenhurst knew he had nothing much more to fear until they were actually aboard the meat boat. He took his place with the other four around the viewing bowls which flooded them now in bright blues and vivid pinks, adjusting to a formal plum colour as Paul Minct stroked his backupper to make shapes from the enlivened dust. Some of the images were familiar but many were not. Sam Oakenhurst found them obscene.

'We have agreed a common principle, my dears,' Paul Minct seemed a little sanctimonious. 'And must stick to the rules we form here tonight. Or we shall be lost.'

'Do we need to be reminded of that?' Sam Oakenhurst was almost irritable as he studied the bowl, finding some strands on the screen he could use. He wove a showy, challenging pattern.

'We are a team, Mr Oakenhurst.' Paul Minct seemed pleased by this offhand display. 'We can afford no weak links. No, as it were, anti-socialism.' Sam Oakenhurst guessed Mr Minct had found a tune which he must now rehearse for a while. Mr Minct searched under his veil and plucked at his hideous jowls.

Unusually alert, Sam Oakenhurst studied Paul Minct's companions and detected a tremor of victorious malice in Major Moyra's face. The Rose's warning was confirmed. Certain of his allies, Paul Minct was celebrating a premature triumph.

It will be on board the meat boat. That has always featured in his scenario, I think. I don't know why, save that he follows a personal aesthetic. Mrs von Bek gave her own attention to the bowls and began a detailed weaving, a story of a planet and its doom, a wonderful miniature. Sam Oakenhurst understood that now she, too, had issued a challenge to Paul Minct. These were the gentle beginnings, the courteous preliminaries of the game.

Upon Mr Minct's irrational insistence they began the first stage of their simulation, producing a reasonable version of the Biloxi Fault and some sort of boat in which to brave these self-created dangers. 'Now we sail into Mustard Splash!' declared Paul Minct, their captain. 'These murky walls will part, thus!' A magician, he revealed the blinding azure of a vast colour field. 'We shall follow a river – thus – ' A hazier network of silver streams which, with his characteristic crudity, he made into one wide road. 'This line will respond to the meat boat's unique geometry. And now we must do our best, dear friends, and make the most of our creative imaginations, for our quest lies even *beyond* the fields of colour – to find eternal life, limitless wealth! There one shall come in to one's true power at last!'

Later, in their cabin, Sam Oakenhurst and the Rose agreed that the exercise had been a complicated sham, a violent and exhausting process with no other purpose, as far as they could tell, than to display Paul Minct's artistic skills. 'That was not the Fault,' she said. 'Merely a surface impression and a bad projection. It was an *arcadium*, no more. Almost an insult. I wonder why? To convince us? To confuse us? To terrify us? He knows in his heart what truly lies beyond the Fault.'

They were lying together on the wide bed, the light from the swamp-cone turning her brown skin into semi-stable green and giving her face a deep flush. 'He still needs our good will, Sam. He had expected your challenge no more than had I.'

It had hardly been a challenge. Mr Oakenhurst, hyped on the sensations of his reunion, had merely wished to show that he no longer feared Paul Minct. He had risked their lives on a vulgar display and he now admitted it.

She began to laugh with quiet spontaneity. 'I have a feeling he did not care to notice, anyway. He was preparing his talents for his demo. Let that hand ride for a while, Sam, and we'll see what happens.'

He marvelled at her beauty, the peerless texture of her skin, her natural, sweet scent, the ever-changing colours of her flesh, and he knew that his feeling for her was stronger than his bond with the *machinoix*. Stronger than with his own species.

'We are defenceless if he decides to take us before the meat boat leaves,' he said. 'I'm pretty scared, Rose.'

'The best way to get out of trouble is to take a risk based on your judgement. You know that, Sam.' Her touch was a petal on his thigh. 'Take another risk. An informed one, this time. Make a change. What can you ever lose? Not me, Sam.'

She began to notice the tiny, symmetrical marks on his stomach, like stylized drops of blood.

He refused to tell her what they were.

17. EXITOS DE ORO

THE MEAT BOAT left two days later from the quarantine dock, its brooding, over-decorated reptilian bulk almost filling the ancient channel. It was lying low in the water, giving the impression that it had just fed well.

In common with the others, Paul Minct had to steady himself against the smell from the holds. He held a huge nosegay of mint and rosemary to his hidden features, while the strength of the perfume sprayed about by Major Moyra was equally hard to stomach. Jasmine Shah contented herself with her fan and some smelling salts. She seemed lost in her own small fantasy.

They were led aboard by an obsequious whitey tattooed with the *machinoix* livery. The extravagantly furnished passenger quarters were clearly designed for the unwholesome comforts of the *machinoix*. It was a great honour, Sam Oakenhurst told them. The majority of quarters reserved for the *machinoix* were less comfortable. And there were quarters for the blankey slaves much closer to the meat.

He and the Rose stood together in the centre of Paul Minct's cabin while the huge creature prowled about the edges, the nosegay still pressed to his beaded veil, inspecting the peculiar cups and little needles placed everywhere for a guest's casual convenience. Sam Oakenhurst reached down to a tiny table and picked up one of the razor-edged shot glasses. He gently touched it to the back of his wrist.

'These colours are so muted,' declared the Rose. 'So gorgeous. So rich.'

'There's no-one doubts the *machinoix* ain't *rich*, Mrs von Bek,' chuckled Jasmine Shah, crowding in with Major Moyra to admire the vast chamber. 'As Croesus, they say.'

'Could buy and sell the Republic of Texas, even in my day,' Major Moyra agreed. 'But they don't mess with human politics much. Ain't that so, Mr Oakenhurst?'

'That's so, major.'

'Built for a giant and furnished for dwarves,' mused Jasmine Shah, making her own tour.

The atmosphere was one of general bonhomie as the would-be murderers saw their end-game laid out, already won.

Their adversaries' confidence could be useful to them, Sam Oakenhurst decided, and later in their own cabin, Rose von Bek told him she had decided the same. 'Their eagerness and anticipation can become our weapon. But it is three days to Biloxi. When will he strike, do you think?'

Sam Oakenhurst made a lazy gesture. He thought it would not be immediately. For the first time he was calmly ready for death. He did not much care how he died. He also knew that he could not accept death while his obligation to the Rose remained. He must make himself worthy of her.

She detected a certain heaviness in his manner. He assured her that he had never been on better form.

While a blankey, smelling strongly of meat, prepared their bed, Sam Oakenhurst said aloud: 'If Paul Minct hopes to seduce whiteys to his cause he cannot know the *machinoix*. This fellow and his kind are as loyal to their masters as anyone can be. Disobedience or treachery is inconceivable to them. They would be disgusted and terrified if it was suggested. The *machinoix* never put their own to work on the meat boats. They trust their whiteys absolutely. There is no reason why they should not.'

'Paul Minct must have some understanding of this. How does he think he can force them to divert the boat and sail into the Fault?' The Rose shook her head.

'Whether or not he plans to enter the Fault, he is without a doubt planning to trap us. He cannot see how we can escape and is happy to take his time. Yet why should he go to such lengths to kill you, Rose?'

'He must be certain. And it is in his nature to make such plots. He knows that I have pursued him through the myriad branches of the multiverse and that I am of the Just. I must put an end to him, if I can. Betrayal is a sophisticated and legitimate art which he practises merely for the pleasure it gives him. But he has another ambition I cannot fathom, as yet.'

'What did he do to you that you must punish him?' Sam Oakenhurst asked.

'He educated me to betray myself and thus to betray my people.' She spoke softly, economically, as if she could not trust her voice for long. 'The story I gave at Brown's was true.'

'And these other stories? Are they true? What we saw at Poker Flats?'

'Myths,' she said. 'True enough. They describe the truth.'

'And what does Paul Minct describe?'

'Only lies, Sam.'

With hideous dignity the whitey bowed and left the cabin.

18. MON BON VIEUX MARI

'WE WERE CALLED the daughters of the Garden, the daughters of the Just,' she told him. 'We reproduced ourselves by the occasional effort of will. We understood the principles of self-similarity. I suppose you would call it an instinct. There is no particular miracle in being, as we were, part flora, part mammal. Such syntheses are common to the worlds I usually inhabit. Paul Minct made me cross so many scales and forget so many lives to reach him. The stories are always a little different. But this time, I think, we shall achieve some kind of resolution.'

'Surely, we are something more than mere echoes . . . ?' Yet even as he said this Sam Oakenhurst felt oppression lifting from him and a rare peace replacing it. In combination with what the *machinoix* had given him, he found still more strength. He had reached a kind of equilibrium. At that moment nothing was puzzling. But was this merely an illusion of control? What she had told him should have dismayed him. Had her madness completely absorbed him?

'Our science was the science of equity,' she continued. 'We were the natural enemies of all tyrannies, no matter how well disguised. Our world occupied a universe of flowers; blossoms and leaves were woven between blooms the size of planets. Paul Minct allied himself with a devolved race whom we knew as Babbyboys and these he ultimately unleashed upon our world. Just before he committed that crime he was my lover and I taught him all our secrets.'

'And your sisters?'

'Our whole universe was raped. I am the last of it.'

Until then Sam Oakenhurst had been unable to imagine a burden greater than his own.

19. DANS LE COEUR DE LA VILLE

'WE ARE PLAYING charades, do you see!' Paul Minct's mask glittered with a kind of merriment. 'Major Moyra is in the part of Little Fanny Fun, while Manly Mark Male is played by our own dashing Jasmine Shah! But who shall play the rival? Who shall play Handsome Harry Ho-Ho? You know this one, Mr Oakenhurst, I'm sure.'

'Those tales no longer fascinate me, Mr Minct.' Sam Oakenhurst stood just within the cabin door. The three would-be murderers had pushed away furniture and draperies and made a stage of a broad, ebony table, its legs carved with a catalogue of *machinoix* delights. It was on this that the two performed, while their superior applauded from an asymmetrical couch he had made comfortable with the sanctuary's afterlife cushions.

'This is disrespectful to your hosts.'

'Oh, Mr Oakenhurst, we shall not be going back to New Orleans! We're on our way to the Fault to find the Holy Grail, remember?' Major Moyra bawled in open contempt and unhitched her gaudy skirts.

The Rose stepped up, anxious to end this. 'Crude entertainment for a mind such as yours, Paul Minct. Or is this merely a *leitmotif*?'

'You are too judgemental, Mrs von Bek.' Paul Minct turned his glaring mask this way and that as if he could barely see through the holes. 'You must be more flexible. Only flexibility will enable you to survive the perils of the Fault. Come now, join our little time-passer. Choose a character of your own. Pearl Peru? *The Spammer Gain?* Corporal Pork? Karl Kapital?'

'I have nothing further to take from this,' said Sam Oakenhurst. 'And nothing to put in. Play on, pards, and don't mind me.'

'Play for the hell of it, then!' Jasmine Shah sprawled her painted legs over the table. 'Play. Play. What else is there to do, Mr Oakenhurst?' Her yellow eyes were sluggish with guilty appetites. His anticipated death was making her salivate. 'Taste something fresh.'

The killing ritual was beginning. And so they sat obediently until they were called and Mr Oakenhurst was a somewhat wooden Harry Ho-Ho, while the Rose became Pearl Peru to the life, telling the first tale of *The Spammer Gain* and how her fishlings were stolen. Enough to distract Paul Minct a little and make him clap his pale hands together. 'You are a natural actress, Mrs von Bek. You missed your vocation.

'I think not,' she said.

'There, pards, we've proved ourselves easy sports,' announced Sam Oakenhurst, 'but now we must come to business. We are here to discuss the part of our plan where we take over the meat boat. Are the whiteys bribed, yet?' Mr Oakenhurst found himself again speaking from impulse. His tone was sufficient to let the *enmascaro* know that Sam Oakenhurst was making a call.

'Not yet,' said Paul Minct easily. 'There's time enough, Mr Oakenhurst. Let us relax.'

'We no longer accept you as our director.' The Rose swung down from the table as Paul Minct, gloating in a supposed small victory, displayed his surprise. But he recovered quickly.

'Here's a better game than I anticipated.' Mr Minct calmed his two shadows with a casual hand. They were both thoroughly alarmed. Evidently they had not once considered a play made at the opponents' convenience.

Caged light, fluttering in the woven flambeaux, cast the only movement on Mr Minct now. His body was still as stone. As if he hoped to stop time.

'This is not like you, Mr Oakenhurst.' The Rose was amused.

'Not like me at all.' He turned to address the *enmascaro*. 'A surprise play, eh, Mr Minct?'

Eyes moved like quick reptiles behind the mask. The curtain over the mouth rattled. 'Just so, Mr Oakenhurst.'

Sam Oakenhurst hardly knew what to do next. He felt a rush of elation. He was in control of his terrors.

20. AIMER ET PERDRE

IT HAD NEVER been in Sam Oakenhurst's nature to decide the first move. Paul Minct had relied on that while certain the Rose would not make a play before Mr Oakenhurst. But now, equally unpredictable, Paul Minct produced the little OK9 he had once recommended to Mrs von Bek and he took a step back to cover them both. 'This is not my style, either, as you know. But I'm willing to change if you are. That's the basis of a relationship, as I tell my wife. No wands now, Mrs von Bek. This beam is wide and I will resort to brute murder if I must. I have a vocation to fulfil. An oath.'

'Ah!' exclaimed the Rose in surprise. 'This one has a conscience!'

'I had such hopes for your death, Mrs von Bek. Mr Oakenhurst would have appreciated what I made of you. We have a little time before we prepare the sacrifice. Not much, but we must make the best of what God sends us.' He signalled to Major Moyra and Jasmine Shah. Then suddenly he was still again, as if stabbed.

'That is the one,' said Sam Oakenhurst to the *machinoix*. 'He is not my friend.' He watched incuriously as one oddly jointed jewelled hand closed over Paul Minct's wrist and squeezed the gun free while fingers felt through the beads deep into his mouth and throat.

Rose von Bek looked away from Paul Minct and, with Swift Thorn, brought Major Moyra and Jasmine Shah merciful deaths. In the last moments the game had been unpleasantly easy as often happens in a spontaneous end-move. When the Rose looked back she saw that Paul Minct had been returned to his seat. He was not dead, but his cold eyes begged for her mercy. The rest of him had been expertly snapped here and there. He was little more than a heap of broken bones but he would live indefinitely.

Mr Oakenhurst bowed low before his invisible kin.

The voice which came from the folds of drapery behind the table was musical but oddly diffident. 'We shall put those two with the other meat.' There was a long pause, then: 'The broken one is yours, if you wish.'

'Thank you,' said the Rose.

'No thankings, no,' said the *machinoix*. 'Not need. I am the same. Same. You. You.'

In the following silence the Rose said: 'Where has she gone?'

'To rest,' Sam Oakenhurst told her. 'She has used up pretty much all her strength for a year. What will you do with him?'

'Eventually I must kill him. I have that much compassion left. But it will take me a while to find the necessary resolution.'

Sam Oakenhurst stepped aside to let the whiteys drag the corpses off. 'Nature resists linearity. Why didn't you understand that, Paul Minct? What was your plan? What did you intend to sacrifice and to whom?' Approaching the couch he reached to Paul Minct's head and touched it in a certain way, allowing the lips to move.

'The meat was for the Fault.' His suffering made Paul Minct obedient now. 'The Fault is a sentient creature. Five times I fed it. This sixth time was to bring me my reward, for I would be sacrificing the Rose, my mortal enemy, body and soul! And what rarer sacrifice? For the Rose is both the last and the first of her kind. Then I should have been permitted to sail through the golden branches into the Great Cup and know my whole power!'

'You must tell me the truth,' she said. 'It will make me more merciful. How did you plan to take over this boat?'

'I placed no faith in bribes or whitey revolt. I simply made adjustments to the steering gear. That is why this boat is now on inevitable course for the Fault, under full sail. We shall keep our original bargain, ma'am. But you never did confront me, Sam. Not really.'

Mr Oakenhurst silenced Paul Minct's mouth. The man's bravery was more impressive than his judgement. 'We are to be your sacrifices, still? I think not. Eh, Mrs von Bek?'

The Rose frowned at him. 'It is either the Fault or drown. Have you no curiosity, Sam?'

'There are innocent lives in this!'

'They will not die, Sam. That's merely a conception of the Singularity. You have already discovered the benefits of mutability. The Fault will either translate us or reject us, but it will not kill us. And there's every chance we'll remain together. We must have the will for it and the courage to follow our instincts.'

'I must return to New Orleans,' said Mr Oakenhurst. 'There is a debt outstanding.' He looked with hatred into Paul Minct's agonized eyes.

Again, he began to doubt his judgement. What good had his decisions been now they were heading helplessly into the Biloxi Fault? He turned to ask her how much time she thought they had, when the whitey bos'un shuffled down the companionway and crossed to the door, kneeling with bowed head before Sam Oakenhurst and the Rose and not speaking until Mr Oakenhurst gave permission.

'Respectfully, master, our meat boat is about to be a-swallered by the Biloxi Fault.'

'Remember!' she called, as she followed him up the narrow ladders towards the bridge, 'It is only a matter of scale and experience. You are not a fraction of the whole. You are a version of the whole! Time will seem to eddy and stall. This is scale. Everything is sentient, but scale alters perception. The time of a tree is not your time.' It was as if she shouted to him all she had meant to teach him before this moment. 'To the snail the foot which comes from nowhere and crushes him is as natural a disaster as a hurricane and as impossible to anticipate. The time of a star is not our time. Equity is the natural condition of the multiverse. There are things to fear in the colour fields, *but not the fields themselves*!'

Now he was on the top deck, heading for the bridge, the vast black sails bulging overhead as the freak wind took them more rapidly towards the Fault than ever Paul Minct had planned. The massive presence of the Biloxi Fault filled their horizon, all bruised colours and sharded light, yelping and gulping the ruins of star systems and galaxies as the meat boat sailed inexorably towards the lava-red glow of Ketchup Cave.

'I will remember all your lessons!' He took the wheel from the terrified whitey, but it would not respond to his straining movements. The boat dipped and rose on a sudden tide while the wind threatened to tear the sheets from her masts. 'Help me,' he said, as the whitey ran below. She came towards him. Then something soft had batted the meat boat into the middle of the bloody blossoming field. Yet the vessel maintained her original momentum, travelling steadily under sail. They could see nothing but the surrounding scarlet. When they spoke their voices were unfamiliar and used new but coherent languages. Sam Oakenhurst felt his stomach peeling open, his entire flesh and bones skinless to the flame. He fell backwards.

He tried to look up beyond the sails and saw something moving against the scarlet. A huge owl. He shuddered.

Now the Rose had her hands upon the useless wheel. Mammalian only in broad outline, she appeared to curl her limbs and cast roots into the steering machinery, as if seeking the whereabouts of Paul Minct's tamperings. Her scent enraptured him. It was thicker than smoke. Something vicious and insistent threatened nearby and was dangerous, some version of Paul Minct. The Rose pulled mightily on the wheel and this time the meat boat responded, gliding into a sudden field of blue populated with the black silhouettes of mountains shifting constantly in perspective, and then descending into a maelstrom of purple and white, soaring into field upon field of the vast spectrum, turning and wheeling until Sam Oakenhurst had to take his eyes from her to lean over the side and throw up into an infinity of lemon yellow spheres and witness his own vomit becoming another universe in which uncountable souls would live, suffer and die until the end of time, while the sounds that he made would eventually be interpreted by them as evidence of a Guiding Principle.

The Rose was laughing. Sam Oakenhurst had never seen a creature so filled with joy, with the rage of risk and skill which marked the greatest *jugaderos*. He had never known a creature so daring, so wise. And it seemed to him that some new strength bound him to her, through all the colour-flooded fields of the multiverse. And then she began to sing.

The beauty of her song was almost unbearable. He began to weep and his tears were blinding quicksilver. It was as if she had summoned a wind and the wind was her voice calling to him.

'Look up, Sam! There, beyond the colour fields! It's the Grail, Sam. It's the great Grail itself!'

But when his eyes were clear of tears Sam Oakenhurst looked up and all he saw was a lattice of light, like roots and branches, twisting around them on every side, a kind of nest made of curled gold and silver rays. And through this, with happy ease, the Rose steered the *machinoix* meat boat. Her hair was wild around her head, like flames; her limbs a haze of petals and brambles; and her song seemed to fill the multiverse.

The meat boat was a fat brazen lizard crawling over the surfaces of the vast fields, following the complex river systems which united them, replenished them, blending with new multihued mercury fractures running through a million dimensions and remaking themselves, fold upon fold, scale upon scale, until they merged again with the great main trunks, ancient beyond calculation, where (legend insisted) they would find the final scale and return, as was their destiny, to their original being: reunited with their archetype; no longer echoes. 'And this shall be called the Time of Conference,' said the Rose, bringing the meat boat down into a clover field of white and green. 'The Time of Reckoning. That, Sam, is the fate of the Just.'

He had managed to reach her and now sat at her feet with his arms around the stem of the wheel. He watched her as a new force took hold of the boat. A sudden stench came up from the holds, as if something had ruptured. She struggled with the wheel. He tried to help her. She sang to whatever elements would hear her but she was suddenly powerless. She shook her head and gestured for him to relax. There was nothing more they could do.

'We can't go any further now, Sam,' she said. 'We're not ready, I guess.'

'*Not you yet. No, no, no.*'

Turning with sudden recollection they saw oddly shaped jewelled hands disappearing below. How long had the *machinoix* been with them?

'She must be close to death,' said Sam Oakenhurst.

'Can you help her?' asked the Rose.

It was only then that they saw the shapeless ruin of Paul Minct, its upturned mask a blazing battleground of brands, its eyes enlivened at last with the fires of hell.

The Rose made a movement with Swift Thorn. There came a jolt, like a mild shockwave. Sam Oakenhurst felt water wash up his legs and reach his back.

He heard the sound of a tide as it retreated from the shore and he smelled the salt, the oily air of the coast. He opened his eyes. The boat was gone.

Eventually his vision adjusted. He understood what had happened. He lay on his side in the water, as if left there by a wave. A little above him, on the beach, the Rose was calling his name. 'Sam! The Fault has taken the meat boat.'

'Maybe Paul Minct achieved his ambition?' Away in the distance were the tranquil skies which marked the Biloxi Fault. Mr Oakenhurst turned on to his back. He began to get to his feet. He shuddered at the state of his clothing and was glad there were no witnesses to their coming ashore. The Rose appeared unaffected by their adventure. Taking his hand she waded briskly through the shallows and brought them up to the tufted dunes. A light wind blew the sand in rivulets through the grass.

'The meat boat was accepted and we were not. Whose sacrifice?' She pointed. 'See! We have Biloxi that way, New Orleans the other! We shall go to the Terminal, Sam. I have a purpose there.'

'I cannot go there yet,' he told her. 'I must go to New Orleans. Is it too much for me to learn? Too much that is novel and incomprehensible?'

'Ah, no, Sam. You already know it in your bones. Come on to Biloxi, mon brave. Later, maybe, you go to New Orleans, when I can come with you.' Standing against the yellow dunes, her hair still wild, a red haze in the wind, human in form but radiating the quintessence of the rose, all its exquisite beauty, Mrs von Bek made no indirect attempt to persuade him, either by gesture or word, and for that he loved her without reserve.

'You must go alone to Biloxi,' he said. 'There is a price for our salvation and I return to New Orleans to pay it.'

'Oh, don't go, Sam.' Clearly she found this request almost distasteful, though she had to make it. 'Are you sure this is nothing more than your own addiction?'

'On my honour, I swore to help you. On my honour, I must keep my bargain with those who helped me fulfil that pledge to you.'

She accepted this in silence, but it seemed to him that he had wounded her or that she disbelieved him. He said more softly:

'I will meet you at the Terminal. It is not my life I owe them, but my respect. I must acknowledge their sacrifice. Courageously they defied their most powerful taboos to do what I asked of them. And here we are, Rose, thanks to their courage.'

'And ours, Sam. I would return with you now, but I, too, am bound to a promise. If I lived after my business with Mr Minct I said I would deliver a message to Mr Jack Karaquazian at the Terminal Café. So I must make my way there and, yes, I will wait for you, Sam, at least until the boredom grows intolerable.' She smiled. 'Yes, I will meet you again, whenever our luck will have it so. Then, I hope, you will want to come with me, beyond the colour fields, beyond the universe known as The Grail, to the wonders of the Second Ether, where plurality forever holds sway. There you will discover what it is to be *jugaderos* and paramours, Sam. What it is to be alive! There's more than me in this for you, Sam.' Her lips released a sigh.

'Well,' he said, 'I think you will not forget me, Rose. You know who I am.'

'By and large, Sam.' She turned away.

As he put the Rose, the ocean and the dunes at his back and took the broken old road towards Louisiana, her voice returned to him on the wind.

'*Ma romance, nouvelle romance. Ma romancier, muy necromancier. Ma histoire, muy histoire nouvelle. Joli boys all dansez. Joli boys all dansez. Sing for me, olé, olé. But they shall not have muy vieux carré. Joli garçon sans merci. Pauvre pierrot, mon vieux, mon brave. Petit pierrot, mon sweet savage. Le monde est fou. El mundo c'est moi.*'

There was to be a final miracle: It seemed to him that the distant yell of the Biloxi Fault took fresh harmonics from the Rose's song and amplified and modified it until for a while a vast unearthly orchestra played the old tune, told the old story of lies and truth, of betrayals and sacrifices, of quests and oaths, of love and loss and resolutions that are not always tragic. The old story which is echoed by our own.

This sequence began with *Colour* and will end with *Routes*. Thanks to Los Tigres del Norte (Musivisa), Mamou (MCA Records), The Movies Sound Orchestra (Yel) and the bands at Michaux's, New Orleans.

In April 1994, I reminded Rob Holdstock that I would very much like him to write a story for this volume of New Worlds.

He replied on June 11.

David Garnett

Dear David,

Thanks for your note and I'm sorry to have been so slow responding. Two reasons for my distraction: first, the story I'd *planned* to show you ('Merlin's Wood') grew into a novel! And secondly, that business at Hockley Mere in Norfolk, I mentioned to you, has been taking some interesting twists and turns. I'll be getting back into Science after twenty years! Real Soon Now . . .

It occurs to me that the letters from the paleo-botanist who contacted me might be of interest, since they deal, as does the whole Hockley Mere 'event', with a subject close to the modern SF heart.

I enclose her side of the correspondence; see what you think. In any case, I'll be in touch in July.

All the best

Rob

The Charisma Trees

Robert Holdstock

(Letters from Rebecca Knight of the Department of Botany, Cambridge University, 1992–1994)

August '92 (letter)

Dear Rob,
Thanks for the book, but especially thanks for your time and work with Phil and myself at Hockley Mere. As you've no doubt discovered, taking peat-samples from thinly wooded Norfolk Fenland is laborious, wet, tiring on the arms, and very, *very* dirty! Thank God for the Dancing Poachers pub, even if it is a gathering point for the metal-detector mafia, the bloody treasure hunters! Anyway, more to the point: our research prcject is not just one page further along, thanks to your efforts – it's beginning to take a whole new direction! There was something very strange and very exciting in one of the samples we took that day. I'll get to it in a moment.

For your information, since you've asked, the cores you took were two inches in diameter, went forty feet deep, reaching down through one hundred and fifty thousand years of time, more or less. We have some horrendous names for the feet and inches along that core which mark out the centuries: *Alerod* and *Windermere Interstadial* (those were the warm times); *Older* and *Younger Dryas* (the woody times); *Devensian*, *Flandrian* and *Holocene* . . . it goes on!

So you have sampled oak and elm wildwood at a time when only boar, bears and *beavers* hunted the magic groves. Oh yes, there were beavers at work in Norfolk a hundred thousand years ago, same style of dams, same effect on shaping the woodland around the rivers as you get in Canada.

Anyway, your core was a fine sample, and an interesting one. A 'good call', as we Americans say. It has a charcoal line in the Older Dryas, followed by an inch of grassland pollen: this means that about a hundred thousand years ago the forest around Norwich burned down – a ferocious fire, by the looks of it, very localized, quite inexplicable. The area never recovered. The climate cooled, and a sort of cold savannah took over; an open grassland scattered with stands of beech and silver birch, patches of scrub-oak and wych elm, acting as shelters to ungulates, rodents and birds of prey. This was *rich* grassland, though, and would have been grazed by many species of creature, mostly now extinct.

But most interesting of all, we've found the pollen of an equally extinct tree, a shade-tolerant ecotype of *Corylus avellana*: yes, the famous and magical British hazel, the sacred Tree of Avalon, whose nuts carry wisdom and inspiration and whose twigs can find water and make rain!

We think the ecotype must have developed and spread from a single *refugium* (that's the academic's word for the first seeding-place), which was light-starved. In other words, this tree had stamina. Or to put it another way, it had a versatile gene pool.

No: I *don't* intend to get into the debate about DNA and magic attributes! Save that for your novels!

At the risk of boring you with facts (I know you prefer your *own* facts to anyone else's), let me take a moment to walk you through some ancient echoes, just outside Norwich.

At fifty thousand years Before the Present, primary oak and elm returns to what for millennia has been a rich grassland, so you can imagine the Fenland as now being a stifling, unbroken forest in three layers: a gloomy and dangerous underwood of scrub-hazel, juniper, crab-apple, maythorn and holly – below a vast sprawling canopy of oak, elm and lime, a sea of foliage that is penetrated vertically by oaks of enormous size! Grandfather trees, as they would be called in the Amazon rainforests.

But these oaks must have been *phenomenal* – nearly two hundred feet of vertical trunk, and then a vast but compact head of twisting branches, gnarled bark, leaf mass, fungal extrusions, *hollowings* and hollows in the mass. Mini-ecosystems, in other words, hovering above a broken and restless landscape of canopy and nests. (Oh yes: did I mention that we find evidence that the upper canopy was used like a *land surface*, swarming with birds and light-boned mammals, running the leaf mass above the half-light of the wildwood below, where the *big* creatures hunted?)

The core-sample you took – so much work for eight hours, so many pints that evening! – shows that during the last hundred and fifty thousand years, Eastern England was covered four times by a massive wildwood. But each period of afforestation lasted no more than ten thousand years before giving way to tundra, or cold savannah.

I know you don't agree with me, but the wildwood is only an *occasional* visitor to the Earth. Because it's long-lived in human terms, and humans achieved consciousness during its last and latest visit, we think of it as *the* natural state, but the wildwood really is only one face of an Earth that is continually playing with its options. Savannah, in the heat, and tundra, in the cool, are the *real* landscape, the most cost-effective if you want to think of it in those terms. I know we all worry about the loss of forests – their beauty, their biota, their diversity, and their function as *refugia* for human populations who have become of interest to anthropologists, if that's something you can sanction. But the Earth itself seems to recognize that big forests are simply one extreme of the Life-Fluctuation norm – deserts being the other – and so what we *should* be concerned with is the *concreting* of the Earth. As long as we have fields of grass to dream in: No problem! When the fields go . . . Problem!

October '92 (letter)

Dear Rob . . . I've just been to a seminar on the whole Hockley Mere site, and here's some information closer to the heart of a Celtophilic, nostalgic old archaeo-culture-vulture – your core, which reached down one hundred and fifty thousand years into the past, began its journey through a vertical cut of *human* time. In the top four feet you managed to pass through the site of a Civil War skirmish, then through one of King John's camps (a small coin has been found); there are traces of a seventh-century settlement, possibly Efringdun, and a Celtic shrine, Icenian, probably associated with Boudicca or her husband, Prasitagus, and dedicated to *Mabon*. Below that, a Bronze Age cemetery with burnt offerings and obsidian beads; then a flint workshop, probably five thousand years Before Present, and finally a shell midden, almost certainly Mesolithic; a community of fisherfolk and hunters that had lived here when the coastline of Norfolk came a lot further inland – before Cromer, before Great Yarmouth!

It's like a new excursion into Puck of Pook's Hill, isn't it? Downwards through time.

A foot below these echoes of Kipling's journey, the wildwood, according to its pollen record, is strong and free, reaching to the edge of the ocean itself. But six inches below that there is nothing but the signs of ice and desolation – namely sterile clays and gravels. Then, ten feet down – about twenty five thousand years ago – we find not just the wildwood again, but fire and flint!

Dear God, we think of Ancient History as Stone Age, Stonehenge, Bronze Age, Romans, Trojans, King Arthur, Robin Hood – Abba! But here, *before* the Ice Age that shaped your country as you know it, someone *lived*, made tools, burned a clearing to construct a shelter, someone *echoed the beaver*, forgotten folk shaping the land by making their refuge out of the *product* of that land.

It makes me think of the question you posed to us that final night in the pub, before you left: what did they dream of? Where are their dreams now? How do we *look* at the land in the right way to see what they might have left for us? (I'm talking forgotten folk here, not Abba . . .)

November '92 (letter)

Rob . . . really bad news: three evenings ago, the treasure hunters came, metal detectors in profusion. There were five of them, possibly more, since one kept talking into a mobile phone. Typical Nighthawks – leather masks painted with bird features, army-surplus anoraks, 'bovver boots' and motorcycle chains. They smashed the last two cores we'd taken – the others, fortunately, had already gone to Cambridge – and burned our tents. They said we were trespassing on a 'listed site'. When Phil pointed out that Hockley Mere was nothing of the sort, and he'd know because he'd done the routine search, as he did before sampling from *any* part of the land, he got two broken teeth and chain burn round his neck for his protest.

They waved a map of Britain at us – it was covered with circles, thousands of them. 'Listed sites! Listed sites!' the leader chanted.

Phil did absolutely nothing physical. He just kept arguing with them. This *was* a site of archaeological interest, he roared at the leader, as the recent core-sampling would suggest. But it wasn't yet a listed site, as they must well have known. If they'd found evidence of a settlement, they should report it to the British Museum and immediately stop all metal-detecting work at the site. The only thing their map showed was archaeological sites that had been tentatively identified from the air, or by bastards like them with metal detectors, none of which had yet been officially excavated, and which in most instances were probably not even *known* officially.

Then he called them 'nothing more than thieves!' 'Pillagers!' he shouted, 'Don't pretend differently.'

That's when he got an old-fashioned police baton in the mouth, and four hundred pounds' worth of dental work. He's defiant though. This country's heritage *is* being mined for gold and silver, while 'dull' things like clay plaques with scrawled writing on them, lifted from a Roman site, or boot buckles from a lost medieval village, get dumped in what the Nighthawks call Bad Find Pit.

From a stray comment heard before he was beaten up, Phil thinks Bad Find Pit is somewhere in the West York Moors, a deep ghyll of some sort, maybe even Gaping Ghyll itself. The ultimate votive-offering shaft! If that sounds flippant, I don't feel flippant. I feel sick . . .

February '93 (fax)

. . . Do you remember the pollen of *Corylus* we found? Curiouser and curiouser . . . This ecotype of the magical hazel hasn't been known for a hundred thousand years, but its DNA, in the pollen we extracted, was still intact and viable. It had been preserved in a sugar – trehalose, I think – which doesn't crystallize but instead forms a sort of *glass* – it protects molecules, even complex ones, by forming hydrogen bonds with macromolecules in place of water. That's how seeds, frogs, even some reptiles survive droughts in non-active metabolic states for decades . . . but one hundred thousand years!

Apparently there are stands of *Corylus* all over the world, seeded from a Hockley Mere sample taken ten years ago. (No: I'm afraid it wasn't a new discovery after all.) It's a fast-growing tree, unlike modern hazel, and secretes organic matter in the same sugar-glass, presumably to protect itself against insect parasites – rather like resin, I suppose, although it must also *attract* creatures, I'd have thought. Do you remember visiting Wytham Woods outside Oxford? We got permission to go into the wildwood *refugium*, the few acres where they're leaving the wood unmanaged for the foreseeable future, and at one point we were both almost speechless with a sense of belonging, of beauty, of being almost in a New Age fever of closeness to nature. You wanted to hug the trees, you said. In fact you did, and got very sticky as a result. Well, that was the *Corylus* refuge. I'll try and find out more and let you know.

April '93 (letter)

. . . I was talking with David Bellamy at a faculty supper. Apparently on the island of Tasmania there's a swathe of forest that no lumberjack will touch, or even go near. These are hard-assed, hardwood-hating, moneyseeking, western, 'exploitation-vegetation' (as we call the logging companies). But they won't access Gordon Valley for love, money, or even more money! And the place is riddled with archaic *Corylus*, seeded there in '82, and now widely spread. Each *Corylus* hazel seems to create a circle of protection among the native trees, which include mahogany and the so-called Dragon trees with their huge buttresses, a circle about four hundred yards in diameter. Bellamy said he'd heard these called Charisma Zones. To go into them was either frightening or awe-inspiring. He said he'd wanted to stay in the valley for ever and had to forcibly control what he called an emotional-overload in order to get out. But – loggers unwilling to cut the trees? Odd, to say the least.

At the same supper, listening to the same conversation, was Jack Cohen, an embryologist and science-fiction fan, I think. Do you know him? He apparently goes to sci-fi conventions and gives crazy, right-on lectures about alien biologies. He'd heard that the *Corylus avellana* seeded in Tasmania are transgenic, he's not sure how, and will arrange for me to meet Crick's assistant in the Botany department. They're playing with all manner of genetic matchmaking, as they call it, of plants.

May '93 (letter)

. . . It's human DNA! I can hardly believe it. The *Corylus avellana* archeotypes have been 'infected' with twenty gene-sequences selected from various human chromosomes (I was told which ones, but it didn't mean a lot to me), complex sequences that between them contain some, though not all – but *enough* – of the coding that combines to create the chemical and behavioural attributes we call *charisma*; the effect that some people have when they walk into a room, or talk to you – you feel drawn to them, you feel in their shadow, but you're content, it's a form of nurture – you can't touch, but they can hold you so close. They can elicit fear, or respect, but mostly *well being* – what Americans are increasingly calling the feelgood factor, as Hollywood's own charisma cuts through the neural networks of the American psyche, leaving only sentimentality and redemption as the Theme of Life.

Charisma!

They've apparently set up small intrusions of transgenic hazelwood in fifty forest locations, each with the Group-DNA-sequences from a different charismatic individual.

The way it works is to do with the trehalose sugar-glass. The hazel tree *exudes* the charisma factor, which is protected in fluid glass and contained in molecular tubes of Buckminsterfullerine, a complex of hexagonal and pentagonal carbon rings that form together like a football but which can also link to form incredibly resistant, single-molecular thickness tubes, theoretically with no limit to their length! Each breeze in the rainforest, or temperate woodland, carries millions of these charisma packages to the foliage of the native trees, where they're absorbed through pores into the leaves, and disseminated through the sap system to individual cells. The 'bucky-tubes' seem able to enter the transport systems of each plant cell through the exits in the cell membrane from the reticular system, which accumulates and pumps out cell products. Everything is in reverse, then – the human genes, linked with *Corylus avellana*'s reverse transcriptase and a so-called 'seek and find' gene that targets the nuclear membrane, enters it, and allows for the stitching into the cells of the tropical hardwood (or whatever) of the viral DNA, thus allowing a gigantic and long-established hardwood to produce some of the thousands of human pheromones that can combine to create the aura of *charisma*.

By the way – you remember the *refugium* in Wycome Wood? When you hugged and kissed the trees, and called them 'wonderful' and 'so, so precious' and 'my special luvvies'?

They were carrying the pooled DNA of five years of British Oscar winners!

September '93 (letter)

. . . It's not easy getting details of the charismatic *Corylus* intrusions. The original requests for DNA were made surreptitiously, but the 'Charisma Set' got to hear of it, through the grapevine, in no time at all. There were *thousands* of applications to donate DNA – from politicians, actors, explorers, religious leaders, ex-hostages, painters, writers, newspaper moguls, athletes, comedians, TV presenters – it's astonishing how these people define their own charisma. How many *believe* the fake charisma of public notoriety is somehow to do with them.

Of course, money talked in its own persuasive dialect, as has politics, which is to say 'blackmail'.

But on the whole, the charisma – which of course is to be used to *protect* and *preserve* the woodlands – has been acquired by general agreement.

A notable success, for example, is the Clint Eastwood *Corylus* pinewood up in Montana. They call it Make-My-Day wood, and it's flourishing – mainly because no one dares go near it.

The various GellerGroves – using Uri Geller's DNA – are also having a remarkable effect. Although his spoonbending was probably a trick, his ability to stop wrist-watches seems to have been genuine. But inside a GellerGrove, time doesn't just *stop*, its accumulated events *vanish*, facilitating peace meetings between enemy states that can be undertaken without the burden of history.

The hugely promoted Papwoods of Madonna have been successful too – they're so tacky and forgettable, nobody bothers with them.

Not all the *Corylus refugia* are working as well as these. The so-called Ed Kennedy copses in New England have deteriorated into shallow lakes and marshes, now used by the locals to dump their old cars. And four hundred miles from Manaus, in the Caruari region of the Brazilian rainforest, the charismatic *Corylus* intrusion actually seemed to *encourage* the loggers and drug companies in the mindless exploitation of the local flora, causing much suffering. After several years of such abuse, however, the *Corylus* were suddenly found strangled with creeper; Thatcher wood has now been deemed a failure and will be cut down.

November '93 (scrawled letter)

. . . I can't bear it. I've been hysterical with rage for a week. I should have written to you at once, but sometimes I'm not strong enough to face my own despair.

Phil is in hospital, very badly hurt. He went back to Hockley Mere to take a second core, to try to establish if the charcoal feature that was discovered when you were with us was the result of human clearance by a *Sapiens* group, closely related to *Sapiens Neanderthalis*, remains of which have recently been found in abundance in Spain; it's a human group which might have spread over the fabled landbridge between Brittany and Dorset that we now know existed 80,000 years ago.

The Nighthawks must have been waiting for him, or perhaps he disturbed one of their digging operations. They threw him in the shallow mere, tied up with oiled motorcycle chains, and his skull cracked by a blow from a flint hammer, which they discarded. They'd stuck a red-kite's carcase on an ash-pole by his unconscious body, carved with – can you believe it? – early Latin. The words meant 'Finding is keeping. If you spy, you die.'

The arrogance, the confidence in this display of territoriality, seems to confirm what Phil always suspected – it's the millionaire collectors, the black market, the art world that is behind the Nighthawks. And our government gets a nice little earner in tax to deny it's happening, because questions aren't asked, and objects don't have to be catalogued, just so long as the monetary transaction in 'sale of art' appears on the simplest of tax forms. We're so obsessed with the fine details of select committee reports, rulings, debates and decisions on our heritage, that we forget how easy it is to bribe the establishment to ignore the question of *what* is being traded, or exploited, by simply being honest about the amount of money its being traded *for*!

Late February '94 (fax)

. . . You remember the woods near Hockley Mere? Three sets of men's clothes – leathers, underclothes, masks, boots, chains – plus metal detectors were found in a *Corylus* grove, strung to branches with ivy, just last week. No sign of bodies, or signs of a struggle. And it turns out it's a Charisma wood too! But there's a certain cageyness about exactly *whose* charisma. There are five 'closed files', according to Jack Cohen. Five woods, world-wide, that are 'outside' the main experiment. Cambridge is completely silent on the nature – even the location – of those five. Hockley Mere has 'leaked' – in part at least – but I hear already that the army is moving in.

What happened to the Nighthawks? Charisma can't *kill*, can it? It can't be the *trees* tying the clothes up . . . Can it? What happened to the bodies?

Later note by post:

I just found out Phil was down there at the time, went there after discharging himself from hospital. But he wasn't around when the discovery of the discarded clothes was made, or at least no one saw him. He's not been seen for several days, in fact. I'm seriously worried, now. I'm going down to Hockley Mere to take a look – I'll call you tomorrow if all's well.

March '94 (handwritten notes on lined paper)

. . . The whole area around Hockley Mere has been sealed off: lakes and woods, fields and farms, the army and police are everywhere, and rangers, and paramilitaries. It's like a scene from a movie. Army trucks are in and out along the main road in a constant stream.

I caught up with Phil in the Dancing Poachers. He's managed to dig in, at Hockley, a sort of hide, close enough to the woods to see the activity at closer hand, but it's risky.

The main thing he's observed is that a stretch-limo arrives every day, driving slowly into the cluster of lorries, portacabins and tents that have been erected at the lake-side perimeter of Hockley wood. Always a cluster of people around the limo, and much activity out of sight, moving towards the woods. Who's inside, Phil hasn't seen or managed to find out yet.

Meanwhile, locals talk about the two lost kids, both in their teens, both keen on fishing in the scatter of ponds around the main lake itself. They'd gone missing three days before. Just their clothes found, neatly packaged at the woodland edge . . .

March '94 (postcard)

Two army privates, who came into the Poachers for a drink, were talking about 'missing' friends. They were getting scared of the Hockley Mere duty, talking about asking for a transfer. They clammed up when Phil came and sat down nearby, but the landlady, an easy-going woman, got talking to them later. Five of their unit have gone missing, it seems, and the rest are badly affected by going *anywhere* near the trees – a dizzying sense of dislocation, void, emptiness, a feeling of being far flung, helplessly travelling towards a strong, guiding light.

March '94 (postcard, same post)

Out of body experiences? Or maybe that odd experience during near death when you seem to be going down a tunnel towards an 'angelic' light? Who knows? I can't get close enough to find out. Rumour in the 'scientific' world, by the way, is that the charisma is Billy Graham's, but I'm sure Praise-The-

Lord wood (the trees wave their upper branches in unison) is in the USA somewhere.

Early April '94 (fax)

. . . Curiouser and curiouser: a constant stream of experts on what I hear is being called 'Imaginative Time' are being bussed in from around the world. Many of them stop off at the Poachers'. By all accounts they are as confused by the happenings at the Charisma wood as the locals.

You'll probably know some of the writers among them: they've been brought in because of their expertise in the relationship between time and imagination: Aldiss to advise on the Jurassic; Priest on the Edwardian; Moorcock and Silverberg on the End of Time itself; Kushner and de Lint on time as it runs in the realm of Faerie; Tuttle on lost futures; Bear, Baxter, McAuley on Big Science. Several others. There are musicians – Birtwhistle, Chris Dench, Laurie Anderson, the younger Taverner, folk singers plus pipes and hurdy-gurdies, Aboriginal musicians plus flutes and drums, Hawkwind.

All of them go into Hockley wood, near the shallow lake, and sometimes you can hear music. On their return they are debriefed at length before being bussed to their hotel, exhausted and frightened, and sworn to secrecy.

April '94 (postcard)

Two of the writers have vanished: just their clothes found, oddly intertwined, plus a few frantically scribbled sentences from each, nothing coherent, although in the man's case, startlingly enigmatic. They'll be greatly missed by their fans.

Late April '94 (scrawled letter)

. . . A great deal of consternation. Rumour has it that something in the charisma of the wood is functioning in a way that was not expected. Each day, the stretch-limo brings the Charisma Source, the only man who can control his inadvertent creation. Master of the Id! In the Dancing Poachers, the talk is all of the stars 'spinning and swirling above Hockley, like a heavenly whirlpool' a phenomenon witnessed by several local – and sober – people, although the effect lasted for just a few seconds.

A friend in the department of paleontology at Cambridge, someone who's always on the case in his quiet manner, has slipped me a note: new studies of bone fragments, collected in Victorian times from pits and excavations in the

Hockley area that probably reached, during the digging, to levels representing fifty to one hundred thousand years Before Present, seem to be of *modern man*. Something about the teeth: lacunae in two molars show signs of having been produced by a metal drill! Sounds like one of those urban myths, doesn't it? But there's a real buzz of activity in the department. *Someone*'s taking it seriously.

By the way, I see *you've* been invited to participate, along with others on the new list. Let me know when you're coming to Hockley.

May '94 (letter)

...It's Hawking's! The charisma DNA, I mean. The Cambridge mathematician who has visualized so much of the beginning of the universe. It's Hawking himself who arrives each day in the stretch-limo. He's trying to reverse the defensive field of the charisma trees at Hockley, to make them bring back the lives that have been set adrift in time!

It was so obvious, I suppose. Hawking's charisma is substantially related to his imagination, and his total engagement with Imaginative Time, an expression that turns out to be *his* coinage. The hazelwood has formed a tunnel from the beginning to the end of the universe as it exists for the *wood*, and they use it, as do all the *Corylus* woods, to protect themselves, not understanding – how can they? They are not sentient – that they are destroying life.

May '94 (postcard)

One of the writers who disappeared three weeks ago has returned, grotesquely naked and dishevelled, aged by many years, his flesh hanging from him in fatty rags. He stumbled from the wood clutching a strange flower, and was hastened away to the interview rooms to tell his story. I hear that he is insisting on 'going back' – he's met someone – but he will not say to where. Something has happened to him and he no longer belongs in his own time. But he has been through the tunnel and survived! I hear talk that it is the trees *themselves* that have brought him back and sent him as an envoy, an emissary, to communicate with Hawking about what must be done to protect human life, while the imagination is allowed to access the views of past and future inside the hazelwood. Perhaps sentience exists after all!

June '94 (scrawled letter on back of manuscript sheet)

Rob – This may be my last letter – not sure – Phil has found a way through the military fence. We're going into Hockley wood tonight. It's an opportunity that we have to take – I can't explain it except to say it *feels* right. I'm drawn to Hockley. Charisma? Of course. But I don't want to think too rationally at the moment, I just need to hold Phil's hand and enter the flow of time. I know you're coming up soon, but I really can't wait for you. I have to go *now* into the flow.

By all the signs, that flow is *backwards*, and to that time of the intriguing forest fire, which I now think was probably started by the first unwilling travellers, the Nighthawks. I want to come back, of course, but . . . well, there's no guaranteeing. How to communicate with you from so far in the past I haven't a clue, unless I scratch a letter on *ivory*. I'm prompted to suggest this by something Phil heard from the Nighthawks, way back, when they tried to kill him. They'd been over the Hockley area pretty thoroughly, but mostly Bad Finds: and the Bad Finds included a stack of bones with what looked like writing on them, which they assumed were some 'freak show' and were disposed of.

If you ever locate Bad Find Pit, search among those bones for a letter from Rebecca.

I hope you don't get asked for postage!

Rob Holdstock's penultimate words to me were: 'I'll be in touch in July.'
I'm still waiting to hear from him.
Somehow or other.

David Garnett
Three Chimneys
Ferring
September 1994

Inside Outside

David Langford

It is well known in certain circles that all science fiction is trash, since it's always possible for an 'outside' critic to give it the quick once-over and discover a book that doesn't meet selected literary standards. Like travel journalists summing up an entire country's unmistakable state of decline after a 24-hour stopover and two conversations with taxi drivers, such visitors unerringly find what they expect.

The converse argument that the bad non-genre books X and Y and Z condemn all 'real' fiction by their mere existence is never seriously advanced, but is worth keeping in mind as a parable or thought experiment.

Now there are a number of well-worn debating points to be made here about the dread walls of the sf genre ghetto, but this logomachy seems outdated. Sf these days is a fuzzy circle on an imaginary Venn diagram of literature. Some writers play around in its broad, ill-defined borders and are called 'slipstream': Christopher Priest's *The Affirmation* (1981) is an excellent example. Some stand just within the border zone, but with much still depending on which way they happen to face: Robert Harris in *Fatherland* (1992) uses the traditional sf device of an alternative history but aims his story more into the overlapping Venn circle of thriller/detective fiction.

And certain writers wander deep into sf while resolutely claiming that they are doing no such thing. Whitley Strieber, for example, writes about literal flying saucers and presumed aliens in *Majestic* (1989) but has been heard to argue that this novel is by no means nasty old sf because, being based on the 'true' story of the ever-controversial 1947 Roswell UFO incident, it's *set in the past*. P.D. James once insisted on TV that her *The Children of Men* (1992), despite inhabiting a recognizable and indeed over-exploited niche of bleak near-future speculation, is not sf since it contains neither spaceships nor robots. One rather assumes that the late great Anthony Burgess might have had his own sf excursions slightly in mind when he praised Brian Aldiss's 1978 *Enemies of the System* (set 1.09 million years hence and featuring faster-than-light interstellar spaceships) as ' . . . rich, allusive, full of real people and unfailingly interesting. It is not, then, real SF.'

Turnabout is fair play. Critical tourists in sf reasonably insist on applying literary standards. Literary visitors to the genre can hardly complain if we apply the related sf standards, those rules of thumb that codify gut feelings about what makes sf work. Some of the pitfalls, in no particular order:

• **Information feed.** Writers accustomed to telling the reader highly subtle things about characters' relations, through natural-seeming nuances of narrative or dialogue, can go bananas when confronted with the task of conveying a new chunk of history, a new society, a new world. They may not descend to lines like: 'Er, tell me again how the present war came about, as though I knew nothing of it' . . . but some come fearfully close.

Robert Harris in *Fatherland* has a relatively easy task in this area; the alternative history where Hitler won is all too imaginable. Harris handles the mechanics well, neatly allowing a tourist guide to describe the ghastly architecture of Albert Speer's planned post-war Berlin – including a genuine sf *frisson* concerning the Great Hall of the Reich, largest building in this world, which when crammed with a rally of 180,000 Nazis develops its own internal rainfall. After which the book heads off into thriller territory and the sf critic says farewell.

• **Consistency with natural law.** This largely means internal consistency rather than slavish adherence to physicists' current snapshots of how things are. A faster-than-light spaceship is a legitimate plot device – this *is* fiction, and General Relativity may not be the last word on the cosmos. Writing about a spacecraft that lands on the surface of the Sun (which has no surface) is harder to justify.

A oft-cited example is that of Piggy's glasses in William Golding's remotely science-fictional *Lord of the Flies* (1954). Piggy is short-sighted; his spectacles thus have concave lenses which will spread rather than concentrate sunlight, and can't be used to start a fire. This is a peripheral blemish, a small solecism which by no means destroys the book as some sf pedants have claimed. Oddly enough, the problem was solved better on another fantasy island which Golding surely knew: that of J.M. Barrie's play *The Admirable Crichton* (1902), where resourceful Crichton plausibly contrives a lens from two watch-glasses with some water between them.

• **Consistency with the present.** This could also be called common sense. Much writing about tomorrow seems instantly archaic because the author hasn't assimilated the 'givens' imposed on the story by today. It isn't necessary to take this as far as those cryonics enthusiasts who are so keen on their plans for frozen immortality that they will rubbish any imagined future which fails to centre on an ever-growing reserve of corpses in liquid nitrogen.

But today's proliferation of personal computers and the Internet *does* strongly imply a data-riddled millennium where virtually every literate person with an income will be linked into the global web. (As I write, a million new users are joining the net each month.) Near-future sf can't afford to leave this out of the reckoning – unless, as in *The Children of Men*, a convenient disaster or social collapse can help sidestep the issue. So many writers have devastated half the world in order to produce a future sufficiently crippled to be easily imaginable. I've done it myself. We are all guilty.

Another author praised outside sf is Kathy Page, whose *Island Paradise* (1989) comes with a warm plug from Malcolm Bradbury. It's well written; the low-key dystopian scenario (of which more below) is convincing enough; and then we learn that this over-governed world has a secret nuclear arms dump into which large, informal parties of dissidents can wander at will to carry off the conveniently miniaturized doomsday weapons, in backpacks. The only thing missing is a sign saying 'Please Take One'. To the innocent eye of the sf reader, this is plotting that simply will not do.

• **Futurespeak.** Jargon – especially scientific or pseudo-scientific jargon – must be worked over and subjected to plausibility tests until something reasonably credible emerges. Slang is folk poetry: perhaps the real thing can be created only by poets (later on we'll remember that Marge Piercy is a poet of some note). The real-life tendency of capital letters to fade into the lower-case undergrowth should also be noted.

Here's a fine novel studded with micro-lapses of invariably capitalized terminology: *The Handmaid's Tale* (1985) by Margaret Atwood, of whom the *SF Encyclopaedia* remarks that her 'attempts at the language of genre sf are not unembarrassing'. There are religious outbreaks called Prayvaganzas, the poorer chaps' women are Econowives and the democratic tearing-apart of a victim by a mob is Particicution. People don't phone but use the Compuphone, not to mention banking at the Compubank and sticking their credit cards into a Compubite – all reminiscent of those pseudo-futuristic prefixes in pulp sf, like 'space-rations' and 'plasti-boots', or the omnipresent 'synthi-' in Judge Dredd comics: 'synthinylon'.

Island Paradise, already mentioned, has a humane voluntary-euthanasia programme whereby they don't cart older folk off to lethal chambers, but, instead, a social worker comes round and nags you to do the decent thing. This is portrayed in terms of Timely and Untimely Deaths, the former being the Price of utopia – awkward capitals again, as though today we went on about Pensions and Bus Passes. This book also speaks of power (that is, Power) being imported from 'Planet Three'. Ignoring the impossible economics of shipping power across interplanetary space, the suspicion here is that Kathy Page somehow got the idea that mentioning Venus or Mars would be *too sci-fi* – and so she substituted this colourless yet deeply unbelievable name.

• **Unrepeatability.** If an sf story depends on an event or discovery that is billed as unique and never to be repeated, there had better be a good reason why. 'The secret of the deadly Wibble Ray, which could so easily have ended all life on Earth, died with Professor Jones. The horror is over for ever.' No, it isn't: some other damned researcher in some other country is busy inventing the thing all over again. Scientific genies are not so easily coaxed back into the bottle. Examples will follow.

• **Uniformity.** Sf often deals with the actions of large numbers of people: a whole population responds to global threat or the apparition of Elvis in the sky. The point here is that people are very diverse. Only lazy writers give us stuff like: 'The entire world was convinced at once by President Spong's call for universal overtime without pay in order to defeat the Vegan economic assault.'

Our remaining specimens deserve examination at greater length. The following selections were made by a computer randomization process not wholly uninfluenced by what I actually had available.

The Children of Men by P.D. James was a UK paperback bestseller in spring 1994. Essentially this is the standard sf novel of sterility, strongly reminiscent (to genre readers) of Brian Aldiss's 1964 *Greybeard*. The book is well written – perhaps too much so in places; as John Grant observes, some of the more mannered passages would definitely have rated three stars if included in *Cold Comfort Farm*.

Strangely, there is a terminological glitch on the first page. After a striking enough opening about the death of the last-ever man to be born, the narrator mentions hearing this on the 'State Radio Service'. Later we meet the 'State Security Police'. But this is Britain – Britain under a dictatorship, admittedly, but even a very stupid dictator (and this one is reputedly a genius) won't go around changing institutions' names merely to make them more science-fictionally sinister. Of course the State Radio Service and the SSP – note that SS! – would be soothingly called the BBC and the police.

Next comes a whopping information dump. The protagonist begins a painstakingly literate diary and records in merciless detail the history of the world from now to his present day of 2021. Not for posterity, because there won't be any – and just in case, he announces his firm intention of burning the diary. Meanwhile, he shows an uncanny ability to give just the background information that might be required by a reader situated in the early 1990s, almost as though his hand were being guided by some omnipotent Author . . .

The story he tells is pretty odd, too. All human sperm ceased quite suddenly to be fertile by 1995, now subtly renamed 'Year Omega'. It's a *possible* premise, though such absolutes in biology are to be distrusted. The cutoff has to be absolute for James's plot, which requires a Last Generation and no distracting kids around for the big event, subtly hinted by the fact that while Part 1 of the book is called 'Omega', Part 2 is called 'Alpha'. Therefore, testing our credulity to the limit and beyond, it is stated that even artificial insemination or *in vitro* fertilization using frozen sperm from the potent days won't work. One fights to resist the image of an offstage fleet of alien spaceships manned by robots and broadcasting infertility rays.

We also have a touch of what I've called the fallacy of uniformity when it comes to the Omegas, as those born in Year Omega are subtly named. Every member of this Last/Lost Generation was, it seems, thoroughly pampered (unbelievable uniformity of parents world-wide), and now in their maturity they are without exception unusually beautiful (no explanation for this) and menacing, the epitome of the Youth Problem. Credibility would be much enhanced by permitting a reasonable percentage to be overweight; have acne; prefer rock-climbing, tiddlywinks or reading detective stories to the bouts of orgiastic violence so necessary for a further kink in the plot of *The Children of Men*.

Unrepeatability is another of the sf touchstones listed above. Warning bells ring under this heading when we hear of the one remaining secretly fertile man in the world: what, just one? And gosh, he's dead now, so we have to hope the one pregnant woman's baby is a boy. But after the abrupt way human reproduction was halted, there's a broader implication that the displeasure of God has now ceased, or the aliens have turned off their sterility rays, and that if one chap is functional then lots more probably are. This detracts somewhat from the tension of the final chapters – though there's a wonderful pulp-sf bit where the dictator himself, who personally controls the entire security forces of Britain, turns up alone to shoot it out with the protagonist.

The book is often finely written; there are excellent character touches and poignant images of Oxford in decay ('just like *Greybeard*,' mutters the unregenerate sf fan); but there is also this nonsense cluttering up the plot. Nonsense, too, which one would expect an sf editor to sort out before publication. Is it significant that *The Children of Men* was first published by Faber ('just like *Greybeard*'), which no longer has an official sf list or editor?

Martin Amis avoids the difficulties of dealing with the future in *Time's Arrow* (1991) by running his story backwards from the present day into the past. This is not a cop-out (Amis knows his sf) but an attempted *tour de force*, the telling of an entire life from a time-reversed viewpoint.

Time running backwards is hardly a new sf idea. Brian Aldiss – that man again – toyed with it in *An Age* alias *Cryptozoic!* (1967) but cannily avoided taking the actual narrative into reverse; Roger Zelazny, J.G. Ballard and others wrote short stories on the theme; Philip K. Dick's unusually eccentric and flawed *Counter-Clock World* (1967) revolves around life-spotters rescuing the awakening dead from their graves and librarians erasing texts to expunge knowledge for ever. There was even a 1989 episode of *Red Dwarf* called 'Backwards'.

The familiarity of the idea is no obstacle here: Amis is gifted enough to get away with a great deal, and it's good to see him come to grips with the technical challenge of time-reversal . . . for a while. What he sinks into might be called the pitfall of the prolonged conceit – as with those early sf writers who so much loved the ingenuity of their One Big Idea that, to them, the story seemed to require only that this notion be laid out at length on the page and admired from every angle.

Thus whole chapters of hyperkinetic Amis prose and clever postmodern bits come to seem a desperate waltz of distraction, smoke and mirrors to obscure the fact that uneventful decades told backwards are not really more interesting than their forwards version. Successive shocks of reversed bodily function have a diminishing effect (and we are spared nothing, not even the preliminary to a good backwards puke as the protagonist pulls the toilet handle and 'The bowl filled with its terrible surprises.'). The sf reader begins to shuffle slightly, remembering perhaps that *Counter-Clock World* also had a plot going before the end of chapter one.

The identity of the narrative voice who inhabits the protagonist is a dodgy philosophical problem. Like all those convenient amnesiacs in sf, this personality's memory (none) and abilities are determined solely by the story. He is not the protagonist retracing his own timeline, since it is required that he should not know the appalling past that is his future. Equally, he's not a brand-new soul whose reversed experiences begin with the protagonist's death, since like a computer he comes prepackaged with useful functions: English, general knowledge, moral views, the sense that things are going backwards, and a tiresomely constant capacity to be surprised by this. Well into the narrative he's still referring to post-coital languor as foreplay (which is quite witty) and mentioning that the protagonist has 'jumped the queue' (which seems dumb: joining the queue at its head is the norm in retrograde time and the narrator should by then be entirely used to it). An important nightmare of the protagonist's, foreshadowing or postshadowing that nasty area of the past, is played in forwards time for no apparent reason other than to give the reader a better chance at understanding. There are other small niggles. Backward ran dialogue until reeled the mind . . .

At the heart of the book, when time has rewound to 1944, comes the short story for which the rest of *Time's Arrow* is an elaborate frame and apparatus of translation. It is the reversed story of Auschwitz, made hideously lyrical by its presentation as a sort of joyous creation myth. Men of infinite compassion and power cause a whole race to be born from flame, etc.

I truly don't know whether all the rest of the laborious backward narrative is justified by this segment of ironic distancing taken to a point beyond irony. The Holocaust is one of the major arcana of the twentieth-century cultural pack, a card that may be devalued by playing it too often – at risk of spreading a further blur of familiarity over the reports of people like Primo Levi who were actually there.

(Yes, this card is also played in *Fatherland*, but very discreetly; not, as it were, face up.)

Nietzsche said: 'if you gaze for long into the abyss, the abyss gazes also into you,' although I believe he said it in German. Perhaps my worry is that if you gaze for long into the abyss, the abyss begins to look ordinary or even boring.

The winner of the 1993 Arthur C. Clarke Award amid some slight controversy, Marge Piercy's *Body of Glass* (1991) comes from an author already known in sf for *Woman on the Edge of Time* (1976) – though most of her work lies outside the genre and, for many, the sf bits of *Woman . . .* were the least convincing.

Most of *Body of Glass* works rather well, with its free rendition of the story of Rabbi Loew's golem in seventeenth-century Prague linking nicely with the exploits of the 2059 cyborg Yod to whom the old tale is being told, and who like the golem is created to defend a threatened Jewish community. The historical resonance is effective enough to quell carping critics who might suggest that Yod, being primarily designed as a self-acting AI weapon to be deployed in cyberspace, hardly needs a perfect humanoid body at all – let alone one capable of tireless yet tasteful sex. John Sladek's argument is also valid here: that we *will* create anthropomorphic robots when we can, because the idea is so fascinating.

Similarly, Yod's final sacrifice to save the community has been criticized as unnecessary, since (being an artificial intelligence) he could be multiply copied, downloadable into other cyborg bodies. Yes indeed, but he explicitly chooses suicide and also takes pains to bump off his maker and destroy the manufacturing records, because Yod himself has come to disapprove of having been created as a weapon. There is a hint of the uniqueness pitfall discussed above, in that now it's known that Yods are possible more will surely be built, very probably by the nasty conglomerates against whose depredations Yod was made as a counterweapon . . . but that's the future, after the book ends.

What is a little dissatisfying about Piercy's novel is that her whole picture of state-of-the-art 2059 cyberspace comes straight from the work of our very own sf visionary and technological know-nothing, William Gibson. This is implicit in the text ('She called up the time on her cornea') and explicitly acknowledged: 'I have freely borrowed . . . I figure it's all one playground.' Which is fine, except that the real world of the net has already read Gibson and moved on.

The threat against the lovable Jewish commune of Tikva, where people embroider folksy computer software better than anyone else in the world, consists of net-riding information pirates who lethally invade Tikva's local cyberspace work-zone. Such a killing mode of attack is not yet with us, but we already have the defence – you pull the plug and disconnect your local computer complex from the net. Or, with more sophistication, you work behind 'firewall' systems that allow data in and out without surrendering program control to any outside source.

I suspect that Piercy is one of the many people who haven't quite got the hang of the difference between data and programs. When Yod and friends electronically invade the cyberspace of the wicked conglomerate Yakamura-Stichen, they do so 'along the com-con channels, to pass in with messages. There was no way a base could distinguish between legitimate entering data and folks along for the ride.' Right. They have transmitted computer simulacra of themselves as data, like a multi-gigabyte electronic mail message. The next step is presumably for this data to be run as an executable program within the Y-S system – otherwise it just lies there, inert. Who is going to run it for them? 'Hey, that's interesting, an anonymous friend has sent me this 15 gigabyte program file – I wonder what it does? Let's try it and find out . . . '

For the rest: the street slang is pretty good, although I couldn't swallow the Glop – would you? This is the name for an extended urban blight closely resembling Gibson's Sprawl, based on the term apparently on all street folk's lips until shortened by usage: 'megalopolis'. Hmm. Least convincing future scene-setting: I imagine one must need a good eye for fashion to spot that a silk robe is 'from the mutated worms that were the rage'.

Body of Glass is nevertheless an enjoyable and satisfying book despite wonky technological premises.

There is another oft-told tale lurking in Paul Theroux's *O-Zone* (1986): the thuddingly familiar sf yarn of the very bad place, the feared land beyond the pale, which when confronted at ground level turns out less awful than expected – indeed rather a good thing, whose noble savagery makes a man of you. O-Zone is this place, a chunk of midwest America (Ozarks) closed off 'for over fifteen years' after an escape of radioactive wastes. Wastes with short half-lives, presumably; their impact on the plot is zero.

Theroux is never less than literate, but his narrative has strange dips and lurches, with dense pockets of exclamation marks. O-Zone! Think of that! They were here, here in O-Zone! In forbidden O-Zone itself! It may be a sign of not wholly thought-out sf that the first party to be issued an Access Pass and allowed to land in O-Zone after its long seclusion are not official explorers, nor investigators checking whether the land is commercially reclaimable, but tourists out for fun.

Besides O-Zone the USA comprises sealed, fortified cities of the decadent rich, who evince decadence by doing things like walking around naked except for masks. There is also 'Godseye', a semi-official organization of futuristically armed psychopath vigilantes whose hobby is to blast, stun or incinerate anyone seen behaving suspiciously on the streets – e.g. running in terror, looking like a member of the underclasses, or standing too close to such a suspect person. (It seems a distinct flaw that these weapons freaks never, ever compare their beloved killing tools in terms of brand names, but go on about generic burp guns, particle beams, stunners or lasers.) Later we visit a community echoing the wonderfully banal American Good Place of a thousand ungood sf novels, a town where people go to church, eat nice home-made pies, wear decent, old-fashioned guns with real moving parts . . .

The story is burdened with one of the most tiresome characters in recent sf – Fisher 'Fizzy' Allbright, teenage physics genius and brat, whose neurotic inability to cope with human relations goes beyond parody. Naturally he's soon dumped in O-Zone and forced to get along with some of its native hunter-gatherers over the course of a lengthy trek, maturing slightly in the process. One marvels at the good nature of the Zone dwellers, who put up with Fizzy calling them aliens (city jargon), monkeys, herberts, dongs, tools, whackos, jigs, dipshits, shit-wits, etc, and at no time drop him down a deep hole. There is a complementary strand about the O-Zone girl called Bligh who is taken off to the joys of city life, but she seems almost devoid of personality, and barely reacts.

O-Zone's science is quite remarkably unconvincing, conveying the impression that Theroux regards lasers, particle beams and fibre-optics as all very much the same thing. Fizzy's deep knowledge of particle physics seems to be based on study of E.E. Smith or Hugo Gernsback: 'It's fibre-optics, fuck-wit . . . This weapon can do it. We just program it to fire a continuous exode full of antigons.' When someone who knows a little physics complains (as did I) that he's never heard of antigons, the reply is, 'I only discovered antigons last year, wang-face!' What the weapon, a particle-beam handgun with a ludicrous seven megawatt output, is being programmed to do is to bend the lethal laser beam that runs near ground level around the O-Zone perimeter, so the party can slip under it and escape. Why they can't jump over it is unclear, but using a particle stream to bend a laser ray makes as much sense as trying to deflect light with a magnet. And it would have taken very little research to ascertain that, far from being silent and invisible, the mooted laser and particle beams have power densities that would violently ionize the air in something like a continuous, noisy lightning bolt.

O-Zone has a worthy stance, a general worrying about dependence on technology and the resultant depersonalization. Its tiresome length and its over-familiarity to any sf reader must count against it, though, and the technobabble smells of that dangerous attitude, 'I can put down any old rubbish – this is only sf.'

Nicholson Baker's *The Fermata* (1994) uses yet another premise with deep sf roots. H.G. Wells started this particular hare in 'The New Accelerator', his account of a potion that temporarily speeds one's biological clock by a factor of thousands. Like a conjuror, Wells distracts you from the absurdities by keeping the story short, thrusting one surprise consequence under your nose (the accelerated experimenter's trousers begin to smoulder as they whiz around) and concluding with a spectacular diversion in the form of a practical joke. Much practical joking also features in the best and funniest treatment of the notion, John D. MacDonald's sf thriller *The Girl, the Gold Watch and Everything* (1962). Here the speed-up is wisely rooted in physics rather than biology, with some (though not too much) thought given to its effects: the super-accelerated hero finds the slowed outer world dull and red, while objects seem to have huge inertia and speedy things like bullets do visibly move even from the fast-lane perspective.

Baker's endlessly prattling hero Arno Strine does not merely slow external time but stops it completely, through a mere effort of will and belief. He calls his private time-zone the Fold or Fermata, in which he lives and moves while the universe outside is static. There are periods when he can't enter it and needs to find a new focus of belief (ranging from simple gestures through gadgets – transformer, rocker- switch, fingernail clippers – to odd or fetishistic acts like stitching thread through his skin). One sees the dramatic opportunities: Strine will be unable to enter the Fold when he urgently needs to; will exit into real time at an inconvenient, embarrassing or downright dangerous moment through failure of concentration . . .

No, none of these possibilities is followed up. For a man with super powers, Strine lives a life oddly short on drama – perhaps because his moral sense won't let him use the Fold to steal, and he even feels intensely guilty after dealing with armed muggers by halting time and lashing them by their goolies to a signpost. However, Strine's otherwise rigid code does let him use stopped time to remove women's clothing; also to fondle them all over, explore their orifices from 'ane' to 'vadge', spy on them in the bath, attach electric sexual stimulators to them as they ride on public transport, cause subliminal flashes of rude photographs in their field of vision, scrawl dirty comments in the margins of books they're reading (although not books written by women, which would be going too far), ejaculate all over them, affix exotic 'nipple nooses' during bookshop signings (Anne Rice of all people is singled out for this fate) . . . the list goes on.

Not much drama, but a great deal of fuzzy embarrassment for the reader; one hardly knows whether it's the narrator's or the author's painful transparency that is so uncomfortable, most especially in the dildo-infested porn fiction – included in full – which Strine writes to excite women whom he can then watch masturbating. How different, how very different, from the home life of our own dear Queen.

Best coinage, all too appropriate and evidently loved by the author since it's repeated several times: 'chronanism'. Worst euphemism, by a hair, out of an enormous selection: 'my triune crotch-lump'.

Excuse me, I was talking about the sf content. Of course *The Fermata* is pure fantasy, but there is the occasional rationalizing mention of physics. Baker is savvy enough to consider that if all time-flow ceases outside Strine's body, he'll be trapped in a form-fitting bubble of frozen air. So our chronanist's immediate vicinity is not quite halted: women aren't rigid statues but conveniently warm and soft, while equally conveniently failing to be conscious. Far enough from Strine himself, the stasis is total. There is some babble about Polaroid photos taken in the Fold not developing properly. Taps merely trickle because 'water pressure is never good in the Fold' – nonexistent, surely, cut off at the time-frozen main? Electrical supplies are similarly fudged when Strine wants to use his word processor.

Thought experiment: safe in the Fold, Strine strips a woman and gropes her for an hour. All this time she is warm but not breathing; it is uncertain whether her heart beats. Are the inner chemical furnaces at work, burning sugars to generate warmth? If the answer is no, she ends up probably dead from hypothermia; if yes, definitely dead from anoxia. You choose.

Thought experiment: Strine halts time out in bright sunlight. An infinitesimal fraction of a second later, total darkness must surround him (the Sun is not in his immediate vicinity) and the only illumination is infra-red blackbody radiation from Strine himself and any women unfortunate enough to be adjacent. Blackout.

All this shows the superiority of Wells's and MacDonald's device of slowing down exterior timeflow (or speeding interior time) by a large amount, rather than introducing the awkward factor of infinity.

But what's the use? *The Fermata* genuinely is about sexual fantasy and nothing else, and even there refuses to explore any dangerous edge (compare Alasdair Gray's harrowing 'slipstream' *1982, Janine*). Its shallowness runs deep. Even one's growing hope that Strine will eventually meet a sharp comeuppance is frustrated – in fact he postmodernly gloats over this. That's the joke: a practical joke on the reader.

Now would be the time for some lofty generalization about these sf or sf-like works written by – let's not say outsiders, but writers other than the usual genre suspects. The exercise is futile, though: even this small sample is too diverse for facile summary. Just like science fiction, really.

The Final Word

Michael Moorcock

A long time ago someone asked me the schedule and policy of *New Worlds*. My answer was 'erratic', and 'optimistic', which isn't a formula you often come across in *Writers' and Artists' Yearbook* but it does appear to be a formula for survival. In fact for the past quarter of a century whenever someone tried to put *New Worlds* on a regular schedule, it didn't so much die as faint with shock and have to be revived, sometimes years later. Admittedly, we pretty much missed the eighties altogether, which is probably how many of us would have wished to experience the insane simplifications of the Reagan/Thatcher decade which reintroduced tribalism and the blood-feud into modern politics.

It's thirty years since I edited my first issue of *New Worlds*. I was proposed as editor by Ted Carnell (who had edited the magazine and its companions for some twenty years). I remember that I was rather reluctant to take the job. I had lost interest in science fiction. I had lost hope in its ability to revivify or even become the mainstream. I had attended conferences when Ballard and I had planned to discuss the literary possibilities of the form, and most of the other writers wanted to discuss how to break into TV writing. I wasn't sure I could do anything worthwhile with the magazine. As it happened, the writers eventually began to emerge and a lot of what they produced was everything I'd hoped for. I particularly remember the excitement of reading Disch's *Camp Concentration*, Harrison's *Running Down*, Ballard's concentrated novels which became *The Atrocity Exhibition*, Bayley's stories which were to appear in *The Knights of the Limits*, Aldiss's *Report on Probability A*, Spinrad's *Bug Jack Barron*, Sladek's *Masterson and the Clerks* and Zoline's *The Heat Death of the Universe*.

Not that everyone who attended science fiction conventions would agree that such work was sf, or even speculative fiction. Once a whole group of fans came down to a Brighton Arts Festival to demand of *New Worlds* and its writers that we 'return' sf to them. I wasn't aware we'd rustled it.

Michael Kustow, then director of the ICA gallery, said that he'd experienced something similar when he had run the Royal Shakespeare Company in Stratford. Dedicated fans, he said, never wanted anything new. They believed Shakespeare to be theirs and resented any tampering. He called this 'the anxious ownership syndrome'. It was never the general public who complained, he said, only those who for some reason had identified the stuff (sf or Shakespeare or religion) so thoroughly with their own personalities that any change was an attack on their very being . . .

That particular form of insanity is no longer as evident as it was and the messianic element of sf fandom appears to have discovered scientology, *Star Trek* or some other low-level quasi-religion to occupy its time. But it was never surprising that so many sf fans were of that persuasion, for there has always been a strong visionary element in sf and it is this which initially attracted many of us to the form. It is what continues to attract people to Ballard, Banks, McKay, Ackroyd, Nye, Rushdie, Carter and many of the writers who now dominate fiction in Britain.

It's probably fair to say that the film *2001* had a profound effect upon the public vision of the future which would not be challenged until *Blade Runner* set the tone for the eighties. Bleak as that vision was, it was far more sophisticated than Kubrick's celebration, and where his film had been dominated by a kind of technoporn, Ridley Scott's was primarily about human beings coping with the excesses of other human beings' greed, and represented an important change of emphasis. Just as *2001* gave birth to billions of words of 'hard' sf, so Scott's film has spawned its cruder clones and inspired an equally boring sub-genre. Such public visions set the tone for most genre fiction, but it was left to *New Worlds* and those like it to encourage individuals to express their own private visions, to reject the conventional and to write for themselves. Which is probably why *New Worlds* and its writers never had the immediate success of those who were only too pleased to offer genre ingredients over and over again. Yet it's interesting to note how relevant they are to the present, when most of the bestsellers of their day have disappeared.

I have a feeling that many of the stories here will stand at least another reading or two in years to come. Obsessive, idiosyncratic, bizarre and odd as some of them seem (and this edition contains a batch of my very favourite writers, including Barry Bayley, who continues to astonish me), they are the visions of individuals who will retain their readership long after the massive bestsellers have gone the way of Ouida, Marie Corelli, Hall Caine and Warwick Deeping, all of whom sold in their tens of millions in their own particular golden age. Without David Garnett and *New Worlds* some of these stories would not exist. Without you, *New Worlds* would not exist. We're all in this together. I hope you found this especially fine collection as satisfying as I did.

Michael Moorcock
Lost Pines
Texas
Spring 1994

MICHAEL MOORCOCK now lives in Texas, Majorca and London. His most recently published novel was *Jerusalem Commands*, the penultimate book in his Colonel Pyat tetralogy dealing with the Holocaust and its causes. *Lunching With the Antichrist*, stories about the von Beks, Becks and Beggs, will be published later this year by Mark Ziesing Books and *Blood, A Southern Fantasy*, will be published by Orion Books early in 1995, including all the material so far published in *New Worlds*. Other forthcoming titles are *Fabulous Harbours* and *The War Amongst the Angels*.

Still available . . .

The first three volumes of

NEW WORLDS

NEW WORLDS 1	VGSF £4.99
Introduction	Michael Moorcock
Immaculate	Storm Constantine
Any Major Dude	Paul Di Filippo
Heat	J. D. Gresham
Floating Dogs	Ian McDonald
Übermensch	Kim Newman
Indeterminacy	Jay Summers
Colour	Michael Moorcock
The Descent of Man	Matthew Dickens
Something Sweet	Simon Ings and Charles Stross
FOAM	Brian W. Aldiss
SF Novels of the Year	John Clute
Past, Present and Future	David Garnett

NEW WORLDS 2	VGSF £5.99
Introduction	David Garnett
Innocents	Ian McDonald
Brain Wars	Paul Di Filippo
Corsairs of the Second Ether	Warwick Colvin Jnr
Ratbird	Brian W. Aldiss
Candy Buds	Peter F. Hamilton
Great Breakthroughs in Darkness	Marc Laidlaw
Bruised Time	Simon Ings
Virtually Lucid Lucy	Ian Watson
The Face of the Waters	Jack Deighton
Inherit the Earth	Stephen Baxter
A Gadget Too Far	David Langford
Joe Protagoras is Alive and Living on Earth, and	
The Name of the Game is Death	Philip K. Dick
Introduced by	Paul Williams
Illustrated by	Jim Burns
Afterword	Michael Moorcock

NEW WORLDS 3	VGSF £6.99
Introduction	David Garnett
Spare Capacity	Peter F. Hamilton
Gap-sickness	Graham Joyce
Friendship Bridge	Brian W. Aldiss
The Mechanic	Gwyneth Jones
Tolkowsky's Cut	Simon Ings and Charles Stross
On the Shores of a Fractal Sea	Graham Charnock
This is the Road	Jack Deighton
Streetlife	Paul Di Filippo
Children of the Revolution	Paul J. McAuley
SF Novels of the Year	John Clute
Afterword	Michael Moorcock